D0051465

JONATHAN MABERRY

RAGE

JOE LEDGER AND ROGUE TEAM INTERNATIONAL

 ST. MARTIN'S GRIFFIN
NEW YORK

First published in the United States by St. Martin's Griffin, an imprint of St. Martin's Publishing Group

RAGE. Copyright © 2019 by Jonathan Maberry. All rights reserved. Printed in the United States of America. For information, address St. Martin's Publishing Group, 120 Broadway, New York, NY 10271.

www.stmartins.com

Designed by Jonathan Bennett

Library of Congress Cataloging-in-Publication Data

Names: Maberry, Jonathan, author.
Title: Rage : Joe Ledger and Rogue Team International / Jonathan Maberry.
Description: First Edition. | New York : St. Martin's Griffin, 2019. | Series: Rogue Team International; 1
Identifiers: LCCN 2019028349 | ISBN 9781250303578 (trade paperback) | ISBN 9781250303585 (ebook)
Subjects: LCSH: Biological weapons—Fiction. | GSAFD: Science fiction.
Classification: LCC PS3613.A19 R34 2019 | DDC 813/.6—dc23
LC record available at https://lccn.loc.gov/2019028349

Our books may be purchased in bulk for promotional, educational, or business use. Please contact your local bookseller or the Macmillan Corporate and Premium Sales Department at 1-800-221-7945, extension 5442, or by email at MacmillanSpecialMarkets@macmillan.com.

First Edition: November 2019

10 9 8 7 6 5 4 3 2 1

This is for my literary brother, Henry Herz
Friend, colleague, coconspirator
and cohost of the Writers Coffeehouse at
   Mysterious Galaxy Bookstore in San Diego.

And, as always, for Sara Jo

ACKNOWLEDGMENTS

The Joe Ledger novels could not be undertaken without the help of a lot of talented and generous people. In no particular order, then . . .

Many thanks to John Cmar, Director, Division of Infectious Diseases, Sinai Hospital of Baltimore; Dr. Steve A. Yetiv, Professor of Political Science, Old Dominion University. Thanks to my friends in the International Thriller Writers, International Association of Media Tie-in Writers, the Mystery Writers of America, and the Horror Writers Association. Thanks to my literary agent, Sara Crowe of Pippin Properties; my stalwart editor at St. Martin's Griffin, Michael Homler; Robert Allen and the crew at Macmillan Audio; and my film agent, Dana Spector of Creative Artists Agency. And special thanks to my brilliant audiobook reader, Ray Porter. Thanks also to Corky King, Ahmed Othman, Caroline Shehata, Janice Breitkopf, and Kellie Hollingsworth.

ALEPPO, SYRIA

PART ONE

My first wish is to see this plague of mankind, war, banished from the earth.

—GEORGE WASHINGTON

CHAPTER ONE

If the world is on all four wheels and nothing is burning, you'll never hear from guys like me.

But, let's face it, when's the last time that was true?

CHAPTER TWO
ALMANZEL CAFE
ZOHER IBN ABI SOLMA ST
ALEPPO, SYRIA

So . . . they dragged me out of the back of an Iveco LMV that smelled of dog piss and human blood. Even with a black bag over my head my eyes were watering. Can't begin to imagine how the four soldiers who nabbed me dealt with it. Maybe psychopaths don't care about smelly cars.

Or, then again, maybe they do. Psychologically-speaking I'm a bit of a freak show myself, and it bothered me. Be kind of funny if I was crazier than a bunch of henchmen working for President Assad.

Musings of a guy about to be tortured and killed.

My hands were zip-cuffed behind my back. The beating they gave me was, I can assume, just a sort of greeting. Welcome to Syria. That kind of thing.

I heard them open a heavy door and then heard it slam shut behind. Heavy locks and the dull thud of a crossbar being dropped into place. I stumbled along with two of them holding me under the armpits. Counting my steps, numbering the hallways and turns. Down one flight, two, three. Deep under somewhere. The place smelled a lot better than the vehicle except for one place where there was a heavy, rancid stink. It wasn't a dead smell. Not exactly. Not like a corpse. It was more of a gangrene stench, and I wondered if maybe some injured prisoner was locked up, rotting in the fetid darkness. But we moved on and soon I could smell more wholesome things—wheat flour, lentils, figs, and coffee. A lot of coffee. Smelled good, and I could use a cup and a nice pastry. Maybe a *namoura* with some nuts on top. Yum.

Another door opened. Creaky hinges.

"*Daeh hunak*," said a voice. Male, middle-aged and authoritative, speaking Syrian Arabic. "*Daeh fi alkursii*."

They did as they were told and put me in a chair. There was a whisk of a knife to remove the plastic cuffs and then a metallic clink as steel cuffs were snapped too tightly around my wrists, threaded through the back slats of the chair. They were being very careful. Then the same voice said, "*Khale alghata'*."

Take off the hood. Which they did.

In any hostage situation, it is generally not a good sign when they let you see their faces. It does not, as the saying goes, bode well. One is expected to be filled with a reasonable amount of dread. No problem then. I was sweating heavy-caliber bullets and I'm pretty sure my sphincter was never going to unclench. Ever. Even if I lived through this.

I blinked my eyes clear. They had me in a small storeroom that was stripped of everything except shelves, the chair on which I sat, and a wooden table on which were the kind of items you never want to see outside of a horror movie. They were laid out to impress me, from the scalpels all the way to the bone saw. Eloquent. And, weirdly, a bottle of Diet Coke.

The middle-aged man stood with his back to me. He was average height, slim, wore khakis and a white shirt. I watched him remove a blue sports coat, shake some cellar dust from it, and hand it to a guard. His shoes were highly polished and his wristwatch was expensive, a Tag Heuer Monaco that had to run forty grand. A lot of watch for a guy who was supposed to be a civil servant . . . but, let's face it, corruption came with perks. Kind of the point.

The four men who brought me here were dressed in clothes so obviously nondescript they might as well have worn uniforms. Jeans, dress shirts, sneakers. They moved like military, so they weren't fooling anyone.

The middle-aged guy spent a few moments arranging the instruments on the table. Straightening them, picking one or another up to examine as if they were items at a juried craft fair and he was a discerning buyer. It was all a bit of theater. Psychodrama to unnerve whoever might be cuffed to that chair. I doubted I was the first person to attend this show.

Turn around. I willed him to get on with it. *Turn around and let me see those baby blue eyes.*

Hoping they would be blue eyes. Just like I was hoping there would be a white streak in his mustache. If, in fact, he had a mustache.

Turn around, Bright Eyes.

And . . . now I had the damn Bonnie Tyler song playing in my head.

He turned. I almost smiled. He had the biggest, brightest, sunniest blue eyes you'd ever want to see in the face of a practiced torturer and state-sponsored terrorist. And the white streak? Yup. Just under his left nostril.

Qasim Almasi.

And he held a slender boning knife the way a conductor holds a baton. Ready to make music.

"We were very clear," he said, still speaking in Arabic. "They were to send no one. No police, no military."

"That's not what I am," I said in the same language. I tweaked it with a vaguely Eastern European accent.

"My men said you moved like a soldier. You spotted them following you, tried several very professional methods to evade pursuit, and had an unregistered disposable phone."

"Not a soldier," I repeated. "I'm private security."

"Security for whom?" asked Almasi. "We were very specific when we spoke to her father."

"I know, but I'm not working for Mr. Jacobsen."

He touched the point of the boning knife low so that it rested very lightly on my crotch.

"Then who *are* you working for?"

I smiled. "I work for Overlegen Kjemi."

That hung in the air for a moment. Overlegen Kjemi was the Norwegian company that made industrial pesticides and agricultural antifungals. Oliver Jacobsen was a journalist who'd infiltrated the company to gather irrefutable proof that a new generation of weaponized mycotoxins were being developed for sale to the Syrian government. These biological agents caused immediate anaphylaxis. Unlike

sarin gas, which was President Assad's favorite toy for urban pacification, these fungi were specifically designed to look like a natural mutation. Better murder through chemistry.

Jacobsen got out with a lot of information, enough to put the entire company out of business and its executives in jail. It would also get the United Nations to stop fucking around and step in to take Assad down.

Assad's spies got wind of it almost too late. They tried to pick up Jacobsen, missed him by three minutes, and kidnapped his only daughter, Astrid, instead. The deal was simple—Jacobsen had to turn himself and all of his research in to Assad's goons. That included email passwords and all other access that would prove that he had no copies and had sent no story to his news service. Fail to do so, and Astrid would be gang-raped, tortured, and dismembered, all of which would be recorded on high-def video for her father to watch.

The boning knife pressed down.

"Why would Overlegen Kjemi send a field agent?" asked Almasi. "We are handling it. Don't they trust us?" He contrived to look shocked and hurt.

I shrugged. "Because they don't trust anyone. Would you?"

Almasi smiled. "And what is your brief?"

"To find where the girl's being held. Make sure she's alive."

"And what does her being alive matter to you?"

"Because her father hasn't turned himself in yet," I said. "And there's no chance at all he'd do so without proof of life. He's going to need that. I mean, come on, we all know he's a dead man as soon as this deal closes. There's no reason to keep him alive and a lot of good reasons to cut his throat as soon as you have his files. Knowing he's walking into a death trap, he's got to believe his sacrifice will be worth it. So, yeah, he's going to want to see her alive. He's probably going to push to see her in person before he gives you the last passwords. My bosses sent me to make sure your team wasn't going to screw the pooch."

He considered that for a moment, then stepped back. He didn't put the knife down.

"Bottom line here," I said, "is that if this hits a speed bump the guy who signs my paycheck goes away for life. Our whole company goes belly-up, and you boys will need another group of mad scientists to cook up your next batch of party favors."

JONATHAN MABERRY

Almasi turned and spoke to one of his men in rapid-fire Circassian, which is a language used in some villages in the Aleppo suburbs. I didn't understand a word of it. Not one of my languages. Then Almasi held a cell phone out to me. A man was yelling something harsh, but clearly not into the phone. Then a woman's voice—young and frightened—pleaded for help in Norwegian. I'd heard tapes of Astrid Jacobsen. This was her.

There was some yelling and then Astrid screamed in serious pain.

Almasi ended the call.

The sound of the scream seemed to hang in the air for a moment. Faint, but definitely not an echo from the call. I heard the scream wind down and disintegrate into weeping.

Astrid was here.

I smiled. "Thanks," I said.

Almasi raised the boning knife.

"Whoa," I yelped, "what gives?"

He approached slowly. "I want you to give a message to your employers," he said, still smiling. "I want you to explain that sending you was clumsy and stupid and that we will not tolerate any further—"

There was a click.

And a rattle.

And then a metallic click-clack.

It stopped him and his eyes flicked down to the floor. The guards looked down, too. My handcuffs lay there.

Fuck it, I was a cop and then a SpecOps shooter for a bunch of years. If I couldn't get out of a pair of handcuffs then I wasn't even trying.

I smiled and said, "Oops."

CHAPTER THREE
ALMANZEL CAFE
ZOHER IBN ABI SOLMA ST
ALEPPO, SYRIA

As I came up off the chair I kicked it backward with my heel so that it hit one of the two guards on my right, used the same foot to kick the kneecap loose on the front guard on my left, and stepped into

Almasi and punched him in the throat. Not a killing blow, but hard enough. He gagged and stumbled back; I snatched the boning knife from his hand, pivoted, and stabbed it into the eye socket of the first guard to reach for me. Then I grabbed a meat cleaver and a big ·butcher knife from the table.

They had guns, but they'd been slung. I'd been a beaten, cuffed prisoner and there were five of them. In their minds I was just a desperate prisoner making a last desperate attempt to escape. I gave them no time at all to correct their mistake. The guy with the broken knee tried to grab me as he fell, but I kneed him in the face and buried the cleaver in the shoulder of the man behind him. The heavy blade chunked through meat and bone, and blood shot all the way to the ceiling.

I whirled toward the fourth man, the one I'd kicked the chair at. He was bringing his weapon up, but I was three feet away and I had a blade. They don't call it a butcher knife for nothing.

As he fell with nothing but a string of gristle keeping his head on, I turned and drove the knife between the shoulder blades of the guy with the broken knee.

Then I kicked Almasi in the balls. Mostly because I could. Took a short, heavy knife from the table and cut the throats of every man who was screaming.

Total elapsed time? Maybe three seconds. You don't want fights to last longer than that.

Almasi was trying to breathe and trying to crawl, failing at both. His face was an awful shade of mauve. I used to have a car that color. It was a worthless piece of shit, too.

I tapped a mole on my tragus, the little flap of skin and cartilage on the outer ear, and said, "You get all that?"

"Roger that, Outlaw," said a voice in my ear. "We have a medical team en route. ETA four minutes. Havoc Team is six blocks out."

"Tell Havoc to close on my location but not to enter until I give the word."

"Copy that. I have four pigeon drones in the air. Running thermals. Ground floor has one signature and a heat bloom consistent with a bakery oven. According to your RFID chip, you're on the bottom of three subfloors. Picking up multiple signatures on the top floor. Count sixteen signatures. Count twenty hostiles on sub-one, but scans can't read any farther down."

"Swell," I said. "Make sure Havoc brings their toys."

A deep voice said, "We brought *all* the toys, Outlaw."

Nice to know that my team was on the same channel and that the building structure wasn't blocking anyone from the party. That deep voice belonged to Bradley Sims, known as Top to everyone, but his combat call sign was Pappy because he was the oldest field operator anyone knew. Looking at fifty, but not where it showed.

"Other kids in the playground are Republican Guard in civilian clothes," I said. "Heavily armed."

"Sucks to be them, then," said another voice. Younger, with a Southern California surfer drawl. Harvey Rabbit—sadly, that was his actual name. We called him Bunny in every situation other than when we were out on a gig. His combat call sign was Donnie Darko.

I took the weapons away from the soldiers, checked the magazines on a Makarov PM and tucked it in the back of my belt, and pocketed four spare mags. Took the heavier Browning Hi-Power and slid it between belt buckle and belly. Only three magazines for that, but they held thirteen rounds each, as opposed to eight-round mags for the Russian gun. The long guns were AK-104s with thirty-round mags. I had no idea how many more of Almasi's goons were in the building.

Listening at the door got me an earful of silence. Apparently no one comes to investigate screams in a place like this. I looked down at Almasi. That was going to be unfortunate for him.

CHAPTER FOUR
ALMANZEL CAFE
ZOHER IBN ABI SOLMA ST
ALEPPO, SYRIA

Almasi was chatty.

Might have been a revelation for him, if he appreciated the irony. Torturers tend to think that they could endure the kinds of physical horrors they inflict. I mean, sure, deep down they know they can't, but projecting the air of confidence goes with the job.

When it comes right down to the point where scrotum and knife blade are introduced, they're not at all interested in you swiping left. Or right. I didn't have to draw a single drop of blood before he told me every goddamn thing I wanted to know. And some stuff I didn't want to know. Maybe he thought if he kept telling me stuff I wouldn't kill him.

Hope springs eternal. Arteries do not.

I patted his twitching corpse down and took a cell phone. The fact that it was password protected didn't mean a damn thing to me because Bug and his team laugh at that kind of security. Once I got out of here and plugged the cell into a MindReader uplink, the encryption would get its ass kicked. I left the room and did a quick check on the hallway. Clear. Took a moment to orient myself. From what I remembered of the route here, they'd brought me in from my right. The scream I'd heard was to my left. Not close, but close enough to have been heard through closed doors.

I tucked the stock of the AK-104 into my shoulder and went hunting. Running quickly, taking a lot of small steps instead of big ones in order to maintain contact with the ground for shooting stability.

The basement was cool and clammy but there was a definite smell of baking bread. Faint though. Probably ground level. Either a restaurant or café used as a front for dirty work like this. Oliver Jacobsen was semi-blackmailing us. He had the data on Assad and the chemical company, but he wouldn't give it to us—or anyone—as long as Astrid was in danger. Couldn't entirely blame him.

I'm coming, I mentally promised the young woman. She was seventeen. A smart, pretty teenager who expected to grow up and have a life unpolluted by monsters. The kind of person who stopped believing in monsters in her closet or under the bed long ago. Sad truth was that there were much worse monsters in the real world. Some of them ran corporations like Overlegen Kjemi. Some were immoral psychopaths like Almasi and his goon squad. And some were heads of state.

Some monsters, though, were on her side.

I moved through the shadows.

The hall ended in a T-juncture. The left-hand side ran forty feet and ended in a row of pallets stacked high with sacks of flour and large tins of olive oil. The right side led to a single door fifty feet in. There were two guards in front of it, both with rifles. As I knelt at the corner I could hear them talking about last night's football match. Iran lost to Japan by a single goal. The guard on the left won five thousand pounds. The Syrian pound is for shit, so that was about ten American dollars. Seemed to matter a lot to him, and he thought the referee was on the pad. The other guy was nodding the way people do when they disagree but everyone's holding rifles.

I had one, too.

I stepped into the hallway and shot them both.

Then I ran like a son of a bitch and emptied the rest of the magazine into the door lock, blowing it apart.

There was a burst of automatic gunfire from inside, and I shifted sideways to avoid lead and splinters. The angle of the shots told me a lot. Hopefully enough. I dropped the rifle, drew the Browning, and went in low and fast, pivoting and squatting as I went through the door, gun in both hands. There were two men in there. Both had rifles. They stood behind a slim blonde with a torn blouse and blood on her face. They fired chest-high, aiming where they assumed I'd be. I fired at where they actually were. The 9mm rounds punched through their faces and blew out the backs of their heads.

I spun to make sure there was no one behind the door. There wasn't.

Astrid Jacobsen screamed at the top of her lungs. Of course she did.

I put a finger to my lips. "My name is Colonel Joe Ledger. I'm a friend of your father. We're here to get you out."

Astrid stopped screaming. Gaped for a moment, then whispered, "Papa . . . ?"

"He's waiting for you at a safe house," I told her. "We'll take you to him."

She looked past me to see who "we" was. I winked, tapped my earbud, and said, "Package secure. Need exfil now. Kick the doors and make some noise. The only friendly is with me. Designate all others as hostiles. Go weapons hot."

I wanted to say something like, *"Cry havoc and let slip the dogs of war,"* but you have to read the room. I mean, I'd already winked, and that was pretty corny.

Upstairs I heard an alarm go off. I heard explosions as doors blew inward. Then gunfire echoed through the dusty halls.

CHAPTER FIVE
ALMANZEL CAFE
ZOHER IBN ABI SOLMA ST
ALEPPO, SYRIA

It got real damn loud.

Alarms began blaring, as if anyone needed proof that bad shit was happening. I heard doors bang open and men yelling. There was the rattle of automatic gunfire upstairs and booted feet pounding down concrete stairs.

"Get behind this wall and stay down until I tell you to move," I ordered. Astrid paused for a long moment, trying to shift gears and grinding the clutch. "Do exactly as I say and we will get out of this. Now, get down."

She did.

Smoke was funneling along the hall, driven by the pressure of movement and the force waves of the breaching explosions from upstairs. I could see shapes moving toward me but there is a moment in these kinds of situations where you can't tell if it's the cavalry riding to the rescue or bad guys coming to kill you. I tapped my earbud.

"Havoc Actual to Havoc Team," I growled. "What's your location?"

"Two floors up, Outlaw," came the reply from Pappy. "Meeting heavy resistance."

"Is there anyone from Havoc Team in subbasement two?"

"Negative, Outlaw, we're all up here."

"Very well," I said, unhappy with that news. "Coming your way. Havoc Actual plus one. Will let you know when we reach the ground floor."

The hallway bent ahead and then stretched into darkness punctuated by the meager yellow light of low-wattage bulbs in wire cages mounted on the walls. There were doors on both sides of the hall, which is always a scary thing. You never know who is going to come out of them, and with Astrid behind me I couldn't safely check and clear each one. That meant I could not guarantee the protection I'd promised. I gave her some quick instructions about how to move with me and not hamper what I do.

We moved. I followed the barrel of my gun, but every dozen steps I turned and brought it up again as I scanned behind us, dipping the barrel each time to prevent it hitting a wall or other obstruction. Rinse, repeat. It was a long hallway, but it matched pretty well to the distances I'd calculated when they were bringing me in. If I was right, there would be a right turn ahead and then some stairs.

The toughest part in a recovery operation of this kind is the speculation about what—or, more to the point, *who*—might be behind some of those closed doors. Could be a couple of squads of Assad's soldiers polishing their bullets. We moved as fast as we could.

At the end of the hall I stopped because there was a side corridor going off to my left that I hadn't been aware of on the way here. Or, maybe I had. I'd smelled something rancid for a moment on the way in. I'd assumed it was a prisoner in a cell, dying or maybe long dead.

We crouched near the mouth of the corridor because I could hear voices talking excitedly; and I caught snatches of what they were saying. Demanding answers to what was happening upstairs. Demanding protection. But I also caught individual words like "samples" and "evacuation."

I gestured for Astrid to be still and silent. She nodded, but her face was filled with terror. I pivoted on the balls of my feet and did a quick-look around the corner, then leaned out to look in through an open door. I couldn't see much, but what I did glimpse looked like a laboratory. There were tables covered with high-end laptops and a pretty elaborate industrial chemistry setup. A guard stood outside, turned away from us, looking into the room, jabbering on his cell phone, demanding to speak to his lieutenant. I wondered if that lieutenant had met my friends upstairs, because if he had then soldier boy here was going to need a really good calling plan to reach him in the afterlife.

I really wanted to have a look inside that lab. Its presence here, so close to where Almasi had brought Astrid, seemed suggestive. So, I pulled back and leaned very close to the girl.

"Listen to me," I said, speaking very quietly instead of whispering because the sibilance of whispers carry farther. "There is a guard around the corner and I need to deal with him. Do you understand what that means? Just nod."

Her eyes were huge and filled with the tears of fear and horror, and she began to say something, but stopped herself. She was impressing the hell out of me. She nodded.

"I need you to stay right here. Do not move. Do not follow me. I'll be back very quickly. Nod if you understand."

She did.

I gave her the patented Joe Ledger smile. The one that crinkles the corners of my eyes and looks like a poster for good dental hygiene.

My stolen weapons had no sound suppressors, which left me with a "fuck it" approach. So I wheeled around the corner and ran straight at the guard, opening up with the rifle, with the selector set to two-round bursts. The bullets hit him center mass and blew a big hole through his spine and heart. He fell and I was through the door, taking in everything in a split part of a second.

There were five long tables filled with the lab equipment. Six tall glass tanks were arranged almost like a brewery, with pipes and hoses going everywhere. Some of those hoses were socketed into the walls of three small cells built into the right-hand wall, each with glass walls and heavily locked doors. Through the glass I could see figures—prisoners or test subjects, or both. Some kind of gas or vapor was hissing into the tanks. The prisoners saw it and freaked out, beating with bloodied fists to try and get out. Each prisoner's face was twisted into a mask of terror and fury. There were biohazard symbols stenciled on everything. There were five people in white lab coats and four uniformed guards with rifles. They were all frozen in a microsecond of shock—the lab geeks stuffing papers into leather cases, the guards realizing that I had my gun leveled and theirs were still slung.

The frozen moment burst apart. The guards raised their weapons fast, but then hesitated because the glass tanks were behind me. I could see the indecision ignite in their eyes. I did not hesitate and opened up on them, hosing them with the AK-104. Their indecision was fatal.

But as they fell, two of them jerked fingers on their triggers and bullets hammered into the scientists, who went spinning away, red poppies blooming on their white lab coats. And some of their wild rounds hit the lab equipment. I emptied an entire magazine, spraying everyone I could hit. In the space of two seconds the room went from urgent uncertainty into a madhouse of exploding glass and metal. Laptops erupted in showers of sparks, rounds ricocheted off the machinery and walls and the curved faces of the tubes. Two of my bullets exploded the glass on one of the holding cells, releasing a swarm of flies, a much greater stink of living rot, and a prisoner who—insane with pain or fear or outrage—grabbed one of the soldiers and dragged him over the jagged teeth of the broken pane. The prisoner began punching the soldier with both fists, screaming incoherently, brutalizing a man who was probably already dead.

I shot the rest of the scientists, but saw that the guard's wild rounds had driven big cracks into one of the tubes. I said, "Fuck this," and got the hell out of there.

Maybe I did some good by ruining this little mad science project, or maybe I made a big goddamn mistake. Couldn't unring that bell, though, so I hooked Astrid under an arm, hauled her to her feet, and we ran.

Behind me I heard terrible screams and something that was so weird and out of place that it chilled me to the bone.

Laughter.

High, shrill, twisted, and filled with a madness beyond words.

CHAPTER SIX
ALMANZEL CAFE
ZOHER IBN ABI SOLMA ST
ALEPPO, SYRIA

We ran down the hall, wheeled around, and saw the steps at the end of another short corridor. There were two closed doors, one on either side, and the sounds of a fierce gunfight rolling down the stairs.

"Get behind me," I ordered. "Keep your hand on my back."

Before we got five steps, one of the doors opened and four men erupted from the room, firing as soon as they saw us, filling the air with hot lead, stone splinters, and choking dust.

I killed the first shooter and his next rounds hit the floor as he fell. Another man tripped over him and went down, so I ignored him for a moment and killed the two men behind him. Then I crouched and put three rounds center mass as the fallen man struggled to his feet. They were shooting through the dust and smoke that swirled around them. I was hunkered down in the shadows. They missed; I didn't.

Then I was up, swapping magazines, moving forward into the gloom, firing as more people came out of the other room. Two people in civilian clothes—both with handguns—fell, one with a scream and the other with a curse. I ran along the hall to the two doorways, saw that they were empty, then moved back to the dead men and took as many fresh magazines as I could cram into my pockets. I did fast pat-downs in the hope they were wearing body armor under their clothes. Would have been nice to have some for Astrid and me, but they had nothing.

Astrid was completely terrified and her body shook as if this was all happening in an industrial freezer. There was a jumpy quality to her eyes, but she wasn't crying. She wasn't being hysterical. That spoke to a deep core of strength beneath the youth and the shock. I've seen adults, including some people who you'd expect to be towers of strength, crumble in situations less horrific than this one.

"Stay behind me," I ordered.

We moved back to the T-junction and then along the corridors back to where I'd left Almasi. As we passed the open doorway she gave a small cry.

"Don't look," I said.

But Astrid stepped into the room and stood over Almasi for a moment. Then she spat into his dead face. As she turned I saw a sneer of contempt that was much more refined, controlled. It was the contempt of someone in possession of her emotions rather than a hysterical teen. And I knew that if I could get her out of this, she would be well.

There was another explosion upstairs and the alarm abruptly cut out. I grinned.

"Let's go," I said. "Put your hand on my back. Keep it there no matter what happens. Don't hold onto my belt. Do you understand?"

She nodded, but I made her say it out loud. She did.

We ran along the hall, retracing the pattern of turns I logged while being dragged to the interrogation room. Found the steps and we went up.

The second floor had only two of Assad's soldiers, both dressed as civilians, neither wearing body armor. Sucked to be them.

One of them got off a lucky shot as he went down and the round hit my rifle and tore it out of my hands. My fingers went numb and the strap damn near tore my arm out of the socket. My shot caught him in the same instant, though, and it tore a red hole in his belly. With hands that felt like nerveless balloons I drew the handgun and parked another round in his forehead.

Astrid was sobbing now. Small, choked sobs that sounded like they hurt, tearing themselves out of her chest. I called her name, told her to stay with me, and she did. She was scared, but she was tough.

I tapped the earbud again. "Havoc Actual to Havoc Team, be advised I am in the stairwell with the package. How much shit are we about to step into?"

There was a flurry of gunfire, and then a woman's voice. "Havoc Actual," said Mother Mercy, "come ahead but stay low." She spoke with a terse Mauritanian accent.

With Astrid still touching my back, we climbed the last few steps, and then entered one of the anterooms of hell. Or maybe a slaughterhouse. There were bodies everywhere.

Three men came hurrying down a flight of steps, yelling as they opened up with Kalashnikovs. Mother Mercy fired three shots and they went down. Bang, bang, bang. No fuss, lots of muss, because the rifle blew big red holes in them. Astrid cried out and the hand on my back gripped a sudden fistful of my shirt.

"It's okay," I said. "We'll get you out."

The soldiers had other plans, though, and there were a lot of them. More of the killers were thundering down the stairs from the second floor, but suddenly a monstrous shape loomed like a giant above me.

"Right here, Outlaw," said Donnie Darko, the huge kid from Orange County. He wore loose black clothes, Kevlar chest and limb pads and a ballistic helmet, and in his hands was an Atchisson assault shotgun with a thirty-two-round drum magazine. The big man opened up and filled the stairwell with death. There were screams and then bodies tumbled like a pile of dolls at the foot of the stairs.

Another knot of them came pounding along the left-hand hall and I flattened sideways, pushing Astrid behind me and down as I opened up. I burned a full mag into them.

"I'm out," I yelled as the slide locked back, but Donnie Darko handed a pistol to me. "One-up," he said, letting me know it was loaded and had one in the chamber. Then he moved past us, heading toward the end of the hall, which was shrouded in smoke. "Got an Uber coming. Stay on my six."

"Roger that," I said and moved as he moved.

"Door left," he said as he went along the hall, his shotgun barrel swiveling side to side as he passed rooms filled with death. "Clear. Door right. Clear."

We passed two open doorways through which I could see just how thoroughly Havoc Team had cleared the obstacles.

"Door right," said Donnie Darko, but then Pappy stepped out of that room, fitting a new magazine into his weapon. He was a big black man who looked tough enough to eat iron bars with only a little steak sauce. He saw Astrid, saw that she was unharmed, and gave me a nod.

"Hall's clear for a run to the back door," Pappy said. "Mother Mercy's got a shooting blind there."

He fell in behind Astrid, walking backward, pointing his weapon the way we'd come. A figure came out of the smoke behind us, running low and fast.

"Havoc, Havoc," he called in a thick Italian accent. "Friendly coming in." Then I saw the slim, wiry figure of Jackpot. An empty pouch flapped at his side, which meant he'd been busy laying charges. "*Sta per diventare rumoroso qui*," he shouted as he raced past.

It's about to get loud in here.

Brick dust and gun smoke choked the air but the clouds were stabbed through with the green laser lights from Pappy and Jackpot's guns as they covered our run. There were dead bodies and expended shell casings everywhere. None of the bodies were dressed like my guys.

Suddenly there was a piercing shriek behind us and a figure burst from the stairwell. He was a civilian, unarmed, covered in blood, and his eyes were filled with madness. I recognized him as the prisoner from downstairs who'd brutalized a guard. Two of Assad's men were on the stairs that led to the second floor, and they suddenly screamed and turned their guns on him as if Havoc team did not even exist. They fired but the man was already in the air, slamming into them. The three of them collapsed into a thrashing tangle of screams and blood.

"What the actual fuck?" said Donnie Darko.

"*Move, move, move,*" yelled Pappy.

We moved.

We ran like hell down the corridor. The small, slim figure of Mother Mercy was at the far end, her rifle laid atop a packing crate, and beyond her was an open doorway.

"Shift left," she barked, and we did. Astrid flinched as Mother Mercy fired. She seemed to take her time with it, like there wasn't a battle and smoke and everything around us going to shit. There was nothing hurried about her as she aimed, took a breath, exhaled as she fired. Again, and then again.

I glanced back and saw the escaped prisoner go flying backward with his chest blown apart. Then a soldier's head exploded. And then another died with a big red hole in his sternum. One, two, three. Mother Mercy looked for another target. Killed it. Another. Killed that one, too. It was so calm, so cold, that even to me it was eerie. Snipers are a breed apart from other kinds of soldiers, and some of them seemed to exist in a type of ethereal other place where time and distance were nothing to them. It was a kind of dark Zen, not without its purity, but all the scarier for that.

As I guided Astrid toward the door, we edged around Mother Mercy, who turned and gave us a stare as alien as anything I'd ever seen on a human face. She looked Astrid up and down, saw she was uninjured, gave the smallest of nods, then turned and killed another soldier. All in a strange little moment.

And, call me crazy, I thought I felt something pass between Mother Mercy and Astrid. A kind of unspoken conversation, a telepathy from one person who had survived being held captive by violent men to another. It was a language I, as a man, would never quite understand because no matter what they might have done to me, the experience of women in these situations carries with it a more terrible cost. And it made them citizens of some country which men could be aware of but to which they would never be permitted passage. Some men resent that kind of privacy and intimacy between women, which speaks to a lack of insight and empathy that runs miles deep.

"Go," said Mother Mercy. And we went.

A voice spoke in my ear as I peered through the doorway to the street. It was Bug, the RTI computer wizard, working real-time mission support from the TOC. "Havoc Team be advised there are multiple vehicles converging on your location. Count three. Government Otokar Cobra infantry vehicles. Heat signatures times twenty-four. These are active military, guys. No one's trying to hide anymore. ETA three minutes. Get the hell out of there."

I looked up the street and saw our own black SUV come screeching to a smoking stop. The driver, a local asset, yelled out the window for us to haul ass.

I turned to Astrid and gave her a big white grin. "Time to go home."

We ran for the car, with Bunny sweeping the street with his shotgun, ready for anything but seeing nothing. Pappy and Jackpot followed us out and, with me, formed a human shield around Astrid. Then Pappy turned and knelt and trained his weapon on the door as he ordered Mother Mercy to fall back. There were two more shots, and then she burst from the building, her rifle held at port arms as she ran for the SUV. Several figures crowded through the doorway, and I was confused, because two of them wore lab coats. Not the ones I'd shot, but other scientists. There must have been a second lab. They screamed and beat at the soldiers who were first to the door, and the whole bunch of them snagged there, fighting so hard to exit that none of them could. It was a vicious damn fight, too. The soldiers seemed absolutely terrified of the scientists, which was the reverse of anything that made sense.

Pappy emptied his magazine into them, driving the whole cluster back inside in a cloud of blood. Then he whirled and Bunny reached out and hauled him inside as the SUV leaped forward.

"Havoc Team," cried Bug, "you have two Mil Mi attack helicopters in the air. ETA two minutes."

"*Gesù Cristo*," gasped Jackpot.

"Bug," I yelled, "you need to buy us some time."

"Working on it, Outlaw," he told me.

Bug made sure the traffic lights worked for us and he turned all of their cell phones and radios into a scrambled mess of static and ear-piercing shrieks. He kicked his way into the onboard computers of the three approaching vehicles and told them to kill the engines.

The helicopter engines couldn't be similarly stalled, but Bug took charge of their targeting system and we heard rockets exploding a few blocks away.

"Count *two* infantry vehicles," Bug said dryly. There was another rolling boom. "My bad, only one."

Jackpot took out a small transmitter and began pushing buttons. Behind us the entire building seemed to leap into the air in a cloud of dense black smoke veined with Halloween orange and devil red.

The SUV raced away like the world was on fire.

Astrid pressed herself against me there in the backseat and began to weep uncontrollably. I wrapped my arm around her. Mother Mercy turned from the front passenger seat, placed her hand on the girl's shoulder, and we raced away in silence.

INTERLUDE ONE
AREA NINETY-FOUR
SECURE MILITARY BLACK SITE
TRIPLE EYE, ARIZONA
SIXTEEN MONTHS AGO

Dr. Rudy Sanchez sat in an uncomfortable metal chair with insufficient padding. Rudy was not as thin as he once was, and the hard, cold metal made his buttocks ache. The room was chilly despite the blistering heat outside. The steel table was bolted to the floor and set with a D-ring mounted on the opposite side.

The cup of coffee Rudy had brought with him from the warden's office had grown tepid and he suspected that the milk had passed its use-by date. He pushed the cup aside, glanced at his watch, spent a few minutes rereading the transcripts of his previous interviews with the prisoner who was being brought up from his cell. For more than two years Rudy Sanchez had come out to this place to try and unlock the mind of a man he believed to be psychotic and one of the most unrepentantly evil men alive. That was saying something, because Rudy had met people who were true monsters. As this man was a monster.

He heard the clang of a heavy door being slid back down the hall. The guards were coming with their prisoner. Just the thought of it sickened Rudy. It made him afraid, too, but the dominant reaction was one of deep disgust. Even so, he composed his face and settled against the chair back, crossed his legs, and waited.

There was the sound of shoes scuffing on the concrete outside, the scrape of a key as the guard fitted it into the lock, the click of tumblers and the creak of hinges. It called to mind scenes from old black-and-white movies about prisoners in the Tower of London. The door swung outward and four muscular, unsmiling guards escorted a small man into the room. He was thin but not emaciated, a man worn down to piano wire and petrified wood; the kind of man who would always be made stronger and more dangerous by hardship. Weakness did not seem to belong to this man's physical or psychological makeup.

The prisoner shuffled along within the restrictions of the ankle, waist, and wrist chains. He wore a ball-gag because he was a biter. His eyes, however, were calm. Rudy once remarked to his wife, Circe, that this prisoner had the calm and almost kind eyes of a country parson. Sometimes eyes were the windows to the soul, but with this prisoner they were pretty bits of polished glass.

The guards pushed the man into the only other chair in the room, and two of them stood with drawn batons while the others disconnected the handcuffs and clicked them securely to the sturdy D-ring on the steel table.

"Remove the gag, please," asked Rudy. They did so. "Wait outside."

The guards always hesitated on this, never wanting to leave anyone alone with this man. But Dr. Sanchez came armed with all of the authority of Mr. Church, and no one crossed the Big Man.

As always, the shift supervisor touched the butt of his baton to the prisoner's chest and said the same thing he always said. "Behave." The degree of threat in that single word was eloquent.

Rudy waited until the guards left and the door closed. Not locked, not even fully latched, but closed enough for a private conversation in discreet tones. He allowed the moment to change its frequency, to become calmer, quieter, and thereby more personal. It worked sometimes, coaxing the prisoner into having a more conversational discourse. At other times it worked against Rudy, making him feel exposed and vulnerable despite the fact that he was not the one in chains. He wondered what it would be today.

"Good afternoon, Dr. Sanchez," said the prisoner, his manner polite, his voice soft, his eyes filled with the lie of sunshine and smiles.

Rudy searched those uninformative parson's eyes, looking for a hint of the truth behind them. Trying to catch a glimpse of one of the most dangerous killers alive in a very troubled world.

He cleared his throat and tried to sound perfectly normal.

"Good afternoon, Mr. Santoro."

CHAPTER SEVEN
ARKLIGHT SAFE HOUSE
UNDISCLOSED LOCATION
ALEPPO, SYRIA

Oliver Jacobsen held his daughter and she clung to him, both of them sobbing fit to break the world.

At the safe house, a medic provided by Arklight checked the young woman out. She gave me a shake and a tiny smile. The girl had been roughed up but not sexually assaulted. We'd gotten to her in time. It did not give me even a flicker of regret for the damage done to those assholes. There was zero chance she'd ever have been released alive and unmolested. Not one chance. She and her father would have gone into an unmarked grave as soon as the stolen data was turned over.

We left them alone in the living room, and Havoc gathered in the kitchen. The safe house custodian was a hatchet faced woman who looked like she ate babies, but she gave me a hug and a kiss on the cheek.

She, like the medic, was part of a group called the Mothers of the Fallen, which was made up of women from dozens of cultures who had either been rescued from sexual slavery or had escaped. The main organization was focused on healing, helping, reeducating, and working with political groups to try and stop those kinds of practices. And they were making inroads, though it was an uphill battle. The slave trade in the twenty-first century was far bigger than it ever was in the pre–Civil War days. It was a trillion-dollar global market. Which is why the Mothers of the Fallen formed Arklight, their highly militant and extremely proactive response to the ongoing threats. A very smart, very scary woman who went by the code name of Lilith ran Arklight. Any stories you may have seen on the internet conspiracy websites about their body count is seriously underestimated.

I took Almasi's cell phone from my pocket and asked the team tech guy, Jackpot—aka Andrea—for an uplink. He handed me a small device about the size of a postage stamp and thick as three stacked quarters. It had a shape-adaptive plug and I socketed it into the charging port on the cell. Immediately tiny green lights flicked on along one side of the device. I tapped my earbud.

"Bug, sending a data stream from Almasi's phone. I need everything that's on it. Call logs, IMs, and emails. The works."

"On it," was the quick reply. I set the phone down, rubbed my eyes, and followed the smell of coffee into the kitchen.

My team sat around the table and I joined them, each of us letting the adrenaline work its way out of our system. Processing the details happens by degrees and sometimes the best clarity comes from sitting down like ordinary folks to have coffee and eggs and toast. Returning to the real world. Or, at least our version of it.

Havoc was the first of three strike teams in the newly formed Rogue Team International. RTI for short. Seven months ago I worked for the U.S. government as part of the Department of Military Sciences. But increasing red tape and runaway political party politics had made it impossible for us to function at top speed. Which sucked, because we were formed for exactly the opposite. We

JONATHAN MABERRY

were created to serve as an ultra-rapid response SpecOps group, a mix of science geeks and first-chair shooters. I'd run Echo Team for the DMS, and we'd scored a lot of wins against the bad guys, but then started tripping over the red tape.

So, our boss, Mr. Church, pulled the plug, shut the DMS down, and took a core of the old guard with him to start Rogue Team International. We were about a tenth the size of the DMS, but RTI had the advantage of picking our own cases, and moving fast with no oversight but our own. We work in harmony with the brighter lights in the U.N., but we're in no way answerable to them. We can pivot and shoot without anything slowing us down.

It felt a bit odd to roll out with a new team name and new combat call signs for all of us. I'd been Cowboy for years, now I was Outlaw. That handle was a bit of a joke, because on my last official DMS case I'd been hunted as a felon by the Secret Service. They tried to arrest me several times and were spectacularly unsuccessful. Even though the attempted arrests had proved to be illegal, the agents could have handled it with class and professional courtesy. They did not. Instead they came at me in ways that pushed all of my bad buttons. I wondered how they were coming along with their physical therapy. Didn't cry a bunch of tears over anything I did because they dealt the play.

Now I was an international man of mystery. Or something. Now I was Outlaw in spirit as well as name.

The other teams were also in gear, though not running a shooting op. Chaos was involved in a series of training exercises in the Afghan hills with some spooky cats from the SAS and Mossad. Bedlam Team was in Norway in one of those unofficial/official gigs tied to D9, the Denuclearization Agreement Summit with the United States, Russia, France, China, the UK, Pakistan, India, Israel, and North Korea. Officially Bedlam had no status and was not actually there. No paperwork, no designation, nothing. Unofficially, a friend of Church's in the U.S. State Department and another chum working in some unnamed department in the Norwegian government both asked Church for a little help. Not actually security, but boots covertly on the ground in case something weird happened. I was glad I didn't get that gig because it sounds like a yawn-fest. Instead I was having fun in Syria.

The Jacobsen gig was Havoc Team's fifth field op, and it was the first where we'd had to pull triggers. The previous four outings were a cross between useful scut work and trial runs.

I looked around at my crew. Apart from Top and Bunny, we had two new players. Seated in the corner was Andrea, a guy who could best be described as "usefully nondescript." He was medium height, medium build, had medium brown hair and medium brown eyes, and a face you'd forget two minutes after you met him. His full name was Andrea Bianchi, and he went by the call sign of Jackpot because he could not pass a game of chance without betting his paycheck. Craps, poker, arm wrestling, horses. You name it. Andrea was on loan to us from the Gruppo di Intervento Speciale, an elite division of Italy's Carabinieri, which was a branch of their armed forces responsible for both military and civil policing. The GIS were tough sonsabitches and although he didn't look it, Andrea was our utility infielder—he could rig a bomb, cut a throat, or pick a lock with equal nonchalance. He was also able to drive or fly anything with a motor.

The person sitting to my right was his polar opposite. I didn't know her real name, but her Arklight code name was Belle. Short for *La Belle Dame Sans Merci*. In combat she was Mother Mercy. A joke that none of her enemies found funny.

Belle was a Muslim woman from Mauritania whose face and body were heavily scarred from religious torture. She had worse scars than the ones we could all see, because when she was two years younger than Astrid she had been subjected to female genital mutilation. It's a common practice in Mauritania and all the more barbaric for that. Her sister had died from infections resulting from the same treatment. Belle had been severely beaten many times for trying to escape. Probably worse things had been done to her because there are a lot of fucking asshole men who treat women with no flicker of mercy or humanity.

Which is why Arklight sent a team in to bust up a large camp where FGM was carried out. During the battle, Belle picked up a rifle and began killing the doctors and soldiers. She'd never touched a gun before, but had seen them used enough times to understand. The story I got was that she killed eighteen men that day. No mercy at all; but then again those men did not deserve any.

I don't see myself shedding any tears for them, either.

Lilith recruited her into Arklight and spent two years turning her into a very precise weapon. Understand, Belle could have opted out and been sent to one of the camps run by the Mothers of the Fallen where women and girls are given medical treatment, education, training, and protection. That wasn't for Belle. She had a war to fight and, as it turned out, had natural gifts. Good with hands, feet, and knives; but with a gun—any kind of gun—she was the angel of death. Lilith's daughter, Violin, oversaw Belle's training as a sniper. When she exceeded even Violin's prodigious skills, Violin gave her that nickname. *La Belle Dame Sans Merci.*

The beautiful lady without mercy.

Lilith asked Belle if she wanted to join Havoc Team. It was a tough offer, too, because she would be the only woman on our team. There were two women on Chaos Team, and one on Bedlam, but Belle said that Havoc would be fine. The first day we were all on the firing range, she put a grouping of six shots into the groin of a paper target at two thousand yards. That's world class and, as personal statements go, eloquent.

Top, who was overseeing the range practice, put the end of a wooden matchstick between his teeth and chewed it from one corner of his mouth to the other. "She'll do right fine."

For him that was the highest possible praise.

"She brings baggage," I said.

He gave me a long, amused, fatherly look. "Then you two should get along fine. Because, let's face it, you've got enough baggage your own self to open a luggage store."

"It wasn't said as a criticism," I said.

He nodded.

We had room for more players on Havoc, but for now the five of us were a team. Still had some kinks to work out, but when we heard Astrid and her father talking in the other room, we looked at each other, shared nods, shared smiles.

It was good to be back in the game.

CHAPTER EIGHT

TRANSCRIPT OF *ONE WORLD/TWO SIDES* WITH JILLIAN BAKSHI AND DR. ANDY MING

HOSTED BY MITCH GREENFIELD

BLOOMBERG TELEVISION

> **GREENFIELD:** And we're back. We're talking with Jillian Bakshi, senior Pacific trade correspondent for *Forbes*, and Dr. Andy Ming, bestselling author of the book *One Korea?* Jillian, before the break you were telling us about the economic impact of a unified Korea . . .

> **BAKSHI:** Yes, Mitch. It's not as simple as erasing lines on a map or tearing down the guard posts on either side of the DMZ. The Korean War is not over. It never actually ended. There has been a truce— and not a comfortable once—since 1953, and in the time since then, North and South Korea have become vastly different countries.

> **GREENFIELD:** Different in what way? Politically or—?

> **BAKSHI:** In every way.

> **MING:** Agreed.

> **GREENFIELD:** How so?

> **BAKSHI:** Well, South Korea is now the eleventh biggest economy, boasting some of the world's top engineering and tech firms, while at the same time North Korea is a largely agricultural culture with a GDP less than one percent of the South. That puts them on completely uneven footing with little chance of an even integration. It's not like metropolitan New Yorkers and farmers in the American corn belt. The education alone is vastly different, the access to news, freedom of action, and ten thousand other things are different. It would be closer, in some ways, to comparing twenty-first-century America to early seventeenth-century farmsteads.

> **GREENFIELD:** You've said much the same in your book, Dr. Ming.

> **MING:** To a degree. Look, my father is Chinese and my mother is Korean. I've visited North and South Korea a number of times, and have spoken about reunification. I don't advocate a simple erasure of borders, though, and partly for the reasons Ms. Bakshi has discussed. It runs deeper than that, and I'm not just talking about the extreme differences in political ideology. The cultural differences have created two kinds of Koreans. Think about it . . . On one hand you have the farmers in the North, many of whom are not allowed education beyond a certain point and who have been spoon-fed Party rhetoric for so many years that they accept

it as the only possible truth. On the other you have the explosive growth of the culture in the South, which is driven by such incredible tech growth that students often study for ten, twelve, or even sixteen hours a day so they can vie for access to the three big universities. At the same time there is a popular culture that dominates everything. You have K-Pop, runaway fashion trends, web-comics, apps for everything, twenty-four-hour video game saloons, fetish for comics and cosplay. It's called the K-Wave but it's more of a tsunami. Tell me, if you were born and raised in the North, how would you ever assimilate into something like that?

BAKSHI: Much of that is good, it puts the South on the leading edge of cultural and technological change.

MING: Yes, but at a price. The "K-Wave," as it's called, had plenty of problems. I mentioned the hours students study, but this is also reflected in the sometimes brutal hours people work at their jobs. The fashion and cosplay culture has resulted in the highest rate of cosmetic surgery in the world—not just as an attempt at beautification, but to become the characters in pop culture. And we also see one of the highest suicide rates in the world.

BAKSHI: And there are strong movements within the government, the education system, and elsewhere in the South that are working to address these things.

MING: I'm delighted to hear it, but I brought those things up as a way of putting reunification in the lens. Merging such disparate cultures is noble in theory, but in practice you'd have what are essentially pre-industrial peasants colliding culturally with people way out on the chaotic edge of social change, pop culture brand addiction, and a dangerous one-upmanship of social acceptance.

BAKSHI: Are you saying reunification is impossible?

MING: I'm saying it's improbable. Look, we know from observing North Korean defectors that there is a real struggle for them to assimilate into South Korean—and by some extension *Western*—culture. The culture shock causes depression, very often they are unable to find work because they aren't trained in what the South needs of its workforce. There are many cases of defectors returned to the North.

BAKSHI: That can be addressed, though. If the South instituted some kind of affirmative action program that would give North Koreans the chance to learn the skills, more opportunities would open up.

MING: Sure, and you would have a lot of pushback, just as you had in America during its race- or gender-based affirmative action programs.

BAKSHI: Those programs did a lot of good.

MING: Sure, but I've never seen an affirmative action program that was as well written and flexible as it needs to be to keep pace with cultural changes. The South's culture pivots on a dime, so any social programming would need to be equally flexible, and you'd need a massive PR campaign to sell it to the South. And likely to the North.

BAKSHI: That's pretty cynical, Andy.

MING: That's politics, Jillian.

GREENFIELD: We're going to take another short break and when we come back we'll continue with the topic of Korean Reunification, and focus on the military and political ramifications. Stay tuned.

CHAPTER NINE
HOTEL HELLSTEN
LUNTMAKARGATAN 68
STOCKHOLM, SWEDEN
FIVE MONTHS AGO

"I . . . I've never done this before," he said.

Eve had expected the man to say this. It was always in the script, no matter how improvised the other details were.

She had the tab of his zipper between her thumb and forefinger. She leaned forward another inch so that her breath was hot on his cheek, his ear. "Do you want me to stop?"

"No," he said. Almost a gasp, because they both knew he didn't want her to stop. "It's just that I—"

She simultaneously bit his earlobe in a way that disrupted any attempt at coherent speech while at the same time slowly pulling his zipper down. His cock, hard for an hour already, bulged into the opening. Her fingers spread the lips of his fly and closed around his shaft. He wore cotton boxers and she worked her hand along his length. He hissed and arched his back and gasped, and was hers.

Seduction was easy for her. She had the body for it, the face for it, and the heart for it. Eve was thirty and looked twenty. Five-three, a hundred and twenty-six pounds of curves over useful muscle. The best cosmetic nips and tucks in the world, which meant the effect was obvious but none of the surgery was. Her hair, top and bottom, was currently a rich auburn. She had not, of course, managed to seduce everyone she targeted, but her success rate gave her a glow of pride. Eighty-three percent of men, seventy-seven percent of women.

This man was an easy mark.

They kissed deeply, and she knew how to school him into being better at it without making it seem like she was superior. That was a subtle tactic, and it always worked. It empowered men like this. And women, too. They would think they were really good at this, and her obvious reactions would push them closer and closer into commission.

She let the kissing build a little and then she broke contact, bent down, and took him in her mouth while unbuckling his belt and pulling his pants off. His boxers came next. It was a bit awkward because he was pawing at her, trying to get to her breasts. She pulled up her blouse and bra and let him play while she continued to blow him.

"Oh God . . . oh God . . . ," he moaned, making it a litany. A familiar one. Eve was excellent at gauging how close a man was to orgasm, and before things got too far she straightened, pulled her blouse off, reached under her skirt and pulled down her thong, snatching a condom from the bedside table.

"No," he protested, but she gave him a wicked smile.

"It's the wrong time of the month for me. I don't want to get pregnant. Besides . . . they're ultrathin. You'll feel everything, I can promise you that."

She rolled the condom over his erection and then climbed atop him, reaching down to guide him into her. He gasped like a cracked steam pipe and Eve moaned, too. She was very wet and very excited and began riding him, slowly and deeply at first, telling him how hard he was, how big, how good. He had his hands on her breasts, pulling and pinching her nipples, and she braced on his stomach to give her good control over what her hips did.

She made sure to make a lot of noise because even though Adam was very quiet, she didn't want to spoil the moment. She was enjoying herself and didn't want the mark to be distracted until she had what she needed from him.

"God," she cried, "fuck me harder."

He did. The man was so close to me that she knew she could make him come right away if she wanted, but she was selfish. Her own orgasm was poised there, waiting for her, and she set the rhythm that worked best for her. It rose up like a dark wave, chasing all of the light from her mind, sending her into a special, beautiful place of burning shadows. Black, with hints of fiery red.

"Fuuuuuuuuuuuuck," she cried as she came, and her internal muscles clenched him, and that pulled the man up to the edge of the cliff and shoved him over. He came so hard that his back arched and shudders rippled through his body. He screamed louder than she did, and at a higher register, and then grabbed her hips, braced his feet, and lifted her off the bed, thrusting with hard, grunting, powerful attacks of his hips.

And then he collapsed back, sweat glistening on his face and throat as if he'd run up ten flights of stairs. His eyes were glazed and unfocused, and aftershocks trembled in his groin and thighs.

Eve bent and kissed him as she lifted her hips so that his cock, already growing flaccid, slipped out of her. She reached back and slid the condom off of him, pinching it closed so as not to spill a drop.

"Thank you," she whispered as she looked at the bulging receptacle end of the condom. "Wow. You came a lot. You must have really needed this."

"It's . . . been . . . a while," he gasped.

"So," said Adam as he stepped out of the wardrobe, "was it good for you?"

The man screeched in surprise, shoving Eve away and clawing a sheet in front of his crotch.

"What the fuck is this?"

Adam raised the pistol. It was a Bulgarian Makarov loaded with .380 ACP rounds and fitted with a sound suppressor. "This," he said, "is you getting fucked."

"Again," corrected Eve.

"Again," agreed Adam.

"What do you want?" demanded the man. "My wallet's in my—"

Adam sat down on the edge of the bed and placed the barrel of the pistol against the tip of the man's nose. "Shhhh," he said gently. "Now isn't the time for you to get loud. Nope. Silence is golden."

The man looked cross-eyed at the gun. "Please . . . I have a wife. I have kids."

"We know," said Eve. "Elsa is at work. Don't you love how her office is decorated? All those photos of the kids. So cute."

"Very cute," said Adam.

"And as for the girls . . . Who picked out Freja's outfit today? That unicorn top? She's the envy of everyone in daycare. And Maja . . . well, she's always popular. She's so pretty she could wear a burlap sack and the boys would still fall in love. Especially now that she's so grown up. C-cup, I think. Busty for a thirteen-year-old."

As Eve spoke, the man's face drained of all blood, all color, leaving his skin gray and waxy. His mouth moved, forming disconnected words but not making any sound. Then he managed to push out a single word.

"Please . . ."

So loaded with horror, with need, that it sounded as if it was scraped from the rawness of his throat.

Adam moved the pistol, tapping the man's upper lip, his chin, his chest, his navel and then his scrotum. With each tap he said, "Boop!"

It made Eve giggle.

"Don't hurt my family," wheezed the man. "For the love of God, please don't hurt them."

Adam used the barrel to lift the sheet away from the man's flaccid penis. "Impressive junk you got there."

"Not bad," said Eve as she bent and kissed Adam on the mouth. "Yours is bigger."

"Don't care."

"Me neither."

"What do you *want?*" demanded the man.

"Oh," said Adam, "we want a lot. We want more than you're going to want to give. But we don't want to turn this into a long discussion, and I'm pretty sure you don't want either of us to have to insist that you cooperate. You're a smart man, Mr. Lingmerth, so you can probably imagine some of the things we could do to *make* you help us."

"No! Don't hurt them."

"Hurt is a relative term," said Adam. He pulled a cell phone out of his pocket and handed it to Eve, who punched in the security code and pulled up an image. She showed it to Ronald Lingmerth. The picture was a five-year-old mixed-race girl. Medium brown skin, paler curly hair, blue eyes.

"You know this kid, right?" said Eve.

Lingmerth did not want to answer.

"Sure you do," said Adam. "Tuva Johansson. She has playdates with Freja twice a week. Sometimes more. Best friends are such a precious thing." He leaned close and smiled like a wolf. "I bet Freja would be absolutely devastated if Tuva wound up raped and murdered. Bet she'd be destroyed when the forensics techs swabbed your semen out of that little girl's mouth and ass and—"

Lingmerth screamed and lunged for the condom Eve still held. Eve twisted away and Adam hooked his left fist into the naked man's balls with terrible force. Lingmerth emitted an ultrasonic shriek and his whole body convulsed into a tight knot of agony. Adam grabbed a fistful of Lingmerth's hair and forced his head back, emphasizing this by pressing the silencer hard up under the soft palate.

"Shhhh," he said again, leaning on it more now, making it a threat.

Things became suddenly very still. Lingmerth lay there, barely breathing, eyes wide and trapped, heart pounding. Eve got off the bed, crossed the room to the wardrobe, and removed a small biological specimen carrier. When she opened it, tendrils of dry ice vapor curled out like snakes. She unscrewed a vial, upended the condom, and squeezed all the semen out. She sealed the vial, closed the container, went into the bathroom, flushed the condom, and then returned to the bedroom with a towel, which she used to pat her vagina dry.

"You have a choice," said Adam. "Well, three choices. Choice A is you fuck with us, and the cops find Tuva's body with your jism and DNA all over her. You go to prison and your family is destroyed forever. Wait, wait, don't say anything yet. Just listen. Good boy. Choice B is that you try some kind of stunt—like feeding us the wrong information in the hopes that we'll get caught, or going straight to the police to try and warn them in time to prevent our people from doing that to Maja or Freja. What's the consequence for that? Well, it wouldn't be Tuva's pussy they swab your DNA out of. You have three pussies at home, let's not forget."

Lingmerth's face had gone from gray to green and was now an awful purple.

"Or," said Adam, "you go for what's behind Door Number Three."

"You're mixing a metaphor, I think," said Eve.

Adam blew her a raspberry. "Choice C," he said, "is you help us without any games, without trying any hinky shit at all, and then the only people who ever get hurt are people you never heard of. People you've never met. People who don't mean a fucking thing to you. People who, even if you hear about what happens to them, won't be real to you because they belong to a whole other part of the world."

The cell phone rang. Eve answered, listened, said, "Got it, Daddy."

She fetched the biological transport box, took it to the door, opened it, and handed it to someone outside. Lingmerth could not see who it was but had the sense that it was a man. Whoever "Daddy" was. Then Eve closed and locked the door.

Adam removed the gun from Lingmerth's chin. "Get up," he said.

"Don't kill me," cried Lingmerth.

"Get up. Right now."

The man did, and Adam had him sit in the heavy wooden armchair across the room. He fished plastic zip ties from his pocket and held the pistol as Eve used the ties to secure Lingmerth's wrists and ankles to the arms and legs of the chair. Adam produced a ball-gag and Eve fitted that into place as well.

Then Adam set the gun down on the nightstand and began to undress.

"We're going to give you a few minutes to think through your three choices," he said as he stepped out of his dark trousers. He was lean and muscular and looked like he could be Eve's brother. They both had natural pale blond hair and blue eyes.

When Adam dropped his underwear it was obvious he was fully erect. Eve came over to him and they stood kissing, hands roving hungrily over each other. Then they tumbled onto the bed and for the next thirty-five minutes they made love with tenderness and passion. Eve came twice, once when he went down on her and then again with Adam as they coupled on the sweaty sheets. Adam did not use a condom. The only words spoken were a single sharp rebuke when Eve looked over and saw that Lingmerth had his eyes squinched shut.

"Open your eyes, motherfucker," she snarled in a voice that was suddenly inhuman. "Watch us or I'll do things to your children that will *ruin* you."

Then she turned back to Adam, and kissed him sweetly, and they made love.

Option C was always the winner. That's what Daddy had taught them, and Daddy was always right.

CHAPTER TEN
IN FLIGHT
OVER THE MEDITERRANEAN SEA

Bug *bing-bonged* in my ear. "Outlaw," he said, "we're getting a ton of stuff off that cell phone. It was coded and all but . . . well . . . this is me."

"Stop gloating and tell me what you found."

"Almasi was not just working for Assad," said Bug. "He was the point man to oversee the acquisition of a whole bunch of different biological and chemical agents which he's been selling to various clients. The Jacobsen stuff was only part of it. Most of it is referred to by code names or numbers, but there are some messages that name the vendor for some of it."

"You actually got a name?"

"I do," he said, "and you're not going to like it."

"Bug, would you like a long list of all the things I don't like?"

Instead of answering, he gave me the name.

"Kuga," he said.

He was right. I didn't like it one damn bit.

I closed my eyes and considered banging my head against the wall. "How sure are you?"

"Very," said Bug. "The name is actually in a few of the messages we've already decoded. I have the guys working on the rest. They use a random encryption algorithm and—"

"I don't care if they used a Ninja Turtles secret decoder ring. I need everything else you can find on Kuga. Everything, Bug."

There was a pause, then Bug said, "Look, Joe, don't get your hopes up too much. We've been round and round with trying to ID Kuga. Every time we get a whiff he's gone."

"Christmas is coming," I said, "try and spread a little fucking cheer, okay?"

His sigh was long and eloquent and he ended the call.

I was in a comfortable leather seat on a very expensive Cessna Citation X private jet. The rest of Havoc were sprawled asleep in their chairs. Bunny had earphones on, but he'd shifted in his sleep and the left cup was askew, and I could hear the faint strains of Christmas music. "I'll Be Home for Christmas." The Elvis version. The song was always a sad one for me, because I'd spent so many Christmases away from my dad and my brother, Sean, and his family. We all had, and the music, coupled with the after-action blues, painted the moment in shades of melancholy.

My big white combat shepherd, Ghost, was aboard, too. He hadn't come on the last part of the rescue mission, but since we didn't know if there was going to be mission creep—things changing from what we thought and hoped was going to happen—I'd brought him to Syria with me. Mostly, he sulked, pooped, ate too many treats, and slept. I watched his ribs rise and fall, and saw a leg occasionally twitch as he dreamed his doggy dreams.

The plane was silent as a tomb, and I was wide awake.

"Kuga," I said quietly. "Fuck."

Kuga. Jeez. If the devil took human form, he would be Kuga.

And, yes, it was only a code name. It was a Bosnian word that meant "plague," so you can figure it wasn't his actual surname unless he was born into the unluckiest family in history. Unfortunately it was the most common of his many aliases that we had. Kuga. He had a bunch of other nicknames too, but the one that always hit me was the one hung on him by Comtre Admiral Laurent Isnard, head of the Commandement des Opérations Spéciales—France's Special Operations Command. He always referred to Kuga as the "*Concierge de l'enfer.*"

Hell's Concierge.

Yeah, fair enough. If you wanted financing to hire a private army to overthrow an inconvenient African tribal government on mineral-rich land, Kuga could arrange it. If you needed canisters of VX nerve gas to fire into a crowd of worshippers on a holy day, call Kuga—and it did not seem to matter if the worshippers were praying to Allah, Buddha, Shiva, or Jesus. If you wanted some polonium-210 to assassinate a government official, Kuga's your guy. And his name pops up all over the place—Africa, the Middle East, Southeast Asia, among the cartels, and even among some of the mouth-breathing, hard alt-right neo-Nazi assholes in America.

He's never the delivery boy. As far as we can tell he's never gotten blood on his own hands, but because of the concierge services he provides, you could fill about a dozen graveyards, and I am likely underestimating that number. Kuga is the Professor Moriarty of international weapons smuggling. He's the force behind half the dirty deals on seven continents.

He's like an evil spirit in the overlapping worlds of international politics, terrorism, and intelligence. I'd first started hearing that name four years ago, early on in my career as a DMS shooter. Like Moriarty, there is no actual proof that he even exists. One theory is that Kuga is the name for a team; another is that there is no Kuga at all, but that the name is adopted as a reusable stage name for people who do what he does. The Alan Smithee of the terrorism world, except that he doesn't direct bad movies but instead causes very bad things to happen.

He came onto the DMS radar some years back when his name showed up in a few heavily encrypted messages being passed to Otto Wirth, the psychotic aide to Cyrus Jakoby, one of the most dangerous and vile real-world mad scientists we've ever encountered. In those messages it appeared that Kuga was the source of stolen clinical samples of exotic strains of sickle cell anemia and Tay-Sachs disease that were then used to create ethnic-specific bioweapons. Even with our MindReader computer system, we found nothing beyond his mention in those emails.

Then his name popped up in connection with genetically modified Ebola samples used by a terrorist organization called the Seven Kings.

And again, when a bizarre new strain of ultrafast-onset rabies was used by Zephyr Bain to try and dramatically reduce the overall human population as a way of ensuring the survival of the rest.

JONATHAN MABERRY

Kuga. Here, there, and nowhere at all.

Even though the DMS caught and killed the bad guys running those old operations, Kuga, like a ghost, slipped away. We had no photo of him, no physical description, no hard details at all. Even his nickname, though Bosnian, did not mean that he was, in fact, from Bosnia. Kuga used and shed so many disguises that no one knew one thing for certain about him. Hell, he could even be a she, not a he. We simply did not know. Bug's team has pieced together a whole slew of cover names Kuga uses around the world. Marad in the Middle East, Kasallik in Uzbekistan, Izurria in the Basque region, Chuma in Bulgaria, Maras in Lithuania, Veba in Turkey. All of them are variations of "plague."

Kuga. The plague. A merchant of death. Hell's Concierge.

Fuck.

If he was now vending high-end bioweapons to Assad, it meant that things in Syria were about to go from bad to really fucking worse. And it was too soon to tell if our raid on Almasi, and the subsequent liberation of Astrid Jacobsen, was going to substantially derail Kuga's plans. If so, that would be a nice Christmas present to the world.

"Kuga," I said. "Damn."

Ghost opened his eyes, caught my mood, and came over to put his big white head on my lap. Sensing my distress, he then wanted comfort *from* me. I obligingly scratched his neck, but my thoughts lingered on Kuga. About a man who was so clever and so elusive that not even Bug, with all the resources of the world's most powerful computer system, was able to locate him.

As we flew back to Greece I should have been happy, relieved that a mission had gone off so well, with no harm to Astrid or her father, or to my team.

I should have been comforted in the knowledge of a job well done.

And yet I was not.

Bunny's playlist had left Elvis behind and was now playing "I Heard the Bells on Christmas Day," which is the most downbeat holiday song I know. Well, maybe the "Coventry Carol" tops that list, but so far Bunny was two for two with stuff that depressed the hell out of me. I tried not to listen to the lyrics, which were based on a Civil War poem by Longfellow, but the cabin was soundproof and I had no choice.

> *I heard the bells on Christmas Day*
> *Their old, familiar carols play,*
> *and wild and sweet*
> *The words repeat*
> *Of peace on earth, good-will to men!*
>
> *Then from each black, accursed mouth*
> *The cannon thundered in the South,*
> *And with the sound*
> *The carols drowned*
> *Of peace on earth, good-will to men!*
>
> *It was as if an earthquake rent*
> *The hearth-stones of a continent,*
> *And made forlorn*
> *The households born*
> *Of peace on earth, good-will to men!*
>
> *And in despair I bowed my head;*
> *"There is no peace on earth," I said;*
> *"For hate is strong,*
> *And mocks the song*
> *Of peace on earth, good-will to men!"*

I try to be a practical guy. Grounded and whatnot. I try. But, let's face it, I'm working with some broken tools, at least emotionally-speaking. I didn't sign up to fight because I like the color motif in the flag, and I sure as hell don't give a blind fuck about *any* political party. I'm not political. I consider myself a patriot, but when it comes down to it I'm for the people. I know from very personal experience what it means to be helpless or defenseless in the face of powerful aggression and hate. My fight is for the people who can't fight for themselves. That sounds heroic and all that shit, but it's not. Maybe it's me working on some karmic debts. Whatever.

JONATHAN MABERRY

My team are all like me. Battered knights in rusty armor with crooked lances. The windmills we tilt at are intolerance and greed, extremist ideologies, cultural and political madness. We stand together against that, and we have a pretty good track record for kicking ass and taking names. We've saved a lot of lives, sometimes by ending lives. Nature of being soldiers. Most days we can sleep okay because we know that we've done our best.

And some days the world itself takes a breath and whispers a bit of reassurance. Like the D9 summit coming up in Norway. All nine of the nations who have nuclear weapons have agreed to sit down for serious discussions about significantly reducing their nuclear arsenals. The chat around the watercooler was that this was real, not just the usual political circle jerk. That was a good thing. A sane thing.

But some days . . .

Sometimes it doesn't feel like we're on a battlefield facing enemies who are as mortal and fragile as we are. Sometimes we don't seem to be awake in a world of sane people who don't want mutually assured destruction to be our defining political strategy. Sometimes it's like we're ankle-deep in wet sand watching as the water is pulled out by forces wildly beyond our own powers. And somewhere out there, just beyond the limits of our vision, something big and dark is rising up, forming a tsunami of such immense destructive blackness that when it hits, none of our bullets, none of our skills, and nothing of who we are will be able to stop it.

No soldier wins every battle, because life itself is a battle and no one gets out of that alive. Which means that we may fall—no, *will* fall—with no guarantee that anyone will be there to take our places.

I scratched Ghost's head and he looked at me with immense and bottomless brown eyes that were filled with knowing and understanding. And with a resignation and acceptance that was beyond me.

The song ended and was replaced with something happier. Someone was rocking around a Christmas tree as if everything was right with the goddamn world. But that other song haunted me. Darkening the skies through which we flew.

Tired as I was, I didn't sleep at all on the flight.

INTERLUDE TWO
AREA NINETY-FOUR
SECURE MILITARY BLACK SITE
TRIPLE EYE, ARIZONA
SIXTEEN MONTHS AGO

"I'm pleased to see that the physical therapy is proceeding," said Rudy Sanchez. "Are you in any discomfort?"

Rafael Santoro paused before he answered. He always did that no matter how basic or inconsequential the question. Rudy knew that this was a tactic refined by long use. The pause suggested that the person about to speak needed time to think, but that was not the case.

"The surgeons lacked commitment," he said. "That's understandable."

He spoke with a pronounced lisp that was likely a permanent souvenir from what had happened. Seven months ago Santoro stole a spoon from the mess hall, sharpened it, and used it to cut out his own tongue. The prison doctors managed to reattach it, but not well enough.

The lisp was a dangerous element for Rudy. It gave Santoro a softness and vulnerability that were entirely false. And it was a source of guilt for Rudy, because after a series of sessions in which they had begun to drill into the reasons Santoro had become aligned with the international criminal empire called the Seven Kings, Rudy had used Santoro's blind and absolute faith in the woman who the Kings called the Goddess as a lever to crack Santoro open. The killer was deeply religious and still secretly worshipped her, even though she, and all of the Kings, were dead, and the organization destroyed.

The Kings group was built on the bones of ancient conspiracy theories, adopting rituals and practices that were partly to allow the members to hide their true identities, and partly to create a mystique. They used the behavior modification and loyalty-building strategies of a number of history's most successful cults. They had teams of computer experts seed the internet with vague stories of the Seven Kings, and had other teams dive deep into Wikipedia and other online information sites to plant select bits of data. Those computer experts hacked into the host sites to change time codes so that the Seven Kings mentions appeared to have always been there. They went through thousands of university websites, sneaking past security, and changing footnotes and entries in thesis papers. They seeded hundreds of books into the pop culture and conspiracy theory genres, even to the point of influencing revisions of older works published by big houses. It was a long game, taking decades, and costing billions, but it worked.

At the same time, they had people working social media platforms, influencing conversations, filtering data to the press on both sides of political lines. The Kings were not themselves political. Politics was something they could use, as was the media.

Rafael Santoro was there for almost all of it. He had been seduced into the church of the Goddess Eris, and rose to become her greatest apostle. He served Eris' son, Hugo Vox, who was the King of Fear; becoming his Conscience, a kind of advisor. Santoro also formed and trained an elite commando group, the Kingsmen.

Santoro's worst crimes, though, were not even these things. He was used by the King of Fear to create a program of blackmail and extortion that ruined the lives and corrupted the souls of hundreds of key people in business, the media, politics, and more. During his last project, the *Sea of Hope,* he attempted to release weaponized Ebola on a charity fund-raising cruise ship filled with celebrities and the children of the former president. That same plague would have spread to the mainlands of South and Central America, likely killing many millions.

That was Rafael Santoro.

The man who sat across from Rudy was only wearing the disguise of weakness and helplessness. His skin had paled to a prison gray, his cheeks were sunken from frequent hunger strikes, and he had that lisp.

It was important for Rudy to give himself a perspective check before these sessions because most of the work he did was helping victims of trauma. Santoro was not that. Not in any way.

"How are they treating you?" asked Rudy.

Santoro almost smiled. There was a twitch of it on his hard mouth. "Like I deserve. No . . . they treat me better than I deserve."

"Because of the things you did?"

"No."

"Then why do you think you deserve harsh treatment?"

"Because of the things I did not do," said Santoro.

Rudy nodded. "Because the Seven Kings organization was torn down?"

"You are not a naïve man, Dr. Sanchez. You should not pretend that you are."

"Because you did not keep Eris from being killed."

"The Goddess," corrected Santoro.

"You do understand that the 'goddess' was an affectation, don't you?" asked Rudy. "We've talked about this at length. She was a woman. Extraordinary in many ways, but ultimately very human."

"So was Jesus until he received the Holy Spirit, yes?"

"And you believe that Eris ascended to a higher state at some point?"

"The Goddess," Santoro said again, reinforcing the correction by speaking very slowly. He was heavily manacled, but he reeked of threat. Of promise.

"You believe your goddess ascended?" said Rudy, choosing phrasing that would keep the conversation civil.

Santoro studied him as if assessing the degree of implied insult. After a moment he nodded, satisfied with the compromise. "Yes," he said flatly. "She became something much more than human. Anyone who met her would understand that."

"And yet her son, Hugo, the person who, arguably, knew her best, betrayed her and killed her. He was her Judas. The boat she was on was blown to splinters and no bodies were ever recovered."

"Sebastian Gault was fished out of the water," said Santoro. "Or, what was left of him."

"He was," conceded Rudy, "but after an exhaustive search by the Coast Guard, no trace of Eris was ever found."

"Which tells you what?" asked Santoro.

"Which tells me there wasn't enough of her left to find."

"Or that she ascended at the moment of her death."

"I don't think that's reasonable."

Santoro played with the links of his chains for a moment before he replied. "The priests of the temple in Jerusalem turned Jesus over to the Romans. He was betrayed, beaten, humiliated, crucified, and stabbed through the side. He died a mortal man's death and yet rose on the third day. Resurrection happens, Doctor, and don't fool yourself into believing we are no longer living in an age of miracles. As for the Goddess, the fact that people who knew her disliked her and refuted her celestial nature does nothing to shake my belief. People are often blind about the things closest to them. Consider Luke, chapter four, verse twenty-four."

Rudy thought about it, then provided the scripture. "*Truly I say to you, no prophet is welcome in his hometown.*"

"From *your* Bible, Doctor."

"My Bible? It is my understanding that you are also Catholic."

"I was raised Catholic," said Santoro, "but left that false faith when I found the true religion."

"And yet you quote Christian scripture."

Santoro shrugged, an action that made his chains tinkle. "Speak to a man in his own language. The Goddess has only been dead for a few years. There is still plenty of time for her apostles to write a new Bible. A *true* Bible."

"Will *you* write that book?" asked Rudy.

"If I did, Dr. Sanchez, I would not be the first apostle to have done so while in chains."

Rudy nodded. "Have you started writing it?"

Santoro shrugged. "It is not my time and I do not have the materials."

"I can provide notebooks and pencils."

"And while I'm walking in the exercise yard the guards can photograph what I've written for you?"

"Would that be a bad thing? A holy book is there to be read, is it not?"

Santoro gave him a pitying look. "Sometimes I am impressed by your perceptions and intelligence, Doctor, and sometimes you make me wonder if you are a fool."

"Tell me why you think that."

The killer did not meet his eyes and instead spent a long time slowly tracing a circle on the tabletop with a fingertip. When he finally spoke he did not look at Rudy but instead stared into the center of the circle he was tracing.

Without looking up he said, "I'll miss you when I'm gone."

"Gone? Are you expecting a transfer?"

"The roaches talk to me, Doctor," said Santoro. He raised his eyes and instead of the flickers of madness or malice, Rudy saw a man whose face was filled with hope.

"The . . . *roaches* . . . talk to you?"

"Yes."

"What do they say?"

"Many things."

"Would you be willing to share some of those things with me?" asked Rudy.

At first he did not think the prisoner would answer, which is how many of these sessions ended. With an unpredictable and immovable silence. A stopping. Not today, however, for Rafael Santoro leaned close and whispered to Rudy.

"They tell me a great change is coming, Dr. Sanchez. They tell me that the world as we know it is coming to its end and a new world will rise up from it."

"Excuse me," said Rudy mildly, "but we have heard that kind of thing before. From Eris—from the *Goddess*. From others, too."

"That does not change the fact."

Rudy sat back and crossed his legs. "You're a clever man, and a games player. It's always a challenge to know when you are telling me your truth or merely playing a game."

Santoro smiled. "A day will come when you know which is which."

"Oh? And how will I recognize that day?"

"You'll know."

"That's unfair," said Rudy. "At least give me a hint."

Santoro thought about it, or seemed to do so. His eyes filled with strange lights but it was hard to read them. After nearly a full minute, Santoro said, "When the Koreans begin killing each other," he said, "then you'll know."

JONATHAN MABERRY

IZMIR, TURKEY
PART TWO

The agony of my feelings allowed me no respite; no incident occurred from which my rage and misery could not extract its food.

Frankenstein
—MARY SHELLEY

CHAPTER ELEVEN
IZMIR ADNAN MENDERES AIRPORT
IZMIR, TURKEY

Havoc Team took Astrid to the RTI headquarters, which was on Omfori Island in Greece. I didn't go with them. Instead I arranged to meet an old friend in the city of Izmir, Turkey, because Bug found a reference to Kuga having met with Assad's agents there. He did some extra digging and built a pretty good case for Arma Kitap Kafe, a trendy little place, to be a regular hangout for people in the more upscale echelon of the Mediterranean black market.

So, I went to Turkey and was met at the airport by a tall, beautiful, strange, and deeply dangerous woman who I knew only by a code name. Violin.

Daughter of Lilith, and the top field agent for Arklight. We'd met in Iran when one of her field ops collided with mine. Took us a while to sort out if we were enemies, rivals, or allies. Turned out to be a bit of all three, but when things got interesting over there, we went into battle together. There are only three people I can name who I would never—under any circumstances—want to have to fight. Church is one, Lilith is another, and, yeah, Violin is the third. She is dangerous on a different scale than anything that measures me. I'm okay with that.

She was waiting for me at baggage claim. Violin is built like a dancer and moves like one, even when she's killing people. Right now she was dressed discreetly in a long-sleeved blouse, full skirt, and a white head scarf over her glossy dark hair. Ten or fifteen years ago, women dressed in a more secular European fashion, but Turkey has since shifted to religious conservatism. Violin was not the kind to bow to custom unless it suited her, and for now discretion was more useful. I hadn't checked a bag and had only a carry-on backpack, so she fell into step beside me as we headed for the exit.

"Hello," I said.

"Hello," she said and gave me the briefest of smiles—a microsecond of wicked humor—and a flash of dark eyes. We had some other kinds of history, too. Once upon a time. Nowadays I was with Junie Flynn, and happy to be so. And Violin had picked up a stray by the name of Harry Bolt, who was waiting for us outside by an idling SUV. He looked like a shorter Matt Damon, but a Matt Damon who hadn't seen the inside of a gym since high school.

"Hey, Joe," he said brightly, offering his hand.

I wanted to punch him. Actually, most people want to punch Harry. He has that kind of face. Not actually a bad guy, but deeply inept, awkward, clumsy, and—as far as everyone but Violin seemed to think—a liability in the field.

"Hey, thanks for using my real first name," I said, taking his hand and doing a moderately good job of grinding his metacarpals to paste. He winced, partly in pain and partly in embarrassment.

"Um. Sorry. Um. *Fred.*"

Frederick Holmann was my cover. Had *been* my cover.

"Get in the fucking car," I muttered.

He got into the fucking car. Violin took shotgun and I glowered from the backseat as Harry pulled into traffic.

Harry had some interesting history. His real name was Harcourt Bolton, Junior, son of the rather infamous Harcourt Bolton, Senior. Daddy had been pretty much my hero. Actually, he'd been hero to most of the JSOC guys in the biz. Bolton was a self-made billionaire, philanthropist, playboy, and—behind all of that—the most successful spy the CIA ever produced. He was Batman and Tony Stark and James Bond rolled into one. His list of wins was a mile long. There have been movies based on some of his cases, though with most of the details completely changed. Tom Cruise has played two different versions of him, and Matt Damon played another version. Neither was quite as amazing as the real deal.

Except . . .

The real deal turned out to be one of the greatest traitors America has ever had. Made Benedict Arnold look like a natural-born hero. Bolton had used technology stolen from DARPA and some deep-cover black-budget science groups to launch a campaign of murder and terror that came very close to wrecking the country. Many people died. Among the tech he stole was a real honest-to-God mind control process that allowed his agents to hijack the minds of several DMS agents, including Top and Bunny. While under Bolton's control, my guys committed a series of brutal murders. I nearly died from a rare form of influenza, and the DMS was very nearly wrecked.

Harry was, luckily, not his father's son. He was perhaps the worst CIA case manager in the agency's storied history, and his career was only kept afloat because of who his father was. When the DMS took Daddy down, Harry left the Agency.

Here's the weirdest part, though. During that case, Harry met Violin, and somehow *they* became a thing. I know. I've dealt with some seriously weird science-fiction bullshit in my years as a Spec-Ops shooter, but I have never encountered anything as weird as Harry Bolt and Violin as a couple. That just shakes the foundations of reality for me.

I could see Harry checking me out in the rearview mirror. He was sweating.

"You sweep the car?" I asked him.

"*I* swept it," said Violin. "It's clean."

"Good. So, tell me, how is it you're already here in Turkey? Last I heard you were making people unhappy in Saudi Arabia."

"Mission creep," she said. "Man plans, God laughs." She went on to explain that her mother, Lilith, sent her to Riyadh to hunt for some black marketers trying to sell trigger systems for man-portable dirty bombs. The hunt hit a snag when those guys somehow made the Arklight team and decided to set an ambush. As master plans go, it was not a good one, because they grossly underestimated who they were setting that trap to catch. Violin, Harry, and three Arklight field operators took it to the black marketers and their hired thugs in very wet and dramatic ways. The plan had been to capture at least one of them and ask a bunch of questions. You do not want details on how Arklight conducts interrogations. Unfortunately during the fight, one of the hired thugs tried to throw a grenade but got shot the instant he raised up from cover to throw it. The grenade fell and the blast took out virtually everyone. The last of the black marketers was mortally wounded and only managed to gasp out a few words. Just enough to send Violin to Izmir in hopes of setting a trap for Kuga or one of his senior lieutenants.

"When we're done here," she said, "my mother wants me to go to Oslo. Just in case anyone tries to sabotage the D9 summit."

"Does Lilith think that's likely?"

Violin shrugged. "Not really. The security will be massive. People talk, though, and there will be protestors, and protestors are often infiltrated by radicals of the opposing ideology. We may pick up some crumbs of useful intelligence by merging into the crowds and listening to who's complaining the most."

"Long shot," I said.

"Of course it is," said Violin, "and I think it's a bit of punishment for what happened in Riyadh."

"Ah," I said. "Okay, here's what I have." I gave them the latest intel from Bug about possible Kuga sightings at Arma Kitap Kafe. "We even have a possible—and I do mean possible—physical description of our guy."

"Wait, you have a description of *Kuga*?" blurted Harry. "That's fucking cool."

"Don't get too excited. Bug says there's only about a fifty-five percent chance the description is of Kuga himself. Could easily be a lieutenant. What we have is a good-looking white male, late fifties or early sixties, with a short beard, crooked nose, and dark hair. Wears sunglasses, even indoors. Wears a hat. Wears nice suits, but of local manufacture, which suggests he buys clothes when he's in town. Probably doesn't travel with much, because he'd want to fit in wherever he goes. No jewelry except a watch, but we have three different reports on that. Only thing they agree on is that the watch is gold. The guy's weight is approximately two hundred. Broad-shouldered and lean, but moves like he's fit."

"Sounds like a military contractor who moved up from field ops to management," suggested Harry.

"Yeah, that was my take, too."

Violin snorted. "This tells us next to nothing."

"Probably the point," I said. "Kuga is not a social butterfly. For most of the time we knew about him he was just a name behind the

scenes. Then he wasn't even that for a while. Now he's maybe—
maybe—taking a more active role in his own operations. Or he's using stand-ins."

"*Concierge de l'enfer*," mused Harry aloud. "That is the most badass
nickname in the world."

"I'm sure he'd be delighted to know you think so," I said.

"Go ahead and joke, Joe, but it *is* really cool. I need to get a nickname like that. Something people call me."

I almost told him a few of the things people called him, but did
not. It would be like shooting fish in a barrel. No, worse, it would be
merely cruel.

Violin opened a small zippered case and handed me a couple of
items. The first was an Akdal Ghost TR01 pistol, which is pretty
close to a Glock 17. The Turkish military were now using the Yavuz
16, but most of the street players carried TR01s. I tucked it into the
back of my belt and pocketed two extra fifteen-round box magazines. Then she handed back a sweet little Wilson Rapid Response
folding knife. My personal favorite. I clipped it to the inside of my
right pants pocket.

"What makes Bug think that he's our guy?" asked Harry.

"A couple of oblique references cadged from emails and cell calls.
References to 'plague man' or 'Mr. Disease.'"

"That's it?"

"Pretty much," I said. "And the fact that people are markedly def-
erential to him."

"Anyone who flashes money and is willing to slip a few hundred
here or there will get that," said Violin. "Izmir is rife with arms dealers, black marketers, technology brokers, human traffickers, and
they all meet in coffee shops. They all dress well because it makes a
statement."

"Hey," I said, "it's what we have, and it's more than we've ever had
on Kuga."

"If it's Kuga."

"Sure."

"And," said Harry, "Bug said that he got wind that this guy was
going to be there for a meeting today?"

"Yup."

"How sure is he?"

I shrugged. "Not very, but it's what we have."

Harry found an open spot and pulled to the curb half a block from the café. "On the remote chance that this guy you described is even here, so what? It's not like he'll be carrying ID that says *Hey, I'm Hell's Concierge.*"

"If he's here, then we'll just let the moment play out."

"What's that supposed to mean?"

I didn't answer.

We got out and went hunting.

CHAPTER TWELVE

TRANSCRIPT OF *ONE WORLD/TWO SIDES* WITH JILLIAN BAKSHI AND DR. ANDY MING
HOSTED BY MITCH GREENFIELD
BLOOMBERG TELEVISION

> **GREENFIELD:** Jillian, before the break you asked if reunification was impossible. Let's stay on that question, but shift the focus to how the political differences could be addressed.

> **BAKSHI:** Well, first you have to understand the realities of the military situation in the peninsula. South Korea is supported by the United States, as the North is by China. Internally, though, there are decidedly different approaches to the armed forces. For example in the South, all men of appropriate age are required to serve for two years, while in the North it's ten.

> **MING:** That would likely change post-reunification.

> **BAKSHI:** Maybe. But consider the challenges of reconciling the militaries themselves. North Korea has a standing army of over a million, and is believed to have over seven million of reserves. They have over thirteen hundred aircraft, not counting three hundred helicopters. They have four hundred and thirty-plus combatant vessels and two hundred fifty amphibious craft and seventy submarines. On land they have over four thousand tanks, nearly three thousand armored vehicles, and fifty-five hundred rocket launchers designed to deploy multiple rockets. Plus there are reliable intelligence reports of up to five thousand tons of chemical weapons.

> **GREENFIELD:** And nukes, let's not forget those.

BAKSHI: We can't. They have an estimated sixty nuclear bombs, and a wide range of short-range and intercontinental-range missiles.

MING: And in an atmosphere of reunification the reduction and inspection of those arms would be a major factor.

BAKSHI: To what end? Which government will make the call? Can you see the North, which as we already discussed is economically depressed and with an undereducated workforce, willingly give up the one area of superiority they have? Hell, we don't even know where many of those weapons are stockpiled.

MING: Sharing that information would have to be a key element of any reunification agreement.

BAKSHI: Andy . . . I don't mean to condescend, but surely you aren't naïve enough to think *either* side would be that willing to open all doors and invite unrestricted inspection.

MING: If they are in earnest about creating a single Korea again, then yes.

BAKSHI: Well, that's my point. I don't know that enough of the right people really are hoping for that.

GREENFIELD: Are you saying they would oppose its ever occurring?

BAKSHI: I'm saying that I would be amazed—truly dumbfounded—if any reunification plans ever get past a discussion like this. People will talk. People will idealize. And there are plenty of people on both sides of the DMZ who would like their families reunited. But an actual coming together of two such disparate cultures seems unlikely in the extreme.

MING: What about the proposal of a "one country, two systems" arrangement, similar to how China and Hong Kong operate? Hong Kong was allowed to have its own government even after it ceded back to China following the end of British rule.

BAKSHI: That would be closer to likely, but still hard to sell. Kim Jong-un loves control and fears exposure to Western culture. Having two governments but with an open border wouldn't be something that supports his regime.

GREENFIELD: East and West Berlin unified when they tore down the wall.

BAKSHI: Did they really? Have you studied the economics of East Berlin in the years since? The unemployment? The un-*equal* employment? The number of children who struggled in schools once they had to learn the more expanded history and other subjects? The eastern German economy is limping along with few indications that it will change. Some of the money that's flowed from the former West Germany to the former East Germany has gone to do things like rebuilding historic neighborhoods, building new autobahns, and bringing phone networks up to date. But do you know where most of the estimated two trillion dollars has gone? Social benefits such as welfare payments. All of the admittedly good-natured optimism for an economic upswing has failed to yield actual significant or lasting change. That process began thirty years ago, and it was a single city. We're talking about a whole country.

INTERLUDE THREE
AREA NINETY-FOUR
SECURE MILITARY BLACK SITE
TRIPLE EYE, ARIZONA
SIXTEEN MONTHS AGO

Dr. Rudy Sanchez frowned. "The roaches told you? What exactly does that mean?"

Santoro did not answer that question but merely gave an enigmatic smile. Knowing and sly.

Rudy tried another tack. "Then why are you telling me this?"

Santoro smiled faintly. "I know that you despise me, Dr. Sanchez. I have no doubt that if you were a killer—as I am a killer—you would want to stab me through the heart. Your friend Captain Ledger would kill me without a flicker of hesitation. Murdering me would probably make him happy. And your employer, Mr. Church, almost certainly will kill me should he ever come to the realization that I will never again assist him in his campaign against the empire of the Goddess. He does not believe that empire is entirely gone from the earth. He is wise. The Seven Kings are gone, but there are higher powers and deeper truths than the kingdom of Hugo Vox." He shook his head. "But you, Dr. Sanchez, are a healer. You are a good man. Even though I can tell you hate me, as you should, you are never rude to me. You do not abuse me. You have never threatened me."

"Perhaps I'm in the habit of civility and nothing more," said Rudy.

"Perhaps. But even if that is true, it is a pleasant thing. I know that you are aware that I respond to it, and yet you haven't tried to blind-side me with it. You use it to try and unlock what I know, but you don't punish me when I obfuscate. You don't wield it like a whip or hold it out like a carrot. Torturers will do that. *I* have. You do not."

Rudy said nothing.

"And so I offer you this one thing because it is the only form of remittance left to me," said Santoro. His voice was very soft, the room around them quiet.

"What is it you offer, Mr. Santoro? I don't know if I can fully appreciate its value."

"It is a warning, Dr. Sanchez. I know that you are married, I can see the ring on your finger. Your sleeve smells of baby formula, so I can infer a child, yes? You have a family, which is something new because you did not have that when we first came into each other's lives."

Rudy stiffened. "Are you threatening my family?"

For a moment Santoro seemed genuinely surprised. "No, Doctor. I am talking about *your* safety. You. I'm offering you a warning."

"What kind of warning?"

Instead of answering directly, the little killer said, "My own wife is long dead. So are both of my children. They died when my village was burned by men who sought to kill me. They died very badly at the hands of men who understood cruelty . . . as I have come to understand it."

"My God, I'm so sorry."

Santoro shrugged again. "It was a very long time ago. Some of those who committed those crimes were unlucky enough to allow me to find them. I took time with them. A great deal of time."

Rudy wanted to look away from the pain in Santoro's eyes, but he did not. He owed nothing to this man, but he would not look away and in doing so dishonor the woman and children who had suffered at the hands of monsters.

"I was not able to find all of those men," said Santoro. "I was not able to find the person who sent them after me. But the roaches who come and whisper to me in the night promise that they can help me find all of the murderers who have eluded me."

"The roaches tell you this?"

"Yes."

"Why?"

"Do you now want to know 'how'? Or have you already decided that I am insane and this is all academic? Perhaps you think I will make an interesting case study for a report you will file or a paper you will publish—if Mr. Church allows you to publish."

"My question stands," said Rudy. "Why?"

Santoro drummed his fingers in silence, making patterns that Rudy assumed were the notes of some piece of music, but each separate tap was shadow soft.

"I have been offered a barter," said the little killer. "They will tell me where the last of the men who killed my family can be found in exchange for my help."

"Help doing . . . what, exactly? Do you mean in completing the work begun by the Seven Kings?"

Again Santoro did not answer but instead said, "The roaches whispered something very important to me, Doctor. They whispered a truth that *you* did not tell me."

"What truth?"

"They told me that my brother, Esteban, was dead. They said that he had been murdered by your friend Joe Ledger."

Rudy said nothing.

"They said that Ledger cast him into hell."

As Santoro spoke his voice became quieter but his face grew livid, his dark eyes glittered with passion, and spit flew from his lips. Then, all at once he stopped and sagged back, looking exhausted and even a little surprised by his outburst. He tried to touch his face, but the chains did not reach that far, so he bent and placed his face in his palms.

Rudy sat still, watching, assessing, processing. He was troubled and confused. However, before he could ask a question Santoro spoke again. "My warning is this," he said quietly. "Do not stand too close to Joe Ledger. Vengeance is coming for him, and when it comes *he* will kill everyone. You, Mr. Church . . . everyone."

"'He'?" asked Rudy. "Are you saying that vengeance is a 'he' or suggesting that Joe Ledger himself is the threat?"

Santoro did not speak again and after ten silent minutes Rudy Sanchez rose and left the room.

CHAPTER THIRTEEN
ARMA KITAP KAFE
ATATURK CADDESI NO:312 ALSANCAK
IZMIR, TURKEY

I went in first, found a table, and ordered coffee and a couple of *poğaças* pastries, one filled with feta and the other with bleu cheese. No reason I can't have something yummy just because I'm looking for a murderous psychopath. Happy tummy makes for happy Joe Ledger.

There were five other people in the place. Two men seated in the window talking about dips in global currencies. Both were dressed in business suits and had that unique blend of harried arrogance that made me think they were stockbrokers. An older man with the most comprehensively wrinkled face I've ever seen, reading a battered copy of Yaşar Kemal's *Memed, My Hawk*. There had to be fifty yellow and orange Post-it notes sticking out of various pages. A teacher, maybe? A black fly crawled on his shoulder, but he did not seem to notice. A middle-aged woman sat primly at a table near the back, filling out a form. I pegged her as someone applying for a job. Which left the last patron, a short guy wearing a dark blue blazer over a white shirt buttoned to the throat and a small white taqiyah skullcap and—unusual for Turkish men—longish hair that covered his ears. He had a heavy beard shot with gray and wore a pair of steel-rim reading glasses as he made his way through a copy of *Takvim*, a conservative newspaper. He made no eye contact and did not glance around, even when the bell above the door tinkled and Harry and Violin came in.

None of the patrons fit the description of Kuga.

The waitress brought my pastries and refilled my cup. Turkish coffee kicks ten kinds of ass. Thick as mud, with enough caffeine to make my molecules sing karaoke, and absolutely delicious. The pastries were great, too. If it wasn't for the whole "tracking a world-class enabler of terrorism" thing I'd be as happy as a dog rolling in raccoon poop.

I took a pack of Camel cigarettes out of my pocket, looking around for a NO SMOKING sign, didn't see one, and lit one up with a lighter. I don't actually smoke; the cigarettes are phony. They smell like Camels but are actually an herb blend. I held the butt with two fingers, very much in the Eastern European and Middle Eastern style.

The listening device was in the cigarette pack, and there was an Anteater in the lighter. Anteaters are very sophisticated devices that detect any kind of electronics, including active or passive listening devices. A faint screen display appeared on the plastic wrapper of the cigarette pack and it told me that there were no bugs in the joint.

"Outlaw," said Bug's voice in my ear, "everyone in there has a cell phone. We're running IDs on them and working on cracking encryption." I tapped the side of the cigarette pack once to acknowledge, then tapped the surface in the eight o'clock position, indicating where the two men sat relative to me. Bug hummed for a moment and then gave me their names and data. They were, in fact, a stockbroker and a banker. They were also second cousins with nothing particularly hinky in their backgrounds.

I tapped the two o'clock spot, for the old man.

"Retired college teacher," said Bug. "Runs a book discussion group at the local mosque. Political, but not in any alarming way. Average for that part of town. Lives above the café."

Three o'clock, for the bearded man. There was a long pause before Bug replied.

"Okay," he said, "now that's interesting."

I saw Violin look up and glance briefly at me. She was on the same coms channel.

"Took a bit to decrypt his phone and access his account," said Bug. "His name is Bülent Imirzalioglu, with an address in Istanbul. But . . ."

There was no way for me to tell him to hurry up because I was alone and did not want to make a fake cell call just to hide speaking to him. Violin came to the rescue, though. She leaned over and touched Harry's arm. "You've had that menu forever now, darling. Stop dawdling."

Harry, true to form, said, "What? I just—"

She kicked him discreetly under the table. From the wince he tried to suppress she hadn't been gentle.

JONATHAN MABERRY

"Yeah, yeah," said Bug, taking her cue. "Listen, at a glance everything about Imirzalioglu is exactly what you'd expect. Average amount in his bank account, owns his own house and car, donates to his mosque and has some vaguely anti-American stuff on his Facebook page. All normal for a conservative of his age. Nothing too radical, nothing violent, no long-winded political rants. Just stuff. Except I don't like it."

Violin touched a random item on the menu. "And what's wrong with this?"

Harry wisely kept his trap shut.

"Maybe I'm getting jaded in my old age," said Bug, "but it's too neat. Look, I've built a million fake accounts for you guys, and this looks like one of those. Everything looks right, and it establishes the kind of backstory you'd expect for a guy like him. Except that it is one hundred percent perfect, and nobody's life is perfect. Even the imperfections—he buys everything with cash or checks and never uses a credit or debit card—is a little too neatly quirky."

I saw Harry mouth the words "*neatly quirky.*"

"So," said Violin, pretending to touch another menu item, "you think this might trigger your allergies?"

"I don't have any—" began Harry but stopped himself and flushed a tomato red. Violin gave me a tiny apologetic smile. I may have scowled.

But then the scowl turned into a frown because I noticed Imirzalioglu was still reading the paper, and I tried to recall if he'd turned the page since we'd come in. Pretty sure he hadn't. I crushed out my cigarette and lit another, then tapped the three o'clock spot several times.

Violin signaled the waitress and put in an order for two teas and baklava, then asked where the toilet was. She patted Harry on the shoulder as she rose, indicating that he stay seated and inactive. She had to pass by the table where the small bearded man sat and flashed him a bright and mildly provocative smile. The man smiled back, though his was polite. I watched his face as he did it, though, and saw him make direct eye contact with her.

"Pardon me," she said as she moved past.

"Of course," he replied, and I heard the exchange via her tiny mic, which looked like a mole on her upper lip. She vanished into the bathroom.

Gotcha, I thought. The man had spoken Turkish, but the accent was all wrong. Even in two simple words you can tell if you know how to listen. Languages have always been easy for me. My brother, Sean, got the math skills, but I pick up languages—and accents— the way a wool sweater picks up lint. Couldn't tell what his real accent was, but there was no way in hell he was Turkish.

Bug caught it, too, though he used software to assess the accent. "You heard that, Outlaw? I think he's European. MindReader says Portugal or Spain with a probability in the low fifties. Four percent that it's Turkish, so . . ." He paused. "Imirzalioglu's passport shows no trips outside of the country. I'm calling 'phony-baloney' on this clown."

The bearded man dug his cell phone out of his jacket pocket, looked at the screen, frowned, and then glanced covertly around the room. He looked at Harry Bolt and then at me, and ignored everyone else. Then he sent a text and put his phone away. His face was unreadable, but the hairs on the back of my neck suddenly stood out stiff as wires. I unobtrusively took the pistol from my belt and laid it on my thigh with my right finger resting on the loop of the trigger guard.

Imirzalioglu stood up and walked slowly toward me. He kept his hands free from his body, palms out, assuring me that he was not armed.

"You think you are very clever, yes?" he said. Not in Turkish but in English, and now I could hear his accent more clearly. Spanish. Not North or South American, but the accent of rural Spain. He spoke quietly, though, and no one else in the place seemed to take notice.

I used the barrel of the gun to tap lightly on the underside of the table. He nodded without surprise.

"You will not find what you're looking for," he said, waving idly to shoo away a buzzing fly. "Not here, and not anywhere you will think to look."

"I found you," I said.

"I am nothing. I am not *him.*"

JONATHAN MABERRY

"Oh, come on now," I chided, "don't be coy. Call him by his name."

There was the smallest flicker on his face. Not enough to read, but my gut told me it was a flinch, not a smile. "And do you think you know his name?"

"Kuga," I said.

Now Imirzalioglu did smile. It was a very happy little smile, and—weirdly—there was something familiar about it.

But that thought, and just about everything else, vanished suddenly from my head because the old man at the other table suddenly shot to his feet, threw back his head, and let loose a huge scream.

"*You bastards!*" he bellowed. Then he snatched up a fork and charged at Harry Bolt.

In the same instant the two businessmen spilled out of their chairs, overturning their table, and came howling toward me, teeth bared, eyes wild, hands filled with cutlery. One had a knife and fork, and the other had, for some bizarre reason, grabbed a spoon.

They rushed at me as Imirzalioglu backpedaled away, hands up and out, still showing me that he had no weapon. Or, maybe making a statement that a gun was not his weapon.

I whipped my pistol out from under the table, but before I could even point it, the plate glass window behind me suddenly exploded as a storm cloud of heavy machine-gun fire began tearing the world apart.

INTERLUDE FOUR
AREA NINETY-FOUR
SECURE MILITARY BLACK SITE
TRIPLE EYE, ARIZONA
FIFTEEN MONTHS AGO

The psychiatrist was gone.

Dr. Rudy Sanchez's last visit was one month ago to the day. Santoro sat in his cell, wondering if Sanchez would ever come back. Probably. He had planted a worm in the man's mind. He, or the Deacon, would have to come back. They would have to ask more questions. They would need to know. The fact that neither had so far appeared was probably due to some case they were on. Saving the world from the wrong people. That amused Santoro.

The days passed pleasantly for him, and he enjoyed the power he'd taken. It was a lovely drug, old and familiar, and it felt delicious to know that he had cut into the doctor's calm. Making surgical cuts in the mind was always more satisfying than similar cuts made to flesh.

There was a risk, of course, that Sanchez would respond by cutting off all interrogations and visits, but Santoro believed the gamble was worth it. He rarely lost such a bet. If it was up to the doctor, then Santoro was sure that Sanchez would return, and he would be back soon. The Deacon was far more patient, subtle and devious. He could wait. He might wait, letting time and doubt do the bulk of his work.

It did not matter either way, though. He knew that they would never let him out of the cage. Having a game to play, even a long-range one, was something to pass the time. It made him feel a flicker of power. When he worked for the Seven Kings, coercion, extortion, and manipulation were his tools. The slivers of information he had given to Sanchez would work their way under the flesh of both men, and of others in the DMS.

Yes. That felt good.

So he would wait.

Here in the prison. Here in the routine that promised no change, no end. No escape. They would never let him leave his cell. To shower, sure. To walk the exercise yard alone and under guard for one hour a day, yes. But Rafael Santoro was positive that he would never walk out of this prison alive. He had been told as much by Mr. Church.

He thought about that man, and his name. Names. Mr. Church. The Deacon. St. Germaine. The Sexton. Dr. Pope. Colonel Eldritch. So many other names. Santoro knew at least a dozen of them, and he was certain that there were many more, and none of them real, none of them true.

If there was a devil in the flesh, then Church was Lucifer himself. Santoro knew and hated him, and he feared the Deacon as he feared no one else alive or dead. Even the men who had slaughtered

JONATHAN MABERRY

his family did not make him afraid. He merely loathed them. Church was something else. In private interview rooms at the previous black site where he'd been held first, Santoro had seen the man's true face. He was certain few other people ever had. Certainly no one alive.

Church was the devil. He was a monster. Santoro was sure of it.

And Church had promised Santoro that this prison would be his life and it would be his grave. Santoro had only hinted about these things with Dr. Sanchez. He had a suspicion that the psychiatrist did not know who—or what—he worked for.

At night, when he knelt on the cold concrete of his tiny cell and prayed to the ghost of the Goddess, he did not pray for salvation or escape. He prayed for sickness to come to the life of Mr. Church. Sickness and blight. He prayed for the demons of justice to devour the man's loved ones. He prayed that everyone Church loved—if such a monster was capable of love—would wither and suffer and die.

Those prayers gave him strength. His hate gave him power. He believed that if he prayed hard enough and well enough then the Goddess or her saints would hear him.

Each day, Santoro spent his time reading and thinking and hating. Sometimes he would weep when he thought of how he had failed the Goddess. Church somehow knew this, and used it against him, tricking him into saying more than he ever wanted to. But when Santoro cut his tongue out of his own mouth, that had stopped the interrogations. At least with Church.

The pain of that had been . . . *purifying.*

The Deacon had come to see him only one more time after that. The man seemed to grasp that their conversations were over. Santoro expected a bullet from the cold-eyed bastard. He knew that Church would not plead or bully or offer bribes. They both knew it was over.

Instead Church stood watching him from the foot of Santoro's bed in the prison hospital. He stood like a ghost, saying nothing for a long time. Watching. Santoro's mouth was full of stitches, his body shot up with painkillers, his heart turned to stone.

The man stood there, looking at him with those demon eyes. Santoro could never quite remember for how long. Eventually even he could not bear the weight of that gaze and Santoro turned away to look at the wall. When he turned back, ten or twenty minutes later, Mr. Church was gone. Vanished without a sound or a trace.

Perhaps he had never been there at all.

The devil was like that, Santoro knew. Subtle and deceptive and elusive.

Dr. Sanchez was a far less devious person. He was an actual good man. A rarity in the world. It pleased Santoro to offer the doctor the warning, and he would not break his word. He wouldn't go after Dr. Sanchez, and he hoped the man would steer clear of Ledger. If not, then at least Santoro had tried to warn him.

Ledger, Santoro knew, was doomed.

The roaches had told him.

The roaches told him so much.

In the days after his last interview with Dr. Sanchez, Santoro refused to speak to anyone. Not to guards, or the medical staff. He went silent and traveled deep into his own mind.

He only resurfaced to talk with the roaches.

They had been silent for a while, too. Then they crawled out of the cracks in the wall and scuttled onto his bed. They covered his chest and face.

And they whispered to him.

"Tomorrow night," they said. "Be ready. Tomorrow night."

CHAPTER FOURTEEN
ARMA KITAP KAFE
ATATURK CADDESI NO:312 ALSANCAK
IZMIR, TURKEY

I dove forward chased by a thousand hungry teeth of glass.

I hit the edge of the table and fell, dragging it with me, turning it as I crashed down on my back, using it as a shield. The bullets tore it to splinters, but I wasn't hit. I rolled sideways to see four men with machine guns walking toward the shattered window. The two businessmen were down already, their chests torn to red ruin.

Harry Bolt was down, wrestling with the old schoolteacher, while the woman who'd come to apply for a job was kicking them both.

The moment made no sense. Or, not enough of it.

First things first, though, and I opened up on the four gunmen. I took the closest one in the side of the chest and the bullets punched all the way through him and into the man next to him. They both staggered but did not go down. The others shifted their barrels and hosed the place, but I was already moving, scuttling like a cockroach across the floor, trying not to die.

I glanced around for Imirzalioglu, but he was gone. All I saw was a beard lying on a spray of broken glass. Fuck.

The gunmen began stepping over the window frame and I rose up to one knee and fired, but as I did a second gun opened up behind me and suddenly Violin was there. She took one man in the face and throat, and I put two into a second guy's head. They went down and as I swung my gun toward the two injured ones, Violin shot them both. Head shots while walking forward. Four up, four down.

She pivoted and caught the job applicant by the hair, jerked her back with such force that the woman seemed to fly into the air, then Violin simply tossed her away. The woman hit the floor hard, skidded on the sharp glass, but was instantly on all fours, rising, snarling like an animal.

"Watch!" I yelled, but didn't fire because something was wrong about the moment. It wasn't clear if the woman was working for Imirzalioglu, or was somehow caught up in the violence and hysteria of all of this. But as I shot to my feet, the woman ran at Violin, who—cold as an eel—pivoted and shot her in the face.

Harry had managed to push the old man off but seemed unable to actually overpower the guy. Violin shot him, too.

Then the waitress came screaming out of the kitchen, looked around, and ran back. Violin nearly shot her, but paused, because this really *was* hysteria and not another attack.

The thunder of our gunfire echoed for a moment and then a quick and dreadful silence dropped over the café. It was an envelope in which the three of us tried to make sense of what just happened.

Then the silence was broken as we heard people outside yelling, some screaming, and the sound of running feet.

"Out," I yelled, and I grabbed Harry by the shoulder, jerked him to his feet and propelled him toward the front door. "*Go, go, go.*"

He went. Violin and I followed, giving him ungentle pushes toward the car. In seconds we were driving away, me behind the wheel, Harry dumped in the back, and Violin, gun ready, in the shotgun seat.

As we drove, Violin looked at the fake beard I'd snatched up during our exit.

"What," sputtered Harry, "just happened?"

I said nothing and drove.

CHAPTER FIFTEEN
BURJ AL ARAB JUMEIRAH HOTEL
JUMEIRAH STREET
DUBAI, UNITED ARAB EMIRATES
FOUR MONTHS AGO

They came out of the hotel bar, arms linked, laughing, stumbling, laughing harder. There was a hilarious confusion with a revolving door—and a pause mid-turn for a sloppy kiss. Then they were on the pavement. The man, Edward Dexter, CEO of Dexter Tactical and "Dex" to all his friends, was having the time of his life.

The lady was probably younger than Dex's oldest daughter, but how did that matter? The family was back home in Albany and that was a long goddamn way from Dubai. Everything was, in point of fact, a long goddamn way from Dubai. The real world was back there because it certainly wasn't here in the United Arab Emirates.

While they waited for the concierge to fetch a cab, Dex hugged the woman to him, trying like hell to remember her name. Angela? No, that wasn't it. Angela was the lobbyist he banged in Singapore. Ellen? Closer. He thought her name started with an E, but Ellen didn't quite fit. He remembered knowing it three or four martinis back, but with her nibbling his ear like that he wasn't sure if he could remember his own damn name.

The cab arrived and he shoved some bills at the concierge, and the two of them tumbled into the backseat. The woman—Emily or Edna or whatever—gave the address of her hotel, and before the cab was in gear Dex had his hand all the way up under her skirt. She had his zipper down and her fingers were doing really interesting things.

The ride was a blur of colored lights whipping past the windows fueled by his rising need for this woman. She got him so wound up that he had to actually make her stop before he came right there in the cab. And he didn't want to. What he wanted was to get upstairs, pop a Viagra, and then settle down for at least three or four hours of serious humping. That was the plan. Fuck her cross-eyed and then climb back into a cab and get back to his hotel, get cleaned up, get some sleep, and be bright-eyed and bushy-tailed for the meeting with the Saudi princes tomorrow. Dex had a stack of glossy catalogs featuring twelve new models of urban pacification drones that, with certain pricey extras, could be upgraded for military use.

Life, as he saw it, was really fucking grand.

They got to her hotel, which was a bit squalid—though by Dubai standards it would have been on a par with any four-star hotel in New York. They made out in the elevator and then stumbled along the red-carpeted hall to her door.

Inside they kissed for several heated moments and then he excused himself to use her bathroom. Once inside he took the vial of pills from his pocket, popped one, and washed it down with six handfuls of water. Then he washed his face, finger-combed his hair, loosened his tie, and left the bathroom.

And stopped dead.

The big-screen TV on the bureau across from the bed was turned on, with the sound all the way down. On the screen was a woman walking a child to a bus stop. The woman was a little younger than the woman whose room this was. The child was seven. It was obvious they did not know they were being filmed.

The woman was his youngest daughter, Bailey. The child was his grandson, Tyler.

Dex said, "What the fuck?"

The woman he'd picked up at the hotel bar sat fully dressed on the edge of the bed. She held a pistol in her hands. Next to her sat a muscular blond man. He also held a gun. They were both smiling.

"Hi," said Adam.

Eve just giggled.

CHAPTER SIXTEEN
GAZILER CADDESI
IZMIR, TURKEY

Kuga's voice on the phone was cold. Calm as ice.

"What went wrong?" he asked.

The bearded man sat in the backseat of a sedan that sped along Gaziler Caddesi. The driver kept it to three miles over the posted speed, and the car was a Renault, a make and model so common it was virtually invisible. A family car of the right color. Moving with the traffic.

"You saw the camera feed," said the man. He rubbed his chin, peeling away the last of the adhesive.

"The big blond guy," said Kuga. "Was that who I think it was?"

"Yes."

"You're sure?"

"I am certain. It was Joe Ledger."

There were rain clouds in the sky and he leaned close to the glass to look up at them. Dark and troubled, boiling slowly together to erase the light of day.

"Did he make you?"

"No."

"How sure are you?" demanded Kuga.

"Certain."

"*Why* are you certain?"

"He would have reacted differently."

That seemed to wash back and forth between them.

"Why was he there? Does he know about the operation? Is he hunting us?"

"I think," said the bearded man, "that he is hunting you. He was with the Arklight woman. The one they call Violin. And a young man I do not know. He may be a—"

"I know him," said Kuga, and the coldness went colder still.

"Who is he?"

"We can talk about that later. Right now we need to focus on Ledger. Why was he there?"

After a pause, the bearded man said, "Aleppo."

The car drove a whole mile before Kuga said, "Fuck."

"It is only a guess. But the timing . . ."

"Fuck."

"What do you want to do?"

"We can't shift the timetable," said Kuga. "We're already in motion now. We couldn't stop it if we wanted to."

There was a rumble of thunder and the first fat drops splatted against the windshield and popped on the car's roof. Lightning forked in the sky, splashing the road with blinding white light. The bearded man flinched back as if the entire city were burning inside the fireball of a nuclear explosion. The light stung his eyes. The phone connection crackled as if it, too, were burning.

Then, as the light faded and the rain began to hammer, falling in gray sheets, Kuga said, "I'm going to find whatever and whoever it is that Ledger loves best, and I'm going to tear them apart."

"You will turn a madman into a monster."

Kuga's laugh was dark and hard and so damn cold. "You, of all people, should know that everyone has a breaking point. Everyone. Even monsters."

The line went dead.

CHAPTER SEVENTEEN
BARRIER SAFE HOUSE
UNDISCLOSED LOCATION
IZMIR, TURKEY

We went to ground at a safe house run by old friends from Barrier, which is the British counterpart of the DMS. The place was empty, but very cleverly placed electronics signaled our arrival and within a minute the house phone rang. I took the call.

"Hello," I said neutrally.

"What's for lunch?" asked a female voice.

"Bangers and mash," I said, using the current day code.

"Enjoy your stay." That was all.

I used an Anteater to check for bugs and disabled them all, even the ones left by Barrier. Bug would square that with them, and the Brits would understand. Violin made a routine check of the house and then we all convened in the kitchen. Harry was shaken and embarrassed. Violin looked calm—because she always looked calm—but I knew that she had to be as rattled as I was.

I made a pot of coffee while Violin opened a small laptop, which I recognized as an Oracle substation. Oracle was the proprietary computer system used by Arklight and the Mothers of the Fallen. The screen showed a subtly smiling Mona Lisa, which was actually the face of an interactive AI program. Violin spoke to it in a language that maybe six people outside of Arklight could understand. I'm one of them, though I don't think Violin knows that. I played dumb, which is actually easier for me than I'd like to admit. I even whistled while I started the coffee maker and fished in the cabinets for food. Nothing I heard was earthshaking, though. Just Violin logging on and asking for a pickup and forensic analysis of the fake beard. By the time I had lunch ready she'd shut Oracle down.

"Mother won't be happy with how this turned out," she said, placing the beard carefully onto the table.

"Mr. Church isn't going to give me a wet sloppy kiss, either," I agreed.

"Ewww," said Harry.

"Lilith will find some way to blame you for this debacle," said Violin.

"Well, she already hates me, so that's not that big a thing."

Harry snorted but made no comment. Lilith half-assed liked him, but I figured it was more like the affection people have for a mongrel dog rather than as a potential life partner for Violin.

"Will she still send you to Norway for the D9 thing?" I asked.

"Oh, probably. We still need a presence there, but I shudder to think where she'll exile me to afterward."

The fact that she was traveling the world with Harry Bolt seemed like enough of a punishment, but I elected not to say so. Instead, I set a cup and a bowl of canned vegetable soup in front of Violin and picked up the beard. She watched me as I examined it.

"Might get some DNA off of it," I said.

"There's always that small chance," she said, studying me.

"We need to get this to a lab."

Violin gave me a very thin little smile, and that's when I knew that *she* knew I'd understood the call.

"Hey," said Harry, "can someone please tell me what the heck just happened?"

Instead of answering I tapped my earbud. "Bug, have you finished running facial recognition on Imirzalioglu?"

"Yes," said the voice in my ear, "but you're not going to like it. His hair hid his ears and the beard and mustache hid jaw shape, mouth contours, and nostrils. We know the beard was fake, and I bet the hair was, too. The tinted glasses gave us nothing on his eyes except an iffy measurement. I'm sorry, Joe, but there's just not enough unique detail."

"Which meant he was trying to disguise himself knowing that someone might recognize him," said Harry.

"Thank you, Captain Obvious," I said.

"No," protested Harry, "I mean . . . he couldn't have known we were going to be there. So he was in disguise to meet someone else. You think that was actually Kuga himself?"

Violin and I exchanged a look and we both shook our heads at the same time.

"All of the descriptions we've had of Kuga," she said, "said he was tall. This man, at best, was five-eight."

"Maybe he sometimes wears special shoes to make him look taller," ventured Harry.

"He'd have to have been wearing stilts," I said. "Nah, kid, this guy maybe worked for Kuga, but I don't think that was him."

"Whoever he was," said Bug, "he made you all pretty fast."

"He must have been there to meet someone dangerous," mused Violin. "He had the four shooters outside and the fake patrons who attacked us."

"Yeah," Harry said, "about that . . . I know I'm not a genius when it comes to reading a situation, but am I the only one who thinks there was something weird with those customers? I mean, if they were there as backup for Imirzalioglu, then why weren't they strapped? It's not like there was a metal detector at the door. If they were plants, then they could each have had a gun and instead of Imirzalioglu needing an army with assault rifles, they could have gotten the drop on us without a fuss."

"Your puppy makes a good point," I said.

"Hey," groused Harry.

"I was thinking the same thing," said Bug. "Those people came after you with cutlery. I mean, come on, one of those guys tried to stab you with a freaking *spoon*."

Violin, who hadn't seen the start of it because she was in the bathroom, had Harry and me go over everything step by step. I had Bug send the feeds from my body cam to her Oracle station and we all watched it six times.

"Okay," said Harry, "I'm even more freaked out now. Look at how they suddenly go from pretending to be ordinary folks out for coffee to going all apeshit. It's like *bam*, instant psychos."

"Yeah, damn it," I said.

We chewed on it for a bit, but it was obvious we stepped into the middle of something else and things just turned sour for us. A line from that old Lightnin' Hopkins song began playing in my head. *Bad Luck and Trouble, two of my best friends.*

"Keep working on the facial recognition," I said to Bug. "Voice recognition, too. And maybe we'll get lucky and get something from the beard."

"Lucky?" asked Violin with a laugh. "When was the last time *you* were lucky?"

CHAPTER EIGHTEEN

ABOARD *THE SOUL OF PIETY*
KIEL CANAL
RIVER ELBE, GERMANY

Kuga sat in a leather swivel chair in the galley of the expensive yacht, a glass of whiskey in his hand. The Göttingen Festival Orchestra recording of Handel's *Wassermusik* played sweetly. Water slapped against the hull and outside a gull cried its lonely love song, which was answered faintly and far away.

He was a tall man, dressed in a dark blue roll-neck sweater and soft gray wool trousers. The heater was on and the galley was warm. It smelled of honeyed rolls and good bourbon.

There was a sophisticated computer monitoring setup in a corner of the galley, with multiple screens and good sound fidelity. Three different angles of the same video played out, perfectly synced. He watched two men and a woman fight for their lives in a Turkish café far from where he sat. A small muscle bunched and flexed at the corner of his jaw.

When he'd gotten the call that an important meeting at the café in Izmir had gone south very dramatically, he directed his people to send all camera feeds to him. The reasonable assumption was that either a rival team had come to cut into his action—something that was always a danger for someone like him—or that some government cops were trying to make a name for themselves. In either case the bad guys should have been swatted quickly and thoroughly. His very best man was on-site.

But now he was watching the video for the tenth time.

Yes, his man had controlled the situation as much as possible, but he had not eliminated the threat.

Worse, Kuga knew the three people who'd come to the café. He knew them each very well.

That psychopath Joe Ledger.

Violin, the Arklight witch.

And the former CIA agent who called himself Harry Bolt.

Kuga drank his whiskey, refilled his glass, drank it dry. Got more, not even bothering with ice.

He froze the images and touched a screen, touched one of the faces.

"Damn it," he breathed.

He felt something on his face and pawed at it, then stared at his hand. At the wetness of tears that glistened there.

"Goddamn son of a bitch," he swore.

Kuga sat there for a long time, staring at that one face. Letting the tears flow and hating each one of them. He got very, very drunk.

CHAPTER NINETEEN
BARRIER SAFE HOUSE
UNDISCLOSED LOCATION
IZMIR, TURKEY

We stayed at the safe house for a few hours, until Bug assured us that there was no active manhunt for us. The Barrier runner picked up the beard.

Violin and I sat for a while and talked about friends we had in common and people we knew. It was a wistful game of catch-up. Even though we were never officially a couple, there were people who came into our lives around the time we were lovers, and those people defined that time. And, there were people who knew both of us, but separately. She asked about Junie, and I told her about the latest stuff FreeTech was doing to save the world. Once upon a time Violin disliked Junie and saw her as a rival, but they bonded during the Code Zero case and have been friends since.

Violin asked about my brother, Sean, who was a detective in Baltimore. Sean was married to a wonderful woman, Ali; and they had two amazing kids, Em and Ryan, known as Lefty. For some reason Violin bonded with the kids and when she was in town would take them out for long days of mysterious fun, with the kids sworn to secrecy. The kids always came back smiling and laughing, and they loved Violin.

I asked about her mother, Lilith, and Violin's face got a little wooden. "She's fine," was all she'd say. That was okay, it was all I wanted to hear. I was moderately low on Lilith's Christmas card list. Somewhere between Vladimir Putin and Satan.

We talked and talked, but then it was time for her to go. Violin gave me a sweet kiss on the cheek and a warm hug that left me with a fragment of memory of when she and I had been lovers. Harry looked a little jealous, but he had nothing to worry about. The memories of being with Violin would always be in my head, and in a very special place; but I was in love with Junie and when I looked into my own future I didn't see that changing.

But, damn, that hug felt good.

I went upstairs and took a hot shower, shaved, and slept for an hour. Or tried to. What I really did was lay there on the top sheet and stare at the uninformative bedroom ceiling. Not daydreaming about my brother, Sean, and his family, or Violin, or even of Junie. Nothing that pure.

Instead I thought about the man who called himself Imirzalioglu. Did I believe that was his real name? No. After hearing him speak there was every possibility he was neither Turkish nor even Muslim.

He was so familiar, though. Something about him. His voice? Yes. His energy—to borrow something Junie often says. Yes, there was definitely something about his energy, and I was almost positive I'd been in the same place with him before. But where? Why? Under what circumstances? It taunted me because the more I thought about it, the more sure I was.

"Who are you, you son of a bitch?" I said aloud.

His words came back to me. *"You will not find what you're looking for. Not here, and not anywhere you will think to look."*

"Who are you?"

After an hour I got up, got dressed, and took a cab to the airport.

ISLAND OF FROGS, NORTH KOREA

Do not go gentle into that good night,
Rage, rage against the dying of the light.

—DYLAN THOMAS

CHAPTER TWENTY
GAEGULI SEOM
EIGHTEEN NAUTICAL MILES WEST OF NORTH KOREA
SEA OF JAPAN

They called it the Island of Frogs, and Gaeguli Seom lived up to that name. There were frogs everywhere. Toads, too. And salamanders.

The old man, Byeon Sok, liked the frogs. They made the night pulse like a beating heart, even this late in the year. Regular, calm, soothing. Rather lovely as he sat on a stool, chewing on a stem of withered grass and mending his fishing nets. The day's catch was good, and he'd dragged aboard a surprising variety of fishes, including mackerel, saury, pollock, and sardines. Enough to put him ahead of his quota. Seventy percent of his estimated catch was regularly shipped back to the mainland on a government gunboat, and he was allowed to keep anything over that. Some days that meant he and his wife went hungry. He did, too, so the kids could eat. They'd adopted their grandchildren after their daughter died of cancer and her husband was lost in a storm. The children were still small—six and four. Most days Byeon's catch was enough, though. They did not starve. Days like today were rare, though, and the extra put him into a good mood.

He had a little fire in an old gasoline drum and it spilled yellow light and a great deal of warmth all around him, keeping his old fingers pliant and nimble as he worked. A small oil lantern was set on a stump to give him better light for the close work. Byeon didn't need or want much out of life, at least not much beyond what he had. His wife, whom he loved, his friends in the village, plenty of fish in the sea, a warm fire, the stars, and the frogs.

He'd seen a Huanren frog that morning, and they were so rare Byeon had taken it as an auspicious sign, which it proved to be. There were nineteen pounds of fish being cleaned by his wife. She would cook some, smoke some, and salt the rest.

Life, he mused, was good.

Well, except for the flies. They were everywhere, despite the cold.

Swarming and biting. Byeon was a tolerant and generally forgiving man, but he would have been okay with it if the frogs ate every single one of the little bastards. That would make the evening perfect.

Above the tiny island a shooting star scraped like a match across the ceiling of the world. Another auspicious sign. Perhaps tomorrow's catch would be as bountiful as today's. He had a few friends he'd like to gift with some mackerel.

Byeon heard a twig break in the jungle and turned, smiling, expecting it to be his particular friend, Gang. Good old Gang Seon was even older than Byeon. Nobody knew exactly how old, not even Gang. It was a running joke that he was older than the island itself, which had been pushed up out of the water a couple of million years ago.

"Gang, you old goat," he called. "Come and sit down. I have some tea and it's still hot. Or, hot enough anyway."

However, the shape that detached itself from the dense shadows of the jungle was not his friend. It was slimmer and shorter and it took Byeon a moment to make out who it was. It moved to within a few feet of the spill of light from the old man's tiny lantern and then stopped, swaying slowly as if nudged by the gentle ocean breeze. He saw the wisps of long hair dancing around soft shoulders, and could just make out the faintness of a pink shirt.

"Ha-yuen?" he said, surprised to see his wife down here on the beach when there was so much work to be done with the catch at home.

The figure stayed there, moving almost to the pulsing rhythm of the frogs.

"Are you done already?"

There was no answer.

Byeon frowned. "Ha-yuen . . . ?"

She stepped out of the darkness and into the yellow lantern light. Byeon looked at the face of the woman to whom he'd been married for fifty-three years. She was slender and strong, and even age had never taken the twinkle out of her eyes nor hard work drained the uncomplicated happiness of her smile. She'd been his love, his friend, his flower for all these years.

JONATHAN MABERRY

Now, as he looked at Ha-yuen's face, Byeon Sok felt a terrible dread open up in the bottom of his heart. Her eyes were glassy and they stared without blinking. She was smiling, but that smile was . . . wrong. Her lips were peeled back to show her remaining teeth. Bad, like his; gray and rotted.

But red.

The lantern light showed that.

Glistening red. It coated her teeth and lips and ran in lines down her chin to drip onto the front of her blouse. Her hands were red, too.

"Ha-yuen," he gasped, dropping his net and staggering to his feet. "What is this? What's happened?"

Her answer was a sound. The wrong kind of sound. Not a whimper of pain because of some accident. Not a cry for help.

Ha-yuen laughed.

A small, fractured, ugly sound.

Byeon looked at her and then past her. "Where . . . where are the children . . . ?"

Her smile turned into a grin. A huge, crimson smile of awful joy.

"Ha-yuen, *where are the children?*"

His wife threw back her head and screamed.

With laughter.

With such hungry, hungry laughter. And then she ran at him, hands reaching and those bloody teeth opening wide.

CHAPTER TWENTY-ONE

TRANSCRIPT OF *ONE WORLD/TWO SIDES* WITH JILLIAN BAKSHI AND DR. ANDY MING
HOSTED BY MITCH GREENFIELD
BLOOMBERG TELEVISION

> **GREENFIELD:** And we're back. We've been talking the pros and cons of reunification of the two Koreas. Dr. Andy Ming expresses some concerns, and Jillian Bakshi is arguing for it. Many experts have debated the economic benefits versus costs of reunification. While some analysts focus on the tremendous economic potential of a unified Korea, others express concern over the price tag of

bringing North Korea up to the standards of living and education enjoyed in the South.

BAKSHI: And yet we've seen solid steps in the right direction. Leader Kim has pledged to end the testing of nuclear weapons and agreed to dismantle the Punggye-ri nuclear testing site.

MING: Excuse me, Jillian, but geologists have already indicated that the Punggye-ri collapsed some time ago. Kim's offer of dismantling it appears to be greatly disingenuous. And, although he hasn't detonated any new devices, there is every indication that he continues nuclear weapons development. He's made it quite clear he wants the U.S. to remove troops from South Korea before he'll take any real action, and even then I have my doubts.

GREENFIELD: Let's shift focus a bit to China. Kim Jong-un has gone there several times without disclosing the substance of those talks. Some experts have suggested he has been going there to lay the groundwork for reunification, which would necessarily involve China, as they are part of the cease-fire.

BAKSHI: Well, I may lose my optimist card there, Mitch, because I don't think that's why he's been going there. I think Andy will agree with me that he's been called on the carpet by the Chinese president.

MING: We absolutely agree on that, Jillian. His saber-rattling and—excuse the crudity—penis-measuring with the American president got out of hand.

BAKSHI: You're absolutely right. Kim was bringing his country too close to an actual exchange of missiles with the world's unrivaled superpower. A contest that could have forced China into the conflict, and possibly drawn in Russia as well. Even if that conflict somehow stayed non-nuclear, it would amount to World War Three, with China, Russia, North Korea, and possibly Iran and a few other nations, against the United States and its allies. Apart from the appalling risk to human life and damage to the planet, it would destroy the global economy as we know it.

CHAPTER TWENTY-TWO
ELECTRA PALACE THESSALONIKI
9 ARISTOTELOUS SQUARE
THESSALONIKI, GREECE

The note read "All Work and No Play Makes Joe a Dull Boy."

The note had been slipped under my office door when I got back

JONATHAN MABERRY

from Turkey. It was in an envelope that had a room key card for a snazzy hotel. The note was unsigned, but it didn't need to be. I knew the handwriting.

Since I'd already written my after-action report on the flight and had only a loose plan to head to Athens to do some Christmas shopping, I was okay with a change in agenda.

That note made me smile.

I logged onto the RTI server and told everyone who needed to know that I was officially off the clock until further notice. Then I took my chopper to Thessaloniki, which is the second largest city in Greece but one I'd never visited before. The town is lovely but that hotel knocked my socks off. It looms over the Aristotelous Square and looked like a Byzantine palace, with an eye-popping view of the Thermaic Gulf. The hotel, apparently, had a reputation as a romantic getaway, and the cab driver kept grinning and winking at me.

I got out and heard a soft rumble. Above me the sky had gone dark with rain clouds and there was ozone in the air. A storm was coming.

I went in and stopped at the desk to request that a couple of superb bottles of wine be sent up to the room. The woman behind the counter said that wine had already been delivered. She gave me a knowing smile, too.

So, grinning, I went to the elevator and took it to the fourth floor, followed the curving hallway, trying not to break into an actual run. I used the key card and the door clicked softly open. There was a breath of air from inside that was perfumed with Tibetan temple incense and which carried with it the achingly beautiful sounds of the Moscow Symphony Orchestra playing "Claire de Lune."

She was waiting for me by the window, her back to me, long curly hair falling around good shoulders. I closed the door, shrugged out of my jacket, and came to stand behind her. I bent to kiss the side of her neck and she tilted her head to allow it.

"I missed you," I began, but Junie whispered a soft "shhh."

There was no talk after that.

Junie turned her head and we kissed long and sweetly, and it was very likely the most beautiful moment of my life. No drama, no clever conversation, no need for us to be anything but who we are it

Junie Flynn and Joe Ledger. Lovers and friends. Deep lovers, true friends, which means that what there is between us runs so much deeper than physical attraction or chemistry. Everything is built on a foundation of respect and allowing—neither of us tries to change who the other is.

Junie is one of the most intelligent people I've ever met. She is tall, with masses of wild blond hair, the brightest blue eyes in creation, and creamy skin dappled with freckles. She's been through storms, though, and has scars inside and out. She's beaten cancer three times and also survived an assassin's bullet that killed the baby she'd been carrying. *Our* baby. And that injury also destroyed her uterus. Our relationship was not there to create a family. We were family to each other, and always would be.

She wore a blue Japanese robe and stood with her fingertips touching the glass of the big picture window. I touched Junie's shoulders and leaned close to smell her hair. Junie's skin was warm and perfumed. I kissed very slowly, without haste, enjoying the taste of her on my lips and tongue, biting gently. Junie slid the edge of the robe off one shoulder and it draped down. In the darkened window glass I could see her reflection. The curve of one breast—full, delicate, perfect—and the dusty rose of a nipple. I saw her nipple grow hard as I kissed my way from earlobe down along the soft curve of neck. Then I reached around and pulled the loose belt open. The robe parted and its silky length slid down and puddled on the floor.

I caressed her stomach and hips, then traced a line up to one breast, moving along its contour as if sculpting it. The underside, the graceful slope to the erect nipple. I took her nipple between my fingers and kneaded it with great slowness and great care.

She sighed and leaned back against me, breathing harder with each moment, and reached down to find my hardness. I reached around to her other breast and touched it, explored it as if discovering the landscape of her for the first time. Then I touched her face, caressing her cheek and lips. Junie bent and caught one finger between her teeth and bit down, almost too hard, but not. Sweetly, not.

The sky outside had grown dark and now there was thunder away to the east. Deep, strong, but not threatening. Not to us. Junie

JONATHAN MABERRY

turned toward me and unbuttoned and unbuckled me. Then, naked, we walked hand in hand to the big bed.

There is sex and then there is true lovemaking, and that is what we did. We made love. What we each do takes us away from one another for days, weeks, even months. Our relationship is not normal and maybe it shouldn't work. I am a killer and she, in her way, is a kind of healer. But two people do not need to be alike to be in love. They don't need to parallel each other's lives. They don't need to breathe the same air. Love doesn't require that.

When Junie and I are together we re-make the "us" that we were. Always a bit different, because we're realistic enough and adult enough to know that life is always changing us. When we meet again we accept that we will be slightly different people than the ones who last parted.

And so the joining of our bodies was part of a process of reconnection. As that late afternoon became evening and then turned to night, we made love on the big bed. I kissed my way along the constellation of freckles to the soft heat between her thighs, and when she came she cried out my name in a way that both broke and healed my heart.

Then she pushed me onto my back and climbed astride me, reaching down to guide me into her. I brought my knees up to tilt her mouth toward mine. We made love very slowly, with a rhythm unburdened by haste or greed. We were kissing when I came inside of her, and kissing for long, long minutes after that.

The rains came and hammered on the windows.

It ended so slowly. A winding down. Gasping and trembling. Bathed in sweat, painted with the last paleness of twilight. I wrapped my arms around her and buried my mouth in the cleft between neck and throat and kissed my Junie with a thousand small, sweet kisses.

The storm got bigger and winds whipped the rain against the windows. We lay there, holding each other as the sweat dried on our skin, and listened to it. The only word she said that night was my name.

It was enough. It said so much.

CHAPTER TWENTY-THREE
GAEGULI SEOM
EIGHTEEN NAUTICAL MILES WEST OF NORTH KOREA
SEA OF JAPAN

The two figures sat in their rubber boat, engine silent. One of them—a tall young blond-haired man with beefy shoulders who declined to share his real name—watched the island through night-vision goggles.

The other, a slender woman named Ainil Tan, sat hunched over a laptop on which a dozen video feeds were playing out in small windows. The cameras mounted on trees around the island were ultrasophisticated. They captured everything in 1080p high-definition, and the cameras were keyed to adjust colors to compensate for poor light. Everything was crystal clear; and the miniature condenser microphones recorded every cry, every scream, every unanswered cry for help with perfect fidelity.

"We have it," said Ainil, looking up from the laptop. There was obvious fear and nervousness in her voice. "We have enough, let's go."

The man studied the island for a moment before replying. He lowered his glasses and glanced at the video feeds.

"Give it another few minutes."

"But," she protested, "we have enough."

The man's blue eyes looked black in the poor light. "Another few minutes," he said, spacing the words out, giving them each equal weight and inflection. Then he exhaled. "Look," he said with a bit more patience, "I told you that my sources told me that something big was going to happen here and—"

"This *is* big," Ainil insisted. "Oh my God, this is the biggest thing I've ever seen. This will be headline news everywhere."

"But it's only part of the story," he said.

"What are you talking about? Everyone's *dead*."

He shook his head and looked away, toward the beach. "Not everyone," he said.

"What do you mean?"

The man put a finger to his lips and then pointed. She saw him mouth the word "*look*."

Ainil looked. For long minutes she stared through the lens at figures moving along the sand.

Despite being warned not to speak, she repeated, "*Oh my God . . .*"

The man leaned very close and whispered softly in her ear. "*That's* why I wanted you here. Now . . . make sure you're recording."

She was.

Despite everything—her youth, the shock of this, the horrors—she was first and foremost an investigative journalist. Ainil recorded, even as the tears broke and rolled down her cheeks and her heart beat like frenzied fists on the walls of her chest.

CHAPTER TWENTY-FOUR
ELECTRA PALACE THESSALONIKI
9 ARISTOTELOUS SQUARE
THESSALONIKI, GREECE

Junie and I had breakfast in the rooftop restaurant, at a table by the fireplace. I couldn't even spell half the stuff we ate, but everything tasted wonderful. Everything.

We smiled at each other a lot. Those sly, secret smiles of lovers who are so recently from the moments of passion that each can still remember the heat of breath on naked skin, the taste of kisses, the languor of afterglow.

Somewhere between the eggs with *staka* and *koulouris* bread rings, our long, contented silence gave way to conversation. We don't do chitchat, so she jumped right in and talked about a project she was overseeing at FreeTech, which was her company. FreeTech was privately funded and globally positioned. A big part of what they did was to repurpose some of the truly nasty technologies my guys and I have taken away from mad scientists, terrorists, and other various and assorted dangerous nut bags. It always amazed me how much of any given technology could be used to benefit humanity rather than destroy it. FreeTech uses elements of that science, but not to cause misery; no, Junie and her team have made huge inroads into water purification, non-GMO crop protection, vaccinations, and so much more.

She described one sustainable energy project she was about to launch in Puerto Rico. "It's a new kind of solar panel system," she said, excitement sparkling in her blue eyes. "The standard designs of affordable solar panels are really hampered by the Shockley-Queisser limit, which means that if there is a solar irradiance of, say, one thousand watts per square meter, then the maximum power output that the solar panel can produce is only three hundred and thirty-seven watts per square meter. It's all about the physical process of the absorption of a photon to generate an electron, and then pass it to the band of conduction. So far there hasn't been any solar panel manufacturing process or technological development of silicon p-n junction cells that can change this. It's been accepted as a factual limitation, but one of Zephyr Bain's projects had been on the edge of proving that the limitation was only a theoretical boundary of energy conversion. Our people have taken Bain's work and followed it all the way to practical models. We're going to test them in Puerto Rico, and if it works, if there is another hurricane like they had a few years ago, then we can restore the power grid in days rather than months."

"That's awesome," I said, meaning it. And seeing the delight in her face and hearing the enthusiasm and hope in her voice made my heart happy. Not everyone gets to do what they love, and fewer still are able to have their dream job be one that does measurable good on a grand scale. Junie was the polar opposite of the kinds of people I go hunting for. Instead of being a "mad" scientist, she is eminently sane. And, even though her job—and mine—keeps us apart so often and for so long, reunions like this were joyful. They made lonely nights less bleak. Sure, that's selfish, but I never claimed to be otherwise.

While we were talking, Sean texted us, time difference notwithstanding. He was bursting with news that his wife, Ali, was pregnant with their third child, and due in late June. It made me so happy I wanted to cry. Junie and I got on a Facetime call with the whole family and maybe we were a little loud, but the other diners saw how happy we were and most of them smiled and toasted us with coffee or mimosas. A few didn't, and they can go piss up a rope.

The call ended with my promise to come visit soon. I dabbed at my eyes and Junie and I smiled at each other for a long time, holding hands. Being together. Being happy, which is something people who know me only at work might think is a rare state for me. It's not, really. I do this job because of the people I love. Sean and Ali, Lefty and Em. Junie. All of the good ones.

The conversation went this way and that, and shifted subtly toward our new organization as international troubleshooters. Junie was not an outsider when it came to the details of my job. She used to be, as a standard precaution, but when Church formed the RTI he extended her access from Top Secret to Unlimited.

"I spoke with Joan yesterday," she said. Joan being Doc Holliday. Apart from being our science chief and a self-made bazillionaire, Doc is the great-granddaughter of the actual John Henry "Doc" Holliday. Yeah, Wyatt Earp's buddy, from that shootout at the O.K. Corral. The original Doc Holliday had an affair with a prostitute known as Big Nose Kate, and genetics did some weird stuff over the next century and a half and wound up producing a six-foot-one-inch supergenius who looks like Dolly Parton on growth hormones. Her IQ is off the scale, and she has no visible conversational filters. She dresses and acts like a cartoon character, doesn't give a hairy rat's ass about what anyone thinks, and will flirt with anything that has a pulse. During the Deep Silence case, my last for the DMS, she and Junie had become friends. Now they were like sisters.

"Oh?" I said neutrally.

"She told me a little about what you've been through recently. Syria and Turkey," said Junie. "She said that there was trouble each time."

Trouble was a candy-coated word that Junie generally used to refer to cases where I'd been involved in violent action.

"The usual," I said, dismissing it.

Junie searched my eyes for a long time. I busied myself with buttering some toast.

"Joe . . ."

"It's all good," I said. "We all came home. No one got hurt. Even Harry managed not to get his ass handed to him. Mostly."

"Joe." She said it again, changing the inflection, making it a reproof.

I leaned back in my chair. We were in a private corner of the restaurant. No one could hear us if we kept our voices down.

"What's the big deal?" I asked. "It's not like I haven't had tussles before."

"'Tussles'? Really?" she demanded. "You're just going to dismiss everything you went through as if it were two kids shoving each other back and forth during recess?"

"I've been through a hell of a lot worse, baby."

"Don't 'baby' me, Joe. And who cares if you've been through worse. That doesn't change the fact that you've been in two gunfights in two days." She leaned forward and lowered her voice, but infused it with much more intensity. "You've *killed* people both times. And you just wave it off as 'tussles'?"

I set my knife down and stared at her. "What would you prefer, Junie? That I curl up in my closet and cry? That I have a psychic fracture over the realities of doing my job? That I check into a clinic for treatment of PTSD? This is what I *do*. I'm a soldier and a hunter of very bad people. It would be wonderful as hell if we could settle all of our disputes with thumb-wrestling, but they're the ones dealing the play. I don't go in with the intention of pulling a trigger, but I know that in virtually every case that's a possibility. And, for the record, I don't shoot someone every time I go out on a case. Maybe one in thirty times. Maybe more. So why are you criticizing me for what happened over the last few days?"

Junie reached across the table and took my wrist. She gave it a very sharp and very hard squeeze. Deliberately painful.

"You listen to me and hear me," she said in the coldest voice I've ever heard her use. "I was not criticizing you for doing your job, and you damn well know it. Or *should* know it."

"I—"

"No," she snapped, cutting me off, "I'm talking. You listen. If you think I'm attacking you for doing your job, or the way you do it, or doing what you have to do, then you need to check in with Rudy Sanchez and get your wiring fixed. Show me a little respect, Joseph Edwin Ledger. And while you're at it, show yourself a little respect."

"I don't have a problem with self-respect."

"Oh, bullshit. You swing in a range between unfair self-assessment to a kind of professional hubris."

"So humility or pride are character flaws now?"

"When they are distorted so much that you go around acting like killing people is no more significant than swatting gnats."

"That's unfair."

She moved her grip from my wrist to my hand. Not as painful, but intense.

"It's not a matter of me being unfair, Joe," she said in a softer voice. "This is me being scared that you might be in danger here."

I stared at her. "In danger of *what*?"

"Of forgetting what Rudy always says, about how violence always leaves a mark. You used to care about how much damage the things you're required to do did to your heart and your soul. Now, you seem to think you're wearing impenetrable armor."

"I've been doing this for a long time, Junie," I said. "Do you expect me to flinch each time? I mean, shit, do you *want* me to be damaged by it?"

"Damaged? No. Of course not, and you know that's not what I mean."

"Maybe I don't."

A seabird flew slowly past the window, coasting on the thermals, its breast a perfect white. A baby crab wriggled helpless in its beak.

Junie held my hand. Her fingers felt very cold. "Joe, I'm serious about this. You are being too blasé about this. Either you are acting as if gunfights are nothing to you, like you're some hero from a summer blockbuster movie series, or you're hiding from your true feelings. Either way, that's dangerous."

I said nothing because quite frankly until that conversation I wasn't really aware that's how I was coming off.

"Joe," she said in a softer voice that was filled with love and hurt, "I love you with my whole heart. With my *mind*, too, which is even more important. You are remarkable and kind and capable of more tenderness and gentleness than anyone you work with would ever believe. You are also the bravest man I know. But you are human, too. You are not indestructible. If you think there is even the slightest chance that you are becoming disconnected from the truth of what you're doing, from the humanity that made you who you are, then I need you to stop. Take a breath. Step away. Allow yourself to *feel*."

"Junie, I—"

Her blue eyes were filled with love and with pain and with fear. "Joe, *please* promise me you'll talk to Rudy about this."

It took a lot for me to say, "I promise."

It took more to do that than it took to pull triggers in either Syria or Turkey. I knew it. She knew it.

Shit.

CHAPTER TWENTY-FIVE
EUROPEAN CENTRE FOR DISEASE PREVENTION AND CONTROL (ECDC)
GUSTAV III:S BOULEVARD 40
SOLNA, SWEDEN
FIVE MONTHS AGO

They were so deeply in love.

With each other. With what they did. With who they worked for. With death.

She called him Adam. He called her Eve.

Those weren't their names, of course. The *who* they'd once been had been excised from their lives with the same surgical precision they used on jobs like this. Adam had begun that process when he shucked his previous identity like a snake shedding its dead skin. Then he'd helped Eve do the same, carving out the tumor of her past. Cleaning their back trail was easy, even in the internet age. People only thought it was impossible—the internet never forgets, and all that—but it wasn't impossible, merely difficult. And there is a joy in doing something difficult. Ask any gamer. Ask a mountain climber.

The physical evidence took longer. Schools they had each attended. Family doctors, X-rays in dentist offices, therapists, dojos, gun ranges, juvenile detention centers. Everything, though, burns. People with the kind of specific memory that could have evidentiary weight were handled differently. Never the same way twice.

That was the key. Never create a pattern.

Being patternless was very hard work. It was creative work, patient work. Delicious work.

And cruelty—such a useful tool—was an art. Adam and Eve were, without question, artists of superior skill. Joyful artists, too; never brooding. Nor tortured. That was for the canvases on which they wrought their masterpieces.

Daddy taught them how. They loved him for that. For everything. Sure, they were scared of him, too, but everyone who knew Daddy was scared of him. Unless they were even crazier than Adam and Eve, and they knew they were totally, wonderfully batshit.

They could fake sane, though. Like now. They drove past the building in a late-model Volkswagen Golf, which was the most popular model in Sweden. More so than the locally manufactured Volvo. The Golf was white, because that was also the most common. It was a standard model, without too many obvious luxuries. A working person's car. A commuter car of the kind that had every reason to be abroad on the boulevard. The mundanity of it made it virtually invisible despite passing the ECDC building seven times over the last five hours.

Adam drove because he liked to drive. Eve took pictures because she was better with a camera. Neither had guns or knives anywhere on their persons or in the car. There were groceries in the backseat. There was a car seat for a toddler and some well-chewed dog toys on the backseat floor. The junk in the boot was deliberately ordinary—a can of oil, the packaging from replacement wiper blades, a jack, a donut spare, bungee cords, a mangled paperback book—a stained cookbook by Camilla Läckberg.

The ID they each carried was bulletproof. Adam was Ralph Asplundh, a freelance website designer for a manufacturing business; Eve was Léonie, a photographer for commercial real estate. Even deep Net searches would find nothing amiss.

"There he is," said Eve.

Adam smiled. "Right on time."

"He's a good doggy."

He slowed the car so that Ronald Lingmerth saw them. If they'd swerved onto the pavement and rammed him it would not have made Lingmerth jump higher. It was a quiet stretch of street— chosen for that reason—and there was no one to notice. Lingmerth stopped, but Eve shook her head and gave him a huge smile. Adam held up his cell phone as a reminder of consequences, and then blew him a kiss.

"Don't make him piss his pants," said Eve, fighting a laugh.

"Oh, his dick's probably crawled up inside his body by now, so no chance of that."

Lingmerth kept walking, though his gait was strange, as if his hips joints were welded shut.

Eve leaned back against the seat cushions and gave a contented sigh. They drove away, heading to one of their safe houses. There they parked the car in a double-slot garage, got into the other vehicle left for them—a blue Volvo—backed out, and drove away. One of their team would take the Golf and move it along through channels of used-cars lots—after the car had been thoroughly cleansed.

When they were out of the city and in the country, whisking past rows of linden trees punctuated by the occasional alder or birch, Adam's cell rang. Eve took the call and put it on speaker.

"And . . . ?" she prompted by way of hello.

"I . . . I have it."

Lingmerth sounded like a drowning man. Gasping and lost.

"In a secure container?"

"Yes."

"Where?"

"Where you said. I taped it to my inner thigh."

Adam grinned at that. "His dick's bigger than mine now," he said.

"Follow the plan," said Eve. "Take a walk along the boulevard. A car will pick you up and take the container."

"And my family . . . ?"

"We won't hurt a hair on their heads."

"Swear to me," begged Lingmerth.

"I swear," said Eve. "Neither of us will touch your wife or those precious girls. But, Ronald . . ."

"What?"

"You had better be straight with us."

"I am!"

"That container better have exactly what you were supposed to get. Nothing else. Nothing less."

JONATHAN MABERRY

"I did exactly as you said," whimpered Lingmerth. "Please . . ."

"If there is a tracker on it, or a wire on you, then you *know* what will happen."

"Oh, God, I swear to you."

Eve disconnected the call.

They drove for nearly a mile before Adam said, "You're wicked."

She shrugged.

"That whole 'neither of us' thing? That was evil."

"Well, it's true, isn't it?" she said with a sly smile. "*We* won't touch them. *We* will never even meet them."

"Semantics."

"It's what Daddy taught us to say."

Adam grunted and nodded.

Eve turned on the radio and found a station for progressive rock. Dream Theater was playing. Old stuff, too. "Six Degrees of Inner Turbulence." She turned it up. They drove on.

Twenty minutes later they got a call. When she answered it, she heard a male voice, heavily accented. Daddy. "Line?"

"Clear."

"Status?"

"Everything's in the green."

"Excellent," said Daddy. "We are complete here, then. You have both done very well."

"Are you happy with us?"

"Yes, my sweet. I am very happy with you. Now, it's time to clean things up, yes?"

The line went dead. Eve and Adam smiled at one another. Cleanup was fun.

She punched in a number and a woman answered. A young voice, with a Finnish accent that almost, but not completely, hid her native Korean.

"Waiting on the word," said the young woman.

"The word is 'go,'" said Eve. "Actually . . . go play. Have fun. Be weird."

There was a bubbling laugh from the other end as Eve ended the call.

She turned the phone over, opened it, removed the SIM card,

broke it into four pieces, and tossed one piece out the window every few miles. They checked into a bed-and-breakfast and spent the rest of the day in bed. Every time either of them thought about what was happening to Ronald Lingmerth and his family, their passion spiked and they were at each other like wolves.

CHAPTER TWENTY-SIX
PRIVATE AIRFIELD
CORFU, GREECE

I leaned against the curved body of the big, expensive, luxury helicopter, looking casual as fuck, but feeling a thousand little ants of tension crawling all over my skin. And despite the glorious blue of the Mediterranean skies and mild temperatures, I was pretty damn pissed off. Partly because of my conversation with Junie, and partly because we hadn't moved the needle much following the clusterfuck at the café with the bearded stranger.

"Bug," I said with as much civility as I could manage, "I'm pretty sure that I never want to hear the phrase 'we got nothing' again."

"But—"

"You've been saying that to me ever since Turkey."

"Yeah, Joe, but—"

"That's four days, Bug," I said airily. "You have the world's most sophisticated computer, a staff of the brightest nerds on the planet. You have footage from three bodycams for facial and voice recognition *and* you have DNA. And still you keep saying the same thing."

"Sure, but—"

"Do you want to know what I'm doing right now, Bug? I'm buffing my boots so they're nice and shiny when I put my foot all the way up your ass."

Bug gave a long sigh. "It is what it is, Joe."

"That isn't very helpful."

"Okay, let's look at what we have. The name the bearded guy was using, Bülent Imirzalioglu, is bogus. We cracked open every bit of data associated with that identity and found exactly what we expected to find: nothing. Whoever built it was good, but didn't

JONATHAN MABERRY

seem to think he needed to go whole hog, because the identity was disposable. Imirzalioglu—or whoever he really is—probably has a dozen fake identities, and he'll have left every shred of that one behind. As for the physical evidence . . . there wasn't enough DNA on the beard to give us anything. I can tell you more about the adhesive used to attach it and the coffee he drank than I can about him. The facial recognition is a mess because of the guy's disguise, and vocal recognition isn't the most reliable technology no matter what you see in the movies. If that guy's voice had ever been recorded, then he was manipulating it to give a bad read, and that's pretty easy to do. And there wasn't enough to give us a reliable syntax evaluation. All we got is the region around the town of Ainsa in Spain."

"Bug," I began, but this time he cut me off, and it was clear he was as frustrated and testy as I was.

"You want my opinion? This guy *made* you. And I don't mean that he just made you as a cop or agent, no, I think he actually made *you*. Joe-freaking-Ledger. He knew who you were. My sound guys tell me that there was a bit of a tremolo in his voice consistent with people who are very excited. And he came straight over to you, not to Harry. And he didn't blink when Violin went past him to the ladies' room. That guy made a beeline straight to your table."

I said, "Oh."

"Yeah. Oh."

"Shit."

"Exactly," agreed Bug. "And for the record, Mr. Church doesn't think this guy was Kuga. He said that maybe Kuga's been hiring top talent from around the world, so, taking into account how many organizations we've busted up—and, I guess more to the point, that *you've* busted up—there are people out there who know your face. And who want to put some bullets through that face."

"Well . . . moose shit," I said.

"Plus, ever since Lilith's crew took Ohan off the board, most of his top people are probably on Kuga's payroll, and some of them worked with the Seven Kings, Harcourt Bolton, Majestic Three, or the Jakobys. Every one of those guys probably has a Joe Ledger dartboard."

"Big steaming piles of stinky moose shit."

"Yeah," said Bug.

"Well," I said lamely, "keep at it. Find me something."

Bug said something very specific about what I could go and do with an underaged three-legged female goat, and dropped off the call.

I shoved my hands into the pockets of my leather jacket and leaned back to stare at the sky. My Sikorsky S-92A Cougar helicopter was parked on a pad at a private airfield owned by a friend of a friend of my boss. It had a fourteen-million-dollar price tag, but it didn't cost us a dime. We'd confiscated it from a Chechnian piece of human garbage who'd been a player in the human trafficking market. Top and Bunny had words with him and then pushed him out of the door at eight thousand feet. None of us cried about the fact that they apparently forgot to give him a parachute. I wondered how good it would feel to throw the man who pretended to be Imirzalioglu.

But after a few minutes, my thoughts drifted back to the conversation with Junie, and my bad mood soured even more. I mean, was she right? Or was it proof that the woman I loved really didn't know me very well at all?

Not sure either choice was a pathway to happiness. On one hand, I have been doing this for a long time now, and both the DMS and RTI are the kinds of organizations that tend to push a fellow into the path of violent encounters. It's absolutely part of the job description. The fact that I'm good at it means that Church uses me more than some of the other senior operators. Is that my fault? Every single one of our cases is pretty much the SpecOps equivalent of the last inning of the World Series, with two outs and runners on all the bases. I either pitch it right the first time, or very, very bad things happen. Mixed metaphor, but you get the point. They don't put third-string players into that position. I'm first string. Church knows it and I know it. I don't brag about it. I don't think it means my dick is bigger than anyone else's. It doesn't make me a better person. It is, though, a fact of my life.

What, then, should I do? Break down and cry every time I have to put one of the bad guys down? I told Junie that they deal the plays. I react. What level of emotional investment should I be required or expected to make?

On the other hand . . . she also accused me of hubris. That stung more than I'd like. How does one find that line between a confident acceptance of one's own abilities and arrogance?

Challenging and painful questions to wrestle with. Junie was gone now. She'd taken an early flight to Puerto Rico to meet her team, and would be there for at least a couple of weeks, if not a month.

"Fuck," I snarled, almost spitting the word into the wind.

Ghost leaned his big head out of the open hatch and gave a single bark. Not at me and not in response to my expletive. No, it was one of his happy barks. He bounded down to the tarmac and stood wagging his tail as a figure stepped out of a taxi a hundred yards away. Ghost looked at me for approval, and from the way his head and shoulders were juddering I could tell his tail was wagging at warp speed.

"Yeah, sure," I said, "go ahead, you big goof."

He was off like a furry white missile and ran to greet his favorite uncle. Despite my pissy mood, I smiled as Dr. Rudy Sanchez squatted down to intercept the happy dog.

CHAPTER TWENTY-SEVEN
GAEGULI SEOM
EIGHTEEN NAUTICAL MILES WEST OF NORTH KOREA
SEA OF JAPAN
SEVEN HOURS AGO

Lieutenant Ryuk Yeung of the Democratic People's Republic of North Korea stood on the beach and looked at the wall of trees. He had a hand resting on his holstered pistol. His platoon of twelve men and two women were fanned out along the sand, with cold water lapping around their ankles.

"Sir," said Sergeant Ga, "there is something over there. By that boat."

Ryuk looked where the sergeant was pointing. A small fishing craft, old and battered, had been dragged up under the cover of the leaves of a crooked hemlock tree. Nets were draped over the side and around an overturned wooden stool. He walked over, flanked by the sergeant and a soldier with a rifle held ready, and knelt.

There was a small lantern on its side, the wick extinguished and the oil soaked into the sand. The lantern's glass was cracked and speckled with drops of something viscous. More drops were spattered on the side of the boat, and there were dark patches on the sand where even more had soaked in. The cracked glass showed the color in its truest form. The unmistakable color of blood.

Ryuk rose slowly but did not draw his weapon. Blood was not enough to alarm him. Not on an island where everyone made their living by killing something—fish, squid, pigs, chickens. There was always some kind of slaughter necessary for people like this. His own childhood had been on a cooperative duck farm, and he'd waded knee deep in blood and feathers from the time he could walk.

"Leave this as it is," he said. "Let's go find the station keeper."

Sergeant Ga gestured for the platoon to form up. He sent two ahead and the others followed the noncom and his officer.

Although the Island of Frogs was predominately a poor village on a mostly unimportant island, there was a two-man weather station here. The station was not merely there to record weather patterns, of course. Even the least educated islander knew that. It was one of several such stations that monitored movements of undersea craft. Active and passive sonar sensors were positioned at various depths around the island, which was on a spike that rose above sea level but dropped sharply down to a depth of two miles. More than deep enough for submarines and even deep-sea unmanned vessels of the kind the Americans were using for undersea mapping and spying. Lieutenant Ryuk believed that these DSRV craft were looking for the best invasion route.

They followed a well-worn footpath through the dense subtropical foliage. Birds chattered in the trees and the tree frogs gossiped from their hiding places on crenulated bark. Sunlight slanted through the trees and countless bees buzzed around the flowers.

No, thought Ryuk, *not bees.*

He glanced at the insects. They were flies. Blowflies. Many of them, circling in and out of the sunlight. Dipping down out of sight behind the bushes.

JONATHAN MABERRY

Which is when he smelled it.

"Ga," he said sharply. "Over there."

The sergeant and one of the soldiers stepped off the path, guns leveled, fingers laid along the trigger guards. The smell was strong but not yet overwhelming. The lieutenant drifted behind, his gun still holstered, but he'd loosened it. Ready.

But for what?

Surely not even the corrupt Americans would have dared come onto the island—onto North Korean soil—to commit crimes. Not even they would be so bold.

Sergeant Ga stopped in his tracks a few yards ahead. The soldier stopped next to him, both of them leaning slightly forward to look over the leafy top of a dense shrub.

"Ga . . . what is it?" demanded Ryuk, pausing.

The sergeant said nothing, merely shaking his head.

"Ga? What have you found?"

The soldier beside Ga dropped to his knees. He did it abruptly, thudding onto kneecaps. His rifle fell from his hands and landed with the barrel half buried in the dirt. It was such a strange thing, such a shocking breach of military procedure, compounded by the fact that the soldier did not even seem to notice. He stared at something Ryuk could not see.

Stupid man. Surely he'd seen a dead body before, which is what this had to be. Even if Americans had come onto the island and committed atrocities, that kind of overreaction was foolish. And the soldier would pay for it, Ryuk decided.

And yet he did not approach, did not say anything. He was staring at Sergeant Ga, who kept shaking his head. Side to side, side to side, over and over, like a metronome.

"Sergeant . . . ?"

Ga turned slowly, but he kept shaking his head.

"What's wrong with you?"

The sergeant was staring with wide eyes, and yet his gaze did not seem focused on his officer. Instead the eyes went left and right, left and right, following the movement of the man's head. Focusing on nothing.

Nothing.

It was in that moment that the lieutenant realized that he heard nothing. The birds had stopped singing. Even the frogs were silent. The only sound was the buzzing of the blowflies.

And then Sergeant Ga snarled.

An actual snarl. Low and mean and feral, with no trace of humanity. It was a purely animal sound and yet filled with emotion. Not with hunger or even hate. This was a snarl of anger. Of meanness.

Of rage.

With no warning beyond that sound, the sergeant launched himself forward. His weapon was still in his hands, but Ga seemed to have forgotten about it. Or forgotten what it was. He crashed into Ryuk, bearing him backward and down. The officer fumbled for his gun, but lost it as strong white teeth clamped with crushing force around his windpipe. The world went black and red and full of stars that exploded and quickly faded to dying sparks.

His men did not rush to his aid. Not one of them tried to pull Sergeant Ga off of him, or attempted to stanch the blood that geysered up into the late-afternoon sunlight.

They did nothing at all to help him.

They were too busy killing each other.

CHAPTER TWENTY-EIGHT
TRANSCRIPT OF *ONE WORLD/TWO SIDES* WITH JILLIAN BAKSHI AND DR. ANDY MING
HOSTED BY MITCH GREENFIELD
BLOOMBERG TELEVISION

> **GREENFIELD:** Let's drill down a bit more into China's role in all of this. If Korea is reunited, what are the wins and losses for China?

> **MING:** Well, Mitch, despite China being run by a strict Communist party, there is a great deal of diversity of opinion on this topic. Despite state control over the media, various opinions have gotten into media reports, and they're all over the place. Very pro, very much against, and a lot of iterations in the middle. And even with that, the reasons for their stances vary.

> **BAKSHI:** True. I've interviewed a number of investors and business

owners in the region and they see the process of reunification as potentially disruptive to business as usual. Which is interesting, because most projections indicate that business would prosper in the long run and stocks would stabilize if there wasn't as much rampant brinksmanship.

GREENFIELD: Right, so what are the actual pros and cons?

MING: China wants to keep North Korea under its influence. The North is a buffer between South Korea and therefore America. It's a wall.

BAKSHI: Only if Kim can keep his finger off the button.

MING: Yes.

BAKSHI: Kim's inability to be a reliable, though minor, ally, is problematic for China. The presumption is that a unified Korea would inevitably fall under U.S. influence.

MING: Maybe. South Korea became an American ally in self-defense. America stepped in to fight China on Korean soil, siding with the non-Communist South. Their financial and military support is almost entirely predicated on the status quo. In a reunification scenario, there is no reason that South Korea has to maintain that kind of relationship.

BAKSHI: It goes deeper than that. China has been building very strong new economic and diplomatic relationships around the globe. As it becomes more of a global economic entity, the need for it to be overcautious of its border with Korea will fade. This effort is reflected in its business personality, because that is changing the world perception of what a Communist State is. The more they grow their economy through trade with other nations, the more they prove the Communist model without having to do it through force.

MING: True . . . China wants, and indeed needs, to become a solid first-tier economy. It cannot sustain its own population without vastly increased trade. However, they bring so much to the table that they've become very popular as trading partners. Oddly, the model that is working for them is closer to the Fortune 500 capitalist model than anything out of the Communist Manifesto.

BAKSHI: Another pro for separation from North Korea is that Kim is not a very trustworthy neighbor. There is the physical danger of angering the U.S., South Korea, and Japan, but equally as important are the optics. Defending Kim gets harder and harder to spin. North Korea is becoming a costly ally who brings little to the table.

MING: If North Korea stays separate, though, there is a potential big win for China if they are a key player in convincing Kim to denuclear-ize. If they can swing that, they instantly become one of the most important statesman nations. A purveyor of peace and common sense, and—in political perception—able to do something the U.S. has failed to accomplish.

GREENFIELD: Which I guess is one of the topics that will be discussed in closed-door meetings at the upcoming D9 summit in Oslo.

MING: There's another way this could spin. If the Koreas reunited, who's to say that the U.S. will be the only country allowed to nurture? China is right there, they have deep pockets, and they are rebranding their nation. They could help smooth the process of reintegration, reeducation, and rebuilding.

BAKSHI: There is a danger of that.

GREENFIELD: What "danger"?

BAKSHI: North Korea is a nation of twenty-five million people—maybe half of the population of the South and approximately that of Shanghai. It is highly unlikely America will spend the resources to bring it up to a cultural par with the South. And the South itself can't afford to do that. Which means China could step in to offer financial support to the *entire* country. It is, after all, right there. China had its own cultural upheavals and revolutions, and has learned much from that process.

MING: But there is a long-standing relationship with America, and an even longer animosity toward China.

BAKSHI: In 1945 America dropped two atomic bombs on Japan, and now they are one of America's closest friends and allies. The same goes for Germany. In terms of politics, loyalty and friendship are dangerously fickle.

CHAPTER TWENTY-NINE
PHOENIX HOUSE
OMFORI ISLAND
GREECE

"So," said Rudy Sanchez, as he peered out of the helicopter window, "Mr. Church bought an island."

Rudy is my best friend and also my shrink. Well, technically he's the staff psychiatrist for our little quilting club. He's shorter than me, with black hair and a thick mustache that would have done justice to a 1970s porn star; but he has such natural class and dignity that he makes it work. There's a bit of gray here and there, but it's more from hard use than age, because we're both still in our thirties. Not the years, it's the mileage, and even though he isn't a field op, Rudy's gone down a few hard roads as my friend.

He was wearing a wool suit in a dark charcoal, but with a red shirt and an absurdly festive Christmas tie that had dancing reindeer and lots of elves. A gift from my niece that, despite Rudy's usual subdued tastes, caught his fancy. His collection of novelty Christmas ties was beginning to challenge my wardrobe of inappropriate Hawaiian shirts. Sadly, it was too cold for one of those, so I was wearing a flannel shirt and jeans and looked like a beardless lumberjack.

If he noticed my mood, he didn't say anything, and I knew Rudy well enough to know that he would wait for a more comfortable moment to ask what was going on. And, there was every possibility that Junie already called him, so maybe he was waiting for me to raise the topic. Good luck with that.

We were heading across the sparkling blue of the Ionian Sea on a winter morning. The sky was a cathedral ceiling of hard blue, dusted here and there with wisps of clouds that were delicate as bird feathers. Rudy seemed amused by the location of our new headquarters.

"It's really quite lovely, isn't it?" he said in his deep baritone. He sounds exactly like Gomez Addams from the old movies. Similar charm and sense of humor, too.

"Yup," I said. "Eleven hundred acres. Leased from the Greek government for ninety-nine years. We have a special agreement that, for all intents and purposes, exempts this place from all governmental control. It's private in every useful way, and we have permission to build, which is something they don't like people to do. Especially not on an island with ancient ruins. We had to bring in an archaeologist to make sure we weren't turning those ruins into a topless disco."

"Heaven forfend," said Rudy. "How did Mr. Church finagle all of these permissions?" He held up a finger before I could reply. "No, let me guess . . . he has a friend in the industry."

I grinned. Church was notorious for his network of *friends*. Not all of them were actually in some aspect of business. A great many of them were in the world's various overt and covert military services, and—as I've come to learn recently—in useful places in world governments.

"I asked him that, too," I said. "He dodged the question."

"Of course he did."

We watched the island grow from a dot to green lushness as we approached.

I was a little surprised Rudy signed onto the RTI. When Church closed the DMS, I figured my friend would take the opportunity to retire from this kind of life and go back to private practice. After all, I'd more or less shanghaied him into signing on when I was recruited by Church. Unlike me, Rudy is no soldier, and generally lives at a more evolved end of the evolutionary bell curve than I do. His years with the DMS took a toll on him, too. He lost an eye in a chopper crash, and nearly lost his leg. The replacement eye was a nifty bit of Six Million Dollar Man tech that was indistinguishable from the real one—even down to simulated pupillary dilation and movement. But it's fake and it's a reminder that bad things happen even to good people. Add to that the fact that Rudy has a wife, Dr. Circe O'Tree, and a toddler son, and there were a lot of reasons to call it quits.

But . . . he didn't. Instead, Rudy and Circe bought a rather beautiful house in Corfu, where Circe is continuing her work as a top-level consultant on the psychology of terrorism. She splits her time between writing highly classified papers for several United Nations member states and writing nonfiction books on terrorism that tend to leap to the top of international bestseller lists.

Couple of things to add here, though. First, because Circe loves Rudy and Rudy has gotten hurt several times because of his association with me, Circe kind of hates me. A lot. I don't get random invitations for Thanksgiving and Christmas unless Rudy insists. And then there's a fight, so I usually wind up going to visit my family in Baltimore instead.

Second thing is, she's Church's daughter. As far as I know, that makes her Church's only living relative. But they are not close. They are, in fact, as "not close" as two people can get without actively shooting guns at each other.

So, you can see why I was surprised that Rudy signed on. And even more surprised when they sold their place in La Jolla, California, and bought the property in Corfu. To a place, specifically, I can reach by chopper from our new headquarters in less than an hour. When I asked Rudy about that, he gave me a shrug.

Rudy's good at shrugs. Maybe it's a Mexican thing, but he can put half an hour's conversation into one shrug.

"Coming up on it," said the pilot's voice over the intercom. The Sikorsky S-92A Cougar helicopter was tricked out with a soundproof cabin complete with leather seats, a wet bar, and room for nineteen passengers. Currently it was the two of us and Ghost, who was sleeping on a bench seat in the back, his belly filled with Uncle Rudy's organic smoked bison jerky dog treats.

Rudy crowded the window like a happy kid. I could relate. There was a lot to see. The main feature of the island was a castle. An actual castle. Not local construction, you understand. Church purchased a building from Transylvania and had it brought, stone by stone, to the island. The castle had belonged to Francis II Rákócz, a Hungarian nobleman from the early eighteenth century. And, get this, from 1704 to 1711, Francis II was the Prince of Transylvania. Yeah. Like we weren't all going to try and read something into that shit.

Bunny actually flat out asked Church if he was Dracula. The boss withered him with a look. I told Rudy the story.

"*Ay dios mío,*" he murmured.

"I know," I said.

"You realize Mr. Church may be engaging in deliberate obfuscation so that we are all constantly looking in the wrong direction when it comes to understanding more about him."

I gave him the same kind of look Church probably gave Bunny.

"Clearly you have thought about this," said Rudy.

"A bit."

The castle loomed like something out of an old Hammer horror flick. Gloomy and turreted. Closer observation, though, revealed the network of antennas on the roof, discreet surveillance cameras, the helipad, and beautifully sculpted gardens. It looked like the kind of place a rich oddball like Johnny Depp would buy.

"Did Church decide on a name for it?" asked Rudy as we touched down.

"Phoenix House," I said.

"Ah."

I told him that there'd been several choices under consideration, with suggestions from my crew, Bug, Doc Holliday, and pretty much everyone else. Among those were Secret Empire, Dracula's Castle, House of Horrors, Mount Olympus, Avengers Mansion, and House of Pain. Church tended not to comment on our choices.

"Even so, Phoenix House?" said Rudy slowly. "It's a bit on the nose, don't you think?"

"Tell that to the Big Man," I suggested.

Rudy just laughed.

The doors opened and we stepped onto the asphalt of the landing pad, then hunched and jogged through the diminishing rotor wash. Ghost bounded ahead, spry as a puppy—which he was not. He was technically a venerable dog of middle years—and one who'd been stabbed, shot, and otherwise banged up on six of the seven continents—but he only played that card when he wanted to be fussed over. This wasn't a belly rub moment, and he seemed to be having fun. He *liked* this place, and was already making life difficult for the island's rabbit population. He never actually tried to catch or kill one, but they didn't know that, because he tended to chase like a hellhound. The rabbits probably told stories about him. Big damn goof.

"Are you going home for Christmas?" asked Rudy. "I got an invitation from Sean. Something about a big 'Home for the Holidays' thing at your uncle's old place in Robinwood."

"Kind of have to," I said.

He cocked an eyebrow. "Have to or want to?"

"Both. Living out here . . . well, Baltimore seems like it's on another world. So, yeah, Christmas in the country sounds like exactly the sort of thing I need. Who knows, maybe we'll even get snow. Christmas carols 'round the tree. Sleds and snowball fights and the biggest turkey in North America. A freaking mountain of presents for Em and Lefty to open."

He gave me an affectionate smile. "You are a deeply, deeply corny man, Joe."

"I prefer to think of myself as traditional."

"Sure," he said. "Let's go with that."

Rudy stopped a few yards from the ornate front doors and glanced up at the ancient gray walls. He wore a frown that cut lines around his mouth and between his bushy eyebrows. Rudy shivered as if the mild December afternoon had suddenly turned arctic.

"What's wrong?" I asked.

Rudy shook his head. "It's nothing," he said.

I studied his face. "You sure?"

He pasted on one of the fakest smiles I'd ever seen. "Positive. Come on, Joe, give me the tour."

CHAPTER THIRTY
PHOENIX HOUSE
OMFORI ISLAND
GREECE

Phoenix House was a bit of a con man's trick.

Apart from not being a manor house for some rich clown with too much money, it was also mostly show. The upper floors were still under construction and uninhabited except for a nicely appointed guardroom and Church's private apartment. It was also not actually the headquarters of Rogue Team International. No, that was *below*.

One of the reasons Church bought the island was the fact that it sat atop a massive and very deep series of caverns. A couple of million years ago the island was a volcano, but the inner walls of the magma chamber burst through into the Ionian Sea and the volcano kind of melted away. Or . . . whatever it is old volcanoes do. Not really sure of the science there. Point is that there were huge pockets in the otherwise solid strata. The Greek authorities didn't know about it because it wasn't mentioned in any of the geological survey reports that were included in the sales materials. Or, so they said. My personal theory is that Church had that information suppressed by his friends and then eradicated from all records by Bug.

What it left us was room to grow. Not up, but down and sideways.

There was even a channel on one corner of the island deep enough for freighters. So, the same ships that brought in the pieces of the castle also brought in thousands of tons of building materials, equipment of every kind, high-end generators, and everything else you might want if you wanted to turn caverns into a base for the kind of work we do.

Rudy was absolutely dumbstruck. As I gave him the fifty-cent tour, he goggled. Actually goggled. Computer rooms, labs of every kind, comfortable quarters for everyone, a fully functional TOC—tactical operations center—and more. And there were many areas still under construction—a process that was likely to take a couple of years.

At the end of a walkway between massive hydroponic gardens, Rudy stopped and turned in a slow circle. He shook his head.

"The *scope* of this is incredible," he breathed. "The cost . . . How could anyone, even Church, afford this?"

"Well," I said, "it's not like we haven't picked the pockets of some high-roller bad guys over the years."

"Even so . . . this has to be billions. Many billions."

"Many, many billions," I agreed.

"And to set this up so fast. Not just the construction, but the logistics. The planning and design. Hiring the right people. Handling the red tape while keeping so much of it under the radar. Even for him that must have taken an incredible network. An actual infrastructure. This is all so . . . so . . ." He fished for a word, but I supplied it.

"Improbable?"

Rudy cut me a look. "Yes. There is no way all of this was done since closing the DMS."

"Not a chance in hell," I agreed. "Rough guess? Church has been working on this place for maybe ten years, with things kicking into high gear last year."

"Why, though?" But once again Rudy answered his own question. "Mr. Church is the least naïve person I've ever met. He was reading the writing on the wall all this time. Perhaps before he even formed the DMS."

"That'd be my guess." We walked to the end of the path and stood by a railing that overlooked a huge training facility. Much bigger than was needed for three five-person teams to prepare.

"He has big plans," said Rudy. "Though, I remember him saying that he wanted to keep the group small. Like it was when we first met him."

"Small enough to pivot," I said. "He's said something like that fifty different ways. He really wants us to be ready to roll at the drop of a hat."

"And is that likely?"

I nodded. "Yeah. I think so. Kind of proved that with two back-to-back gigs I just came off of. Got a whiff of something, rolled out, did planning on the fly, and resolved everything fast. Tell you, brother, it's refreshing to feel like we're the big cats in the hunt rather than hyenas stealing meat from someone else's kill. I mean, sure, groups like ours are more reactive than proactive—nature of the kind of threats we face—but it feels different. We can move before a dropped match has time to set something on fire. Consider me a fan."

"I'm very glad to hear it, Colonel," said a voice and we both turned to see Mr. Church standing right behind us. Rudy flinched the way people do when Church seems to step out of a hole in the dimension.

Church is a big man. Blocky and solid, though I've seen him move and he is cat quick. His dark hair is streaked with gray and he looks like he's somewhere in his sixties, but middle age doesn't seem to have slowed him much. Or, at all. He always wears tinted glasses, which Rudy figures are used to hide the expression in his eyes. Everyone has some kind of tell, and the leading theory is that Church knows his eyes are his; so he hides them the way some professional poker players do. He wears thin black silk gloves because his hands were badly damaged in one of our old DMS cases. And he wears very expensive though quiet suits and never looks ruffled. That's part of the vibe he wants—or perhaps needs—to convey: He's in charge and he's cool about that.

He offered a hand to Rudy. "Dr. Sanchez," he said, "it is a pleasure to welcome you to Phoenix House."

"I'm pleased to see you," said Rudy, "though I'm a bit overwhelmed by all this."

"Yes," said Church, "it can be a bit much to first-timers."

"You have a secret lair," said Rudy, gesturing with both hands.

"It's hardly that, Doctor."

"No," said Rudy, "it is precisely that. This is exactly what Joe and

Bug have wanted for years. A high-tech secret base in a hollowed-out volcano. If it wasn't so . . . *real* . . . it would be cliché."

I had to bite my lip to keep from bursting out laughing. The two grown-ups ignored me.

"Well, there may be some truth to that," conceded Church, measuring out a slender half inch of a smile. "After all, it was Bug who found this location and brought it to my attention."

"Ha!" I crowed, and was again ignored. Ghost gave me a pitying look.

"However," continued Church, "as entertaining as the thought might be to some, this place was not purchased to satisfy anyone's pop culture obsessions. I can assure you."

Rudy shook his head. "I'm sorry, sir, and I really don't mean to offend, but I have to reiterate—you have a secret lair in a hollowed-out volcano, with a Transylvanian castle as disguise."

And then Rudy burst out laughing. I lost it, too. Even Ghost barked and pranced around. Church endured it. I think he may even have blushed a little. Or maybe it was the lighting.

"Enjoy your tour, Doctor," he said, and turned to walk away. I saw his shoulders tremble though, and by God, I think he was laughing, too.

Sometimes the world really is that goddamn funny.

Until, of course, it's not.

INTERLUDE FIVE
AREA NINETY-FOUR
SECURE MILITARY BLACK SITE
TRIPLE EYE, ARIZONA
FIFTEEN MONTHS AGO

"It's time to go," said a voice.

Santoro came awake all at once. He knew that voice. Voices, really. When he opened his eyes, there they were. The roaches. They were on him. On his body and the bed. On the floor. On the walls.

Thousands upon thousands of them. More than he'd ever seen before.

"I said, it's time to go."

Santoro flinched, realizing that it was not the roaches whispering to him at all. He sat up, scattering scores of the insects, and saw that it was a man who had spoken. A guard, in fact. Santoro fished for his name. Dillon? Yes.

But it made no sense. This was the middle of the night. It wasn't time for a shower, or breakfast, or exercise. He froze there, his heart hammering, unsure what to do.

They've come to kill me, his mind whispered. *This is Church's doing. They've come to finally kill me.*

Santoro immediately knew what was going to happen. He would be led from his cell and then set upon by the other guards. They would beat him to death, or possibly shoot him. Santoro knew that he had no chance against half a dozen burly guards with clubs or shotguns. The report would be that the prisoner attempted to escape. No one would question a death under those circumstances. After all, he had never been formally charged. Santoro was sure that this facility was an NSA black site and as far as the rest of the world was concerned, it did not exist any more than he did. Church would simply erase him.

"Come *on*," snapped Dillon. "What the fuck are you waiting for? An engraved invitation?"

Santoro did not move.

The guard sighed and then leaned toward the bars so that his nose and mouth were pressed as far between them as possible. "I told you," he said.

The man was not looking at Santoro, and it seemed like he wasn't even speaking to him.

The roaches were all still and silent. And *they* were not looking at Santoro, either. All of them—every single one—had their tiny antennae pointing toward Dillon. Then, as if they were all one creature and not thousands, they turned back toward Santoro.

Suddenly they were moving, running all around, scurrying across the floor and up the wall. Forming clusters, forming shapes.

No.

Not merely shapes. They formed letters. On the floor beside his bed and on the three unbarred walls of the cell. The same four letters in each place. The same name.

KUGA

Santoro cried out. A sharp, high, shrill sound like a wounded gull. He slid off the bed and onto his knees.

"Goddess . . . ?" he said, gasping out the question as his heart beat like fists inside his chest.

"It is time to go," said the roaches. Not in the voice of the Goddess. No, the small creatures spoke as one, and in the voice of a man. In Kuga's voice.

"Apparently you *do* need an engraved invitation," snorted Dillon, cracking apart the magic of this moment. He was a burly man with a crooked nose, a lantern jaw, and a North Jersey accent. Not once in all of Santoro's time there at Area Ninety-Four had the guard betrayed even a hint that he was crooked. "Get up and get dressed, brother. This shit's about to get loud and messy and we need to be ready to rock."

Santoro, still confused, leapt up, pulled on his orange coveralls and thin-soled boat shoes.

"Leave everything else," said the guard. "You won't need it."

"But—"

Before Santoro could get the question out the whole world seemed to shudder as something exploded. It was a massive blast, too, and instantly alarms began blaring throughout the prison. Inmates shouted and screamed from their cells, and in the halls was the thunder of running feet.

Santoro gripped the bars, shook them, but they did not budge.

"Wait for it," said Dillon, glancing at his watch. "Okay, now do exactly what I say. No time for questions. Take your mattress, wrap it around you, and crouch in the far left corner. Do it right now."

Santoro did not hesitate. He snatched the thin mattress and curled into as small a ball as he could manage. The roaches scuttled out of the way. However, as he ducked down he saw that the insects were all flowing toward the bars. Were they fleeing or . . . ?

He stared as the roaches reached the bars and began climbing. They flowed in a bristling mass around and around, climbing atop each other until they were five or six deep. Dillon grinned at them and at Santoro, then he sketched a hasty salute and vanished.

Three things happened all at once.

There was another explosion in the prison—somewhere above, on the administrative level or possibly the roof—and the whole building seemed to lift. Cracks whipsawed along the concrete walls, belching dust into the darkened air.

There was the sound of automatic gunfire. A lot of it, and in a variety of calibers. Handguns, assault rifles, and machine guns. Mixed in with that was the distinctive whirling maelstrom of an electric cannon.

But more immediately, more powerfully, the thousands of cockroaches clinging to the bars exploded. Santoro did not actually see it, but he felt it. The force of the blast punched him back against the wall and drove the breath from his lungs. Debris—shattered metal and broken stone—hammered the mattress and set it ablaze.

Dazed, coughing, dizzy, Santoro only just managed to shove the burning mattress away as he staggered to his feet. He immediately fell to his knees, then a hulking shape materialized in the smoky gloom, hooked a big hand under Santoro's armpit, dragged him to his feet, and pulled him out of the cell into the hall.

The sounds of gunfire were muted by partial deafness from the blast. Santoro struggled to make sense of what just happened. The roaches had exploded.

Exploded.

"H-how—?" he stammered.

Dillon pulled him roughly along the corridor. "You want to talk or do you want to live?"

Those words seemed to reach past Santoro's pain and confusion and flip a switch. An old, disused switch. In the space of three yards he went from a stumbling victim to a man running as if he owned the moment, as if he owned *himself* again. By the time they reached the stairs, Santoro was running faster than the big guard.

They ran through smoke and shadows. More explosions rocked

the prison and the chatter of gunfire was continual, loud enough to drown out the screeching alarms. There was a security door to the stairs and it stood open, blocked by a black duffel bag. Another guard was just inside the stairwell, but he lay in a broken sprawl, his head twisted too far around. Dillon snatched up the bag and kicked the door shut. He knelt fast, jerking down the bag's zipper, and began pulling items out and tossing them to Santoro. Kevlar body armor, limb pads, a ballistic helmet.

And weapons. A Sig Sauer handgun and an M4 carbine. There was a two-pocket shoulder pouch fat with loaded magazines for each. Santoro took a pistol and shoved it into his pocket along with extra magazines, and accepted a rifle. He removed the magazine, checked that it was loaded, and slapped it back. The weapon felt as good as a lover in his hands.

Dillon took a rifle as well and looped a second pouch over his broad shoulder. "Here's the plan," he said tersely. "This place is going to shit in a big way. Got maybe six, eight hundred thousand crawlers in here. Bugs and rats."

"Rats . . . ?"

"They carry more C-4."

"Oh . . ."

"We're heading up to the roof," said Dillon. "We got a couple of helos inbound. Full of our guys. They're top private contractors and they are being paid a shit-ton of money to get you out. Big bonuses if you're unharmed. You're not worth a whole lot dead. So, let's help them earn their cash, okay?"

Dillon turned and ran along the corridor on the other side of the doorway. Santoro did not understand this and did not like it, but he was no fool. He ran to catch up.

The corridor ended at another door, and the sounds of battle were so intense that they rattled the door in its frame. Dillon input a code and the door opened. They peered outside to see a tableau of pure carnage. The prison's guards were taking heavy fire from four combat helicopters. The two doing the most damage were a pair of lethal AH-1Z Vipers that hovered above the outer wall of the prison and rained down fire with three-barreled M197

JONATHAN MABERRY

electric rotary cannons. The heavy-caliber rounds punched through doors, windows, and body armor. The watchtowers were gone—blown to flaming debris by Hellfire missiles and Hydra 70 rockets. Massive chunks of the structure had been destroyed and pillars of smoke rose from the burning rubble. Until now Santoro half believed that this was all some kind of deception, part of an elaborate and devious plan by Church to somehow win his trust and open him up. But now he understood that this was an actual rescue mission.

It was Kuga for real. The Seven Kings had used his services a few times, but always at several removes. Kuga had a fetish for secrecy. Santoro had theories on who the legendary fixer was, but that's all they were.

Why, though, would Kuga spend this much money and take these insane risks to free him?

Dillon shoved him along the walkway. "Daydream later," he roared.

Prison guards were pouring fire at the invaders, but they were armed for a riot, not an invasion. Their body armor was designed to stop most conventional bullets, but offered no protection at all from armor-piercing rounds.

Santoro saw the other two helicopters come sweeping around a burning tower. They were muscular Hueys with their side bay doors open. Rappelling lines tumbled out and mercenaries roped down, firing as they landed. Under cover fire from the helicopter chain guns, the soldiers ran across the shattered roof.

But the battle had a third set of players. Two Apache attack helicopters were coming in hard and fast from the west. As Santoro watched, the lead bird fired a Sidewinder that drilled a hole through the air and struck one of the Vipers. The explosion was massive and as the fireball lit the night sky, the shock wave knocked the men—guards and their attackers—flat. The other helicopters rocked and tilted, spilling air as the pilots fought for control.

Santoro saw ropes dropping from one of the helicopters and black-clad figures slithering down, guns spitting fire.

"Who are they?" cried Santoro.

Dillon snarled, sounding scared. "Fuck me . . . I think they're *DMS.*"

Santoro, for all of his courage and strength, felt a shiver of icy fear stab him in the groin. He hissed and almost dodged back away from the door.

"They will slaughter your men," he warned. "They are devils."

"Leave it," yelled Dillon.

Santoro ignored him and opened fire with his rifle. He hadn't fired a gun in years, but that did not matter. He was born to killing and with every squeeze of the trigger he became more fully alive. Men died and in their deaths gifted him with new life. Santoro felt like a vampire, feeding on the life force of these soldiers. He wanted to go down into the heat of this battle, to walk like a prince of death through the smoke and fire, reveling in red slaughter.

DMS agents and prison guards, recognizing a new threat as their fellows died, turned to concentrate their return fire on him. But Santoro knew that he was blessed. He could feel the hand of the Goddess on his shoulder, her words whispering into his ear.

For me, she said. *Do this for me.*

Tears ran from his eyes as he fired. Bullets struck the stone and the pipe rail and ricocheted into the fiery darkness, but none touched him. How could they? His faith had been restored, and with it the power he once owned. The Goddess had not abandoned him. No, she was with him now, in this hour of death and liberation. And so he killed for her. He killed and killed and killed.

And, as if recognizing that a master of death was among them, Dillon's own team redoubled their efforts, and the prison became a true killing ground. Above them, Dillon's helicopters moved up and away from the prison to gain maneuvering room for combat. All of the gunships were firing now, filling the night sky with tracers and the hiss of rockets. The air seemed to explode around them. Shrapnel rained down on the prison, cutting down the guards and Dillon's own troops.

One of the Hueys erupted into a massive fireball, and Dillon shoved Santoro back from the flaming debris. Santoro pulled free of him and ran to where one of Dillon's men was fumbling to fix a new rocket-propelled grenade into the launcher, having failed to hit anything on his first try. Santoro tore the weapon from the man with such force that the soldier fell and struck his head on the pipe rail. Santoro snapped the grenade into place, turned, steadied the stock against his shoulder, and fired. The grenade shot into the air, trailing a serpentine coil of dense gray smoke. The DMS pilot banked hard to try and avoid it but he was a second too late and Santoro's round slammed into the Hydra rocket pod. The massive explosion punched the helicopter sideways in the air. As its flaming mass fell, Santoro saw the faces of the crew catch fire. It struck the wall eighty feet away.

The second Apache fired and took a Viper in the tail rotor, spinning it into a death spiral that slammed onto the unforgiving desert floor.

Six of Dillon's team, encouraged by what Santoro had done, fired RPGs at it and the chopper pilot almost—almost—slipped them all. The last one hit just below the door and the blast sent the pilot flying into the air. He fell in pieces and his Apache landed on top of him.

"Go, go, go," yelled Dillon as his remaining Huey dropped down so that its skids scraped along the wall. Santoro dropped the grenade launcher and ran. Hands reached out to pull him and Dillon inside.

The Viper angled in nearby and fired all of its remaining missiles and rockets, and as the Huey rose the entire prison seemed to be engulfed in flame. Even the stones seemed to burn. The hellish orange glow painted the landscape in fire. Then both helicopters were moving away, accelerating.

Santoro clung to a restraining strap and leaned out to watch. Mr. Church would have people search through the ruins, sift through the ash to look for his body. How long would it take? As if in answer there was another, much larger explosion than any that had come before. One massive corner of the prison seemed to break apart as a massive bloom of fire and heat expanded outward from its core. Walls and turrets disintegrated in a fireball of burning destruction. Shock waves chased the chopper into the air, buffeting it, nearly pulling it down into the fiery hell. Alarms shrieked and the rotors struggled for purchase in the sky.

It was close. So close, but the helicopter rose above the burning fingers of death and moved away into the night.

As the helicopter lifted away, Santoro saw something else that puzzled him. A small knot of armed men were clustered around a tall man who wore prison overalls identical to his own. The man looked very familiar, but Santoro could not place him. He turned toward Santoro and flashed a broad grin, then his rescuers escorted him through rotor wash to a waiting helicopter. It lifted off, and a split second later two more helos came swooping in and fired missiles at the corner of the building where the other prisoner had been. They fired again and again, obliterating that part of the prison. Then they turned in midair and launched a new salvo at the area where Santoro had been held these last years. He stood there, watching the building blow apart as if Satan himself had exhaled his fiery breath at it.

Soon the prison was completely engulfed. The helicopters circled wide and began following the machine the first prisoner was on. Flying in formation. However when they were a few miles from the conflagration, the helo with the other prisoner peeled off and vanished into the night.

Santoro turned once more to Dillon. "Who is in that other helicopter? Who else did you help escape?"

The former guard just grinned. "Here, have a beer." He pressed a cold, sweating bottle into the former prisoner's hand and then clinked his own against it. "Welcome back to the world. Things are going to get real fucking interesting."

Dillon threw back his head and laughed at his own cryptic joke. The choppers turned off their lights and flew like phantoms through the night.

CHAPTER THIRTY-ONE

GOSEONG DINOSAUR MUSEUM
618 JARANMAN-RO, HAI-MYEON
GOSEONG-GUN
GYEONGSANGNAM-DO, SOUTH KOREA

Ainil Tan was pretty sure someone was going to kill her.

She stood in the empty main hall looking up at the fully articulated skeleton of an allosaurus. All teeth and claws. An apex predator from the Jurassic period. One hundred and fifty million years ago this creature was the terror of any land it inhabited, fearing nothing. For Ainil there was nothing that could be a sharper contrast to who and what she was. Ninety-three pounds, five feet tall but only when wearing thick-soled sneakers; twenty-two years old, with no combat skills at all. She did not know a single martial arts move, had never fired or even picked up a gun, and could barely cut bread with a knife.

All she had was her camera and her computer.

"Careful," said a voice behind her, "he looks hungry."

She screeched and jumped, then whirled as a man came up behind her. A chubby man in a uniform stood there, looking aghast.

"Oh . . . hey, I'm sorry," the man said quickly. It was Hyuk Cho, the nightshift guard. "I was just playing. God, I—I didn't mean to scare you. Are you okay?"

She wanted to punch him. She wanted to run. Instead she forced a smile. Her heart was hammering and it took real effort to take a full breath. "No, it's okay," she lied.

"You sure? You went white as a ghost."

"Really, it's cool. I'm fine."

They spoke in Korean, which she could manage with a heavy accent. Cho was a local guy. Lumpy and dull, but friendly enough, and he was often the only other person in the museum during these long nights. Normally the quiet and privacy worked for Ainil. Right now she would have liked the place to be filled with five hundred noisy kids and a bunch of parents or schoolteachers. Witnesses, every one of who would have a cell phone camera. The modern safety net.

The guard licked his lips. "Are you sure? It was stupid of me."

"No, it's fine," she said, touching his sleeve, then fished for a lie to make sense of her overreaction. "It's just this place gives me the creeps. All these . . . monsters."

A slow, relieved smile found its way onto Cho's doughy face. "You're still new here. You get used to these cuties." He nodded to the allosaur. "And, once the tourists are gone this place can be pretty creepy."

"Yes."

He cleared his throat. "So . . . you're okay?"

"I'm fine. And I'd better get back to work."

Ainil gave Cho another weak smile and half a bow, then hurried toward the small office reserved for the I.T. people. She had to run a program on the demographics of the customers, enter all the email addresses from the sign-up sheets, and send them emails with dinosaur information and clickable links to membership and donation pages.

She could feel the guard watching her.

He's not one of them, she told herself. *He's too young.*

In the reflection of the glass door to the computer room, she saw him standing there. Still watching.

If he was one of them I'd already be dead.

That was true enough. Once the museum closed the rest of the staff got out of there pretty quickly and the doors were locked. She was lucky she'd gotten here on time. It was close. The man with the boat knew how to slip past all the spotter planes and watching eyes and had gotten her from North Korean waters to a secure section of coastline down here where her car was discreetly parked. She'd broken so many laws that she lost count, but her fear was not of the police or the border patrols for North or South Korea. It was *them*.

They would want her stopped. They would want her dead. Not just silenced, but killed.

She had no idea who, or when, or where, but someone *would* try. They would have to try. If she was in their place, she would, too. Well . . . if she was a government flunky and sociopath. And now there would be four sociopaths making calls to have her found and killed.

As she locked herself into the computer room, Ainil tried to tell herself that she didn't care. That she was too hard to find, too anonymous, too much of a nobody. After all, she worked in a dinosaur museum. Who would ever think to look for her here?

When she peeked through the blinds, she saw the guard turn and walk slowly away. Beginning his rounds.

Please, please, please, she begged silently. It felt like a prayer, but to who? She had no faith, no religion.

She removed her tablet and set it on the desk next to the museum's tabletop workstation. Then she took the thumb drive from a hidden compartment in her purse. It took every ounce of her courage to attach it to a small rerouter device and then plug it into the tablet via a short cable.

"P-please," she said aloud, hearing that word stutter and falter. She took a ragged breath, nodded to herself, and then tapped the keys to upload the video file to an email. It took even more courage to hit Send.

Then she quickly disconnected everything and stashed the thumb drive and re-router back into their compartments. It was done. There was nothing more she could do but wait. And pray to an empty heaven that someone would listen.

Pray that the world wasn't about to end.

Fearing, though, that despite everything she'd done and all the risks she had taken, that it was already too late.

CHAPTER THIRTY-TWO
EMBASSY OF THE UNITED STATES
188 SEJONG-DAERO
SEJONGNO, JONGNO-GU
SEOUL, SOUTH KOREA
FOUR HOURS AGO

Julian Paek had been the ambassador to South Korea for sixteen months. He liked the job. Not *loved* it, but he was getting there.

Although he was very much an American—third generation, from Georgetown—Paek loved his heritage. His family spoke Korean and English almost interchangeably at home and at holiday gatherings. Paek knew the history of Korea going all the way back to Gojoseon, and as an undergrad considered pursuing a degree in Korean studies. The law called him with a clearer voice, though, and he went into immigration law and later, international politics. He'd worked his way up through various offices over the years, aiming his career at a new target: the job he now had.

He knew that his tenure would not outlast the current presidency, but it was a joy of a job. Challenging in interesting ways, despite some frustrations related to the ongoing denuclearization talks. Paek did not personally believe that North Korea would ever stop their nuclear program. Rather the reverse. And although that made him a bit nervous, it was unlikely the North Koreans would drop nukes on their own doorstep. He saw it as sword-rattling by a fragile regime that was only still in existence because China was propping them up. It was all a way of waging an economic war against America without anyone actually dying.

That worked for Paek, because it meant that his job was never going to be boring. And once his term was over, he would be able to slide right into the private sector with a seven-figure salary at any of the corporations doing trade here in Asia.

Life, as he saw it, was pretty damn good.

He was drinking tea and listening to a recording of the Bucheon Philharmonic Orchestra's superb Mahler series when an email pinged. He frowned at it, because of what was written in the subject bar.

READ THIS NOW—CRISIS

All caps.

Paek very nearly dismissed it as spam. Although the embassy's spam filters were excellent, some junk always managed to slip through. If he'd been even a little busier he might have ignored it, or put it in a folder for his assistant to read and vet.

But something about it tickled at him in the wrong way. It gave him a flutter of unease, and so he clicked on it.

A graphic popped up with a logo of a crazy-looking cartoon woman laughing maniacally as she leaned sideways around her laptop. The words "Punk Press" were written in dozens of languages inside little word balloons that rose from the computer and popped. Almost immediately a video began playing, and the first few seconds of it were overlaid by five short sentences.

This is not fake.

This footage was taken this morning.

This is real.

We need you to do the right thing.

You need to stop this from starting a war.

But the email had been simultaneously sent to ambassadors in China and the United States, and to the North Korean government. The video played out and Julian Paek sat there, stunned, horrified. At the end of the video was another message.

This is real. You can tell. You can check.

We don't want to share this with the world because of what will happen.

We sent this to you because you're a good man.

You're always the one to try and calm things down. To keep the fools with missiles from pushing the buttons just to prove how tough they are.

I hope you are the person people think you are.

I hope you understand what this means.

I hope you will figure some way of dealing with this.

If not you... who?

There was more, but it was a set of instructions for where to post a reply.

Julian Paek sat at his desk, feeling faint. Feeling terrified. His hands were shaking when he reached for the phone.

CHAPTER THIRTY-THREE
PHOENIX HOUSE
OMFORI ISLAND
GREECE

I gave Rudy the full tour and then we settled down at a table in the staff lounge. We had an honest-to-God barista coffee roast master. Or whatever it's called. His name is Mustapha and he is a sorcerer of the coffee bean. He is definitely going to be added to my will.

"Just brewed a fresh pot, Colonel," he said, beaming a great smile. Mustapha is short, round, brown, and happy as hell all the time. He took my special cup from below the counter, rinsed it with very hot water, and filled it with steaming and aromatic heaven. The cup was a gift from Bunny. It had a picture of a World War II soldier holding a cup and grinning; the caption is: *How 'bout I pour you a nice fresh cup of shut the fuck up.* I love that mug. It makes my coffee taste even better.

He poured Rudy's from a separate pot, handed me a wire basket of fresh muffins, and gave me a small bag with some grain-free dog treats shaped like little coffeepots for Ghost. I told him that he was a very nice man.

I followed Rudy to a small table by a window. Well, a fake window. It was actually a live feed projected onto a massive video screen framed like a window. It showed an eastern view of the island. Rudy remarked on it.

"This is smart," he said. "Not only are there faux windows like this everywhere, but if my phone's compass app is correct, then they are positioned to show correctly oriented views. It makes being underground tolerable." He touched his hand to the screen and smiled. "The glass is warm, as if the sunlight up there is really light on window glass. Subtle and remarkable."

JONATHAN MABERRY

"Lean close and listen," I suggested. He did, and his eyes grew wide.

"I . . . can hear the waves," he said, grinning like a happy child. "And seagulls."

I winked at him and fed one of the cookies to Ghost. He took it with great delicacy and settled down to eat it in tiny bites. He does that.

"So," said Rudy, settling back in his chair, "you're *Colonel* Ledger now. *Felicidades, mi coronel.*"

"Don't start."

"Seriously, I'm happy for you."

"I'm not," I said, "but Church insisted. He said something about colonels being more widely respected and that taking a new rank would allow me to function more efficiently with governments and groups we interact with, blah blah blah."

His eyes twinkled with amusement. "You disapprove?"

"Fuck, man, I was never entirely comfortable with being a captain. I was only a sergeant in the army and that's the rank I earned."

"You don't feel deserving of a promotion? Even after all you've accomplished? All the good you've done?"

I snorted. "Dude, it's a fake rank. Rogue Team International is a made-up organization, so Church calling me a colonel is about as valid as calling me Grand Pooh-Bah. It's convenient and that's it."

He brushed a speck of something from the sleeve of his suit coat.

"I am tempted to only call you Grand Pooh-Bah henceforth."

"I will hurt you very, very badly."

"Ah, threats of violence," mused Rudy, "the last resort of the macho male over-compensator."

"*And* bury your body where it will never be found," I added.

"I will block out some time later to be afraid." He tore off a piece of a bran muffin, munched it for a moment. Then I saw him smile as he looked past me to where an overweight, somewhat threadbare old marmalade tabby cat lay in a patch of faux sunlight. Ghost went over and laid down next to the cat, and soon they were both asleep like spoons in a drawer.

"Yeah," I said, "Cobbler's still hanging on."

"He's . . . what? Seventeen now?"

"Eighteen last week."

Rudy nodded. He remembered Cobbler as a spry young cat a million years ago. My version of a therapy animal, I suppose. Ghost and Cobbler used to fight like, well, cats and dogs, but as Cobbler's gotten older, the big shepherd has shifted from aggressive to protective.

Rudy leaned back in his chair and gazed deeply into his coffee cup. "I read the field report on the Jacobsen matter and had a phone consult with the therapist assigned to Astrid."

"Astrid's a tough young lady," I said.

Rudy poured a yellow packet of raw sugar into his coffee. Which is odd, because his drink of choice these days is a venti, half whole milk, one quarter one percent, one quarter non-fat, extra hot, split quad shots—two shots decaf, two shots regular—no-foam latte, with whip, two packets of Splenda, a touch of vanilla syrup, and three short sprinkles of cinnamon from Starbucks. The sad thing is the poor beleaguered baristas have to make that crap. Now he was pouring one packet of real sugar into a cup of black decaf coffee. He caught me watching, but made no comment. Rudy likes to mess with me sometimes. Which I'm pretty sure is unethical, since he's my shrink.

"Toughness," he said as he stirred, "is both conditional and relative. Astrid needed to be tough while things were unfolding. That's a survival skill. However, now that she's been rescued, she's having a very hard time adjusting her worldview to fit what happened. Not only was she kidnapped and subjected to physical harm and the threat of sexual violence, but she was also a witness to extreme violence. She saw you kill people."

"Very bad people," I said, pouring milk into my coffee. No sugar. I took an experimental sip. Nice.

"It doesn't entirely matter that they were bad people, Cowboy," he said, using my old boyhood nickname. "Astrid was there when extreme violence occurred. Exposure to that leaves a mark on every person."

"'Violence always leaves a mark,'" I said, quoting his favorite maxim. It made Junie's words echo in my head, and I avoided Rudy's eyes.

"It does," Rudy replied. "And for each person the severity of that

JONATHAN MABERRY

mark is different. For some, it's a badge of honor; for others it is a crippling injury, and there are countless variations in between. You have been marked," said Rudy. "As have I. We are friends and have many shared experiences, but those things we each experienced are unique to us as individuals. You carry your scars differently than I ever could."

"I'm a soldier and you're not."

He smiled. "I did not say you carried them better, Joe. I said 'differently.'"

"Ah," I said. "Right. Sorry."

Okay, that's a point for Junie, I thought.

"Astrid is a teenager," he said. "Her challenge at processing what she experienced is complex." He drank some coffee, winced at the taste, and added a second packet of sweetener. "She was taken to be used as a tool against her father. If her father turned over all his files to save her, then she thinks she would be partly at fault for any deaths resulting from the release of the mycotoxin. She knows her father was willing to sacrifice himself to save her, but at the same time she now knows that her father broke the rules set by her kidnappers by having a rescue mission attempted. There are a lot of subtleties in there that a fragile mind can use to construct more guilt and also resentment toward her father. And, she knows that people were killed by her rescuers. To a person as empathic and sensitive as Astrid, she holds herself responsible for their deaths."

"They were scumbags who would have raped and killed her."

"How does that matter?" asked Rudy. "To her, I mean. They were people. She sees them in a broader framework than you do. She sees their lives, their families—parents, spouses, children. She wonders whether they were truly corrupt or just following orders because there would be consequences for not doing so. And on and on."

I sat back and stared at the air over his head. Ghost got up, came over, and laid his head on my thigh and I scratched his thick white fur.

"Jesus Christ," I said.

"When a team like yours rescues someone," Rudy said gently, "they are rescuing a victim of trauma. The person you bring out is not—and cannot possibly be the person who was taken, and definitely not the person they were in the moments before they were aware they were about to be abducted. Each step of that process inflicts a wound, and the effect is cumulative."

I looked away. He was too compassionate to add something as trite as "as you well know." Of course I knew, and like Astrid I could look back to see the person I was before an act of terrible violence changed the trajectory of my life. When I was fourteen, my girlfriend Helen and I were walking in a park on a lovely spring afternoon, busy with falling in love for the first time, filled with all the excitement and optimism that comes with that bit of magic. Then we were attacked by four older teens. They were bigger and stronger and their minds were furnaces of hatred and awful need. They beat me to a pulp and while I lay there, broken and bleeding, I got to see the process of Helen being destroyed. Unlike Astrid, no one came to rescue Helen.

We both survived the day. Kind of. We were broken and none of the king's horses and none of the king's men could piece us together again. Helen withdrew into herself and, years later, opted out of the whole horror show. I found what was left of her. Cooling, rancid meat that was proof to me that the world could be a dark, ugly, and evil place.

She died, and I lived. I was not whole, though. The initial attack and her suicide splintered me. It was Rudy, then a young resident, who helped me put some of the pieces together, discarding fragments of my personality that no longer fit, and teaching me to make peace with what was left. I had three different aspects to my personality that were so distinct that they had their own names. The Modern Man, the version of me who might have lived a normal life if Helen and I hadn't been attacked. My default personality was the Cop—analytical, introspective, observant, and dedicated to the procedural cause and effect. And then there was the Killer. He was a savage, primal and uncompromising; deeply protective of what he perceives as the vulnerable members of his tribe, and absolutely merciless when he goes hunting for the bad guys. They all warred for control, and Rudy helped me negotiate the terms of our ongoing truce.

I looked back and remembered the day I left the hospital a few weeks after the attack. I went to the closest dojo and signed up. The

Cop part of me became obsessed with learning to be strong because I knew full well the cost of being weak. I became strong, too. I became a monster who fed on other monsters. The Killer emerged through that process. Most of the time I was a creature of peace who loved a nicely grilled steak on Super Bowl Sunday, icy glasses of craft beer, summer days on a sunny beach, and good old-fashioned rock 'n' roll. Until I wasn't. When I rolled into a fight, the Cop tried to keep things copacetic, but when things got freaky he unchained the Killer and let him run wild. And it was that monster who'd rescued Astrid, and it was that monster who helped mark her young soul. Not meaning to, but doing it all the same.

Junie knew all of this, too, and I think I was probably angry with her because her comments made me feel like she'd forgotten or ignored all that. Now I was seeing it differently.

Rudy reached out and laid his hand on my forearm, giving it a gentle and reassuring squeeze. I was in my own head, but he knew the twisted paths my thoughts would take. He let me know that I was never alone.

I opened my mouth to tell him about the conversation with Junie, and to ask his opinion about why my recent gunfights don't seem to have affected me, but I never got the chance. The lounge door opened and the duty officer came hurrying into the room.

"Colonel Ledger?" she said breathlessly. "The Big Man wants you in the TOC right away. Something's come up."

CHAPTER THIRTY-FOUR
THE TOC
PHOENIX HOUSE
OMFORI ISLAND
GREECE

The TOC is the tactical operations center, and it's where all field ops are overseen. It's a big room with a massive bank of high-def computer screens filling one wall and a big half circle of computer workstations facing it on a series of tiers. Looks a bit like mission control for the NASA launches, but maybe we're more high-tech.

Mr. Church stood on the top step beside a shorter, very thin man who had sticklike legs and a weirdly long neck and looked like a wading bird. Maybe an egret, but with sandy hair and steel-rimmed glasses. Scott Wilson was the chief of operations and he was the poor, unfortunate bastard who had to try and fill the shoes of Aunt Sallie. No one could ever do that, of course, and everyone knew it. Wilson knew it, too. Auntie had been with Church for decades and was retired now, working her way through a very slow recovery from a very bad stroke. Wilson, though a former SAS shooter and a bit of a badass in his own right, had no chance with people who'd worked with Auntie. It was like hiring a really tough pit bull to replace a Tyrannosaurus rex. The sense of proportion was all wrong.

That said, Wilson was sharp as hell when it came to mission strategy, especially in the implementation of the latest generation of high-tech combat aides. That included everything from sophisticated computer-enhanced body armor to a slew of specialty tactical drones. And maybe drones were a particular favorite of his because since signing on he'd encouraged Doc Holliday to acquire as many different kinds of drones as she could—from high-flying new-generation predators to swarms of micro-drones the size of houseflies. It was his wish to one day send fewer human assets and more robots into battle. I can see his point, and can certainly admire his goal of preserving human life, but I've dealt with combat drones and it didn't leave me with the warm fuzzies. After all, a good third of that stuff was scary shit we'd taken away from the bad guys in the old DMS days.

Wilson was also much more of a diplomat than Auntie, who was cranky to an Olympic level. Wilson often coordinated interjurisdictional field ops involving thirty different countries and some of America's more covert teams, like Chess Team, Sigma Force, and MHI. Before coming to RTI, he'd been the chief operations officer for Barrier, which was the British group within MI6 that was Church's model for the Department of Military Sciences. So, yeah, he had all the street cred he needed, but even so . . . Auntie, you know? One of a kind.

Church turned as I approached.

"Did Bug get anything on that Imirzalioglu joker?" I asked. "Do

JONATHAN MABERRY

we know who he is yet? Because I'd love to put that son of a bitch in the morgue."

"That bit of mayhem will have to wait, Colonel," said Church. "Something else has come up."

"Shit," I said. "What's on fire now?"

"Currently," said Wilson, "a little nothing of an island off the coast of North Korea."

"Literally on fire?"

"No," said Church, "though that might be better than what we're facing."

"I hate it when you say shit like that," I muttered.

"I hate it when I have to, Colonel." Church gestured to the screen. "This is Gaeguli Seom."

I worked out the translation. "Island of Frogs. Never heard of it."

"No reason you should have done," said Wilson in his crisp Eton accent. "It has a small fishing village with a population of one hundred and eighty-six. Or, at least it did so until last night. There was a satellite flyover using thermal scans and it's currently estimated that the population is zero. That includes, by the by, a platoon of North Korean regulars who were sent in to investigate. And the two-man staff of a small sonar station. The station was established, apparently, to watch for an American submarine invasion of the North Korean mainland."

"Which is never going to happen," I suggested.

"God forbid," snorted Wilson. "To invade North Korea would be to declare war on China. But, the propagandists need to engender fear in order to control the population, hence the sonar station."

I studied the thermal overlay on the image, and saw that a few heat signatures were there, but they were cooling to the point where they'd vanish from the scan.

"Everyone's dead?" I asked. "How? I didn't hear about earthquakes or a tsunami. So, what happened? They have a nuclear plant there that melted down?"

"No," said Wilson. "Apart from the sonar station there is no industry or military presence at all on the island. They don't even have electricity, apart from a few shared diesel generators."

"Then why's everyone dead?"

"We don't know," said Church, "and neither, apparently, do the North Koreans. One of the members of the sonar team attempted to send a distress call, but it was cut off. They sent in a small platoon via boat to investigate, and they failed to report. A second team was sent, this time by helicopter, and shortly after arrival they stopped broadcasting."

I looked at the image and saw that the digital clock was feeding real-time data. "Why am I not seeing the entire North Korean navy converging on the site?"

"Because the upper echelon of that government doesn't yet know about this," said Wilson.

I glanced at him. "You lost me. How do *we* know and they don't?"

"It's complicated."

"Uncomplicate it for me."

Wilson turned to Church and raised his eyebrows.

"Colonel," began Church, "you are aware that I have a number of associates positioned in key places throughout the world. Business, various governments, and so on."

"Your 'friends in the industry.'"

He measured out a microscopic slice of a smile. "Yes. Over the last few years, as the governments of key nations have become increasingly unstable due to election tampering, I've cultivated a new set of *friends*. Diplomats in crucial positions as well as some members of the military of various nations."

"Should I even ask how you manage that?" I asked.

He usually ignores questions like that, but this time he surprised me. "You may be encouraged to know that despite the bluster of a growing number of unstable world leaders, there are a fair number of much cooler heads within those governments. People who have chosen to either remain in place during regime changes, or who have entered into service with a new administration because they believe in the concept of checks and balances. It is no exaggeration at all to say that wars have been prevented by quiet phone calls or coded emails. The global stock market has been propped up at times by a word here, or a warning there. Understand, this is not a network built on party politics—*anyone's* party—or personal gain. These people believe that there needs to be—as you often say—an adult in the room. Or, as Brick likes to say, a designated driver."

"Wow," I said.

"You have no idea," breathed Wilson.

"These people," continued Church, "are aware of the existence of Rogue Team International. They understand that our agenda is to exert agency over global threats that would otherwise be dangerous for any one government to handle. This case may be exactly the sort of thing we formed RTI to address."

"Okay, that's pretty badass," I said. "So . . . who called? And what happened on the island?"

"Second question first," said Wilson. He bent over and used the trackpad on a laptop to change from a satellite view to the feed from a drone that was closer to the ground. The drone flew slowly over a small village that was little more than a cluster of shacks and huts around a central town square.

I watched with a sinking stomach as what at first appeared to be irregularities in the landscape resolved into bodies. Many, many bodies.

In a sick and hollow voice, Wilson said, "As far as we can tell, Colonel, everyone on Gaeguli Seom is dead."

I walked down the steps to stand closer to the screen. It was so densely pixilated that you could actually get within inches and examine minute details. I've been on-site for a lot of slaughters in my time, and I used to be a cop. In essence what I saw was one big crime scene. Bodies everywhere, and even a blind man could see that this had been a mutual slaughter. I walked along the massive screen, letting it tell me a story, and the tale it told was a horror story.

"Jesus Christ," I said, "they all killed each other."

INTERLUDE SIX
IN FLIGHT
THIRTY MILES FROM THE CALIFORNIA BORDER
FIFTEEN MONTHS AGO

Rafael Santoro tried talking to the crew aboard the Huey, but apart from simple politeness no one would engage him in any meaningful conversation. Not even Dillon, who sat in the corner drinking beer after beer. They would not tell him where they were going, who they were going to see, or why they had broken him out of the prison. No one would explain anything about the exploding roaches or rats, and now that he was away from the prison, he took the opportunity to consider what they must have been.

Prior to his incarceration, he'd read about advances in robotics. It was not something of direct interest to the Seven Kings, and his interest lasted about as long as it took to read a magazine article. Now bits of it came back. He closed his eyes and let information float to the top of the troubled soup of his thoughts. There was a word, an acronym.

CRAM?

Yes, that was it. Remembering the full name took a few moments, but it came. Compression Resistant Articulated Mechanism. A radical new kind of designer robot. Very small, and designed to imitate the qualities of actual roaches. Those insects, ancient and beautiful, were designed to survive virtually anything. They can withstand nearly a thousand times their own body weight without injury, and compress their bodies to fit through a quarter-inch gap.

The roaches in the article, though, were very clearly artificial—structures of wire and cardboard. The ones in his cell had looked exactly like real roaches. That had fooled him, and Santoro disliked being fooled. They'd also spoken to him. The voice was soft, soothing, personal; and it had shared so many secrets with him. Quoting scriptures from the writings of the Goddess, telling Santoro things about the Seven Kings that no one knew, not even Church. Over a period of many weeks, the roaches had come to him as messengers of a higher power.

Now he knew that to be a lie. The roaches had been robots, and clearly each carrying a small amount of explosives so that, when clustered, there was enough destructive force to blow open his cell. He assumed the rats were of a similar nature. Smart. Very practical, which is something Santoro always appreciated.

And yet the vermin were a lie. Everything the roaches told him was a lie. The truth may have actually set him free, but there was an insult buried within it. He wrestled with that. On one hand it snapped him out of the religious torpor into which he'd lapsed. On the other, whoever sent them—his mysterious benefactor—had lied to him, using Santoro's faith as a tool of manipulation. That was very nearly unforgiveable.

He sipped his beer and stared out at the darkened landscape. He was free now and he would die before letting anyone put him back in a cage. That included being trapped in a cage of his own beliefs.

The miles blurred into the blackness of the empty land below.

CHAPTER THIRTY-FIVE
THE TOC
PHOENIX HOUSE
OMFORI ISLAND
GREECE

Church and Wilson came down to stand with me. My own words seemed to hang in the air.

They all killed each other.

"So it would appear," said Church softly.

"But . . . how? Why?" I demanded. "A plague of murder? Shit, is this more of the God Machine . . . ?"

"We don't know," said Wilson.

The God Machine was a device created using a dangerous and radical kind of science. One of the effects of it was that it could drive a percentage of the people exposed to it to commit murder or suicide. In our last DMS case, Washington, D.C., was hit with a brutal wave of the God Machine effect. Since then, though, we had gone to great lengths—very, very great lengths—to make sure that all traces and examples of the God Machine were eradicated. We weren't nice about it, either. We broke laws and cut throats and did a lot of damage because that technology was one of the most dangerous we'd ever encountered. And that is saying a whole damn lot.

"'We don't know'?" I echoed. "Well, fuck, man, what *do* we know?"

The screen was so shockingly clear that it was like standing right there among all the death. Scores of bodies, from the very old to the newly born. None of them were whole. They were torn apart. By knives and jagged pieces of pottery, stabbed with farm tools and broken tree branches, beaten with fists and smashed by any blunt object that was apparently close at hand. And many of them—far too many—had been savaged by teeth. The bite marks were there to be read, as were the red smears on dead mouths.

"We don't know anything for sure," said Church.

"At first," said Wilson quietly, "we thought it was more of the rabies."

A little over a year ago I helped break a case involving a global distribution of a weaponized strain of rabies that used pertussis as a delivery system. Groups like FreeTech, the World Health Organization, and others, backed by financial and logistic aid from the United Nations, had virtually eradicated it, but there was always a danger of outbreaks in isolated areas.

"It's not that," I said, "because it affected the soldiers. Any armed platoon would have been inoculated and they wouldn't be overwhelmed by unarmed civilians."

"That was the conclusion we reached as well." Wilson shifted the picture to other places on the island. I saw families locked in the stillness of a terminal death struggle. Children biting the parents who strangled them. Infants ripped to pieces. Young couples locked in sexual embraces while clutching the knives they'd used to murder each other.

"Then this is what? Some kind of new bioweapon?" I asked. "If so, what? Who used it? And to what end? This island looks like it's on the ass-end of nowhere. Why do this?"

Wilson said, "We don't have enough intel to make any good guesses, Colonel. All we know is that it appears to have affected—or perhaps *in*fected—everyone on the island. We know that it has a rate of onset that is both alarming and unnatural. No pathogen in nature could cause such radical and specific behavioral changes as quickly as what appears to have happened here. For a platoon of soldiers to have been affected so fast they could not radio in a report, you'd need a pathogen that hits at the speed of a neurotoxin."

"Show me the soldiers," I said, and Wilson shifted the image again.

There corpses sprawled in silent ugliness along a jungle footpath. It looked like a few had beaten each other to death with their weapons, while others clearly stood a few feet apart and emptied their magazines at one another.

"It's not Seif al Din, either," I said, referring to another and far more dangerous engineered pathogen. Fear of that weapon is what led to Church hiring me into the old Department of Military Sciences. It stood as our "worst-case scenario" since then, and none of us were anxious to find out about something bigger and badder. If it had been Seif al Din, the dead people would still be walking around and they wouldn't have been able to use weapons. "Jesus Christ, what *is* this?"

It was rhetorical by now.

Church said, "I've taken the liberty of alerting Havoc Team. They are loading a helo with weapons, electronics, and hazmat gear. A jet will be smoking on the tarmac in Athens by the time you get there. Bug is smoothing the clearances."

"We're going to the island?"

"Yes," said Wilson. "Your cover is that of a specialized hot zone field team freelancing with the World Health Organization. You are a South African private contractor. Each of your team will have similar credentials. Completely unbreakable."

"Okay."

"You'll fly to Osan Air Base in Pyeongtaek and meet with Colonel Epps, commander of the 51st Fighter Wing."

"He's a friend," said Church quietly.

"At Osan you'll be introduced to Lieutenant Colonel Ho Yongju," said Wilson. "He is a doctor attached to the People's Army Special Operation Force."

I grunted. "We're working with the sanction of the North Korean government?"

"Ho is a friend of a friend," said Church.

"How far can I trust him?"

"As far as your own judgment," said Church. "However, Ho is not a hawk. He has been at his current rank for some time now, getting only lateral promotions because he tends to err on the side of humanism rather than being overtly political. He's never come out and spoken against his government, but it's clear the party leaders don't consider him one of their creatures. He's very good at his job, however, and has taken point on some crucial disease outbreak responses. At a distance he appears to be a moral person trying to do his best in a difficult and restrictive political circumstance."

"Understood," I said.

"Colonel Epps will provide transport to the coast," said Wilson, "where you'll take a non-military RHIB belonging to the WHO."

"What is the actual mission?" I asked.

"Assessment, gather intel, gather samples, and get out," said Wilson. "Take no undue risks."

Church said, "Your coms will be a *team* channel at all times—unless you actively switch to a private channel. It is likely that access to the team channel will be shared with select persons in the governments of North and South Korea, China, and the U.S."

"Well . . . fuck . . ."

"This situation is fragile," Church said, "and transparency might help us keep fingers off of the wrong buttons."

"But, hey, no pressure, right?"

Church measured out a small smile. "You could have chosen a less stressful profession. Lion tamer, bomb disposal . . ."

"Yeah, yeah."

We stood looking at the pain and horror and death on the Island of Frogs.

Church reached out and touched the screen, resting his finger on the image of a Korean soldier who lay next to a comrade he had beaten to death. The beaten soldier's face was literally battered to an inhuman pulp, and the attacker's hands were mangled bits of raw gristle, with pieces of his own bones sticking out through torn flesh. The soldier had a bayonet in his stomach, but it hadn't killed him before he'd done all of that awful damage.

"Before you go, Colonel," he said quietly, "tell me something . . . if you had to put a word to all of this. The emotion of it, what would you call it? Give it a name."

I didn't have to think very hard because one word was painted there on every inch of torn skin and broken lives. It was ground into the bloody dirt and burned into the day.

"Rage," I said.

Church said, "Yes."

I turned to him. "There's another shoe to drop, isn't there? We don't get called in because of shit like this. What's the rest?"

Church gave me a small nod of approval. Wilson used the remote to open a new window on the screen and immediately a video began playing. I stood there and watched in shock and horror as something unfolded that made no sense but was as real as all the other horrors I'd so far seen.

"Oh my God . . . ," I breathed.

"The ambassador of South Korea contacted me because he'd received that video," said Church very quietly. "He knew that I have contacts inside North Korea, and together we came up with a plan that might keep this from starting a war. I need you on the ground on Frog Island. I need you to get ahead of this thing."

I didn't answer. No need. I was already running for the door.

INTERLUDE SEVEN
WILDLIFE ROAD ABOVE THE POINT DUME BLUFFS
MALIBU, CALIFORNIA
FIFTEEN MONTHS AGO

The helicopter did not take Santoro to meet his rescuer. The plan was a great deal more complicated than that. The choppers landed in the parking lot of a large and remote industrial complex in the Mojave Desert in California. There, Santoro and six other people—four men and two women—were ushered inside. There was a surprisingly well-appointed series of room suites, where they were each allowed to shower, eat, and dress.

He stood naked in the shower for long minutes, hands braced on the tiles, head bowed, letting the hot water boil away the memories of prison showers. Dirt, brick dust, gunpowder residue sluiced down his limbs, carrying with them flecks of memories of all of the indignities imposed upon him. They swirled around the drain and washed away.

After many minutes, he turned off the spray, dried himself slowly and carefully on a towel that was so soft it made him want to cry. He found combs, brushes, toothbrush and paste, deodorant, and expensive colognes in a basket on the sink. There was also a voice-activated music system accompanied by a small handwritten note with instructions. Santoro tried it and was delighted with the device.

He cleared his throat and leaned toward a small wall-mounted microphone. "Please play Domenico Scarlatti."

"Which piece by Giuseppe Domenico Scarlatti would you like to hear?" asked a pleasant female voice.

"'Stabat Mater' . . . ?" he said, posing it as a question.

"Playing 'Stabat Mater' by Scarlatti, performed by Stefano Lentini, featuring Sandra Pastrana and the City of Rome Contemporary Music Ensemble." And immediately the music began to play. Santoro stood there, smiling. Dazzled, and for a moment he was a teenager again, standing outside of a music hall, listening to a small college orchestra work their way through the piece. It was a heartbreaking work, exploring the Virgin Mary's suffering at the crucifixion of her son.

"Thank you," he said softly. Not to Mary, or even to Dillon's team. He thanked the Goddess for grinding the gears of the universe to make this happen.

Then he dressed in the Kiton tonal plaid two-piece suit and hand-sewn Italian shoes. He put on the new Cartier Santos watch and matched the time to the wall clock. It matched to the second, a detail Santoro appreciated. He finished dressing and came out of the bedroom just as there was a subtle knock on the door. He opened for a man dressed in nondescript white hotel clothes who pushed in a wheeled cart on which was a lovely breakfast—*huevos a la flamenca*, with tomato, peas, bell pepper, potatoes, chorizo, ham, and onion, topped with eggs and baked so that the egg whites were cooked but the yolk was runny. Perfect. There was toast and jam, and a pot of tea. The waiter bowed and left.

He sat down to eat, washing it down with three cups of tea, listening to the laments of Mary.

An hour later a guard came for him and, very politely, asked him to accompany him outside. There he found a sleek Saab 340 turbo-prop plane waiting. He was the sole passenger.

"What about the other prisoners?" he asked the pilot once he was aboard.

The pilot merely smiled and did not answer. The plane took off and flew all the way to a private airport near Malibu. A brand-new Escalade was waiting, and the driver was as silent and mysterious as the pilot had been, and once Santoro was comfortable, a smoked glass window rose up to isolate him in the back. He could see the outline of the driver speaking on a cell phone, but could hear nothing.

The whole process was, he decided, intended to impress. The silence of the staff was to demonstrate a level of loyalty and professionalism. The attack on the prison showed an investment of money and a high degree of professionalism, as well as meticulous timing. The luxury of the hotel suites inside a nondescript building, the clothes, the plane and this car spoke to an appreciation of elegance, but not an absurd dedication to ostentation. That had been one of Hugo Vox's faults—he always liked to be seen to spend more than anyone else. Everything here was of quality, and that seemed to be the point.

As for the breakfast, that was Santoro's favorite. It meant that someone in this organization had insight into him. He was impressed but also unsettled. Very few people knew that much about him.

Who are you? he mused. *Do I know you? Did you know the Goddess?*

The car took him to a beautiful property on Wildlife Road in Malibu, and this did edge toward ostentation. The place had to have a price tag north of sixty million. They passed through a gated drive and rolled under a lush canopy of trees. The short walk from the car to the house gave him glimpses of the ocean, but once he was ushered into the living room, the glimpse turned into a breathtaking view of the vast blue Pacific.

After being in solitary confinement for so long, the vista was the most beautiful thing he'd ever seen, which, he knew, was again part of the plan. Manipulation as well as a statement.

"It's lovely, isn't it?" asked a voice, and Santoro turned to see a tall, handsome, older middle-aged white man standing a dozen paces behind him. The man wore trousers that were a subtle eggshell shade, a pastel blue shirt, untucked, and no shoes. He looked like a movie star, the kind of actor who would play a president. He walked across the room with the kind of nonchalance that came from confidence. This was *his* place, and his sense of ownership seemed to extend out through the windows, past the sculptured gardens, and across the limitless waters.

The man did not yet offer his hand. Instead he came and stood next to Santoro, looking out at the water. They stood like that for several seconds, watching a group of parasailers fly like prehistoric birds above the waves. Santoro waited out the silence.

"Do you know who I am?" asked the tall man.

"You're the one they call Kuga," said Santoro.

CHAPTER THIRTY-SIX
OVER TURKISH AIRSPACE

It was 5,300 miles from the airfield in Athens to our destination in Seoul. Havoc Team was burning along in a heavily modified Cessna Citation X kitted out with extended-range fuel tanks that bumped its normal range of 3,460 miles to somewhere just under 5,000. We still had to make a refueling stop, but by then we'd be in China. When Wilson said that the clearances would be taken care of, he hadn't been joking. No one stopped us, and at the refuel stop we weren't even asked for papers or told to submit to inspection. Felt good, but also weird. And the urgency of it tended to ramp up the speed with which my gut was clenching into a tight, cold ball of dread.

The bird had an eight-passenger capacity, but there were just the five of us. Like all RTI craft, the cabin was totally soundproofed and rigged with every kind of electronic doodad our science teams could manage. All of it was run by Calpurnia, our AI system. The team were in comfortable butter-soft leather chairs with fold-up desks complete with laptops. All mission briefing intel would later be transferred to smaller flexible computers strapped to our forearms.

Everyone was seated and they all looked at me like the world's most dangerous group of schoolkids.

Top Sims is six feet tall and as solid as a block of granite. He wore loose black pants, a gray T-shirt without logo or graphic, and military athletic shoes that looked like sneakers but had metal alloy reinforcing toe caps and ribs. Nothing to indicate rank anywhere on his clothes. He had dark skin, salt-and-pepper hair cut very short, and a precisely trimmed goatee that he'd recently grown. It gave him a somewhat sinister look, which may have been his point. He nodded to me.

"What's the op?" he asked.

"Yeah," said Bunny, "we loaded enough gear to start World War Three."

"Trying to do exactly the opposite," I said.

"Crap," he said, "I hate it when you say stuff like that."

Bunny was six and a half feet of Orange County white boy, with more muscles than anyone could reasonably use. Someone once remarked that he looked like he could bench-press a school bus while getting a blowjob. Why a blowjob and not, say, a hand job, is one of those things that only ever seems to make sense to cops and soldiers. Bunny was blond, blue-eyed, easygoing and good-natured everywhere except in a fight. He and Top joined the old DMS when I did, and we've walked through the Valley of the Shadow more times than I can count.

Bunny was drinking a Coke Slurpee and gestured with the cup. "Bringing lots of guns to a peace conference? That's new for us."

"It's complicated," I said.

"Ain't it *always* complicated?"

"Welcome to the world of grown-ups, Farm Boy," said Top.

"Bite me, Old Man."

Seated across from them was Belle. At a distance you wouldn't think she was the deadly fighter we all knew her to be. She was a short, very slim woman whose body vanished in baggy clothes; but she was all hard muscle and wiry strength. She did not smile or join in the banter, and rarely spoke at all. Never did. Always makes me wonder what her interior life is like. When you've been that seriously damaged in body and mind, the landscape of your soul can be a pretty damn bleak place. It could well be that every time Belle pulled a trigger on a bad guy she was punching a hole in the dense cloud cover that darkened her life. I felt a strong kinship to her, and deeply admired her courage and integrity. And it made me wonder what Junie would make of her.

Andrea was sprawled across two seats with a leg hooked over an armrest, his foot swinging, and was squeezing a red hand-conditioning ball.

"*So,*" Andrea said brightly, "*chi ha il loro scroto bloccato in uno strizzatore ora?*"

"Speak English," groused Bunny.

"He asked who has his nutsack in a wringer," I said. "And it's a fair question."

"All I can say in Italian is give me more pizza," Bunny complained.

"*Questo perché sei un barbaro,*" said Andrea as he tossed his ball in the air and caught it with his other hand.

"I'm not a barbarian, *stronzo.*"

Andrea gave him a wide grin that showed lots of very white teeth. "And you said you didn't speak Italian."

Top snorted. "Farm Boy here only knows the insults 'cause that's most what people say to him."

"Hey," said Bunny.

Top caught my eye, then gave everyone a glare. "Okay, now all y'all shut the fuck up and let the colonel talk."

I hit a key on my laptop and the aerial view of the island popped onto all of their laptop screens.

"This is Gaeguli Seom," I said, and explained where it was and

JONATHAN MABERRY

what little we knew. I played the videos I'd seen and watched the humor evaporate from their faces. Belle sat up straight and then leaned forward, touching the screen much as Church had.

"*Ya Allah . . . Allah yerhamhom,*" she murmured. *God save their souls.*

"Um, boss . . . ?" said Bunny. "Am I seeing this wrong or did they all kill each other?"

"You ain't seeing it wrong, Farm Boy," said Top. He gave me a hard look. "We talking super rabies here or God Machine or—?"

"I asked those same questions and I'll give you the same answers I got: We don't know," I told them. "The brains at the TOC tell me that there is a low probability this is anything we've seen before. There are similarities, but also notable differences. Onset rates, for example, and notable variations in the way in which violence was expressed. Self-harm as well as outward aggression. Right now we have zero reliable intel about the nature of the threat beyond what's on the video. Whatever it is, there appears to be a one hundred percent infection rate, and a one hundred percent mortality rate. That is deeply frightening."

Andrea held up his hand like a kid in school. "*Perdonami, Colonnello,* but why are we even having a mission briefing on this? This island is in *North* Korea, yes?"

"Yes," I said, "but there are complications."

"Told you," said Bunny. Top ignored him.

I explained the situation with Mr. Church's friends, one of who was usefully placed in the emergency response chain of command in North Korea.

"The North Korean guy is the one who calls the shots on anything related to disease and outbreaks. That means his unofficial job is to prevent North Korea from looking weak and therefore bad in the eyes of the world. So, he is the man who keeps things on the DL."

"Even to the point of not passing this up the party line?" asked Top.

"He's stretching that a bit. Taking some risks," I said. "Which means we have a window of a few hours once we're on the island.

If this outbreak happened on the mainland, or anywhere near a military base, a government hub, or where tourists are likely to be, then he wouldn't be able to contain it at all. So this is an actual break."

Andrea raised his hand. "Teacher—a question? Am I being paranoid for thinking that this outbreak is a bit too conveniently located? A nothing island in the middle of a nowhere part of the ocean, with no one to give much of a muffled fart about what happens there? No cameras, no telephones, no Wi-Fi."

"You are right to be paranoid," I said. "It stinks to high heaven. Which brings me to the next part, and this is where it gets even more complicated."

"Like I said," muttered Bunny.

I tapped a key to send them all the Punk Press homepage and froze the picture there for a moment. "Punk Press is a WikiLeaks wannabe," I explained, "with footprints all through Asia. No one knows who runs it because the feeds get bounced around through a sophisticated network of redirects. All we know is that it's most likely run out of somewhere in South Korea. The uploads are usually done via internet cafés, which means we can't pinpoint their physical location beyond where any given post was made. Watch the video and then we'll talk."

The Punk Press video began with a Google maps satellite image of the Island of Frogs. A voiceover spoke in English, with translation crawls in Korean, Mandarin, Japanese, French, and Russian. The voice had been filtered through one of those apps that made it sound like a robot.

"The following footage," said the voice, *"was taken last night on Gaeguli Seom, eighteen nautical miles west of North Korea, in the sovereign waters of the Democratic People's Republic of Korea. This video contains scenes with violent and graphic imagery that can be shocking or disturbing to some viewers."*

There was a pause as the video shifted from the satellite image to what was clearly recorded with a GoPro camera with a nightvision filter mounted on a small commercial drone. It was all in shades of bright green, black, and white. The lack of realistic colors did nothing to lessen the impact of what was being shown, though; and the warning wasn't really enough. I mean, how could it be?

The footage showed villagers attacking one another. It was an angle on the village square that we'd already seen the aftermath of.

"*This was taken with surveillance cameras,*" said the narrator. "*It shows the people of Gaeguli Seom attacking each other as the result of exposure to an advanced bioweapon. As you can see, the designer pathogen creates an extreme state of violent madness.*"

On the screen there were true horrors. I watched my people as they watched it play out. Belle's eyes were glassy and filled with pain; Andrea tried for a poker face, but he was turning first pale and then green. Bunny sat with his fists balled and a snarl turning his young face ugly. As for Top—he was stone-faced, showing nothing, which meant that he was on one of those deep levels of anger that would need to have an outlet. I could relate.

The video jumped around, showing slaughter all over the island. Attacks with hands, teeth, and weapons of convenience—sticks, rocks, walking sticks, even toys. There were rapes of women, children, and even some elderly men that immediately turned into brutal battering and then ended with self-mutilation. The screams that accompanied the killings. Parents doing awful things to their own kids.

"*After the bioweapon caused these deaths,*" continued the narrator, "*a platoon of North Korean soldiers was sent to investigate. They had no idea what they would find, and were not prepared for a biological threat. They wore no protective equipment or garments.*"

We saw this. A young lieutenant who couldn't have been more than twenty, a slightly older sergeant, and their team. It was an orgy of murder.

"*When this platoon failed to report,*" said the narrator, "*another group was sent in.*"

A helicopter landed a fresh team as dawn was slicing open the horizon. The soldiers were better armed and wore gas masks. They moved like SpecOps, but within three minutes they were all dead or dying. The chopper crew panicked and tried to take off, but when it was a thousand yards in the air the pilot opened the door and, locked in a death struggle with his co-pilot, fell onto the rocks that edged the northern side of the island. The bird itself tilted sideways and broke itself to pieces on the unforgiving ground.

When there was no more carnage to show, the voiceover continued. "*The nature of this bioweapon is unknown. The destructive power of it is obvious. But the question is, who would use such a thing against innocent farmers?*"

A dramatic beat, with a new shot of still bodies lying where they'd died.

"*This is the most terrifying part,*" warned the narrator. "*Punk Press has exclusive footage of the culprits behind this atrocity.*"

"Uh-uh," said Bunny, "this can't be good."

"It's not," I said.

It wasn't.

The night-vision camera now showed a section of beach and an RHIB—a rigid-hulled inflatable boat—bobbing in the surface a few yards out, one man at the wheel. A dozen other figures were milling on the beach. They wore the latest generation of Saratoga Hammer Suits, a flexible combat-appropriate hazmat garment, complete with hoods, gloves, and filtered respirators. The figures all carried guns. Top leaned forward to study the weapons and gave a single, sour grunt.

K2 assault rifles, manufactured by Daewoo.

Manufactured in *South* Korea.

Two of the figures were much taller and broader than the others and they carried Colt M4A1s. The standard weapon of the U.S. Navy goddamn SEALs. There was some hushed conversation, and everyone was speaking in English. Most of them spoke with Korean accents except the two big guys. The conversation itself was meaningless, mostly dealing with gathering equipment and returning to the boat. But the language mattered. The accents mattered every bit as much as those weapons.

Bunny turned sharply to me. "Wait . . . *we* did this?"

CHAPTER THIRTY-SEVEN
WESTOVER AVENUE
WEST GHENT, NORFOLK, VIRGINIA
FIVE MONTHS AGO

They tried to take him in the middle of his morning jog.

Petty Officer Second Class Frank Swanson never made strategic or tactical errors in the field. Even when the real world kicked the shit out of weeks of careful mission planning, Swanson was ready to pivot, to flow, to adapt. He was inventive, careful, and meticulous. When his team went in, they did so quickly and smoothly, and when they left there was no trace.

But this was home. This was Norfolk. This was his own neighborhood, where Swanson lived with his wife, Angie, and teenage daughter. He was at home here, and knew every inch, every street and park and alley. When he was out running he could switch off his combat mind and become Frankie, the redhaired kid who was always inventing schoolyard games over on Princess Avenue. He was the teenager who used to kick so much ass on the tennis court over at Ferguson Reid, and who used to drop three-pointers when he played for the Monarchs. The same Frankie who lost his virginity in the back of a Ford pickup truck parked under the trees by Lambert Creek, and later married that girl when she got pregnant. Love of his life. Angie. Now their daughter, Chelsea, was burning up the track as a sprinter in her senior year. Despite being a foot shorter than her father, Chelsea could not only keep up but had better stamina and never seemed to tire. He suspected she had two extra lungs.

Not that he was a slouch. At thirty-five, Frank was a machine. Top of his fitness goals, and that included a reaction and reflex skill set that had served him very well in thirty-one combat missions.

He was a happy man. Out jogging early on a beautiful spring day, with Uncle Tupelo and Whiskeytown singing in his ears. Frank did not know he was in trouble until they tried to take him.

There were three of them, rising up suddenly from between parked cars, closing around him with speed and efficiency, like they'd done this a thousand times. As smooth as he was when he was on a snatch-and-grab job. Closing fast to give him no time.

Except . . .

Frank Swanson was not average. Not even among his peers in the SEALs. He was a cut above, which is why he was who he was. The brain, even in neutral, was never off-line, and as the two men in front reached for him, his reflexes took over. Part muscle memory and part combat brilliance.

He slapped the closest hand away, using his right to make the contact and then feeding it to his left, which came up under his own right wrist to snag the attacker's left forearm. His body was in motion and as he stepped, his right hand, still open, made a very fast circular motion that ended with a vicious blow to the corner of the first man's jaw. Frank put some hip torque into it and the First Man slammed into the Second Man, jolting him off balance.

Frank kept his grip, using the captured arm like a rudder to turn the First Man while using him as a shield against the Third Man. He thrust First Man toward the Third and gave his own open hand a quick, violent half turn that snapped First Man's elbow like a boiled crab leg. Then he let go of the arm, took Third Man by the head, and jerked him forward with savage force, rising to the toe of his left foot and bringing his right knee up hard. Third Man's nose exploded, but Frank kept his two-hand grip and snapped the injured man forward and down as if he was shaking a blanket out on the ground. Third Man hit the pavement with the point of his chin, which exploded.

Then Frank spun and attacked Second Man, who had his balance back now and was reaching inside his jacket for a holstered gun. Frank pinned the reach hand to the man's chest with a flat left palm and hit him with an overhand elbow strike that dropped Second Man to his kneecaps. Frank boxed his ears, knuckle-punched him in the eye, and chopped him across the throat.

That left First Man on his feet, screaming, clutching a broken arm to his chest. Frank kicked him in the balls with a short snapping toe-kick, then slap-turned him and locked a muscular arm around the man's throat as Frank plucked the pistol from his shoulder holster. He raised the gun—a Glock 26—and began to turn in a quick circle, gun pointing in sync with his sharp eyes as he looked for more attackers.

He saw a fourth man getting out of a parked white van, a strange-looking pistol in his hand. Some kind of dart gun. Frank fired two shots at him, but the man ducked down and back. A car came screaming down the street and even before it smoked to a stop Frank saw doors open and more men pour out. Too many to fight, too many guns.

He fired a couple of shots to buy a moment, then whirled and ran.

They gave chase, but this was his town, his neighborhood. He ran faster than any of them, cutting down back alleys, through yards, making maximum use of cover. His house was close and there were no strange cars, no strange people to be seen. Frank sprinted across the lawn, jumped up the porch steps, banged through the door.

"Angie," he roared, "call nine-one-one."

And then he jolted to a stop as if he'd hit a wall of black ice.

Angie was right there. Seated on a kitchen chair that had been positioned in the middle of the living room. A woman—young and blond—stood behind her. She held a pistol to Angie's head.

A man, also blond and very tan, was beside her. One of his wiry arms was around Chelsea's throat and he had a pistol in his hand. The barrel was pointed at Frank.

"Well," said the blond man with a charming smile, "aren't you impressive as all get-out?"

The woman pressed the barrel hard into Angie's temple. "Drop the gun, Rambo. Do it now. You might take one of us, but the other is going to kill someone you love. And I bet we could get them *both*. Want to find out?"

Frank had no play at all here. He'd been in standoffs before, but never like this. Never with his family. Angie and Chelsea stared at him with a mute terror that threatened to cut his leg tendons and drop him to his knees. It was a level of fear that was totally self-aware, and totally accepting that their death was in the room with them.

The Glock fell to the floor.

The two blonds smiled like happy kids.

"The sad part about all of this," said the man, "is that we had high hopes for you. You'd have been the perfect guy to run our little team. But . . . we're operating on a kind of zero-tolerance policy."

"And you fucked it all up," said the woman with affected petulance. "Dumbass."

"Not that you aren't still useful to us," said the man.

The woman chuckled. It was an ugly sound.

"You get to be a great sales tool for us," the man said. "Don't you think so, Eve?"

"Oh, absolutely, Adam."

They grinned at each other. They grinned at Frank. They seemed so happy. "I'll get the video camera."

CHAPTER THIRTY-EIGHT
OVER TURKISH AIRSPACE

"Mr. Church says no," I replied. "We did *not* do this."

Bunny pointed to his laptop screen. "Yeah, I heard you, boss, but that says different."

"*Bacha ma culo*," said Andrea under his breath. *Kiss my ass.*

"What he said," agreed Bunny.

"How sure is the Big Man?" asked Top. "Last I remember we fell off the Christmas card list of everybody in Washington."

"You know the boss, Top," I said, "Mr. Church has friends everywhere, and a lot of them are deep inside the intelligence communities and the military. If we *were* responsible for this, then somebody on *his* Christmas list would know."

"I hope you're right, boss," said Bunny, "'cause this looks a whole lot like an actual act of war."

"Pretty damn sure that's exactly what someone wants everyone to think," I said. "Whoever our bad guys are, they went to great lengths to sell this. Bug's team is running voice recognition, and so far they have determined that the two American voices aren't foreign nationals faking accents. Bug is sure these are Yanks, but that doesn't mean anything. They could be ex-military. As for getting the right weapons and equipment, I can point you to a dozen black market stores on the Darknet where you can buy that stuff."

"If this footage was taken on the island, does it mean this video *person*," said Belle, leaning on the word, "was there also? Maybe working with them to create a video that would start a war?"

Top turned to her. "We don't know that."

"Oh?" retorted Belle, one eyebrow raised. "What then? They just happen to be there when something like this occurred? Don't be naïve."

"Don't make assumptions," countered Top. "They could have been there acting on a tip. Remember, the video was sent to the South Korean ambassador and not dropped on YouTube. The footage was clearly taken with a drone. That could all have been done to sell the idea of a freelance WikiLeaker wannabe who's really a social media troll for a larger organization. Or it could be an actual good guy. We don't *know* shit."

Belle gave him three seconds of a cold stare and then a single nod. Not sure if that meant she agreed or decided to choose a different hill to die on.

Into the silence I said, "I'm good with theories, folks, but let's not fall to bias in the absence of more intel, okay? Let's keep our minds open to all possibilities."

Andrea said, "*Scusami, Colonello,* but this is still not our matter, is it? If this is already out, then it's up to South Korea and the United States to let the North Koreans and maybe the Chinese check their underwear for stains."

"Normally I'd agree," I said, "but there's a wrinkle."

"There's always a damn wrinkle," complained Bunny. "Wrinkles and complications."

I said, "Punk Press is trying to sell themselves as independent and possibly altruistic. Even if that's a front, as Top suggested, the effect is that there doesn't seem to be a desire to kick-start World War Three, or even relight the burners on the Korean War Part Two. The fact that this was sent to an ambassador, someone widely known as a levelheaded and good-hearted guy, is suggestive. WikiLeaks would have simply sold this to the highest bidder or done one of their big dramatic reveals and things would already be fucked. Personally I wonder if these Punk Press people are even journalists. If they are, and if they're legit, then they may be actual altruists because there is no one—not even *Highlights for Children*—who wouldn't lead with what is clearly a major human rights massacre. You could sell that footage for millions to any news service."

"Okay," said Bunny, "that video is a nuclear bomb. Even if it didn't result in an actual war, the economic fallout would be massive. Our own stock market would tank. But, none of that happened because of how it was sent. And to whom. To diplomats. Have to say there seems to be a lot of hopefulness in that. Naïve, maybe, but optimistic that something positive could be accomplished."

Belle made a sour noise but offered no other comment.

"Timing's weird, too," continued Bunny, "what with that D9 nuke conference coming up. Could this be something designed to piss in that punch bowl?"

"If that video gets out," said Andrea, nodding, "they can forget any talk of denuclearization."

"Agreed," I said, "and the Big Man and Scott Wilson are looking into that. That's secondary, though. What happened on Frog Island is on the front burner. At least for us."

"Got to say," mused Top, "I'm having a hard damn time buying that the SEALs would participate in a mass slaughter of civilians. Sure, they're known for following orders, but something like this shit? Hell, there'd be a mutiny."

"Hooah on that," said Bunny. He was a former Marine and Top, like me, was a former Ranger, but we'd worked with a lot of SEALs over the years—and some ROK shooters to boot—and this smelled wrong to all of us.

"Oh, believe me," I said, "it's way high on my list to get to the bottom of that. And if this is some assholes trying to feed the SEALs to the wolves, then I may have to call in some parachutin' frogmen I know and feed these sonsabitches to them."

"Hoo-goddamn-ah," growled Top, and then punched Bunny on the shoulder.

"So," said Andrea, "who is Punk Press?"

"To be determined," I said. "There are thousands of these Wiki-Leaks wannabes out there, and some of them even do some good. Most are either somebody's state-sponsored disinformation network, or they're earnest but don't really have much of substance. However, we can't disregard that footage. Which is where Havoc Team comes in."

Andrea looked like he was in physical pain. "Does what you're going to say involve us going within two hundred million miles of that Island of Frogs?"

"It does."

"*Merda.*"

"On *North* Korean soil," said Bunny.

"Yup." I explained our cover to them. As you might expect they were less than enthusiastic.

"With or without an official invitation from the North Korea government?" asked Belle.

"Without."

"Donkey balls," said Andrea.

"Our mission is this," I said. "We go in wearing combat hazmat gear. We assess the situation, collect samples, and get the hell out. All data collected will be shared with the four governments." I explained about our WHO cover story.

"That's not going to put the pin back in this," said Bunny. "Heads gotta roll. Those guys on the beach were ROK and SEALs."

"Maybe they were," said Top. "It's staged to look like that. And the fact that someone tipped off these Punk Press fools is telling. Makes me think they were there to make sure someone got the blame."

"Hooah," said Andrea, and even Bunny nodded.

Belle sat with her chin propped on her fists. "Well," she said, "you fellows sure know how to show a girl a good time."

CHAPTER THIRTY-NINE
OUTSIDE OF THE NEW SANNŌ HOTEL / U.S. FORCE CENTER
TOKYO, JAPAN
6:04 A.M. LOCAL TIME
EIGHT WEEKS AGO

The girl asked, "Hey, sailor-boy, would you mind?"

She held her phone out while standing, arms linked, with her boyfriend

The sailor—Petty Officer First Class Cletus Burke—looked at the smiling couple. They were a pair of absurdly good-looking and very fit twenty-somethings who were so clearly happy and in love that it made him smile.

"Sure," he said, reaching for the phone.

Later, he would remember touching it. He'd remember a tiny pinprick of pain. Burke would recall how quickly the day dimmed from sunny and lovely there on the Tokyo side street to utter blackness. He did not remember falling.

7:22 A.M. LOCAL TIME

Consciousness came back to him, but awareness lagged a few steps behind.

It took him long seconds to realize that he was awake and that he was in trouble.

Very, very bad trouble.

In all the time he'd been in the navy, and even during his years of active service with SEAL Team Six, he'd never been taken prisoner. Not once. Not even close. Abduction was something *he* did. At least back then. Now it was something he taught. Snatch and grab. Recovery of hostages and taking of key enemy targets. He was the one who knew everything about how to do this to someone else.

He sat on a heavy wooden chair, secured with turn-upon-turn of gray duct tape. Ankles, thighs, waist, chest, wrists, arms. The tape snaked in and out of the structure of the chair. He could feel that. There was a bag over his head, and when he blinked his eyes clear and looked down, he could see through a narrow gap between the bag and his own chest. The tape was laid carefully over thin strips of white bandage.

So none of the adhesive gets on my skin, he thought.

That was significant. It suggested that his abductors either planned on releasing him without evidence of his being restrained, or that they wanted to leave no useful physical evidence on his corpse. Cuffs, zip ties, rope, and other ligatures always left a mark. Adhesives could be analyzed and inferences drawn. What about the drug used to take him? There were a number of chemical compounds that broke down very quickly in the bloodstream and left no trace.

JONATHAN MABERRY

All of this flashed through his brain in a microsecond.

The bag was opaque, so beyond a bit of his body and the tape, there wasn't much else to see. The floor beneath his feet was soft. Carpet. Short nap, though. Industrial, probably.

The bag smelled of laundry soap and dryer sheets. It was smooth, too, and he realized that it was a pillowcase. Or, maybe a couple of pillowcases doubled up for maximum opacity.

"Here are the rules," said a voice, speaking without preamble. Male voice. Young. American accent. Midwest? Was it the young blond guy? Probably.

Burke waited.

"You're not hurt," continued the man. "You won't *be* hurt if this all plays out the right way. Nod if you understand."

There was no advantage to being contrary at the moment, so Burke nodded.

"I'm going to take the pillowcase off your head. You're not going to yell. You're not going to try and kick up a fuss. You won't like what happens if you do. Give us another nod."

Burke nodded.

A hand abruptly plucked the cases off his head. It came from behind him. Not the man who was speaking. Burke blinked and looked around, taking it all in as fast as possible.

A hotel room. Mid-level, not expensive, not too cheap. Two queen beds, table, and desk chair. Sliding door to bathroom. Windows with no view except sky, so at least third floor or higher. There were four laptops in a row along the end of one bed, but the screens showed only a swirl of colors that moved in slow motion.

The young blond man stood in front of him. He wore the same clothes as before—skinny jeans and a Hawaiian shirt worn untucked—probably to hide a gun; no-brand boat shoes. The shirt's pattern was of palm trees and birds of paradise. Cheap and common. No hat, no watch, rings, or other obvious jewelry. His hands were empty and hung loose at his sides. Maybe twenty-six, but youthful. Good tan, but not tropical. Athletic build. He looked fast, and his arms had wiry muscles, the kind that didn't need to be big in order to be strong.

The man smiled. It was a charming smile, like a Midwestern farm boy on a soft spring morning. Cornflower blue eyes and good teeth.

"Now, you're wondering," said the young man, "why I'm letting you see my face. We both know that kidnappers typically don't. It sets up all kinds of complications."

Burke said nothing.

"And you're probably wondering if it means I'm going to kill you. That would be the normal cause-and-effect logic here. But . . . if we wanted to kill you, let's face it, you'd already be dead."

Burke said nothing.

"You'll notice," said the man, "that there are none of the cliché tools of torture. No pliers or bone saws or any of that shit. No bottle of water and towel to waterboard you. No portable generator or pinch-clips to wire your balls up."

"Ewwww, gross," said a woman's voice behind Burke.

"I know, right?" grinned the man. "So, no . . . this isn't going to be us torturing you. Not that it's completely off the table, mind . . . but I think we can all walk away from this without anyone getting hurt. I do mean everyone."

"What is it you want?" asked Burke. He pitched his voice to sound confident. A reasonable tone of voice. A business tone.

The man nodded, as if understanding and appreciating that bit of subtle manipulation. "Good, good, let's get right to it. We have tickets for the Hakone Daimyo March, and we're burning daylight here." He sat down on the bed that did not have laptops on it and rubbed his palms on his thighs. "I guess I'll start by saying that we know everything about you, Petty Officer First Class Cletus Burke. Formerly an active member of SEAL Team Six; currently a trainer. We know where you work, *when* you work. We know where you sleep, when you go to the gym, and how many sets and reps you do on the circuit machines. We know who your friends are. We know that you like checking out the tits on the lieutenant JG overseeing your training group, but you don't hit on her because you love your wife and you're not the straying kind."

"All sorts of adorable," said the woman, still out of sight behind him. She bent and kissed the top of his head. "It's okay that you look but don't touch. That's healthy. But overall, I'd say you're a keeper."

"You are currently training an extraction team for one of four possible ops in the South China Sea. Your men like and respect you.

No one thinks you're an asshole except one guy—the drone pilot—but he thinks everyone's an asshole, so it's not personal."

Burke waited. He was impressed but also angry, annoyed, and scared in equal measures.

"Now, we don't want you to think that we only have our fingers in your life *here*, so let's look at this."

The man took a small black remote from the night table and pointed it at the first of the laptops. The monitor suddenly switched from the screensaver graphic to a video feed. High definition and full, rich color.

The monitor showed a black-haired woman wearing a floral sundress under a white sweater as she poured raw sugar into a cup of coffee. The image was broad enough to establish that she was at a Starbucks attached to a Barnes & Noble.

Burke's heart nearly stopped in his chest. It jolted so hard that pain seemed to stab him from inside his chest. The man that he was needed to cry out, to shout somehow loud enough to warn her; to protest his outrage. That part of him—the dominant part—who was always a SEAL, a special operator, forced those screams down.

"Always nice to see the folks back home," said the woman. "Sunny Fayetteville, just an easy drive to Fort Bragg. And who do we see here?"

"Why it's Charlotte Burke," said the blond man brightly. "A pretty name. Old-fashioned. And she's an old-fashioned girl, isn't she? Housewife, even in these liberated times. Good wife, good mom. And, for the record, she doesn't cheat on you, either. We would know if she did."

He let that hang.

We would know.

There was so damn much implied in it.

The man held up a cell phone. It was a standard AT&T Samsung Galaxy J3 prepaid phone. A burner like millions just like it that are sold in stores around the world.

"The way this is set up," said the man, "is that I have to send a text several times a day to make sure that Charlotte there remains happy, healthy, and clueless. The timetable for those texts is determined by a random cyclical encoding program, so there's no chance that anyone could beat the clock."

"Why . . . ?" Burke wanted it to come out strong and clear, but it was hoarse. It sounded like the question was punched out of him.

"Wait, wait, there's more."

The blond man pointed the clicker at the other laptops, one, two, three, pausing each time to let the picture resolve.

Click!

On the second screen was his eldest daughter, also named Charlotte but preferring to be called Charlie. She was sitting in a French class, writing notes with a purple ballpoint. She was a younger carbon copy of her mother. Sixteen and lovely, with pale pink lipstick and the single nose jewel that was all she wanted for her birthday.

Click!

The next computer showed a girl about two years younger, with more of her father's olive complexion and dark hair. She was heavier than most of her friends, and was grunting her way around a jogging track. Despite the labored breathing and sweat, she ran well and there was a dreamer's glaze to her eyes. She was Burke's favorite, though he would never have admitted it. About to blossom, just taking hold of her grandmother's creativity. She wanted to be a writer. Danielle.

Click!

By now Burke understood the process, and he knew who would be on the next screen. Aiden. Six years old, smart and funny and energetic. Racing his friends across the schoolyard, always a step or two ahead of everyone else.

"What . . . do . . . you . . . want . . . ?" whispered Burke. Each word tore its way out of his throat. Each word cost him.

"I want you to understand the rules," said the man. "We have people on your family. Teams of people. Enough so that there is never going to be a gap in coverage. You will not know who they are. They are compartmentalized and don't know each other. Everything is handled through encrypted text messages. If there is even the slightest break in the routine then the team will take your family."

Take.

Take.

Burke needed so badly to scream.

"I don't mean that they'll abduct your wife and kids," said the

JONATHAN MABERRY

man. "I mean . . . why would we? What the fuck would we need with them? No . . . I mean take. Here, let me show you."

The man used the clicker to change the images. Again there was a woman and children on the different screens. Not his wife, not his children. But the message was so eloquent.

He knew that it was someone's wife and someone's children. He knew that it was a woman and kids. He could tell that much from the basic shape, from the obvious parts. From what was left.

One of them, the youngest, was still alive. What was left of her was still alive. The video showed the last fluttering trembles of an infant's chest.

Burke had run missions on four continents. He'd killed a great many people. He'd walked through war zones and witnessed horrors like this. But that was war. None of those people were his family. None of them were deliberate stand-ins for his family. The context was what cut the deepest. The context was a towering black monster armed with teeth and claws.

The woman leaned forward, brushing his ear with soft, warm lips.

"Now, sailor-boy," she murmured, "let's talk."

CHAPTER FORTY
PHOENIX HOUSE
OMFORI ISLAND
GREECE

Mr. Church took the elevator to the third floor of the castle. He was alone and deep in thought about the situation unfolding in North Korea, and now there was the added complication of Rafael Santoro's comment. Nothing about either made obvious sense, which meant there were too many unknowns and possibly a clock ticking very quietly but urgently.

The doors opened with a faint hiss and he stepped out into silence. A guard on foot patrol turned to see who came out of the car.

"I'm going to my apartment, Luke," said Church. "Please make sure no one else comes up until I give the word."

"Yes, sir," said the guard. Luke Merishi was a Moran—a Maasai warrior from Kenya—and a former member of the Lion Guardians. His grandfather had been a close friend of Mr. Church and they had worked together to stop a huge poaching ring. The stories told about that mission were a matter of great pride in Luke's family and tribe. When Church asked if Luke would like to come and work for him, the young warrior agreed, and currently split his time between guard duty outside Church's private apartment, and intense training for possible inclusion in an RTI field team. He wore a standard gray patrol uniform but with a red-and-black-checked Maasai sash along with ornate multicolored arm bracelets, necklace, and earrings. He had a pistol in a belt holster and a slung rifle, but also carried a twenty-inch *rungu*, the deadly throwing club made of polished ebony wood.

Church nodded and walked along a hallway cluttered with workman's tools, rolled carpets, paintings still in crates, and cases of electronic equipment waiting to be installed. There was a faint pall of brick dust in the air.

As he approached the door to his apartment the RFID chip embedded in the fatty tissue of his upper arm triggered the security system, and a panel of faux stone folded outward to reveal an off-market biometric scanner. Church removed his right glove and placed the pad of his ring finger on the screen and quietly spoke today's code phrase. The locks clicked and he pulled open the heavy door, which was a slab of steel alloy sheathed in antique hardwood. The door swung shut silently behind him.

Lights came on and Church paused for a moment, eyes closed, collecting his thoughts.

The apartment was very large, with a number of bedrooms, a full kitchen, an elegant dining room, bathrooms, a huge library, a meditation chamber, a gym, and several rooms set aside for his collection of artifacts. There was art on every wall, and some of it quite old. There were only three people ever allowed in the apartment. One was Brick Anderson—Church's personal assistant, bodyguard, and confidant. Another was Mrs. Karasu, a lovely Japanese woman in her mid-seventies whose kind eyes and frilly aprons were an amusing deception. Church had hired her when the woman retired after thirty-four years as a first-class spy and assassin. Even at her age, he had no doubt she could give either Top or Bunny a lesson in unarmed combat that they would never forget.

The third person who he permitted into his private space was one he wished were here now. Lilith. Brilliant, difficult, dangerous, beautiful, and as secretive as he was. She called herself a witch, meaning it in the old way—a woman steeped in old knowledge and wisdom.

"Lilith," he murmured, then sighed. She was with the Mothers of the Fallen, off doing ghastly things to bad men, exacting her brand of inflexible justice. Battling her personal demons.

A soft sound made him turn and he squatted down as his cat, Bastion, a beautiful smoke-gray Scottish fold, came yawning out from behind a couch. The cat walked languorously over and jumped into Church's arms, allowed himself to be petted.

Church rose, holding the cat to his chest. Except for Bastion, the apartment was empty and that was good. He was an intensely private person who habitually kept many aspects of his life compartmentalized. No one, not even Lilith, knew everything about him. That was useful and necessary, but also lonely. Just as Lilith's life was lonely. It was the nature of people like them.

He went through the living room and into the library, closed the door, and placed the cat on the edge of a big teak desk that had been hand-carved from a massive oak tree in 1691. He sat and opened a laptop, then entered his security password. He sent four emails and then settled back and waited for replies. Bastion sat there, washing his face with his paw while staring at an empty piece of air. Church stared at the same place, seeing the same things.

"Calpurnia," he said, activating the artificial intelligence interface, "play Op. 47 I. F Major, 4/4, Molto Adagio."

"Playing," said the soft, lush voice of Calpurnia.

The music, strange and lovely, began to play. A lesser-known sonata for two violins with a bass for harpsichord or violoncello. Church again closed his eyes and let his thoughts drift. They seemed to lift onto a breeze of music and soar far away, to a small island in a troubled sea, where death and heartbreak ran rampant. The croaking of ten thousand frogs offered a counterpoint.

He made a call to a former employee who was living in retirement in Sanibel, Florida. The call was answered by a terse and hostile, *"What?"*

"Mr. Spencer," said Church. "I'm sorry to have to disturb your leisure."

"The fuck you are," growled Jerry Spencer. He had been recruited into the DMS at the same time as Joe Ledger, and had done so under protest. Spencer had been ostensibly a detective from DCPD, attached to a joint task force overseen by Homeland, but his genius lay in forensic evidence collection and analysis. Although Spencer was not officially a forensic scientist, Church had found that his knowledge and—more importantly—his intuition far exceeded anyone else's he had ever worked with. Those skills were only surpassed by his total disregard for authority and cantankerous nature. Spencer was not a nice person, not a polite person, and not in any way agreeable. "Why are you calling me?"

Church explained about the black-site prison, the attack, and the conclusions drawn by NSA and DHS forensics teams that all of the prisoners died during the failed attack.

"Good," said Spencer. "The world's better without them."

"Mr. Spencer," said Church patiently, "I have some reason to perhaps question those findings. I don't have anyone I can rely on to review the evidence and determine if their conclusions are accurate. Quite a lot might hinge on that."

Spencer said nothing for nearly twenty seconds. Church waited him out.

"The National Security Agency and the Department of Homeland Security couldn't find their collective dicks with a microscope and a road map."

Church waited.

"Fuck," said Spencer. Then again, very loud. *"Fuck."*

"I'll send a plane for you," said Church, and hung up before the resulting tirade of profanities could really get into gear.

JONATHAN MABERRY

INTERLUDE EIGHT
WILDLIFE ROAD ABOVE THE POINT DUME BLUFFS
MALIBU, CALIFORNIA
FIFTEEN MONTHS AGO

Santoro glanced at Kuga. At the strong profile and perfect hair, white teeth, and even tan.

He knew the face, having seen it many times in confidential reports Hugo Vox shared with him. It was the same face he'd seen of the man running through fire and smoke at the prison. Vox considered him to be one of the Seven Kings' greatest potential enemies.

The man stood watching him, smiling faintly in a way that let Santoro know that Kuga was aware of the natural thought process. His tan was an excellent fake. A spray, but done with real artistry. Done to match the one Santoro had seen on this man's face in surveillance pictures.

"You were in the prison," said Santoro, not making it a question.

"Yes."

"Mr. Church put you there?"

"Yes."

"Why?"

Kuga smiled. A small, cold, and bitter smile. "I fell from grace."

"You were turned?"

"You mean, was I a spy who was on the payroll of some foreign government? No. Was I blackmailed or extorted by someone like you and forced to commit treason? No."

"Then what?"

The tall man turned and leaned a muscular shoulder against the glass. "I became who I wanted to be," he said quietly. "I was no one's puppet, no one's agent, no one's informant. No one has ever put a collar on me."

"Except Mr. Church," said Santoro.

Kuga shrugged. "Shackles are not a collar."

Santoro raised an eyebrow. "Church didn't break you?"

"Well," laughed Kuga, "not for lack of trying."

Santoro could see that there were small scars on the man's face that were mostly concealed by makeup and bronzer. They had healed well, but their shape and position were telling. At some point, his benefactor had been savagely beaten. There were similar scars on his own face, and Santoro made some logic jumps, putting pieces together. Kuga had not been taken easily.

"I wonder, though," mused Kuga, "about how much he broke *you*. I know you spoke to him, and I have some idea of what he got from you. The Seven Kings organization was dismantled much too quickly for it to be good police work on the part of the DMS. Even taking into account MindReader. No, Church had to get a lot of it from you."

A long line of pelicans drifted by outside. Santoro counted them. Thirty-one. He wondered if there was some cosmic significance in the number, possibly a message from the Goddess. If there was, it eluded him in the strangeness of the moment.

"I'll pay for my sins in my own way," he said softly.

"I don't give much of a damn about redemption, my friend," said Kuga. "I leave that to priests and philosophers. I'm neither. And, for the record, I know about your act of contrition. Your tongue? That must have hurt. I know doctors in L.A. who could fix that."

"I'm not a particularly vain person," said Santoro.

"No, but you sound like you have a mouthful of macaroons."

Santoro gave Kuga a bland smile. He was not a man to rise to an insult, especially when he knew it was a test.

"What is it you want from me?" he asked.

The tall man pushed off the wall and walked slowly across the big living room, his mouth pursed in thought. He bent and picked up a magazine from the coffee table, flipped through it, tossed it down. Then strolled to the wet bar and opened a bottle of eighteen-year-old Laphroaig Islay single malt Scotch. He poured two fingers into a chunky tumbler, sipped the whiskey, hissed mildly the way someone does who hasn't had strong spirits in a long time, took a second sip, and let out a contented sigh.

"One does miss the simple things in life," Kuga said.

Santoro waited.

Kuga took another sip. "I know a lot about you, Rafael—may I call you Rafael?"

Santoro said nothing.

"I know more than you think I know, Rafael," continued Kuga. "Your rather troubled childhood, for example, and what happened to your family. I know about your recruitment into the Seven Kings organization, and your attachment to the woman who called herself the Goddess. I know all of that and a lot more. I know your loyalty to the Kings faltered because you lost faith in the vision of Hugo Vox and you instead hitched your star to the Goddess. I know you are a total badass when it comes to extortion, coercion, blackmail, and murder. None better, and I'm not blowing smoke up your ass when I say that. You could compel Santa Claus to murder babies in their sleep. And as for fighting? Well . . . I know you are one of the deadliest fighters alive. You trained the Kingsmen to be on a par with Delta, which is something most experts would say is impossible. You did it, though." Kuga paused, smiling strangely for a moment. "However, I also know you got your ass handed to you by Joe Ledger."

"Ledger did not beat me," said Santoro coldly.

"Ah, nice to know that pride still lingers. Who was it, then?"

"It was *him*."

Kuga nodded. "Ah. Yes. Well, I guess no one can fault you for losing a fight to the Deacon."

"He is a demon."

"A demon? No. But he is a monster," said Kuga. "If even half of the rumors about him are true, hell, if a tenth of them are true, then he has beaten more dangerous men than either of us."

"He is a demon," Santoro muttered again, but this time Kuga did not dispute it.

"Even as old as Church has to be, he's a spooky bastard, Deacon." He cocked his head and studied Santoro. "Bet you never lost a fight before. That has to sting."

"One day I will drown him in the blood of everyone he loves."

"I like the sound of that."

"Is there a point to this?" asked Rafael, feeling a cold anger rise in him. It made his fingertips ache as if frostbite was setting in. A dangerous sign for him. When he went that cold, when he let that frigidity of emotion own him, then control was lost and he would not take responsibility for what happened next.

"I know a lot about the Seven Kings," said Kuga. "I knew almost everything the Deacon knew, and some things maybe he didn't know. Actually, I know a lot of things he doesn't know. About the Kings, about the old Jakoby operation. And other things. When I went to prison I made sure that I had a way to get myself out. Sure, it took a little longer than I hoped, and it cost a lot more, but I am out. So are you. I had people digging deep into you and feeding me that intel. For example, I know that your brother, Esteban, was involved with the Majestic program. He also worked for me. Bet you didn't know that."

Santoro just stared at him.

"I know that Joe Ledger killed him. Bet you'd like to talk with Ledger about that. One of your *special* talks. The kind you're famous for."

Santoro said nothing.

"Maybe I can arrange that. I have him on my to-do list, and when I get around to him I'm going to have a big comfy chair and a glass of very old Scotch and maybe get a blowjob while I watch you fuck him up so bad forensics won't be able to tell who he is. Sound like a plan? Nah, don't answer, I can see the sweat on your upper lip."

He sipped his drink and smiled at Santoro.

"This name you are using—Kuga—is that really you? Were you always Kuga, or did you acquire it?"

Kuga sipped his Scotch. "I've been Kuga nearly as long as I've been in the game. Kuga and maybe ten other people. I didn't have six other kings, you dig? Just me and a network. The network is still there. What's left of it. The parts that came onto the DMS radar are for shit, just like most of the Kings organization. The Deacon and that fucking MindReader computer are a royal pain in my left nut."

"Which name do you want me to use?"

"Kuga will do. I'm leaving behind a bunch of my old selves. Some are dead weight and some have bull's-eyes painted on them. Kuga, though, hell . . . I paid good money—big money—to keep that about as vague and cryptic as it's possible to get. So much of it is off the Net that MindReader's not going to zero me. Spent forty, fifty million to make sure of that."

"That's a lot of money for a code name."

"It's more than that, Rafael. It's a mystique. People whisper—actually *whisper*—the name Kuga. People get killed for saying that name, and not even by my guys. Sometimes they get their throats cut by people hoping to be seen doing Kuga a favor. It's a self-perpetuating legend. I love the fuck out of it. No, I'll keep Kuga. Plague. That's juicy. And the nickname, *Concierge de l'enfer.*"

Santoro sniffed. "It is a bit melodramatic, yes?"

"Says the former Conscience to the King of Fear."

"Touché." Santoro looked around the opulent room. "As I understand it, Kuga is a fixer, a procurer, a facilitator of things. If so, then your operation relies on clients."

"Very true."

"Do you *have* a client?"

"I do," said Kuga. "And they helped finance the two of us getting out of jail."

"Who are they?"

"We'll get to that."

Santoro clasped his hands behind his back. "Why am I here? Is this a job interview?"

"Of course it is," Kuga said. "But it's more than that. Look, I know you and Esteban had some issues with one another, but he was family. Your only family. And Joe Ledger killed him." Kuga drained the last of the Scotch. "There's actually not much I *don't* know about you. Well, except one thing."

"And what is that?" asked Santoro tightly.

Kuga studied him with cold blue eyes, and Santoro could feel the gaze cut into him like scalpels. This man was getting dangerously close to cutting too deeply. Another nick and the coldness would own this moment and there would be blood and pain. Santoro felt his body shift ever so slightly, his weight moving from flat feet to the balls, knees bending a little, muscles coiling for the leap. Ice flowed through him like floodwaters and at the edges of his vision red flowers seemed to bloom in the air.

Kuga set the glass down and put his hands deep into his pockets. Casual. Vulnerable. Or a trap. Either way, Santoro knew that *he* would kill this man and cut his tongue out and . . .

"What I want to know," said Kuga in a voice that was as smooth and oily as a soiled angel, "is what you would be willing to do to get revenge on the Deacon, Joe Ledger, and everyone they care about. I want to know how far you would go to get revenge on the men who disgraced your goddess and killed your brother. Tell me that, and tell me the truth, and you and I can shake the pillars of heaven together."

CHAPTER FORTY-ONE
PHOENIX HOUSE
OMFORI ISLAND
GREECE

"You have four calls pending in response to your messages," said Calpurnia. "Everyone has signaled that they are ready for a meeting. Shall I activate the ORB?"

Mr. Church rubbed his eyes and then put his tinted glasses back on. "Yes."

The room lights dimmed as the music became hushed. Then two hundred tiny lights ignited from discrete locations throughout the room, and reality seemed to come apart. In truth the ORB—the Operational Resource Bay—was using ultra-high-resolution projectors to create a hologram so real that it was as if Church was transported to another place. The effect was very much like the holodeck in the old *Star Trek: The Next Generation* TV series, or so everyone told him. Church rarely watched TV, but he understood the reference. In actuality the projectors in a darkened room created a 3-D virtual reality experience that allowed people in different places around the world to feel like they were sitting in the same room, without anyone having to use cumbersome goggles.

The system had been one of many advanced technologies brought to Rogue Team by Joan "Doc" Holliday, the head of the Integrated Sciences Division. Prior to joining Church's team, Doc had worked for DARPA, though the ORB was her own property, and she'd made more than two billion dollars selling versions of it to the military and three times as much to game developers, SpaceX, Virgin Galactic, and groups that trained pilots for DSRV deep sea exploration.

Four seated figures appeared in the darkness. Two of them were Korean, one was Chinese, and the fourth an American. The American was the only woman of the group. None of them were heads of state, but were instead the kind of person whose positions of power remained even as political parties came and went.

No one spoke, though they each nodded to the others. The fact that they were patriots to their own nations in no way engendered within them a hostility to one another. Rather the reverse. They shared a common goal, one that soared above political agendas, brinksmanship, or international economics. The Chinese man had suggested a nickname for the group: The Cooler Heads.

When the holograms were resolved to the point of looking perfectly real, Church briefly glanced at each, and then said, *"Factaque pace maestus vigilantiam."*

They each repeated the phrase. *Peace through vigilance and action.*

What Church knew, and the others did not, was that the phrase was an old one, used by generations of people like these through centuries of history.

Peace through vigilance and action.

One of the people, a middle-aged Chinese man, looked around at the others and gave them all a rueful smile. "It sounds so melodramatic to actually say that out loud."

The American chuckled. "I feel just a little bit like a jackass, yes." At sixty, she was the oldest.

"Even so," said a thirty-something man from South Korea, who was the youngest of them, "there are reasons for ceremonies."

"Sometimes," said the very thin North Korean man. "And other times they stand to remind us of the importance of all of . . ." He waved a hand around. "Of this." He and the Chinese man were both in their late forties. "Whatever it is. You still haven't told us."

"Before we begin," said Church, "can each of you assure us all that you are in a secure location and that you've swept it for bugs."

"Is this level of secrecy really necessary?" asked the South Korean, and his counterpart from the North gave him a frank stare, eyebrows raised. "I withdraw the question. Sorry."

They each gave their assurances. There was a soft *bong-bong* in

Church's ear; a signal from Bug that MindReader was reading all of them as clean.

"Very well," he said gravely, "then let us begin. There has been an incident on an island in North Korean territorial waters. This matter was brought to my attention by the U.S. ambassador to South Korea, who is an old and trusted friend, and we can thank him for making so swift and courageous a decision. Had he passed this through ordinary channels there would likely be missiles in the air."

They gaped at him.

"I've never known you to crack jokes, Deacon," said the American.

Church shook his head. "No. This network of ours was not created for anyone's amusement. However, all the ambassador has done is buy us a day or two. After which it *will* have to move through channels. So, by that time we need to have answers and we need a plan. Each of you will need to massage the reactions of your governments. Naturally my people can provide considerable resources to help. But first let me bring you up to date on everything."

He ran the Punk Press video. They watched the images of the SEALs and ROK soldiers on the island and Church watched their faces. He saw the eyes of the Chinese and North Korean men shift from the screen toward the South Korean and American.

"No," whispered America, her face dead white.

"God almighty," said South Korea.

North Korea was shocked to silence, eyes wide and filled with the horror of what it all meant. What it *would* mean.

"This is an act of war," breathed China.

CHAPTER FORTY-TWO
NEW SANNŌ HOTEL / U.S. FORCE CENTER
TOKYO, JAPAN

Petty Officer First Class Cletus Burke sat on the edge of his bed and stared at the floor.

Several members of his team stayed at the same hotel, which was used by active duty and retired U.S. military. His handgun sat on the bed next to him. Ready. Willing. Able. He'd cleaned it more than a dozen times since returning from Gaeguli Seom. He'd removed each bullet from the magazine and reinserted them slowly, as if getting to know the rounds. As if praying to them.

Over the last sixteen hours since checking in he had carefully placed the barrel of the gun against his temple. Under his chin. In his mouth. Twice his finger even curled around the trigger, giving it nearly three pounds of pressure of the five and a half pounds of pull weight needed to send one of those rounds crashing through his brain.

Each time he set the gun down and broke apart into tears. His face was red and swollen from all the times he slapped and punched himself. He had rug burns on his knees from dropping onto the floor—in despair, in prayer.

He did not dare to turn on the TV. The news story would probably have broken by now. With pictures. With video. Proof that the doorway to hell was wide open. Burke hadn't been inside a church for years, not since a friend's wedding, and even then going through the prayers had been rote. His childhood faith in Jesus and Mary and the saints was long gone.

Except now it was as if he lay naked on the floor of the big church he'd gone to as a kid. Naked in body and naked in soul, with all of his sins laid bare. To those long-ignored saints. To Jesus and the Virgin. To God.

"I had to," he whimpered, sliding off the edge of the bed and collapsing into a quivering heap against the night table.

The day, or perhaps his mind, went black for a while and he lost himself in it. Then he was back again, sitting at the small desk in the room, his gun in his right hand. He looked down in surprise and confusion to see that his cell was in his left. Burke had no idea how much time had passed. He could see the time on the phone, but wasn't sure when he'd fallen off the bed, or gotten up. Most of the day was burned out of him. Gone.

He watched, almost like a spectator, as his finger tapped in a phone number. He raised the cell and listened through three endless rings. Burke was about to put the phone down, to end the call, maybe to end himself, when a voice answered.

"Hello?"

"B-Bill . . . ?" whispered Burke.

"Clete?" asked Bill Compton, Burke's former SEAL Team member. A good friend. A good man. Strong. Unbreakable. Reliable. Bill was out of the game now, walking around on a pair of artificial legs. Souvenirs of a mission they'd been on that had gone sideways. Bill was a real American hero. Stalwart. The kind of man who'd never once complained about what he'd lost in the service of what he loved. "Clete . . . is that you?"

"Bill," said Burke, "listen, man . . . I'm in trouble. I need help. I don't know who else to ask."

"Jesus, Clete, what's wrong?"

"Have you seen the news?"

"What news?"

"About Korea? About the island?"

"Clete, what are you trying to say?" asked Bill.

"Christ, Bill, I'm in so much trouble. I need help, I need you to do something for me. Christ, I'm begging you, please."

There was a pause. "Do what, Clete? What is it you need me to do?"

"Charlotte . . . the kids . . . oh, Christ . . ."

"Listen, Clete," said Bill quietly, "take a breath. No, do it. Take a breath. Let it out. You know how it works. Get yourself steady. Good. Now tell me why you're calling."

The old trick worked its magic, but only a little. Enough, though, for Burke to ask his friend for a dangerous favor.

"Bill, listen," he said, "I got into something. Some people threatened to hurt Charlotte and the kids if I didn't . . . didn't . . . *do* something. Something really bad. It's going to be all over the news. I'm done. They're going to arrest me. There's no chance they won't. They could be here any minute. But, Bill . . . the people who did this, they told me what they'd do to my family. They showed me what they'd done to the families of other people who . . . who . . . Shit. Bill, I know this is a lot to ask. A whole fucking lot. But, for God's sake, go get my family. Take them somewhere safe. Don't let anyone near them. Jesus Christ, man, the things they said they'd *do* to them. My wife . . . my babies. I can't . . . I just can't . . . Bill, get my family and take them somewhere safe. I'm begging you. I'm fucking *begging* you. Take my family somewhere safe."

JONATHAN MABERRY

There was a long, long pause on the line.

"Bill, did you hear me?"

"Look, Clete . . . ," said Bill Compton slowly, softly, "didn't they tell you? *Nowhere's safe.*"

There was a sound on the line. A sob. And then the line went dead.

INTERLUDE NINE
WILDLIFE ROAD ABOVE THE POINT DUME BLUFFS
MALIBU, CALIFORNIA
FOURTEEN MONTHS AGO

"How's the pain?" asked Kuga.

They sat on white couches on opposite sides of a big brass Turkish table. Santoro was propped against cushions. His face was swollen and he felt hollow and old. Effects of the surgery. He knew it would pass, but he disliked feeling weak in the presence of this man, particularly since he owed Kuga so much. For his freedom, for protection, and now for the surgery to repair the self-inflicted damage to his tongue.

He'd resisted the surgery, but finally agreed when Kuga pointed out that his lisp would be too unique an identifier. Now Santoro could feel the internal shift to accept it. This wasn't for the sake of his vanity; it had a higher purpose.

"It's merely pain," said Santoro. There was still a bit of a lisp, but only because of the swelling and stitches.

They sat in silence for a while, watching a thin rain fall slantwise across a slate gray sky. The housekeeper—a small woman with a little girl's face and alligator eyes—brought a plate of sandwiches for Kuga and a protein and vegetable power drink for Santoro. In the weeks since coming to the house—which Kuga called the Toybox—he had never heard the woman speak, and had no idea how she knew what Kuga wanted or when. He wondered how all of that worked, given all of her responsibilities. He did not ask about it, though.

When they were alone, Kuga spoke, picking up a conversation they'd been having in installments. "The Seven Kings organization is dead. I can accept that. And I can accept that you provided some of the intelligence that helped the Deacon tear it down. That's yesterday's box score. What I want to know is what's left. Now, before you say anything, remember that I *knew* Hugo Vox and some of the other Kings. Vox was big on the long game. He was the most thorough person I've ever met. Seriously. He spent decades laying the groundwork for what the Kings did. He was subtle and he planned. He did not bully his way into control—he finessed his way in, and by my best estimation, fewer than five percent of the people he owned knew they worked for the Kings."

Santoro shook his head.

"No?" grunted Kuga. "You think it's more than that?"

"Oh, no," said Santoro softly, "it's much less."

Kuga took a bite of a Reuben and chewed thoughtfully. "How much of that apparatus did the DMS tear down? How much did you give them and how much did they find out about from records or materials confiscated?"

Santoro took a long time answering that. He sipped his drink, keeping the wince of pain off his face.

"I told the Deacon everything about the operations related to the Sea of Hope case," he said at last. "I told him everything about the other six kings. I told him everything about five other programs in the works."

Kuga leaned forward. "And . . . ?"

"And it was nothing. Those matters were already falling apart. The DMS would have dismantled those parts of the organization eventually anyway. I gave them enough to make them feel like they had an inside chance of destroying the organization in its entirety." He took a longer sip and swirled it around in his mouth before swallowing, then gave Kuga an appraising look. "You are correct. Hugo was perhaps the most meticulous and forward-thinking planner there has ever been. The Kings fell because he was betrayed, not because he made any great errors. If Sebastian Gault and . . . and the Goddess . . . had not betrayed him, then his plan would have succeeded. That is certain."

"How much of the organization is left?"

"There are dozens of operations planned out, prepared, funded, and ready . . . but sleeping. There are over a hundred mapped out, but with human assets already in place, though most do not know what they are part of. Some are owned outright, others are under the heel of the things they've done that Hugo had evidence of. Many of these assets have worked their entire professional careers thinking they are part of a government division. To a degree they are. They are paid, get benefits, are promoted, and have, no doubt, some patriotic pride in what they do. This is true in America and in many other places. Hugo Vox is their secret god, whether they know it or not."

Kuga waited.

"When viewed from a distance," said Santoro, "more than ninety percent of the Seven Kings organization still exists, still functions, still waits. The network was built to run itself. That is the key, yes? To have people who you trust. Independent thinkers. Running a network like this is not about fear. It is about respect. People will do so much more for someone they love than someone they fear."

Kuga gave him a rueful smile. "I've always found fear to be particularly useful."

"Oh, don't get me wrong, my friend," said Santoro, "fear certainly has its uses. But *true* loyalty, when shaped and encouraged until it approximates religious zeal, ah, that is a far sharper knife."

"Ahhh," said Kuga, "I see where you're going with that. I like it. But what about the information about how to contact these people? What about the protocols governing how to activate these projects? What about the infrastructure of control? The numbered accounts? The encrypted files with all of that information about each person in the network. Did you give that to the Deacon?"

Santoro got up and walked over to the window. Despite the rain there were surfers out, sitting astride their boards, riding the swells.

"No," he said. "I gave none of that to anyone. Everyone else who knows how to access that information is dead."

Kuga leaned forward, forearms on knees, eyes suddenly very bright and intense. "Everyone . . . *else?*"

Despite the pain and the heartbreak he still felt for the Goddess, Rafael Santoro did something he'd had little cause to do in years.

He smiled.

CHAPTER FORTY-THREE

PHOENIX HOUSE
INSIDE THE ORB
OMFORI ISLAND
GREECE

The American leaned forward, her face a mask of anxiety. "This *can't* be us. It can't. Even if this was a deep black operation I would have heard of it."

"How sure are you about that?" asked the Chinese man, his smile completely gone.

"Very," she insisted, and it came out as a growl. "Good God, there's no way this is sanctioned on *any* official level."

"The video is pretty damning," said South Korea. His voice trembled and he reached into a pocket for a handkerchief and mopped sweat from his upper lip.

They all turned to North Korea, who looked sick and pale.

"Even if this is some kind of trick," he said, his voice shaking, "there will be no way to control the reaction if this video gets out."

"Then you have to find a way to make them understand," said America.

"How?" cried North Korea. "Seriously, *how*? I can't see how we could ever stop it. My government will never let this pass. Why would they? Even if they believed it was a fake, this is worth more to them than ten years of missile tests. This is exactly what the hardliners have always wanted. It's exactly the kind of optics they've been praying for."

"Which means my government will have to step up in support," said China.

"I know," said America. "The Korean War will shift back from truce to open conflict."

"At very least," said North Korea, "there would need to be a show of proportional response. Some island in the south or off the coast of the United States would have to be hit. Possibly an aircraft carrier targeted."

"And then that will be war," said America, and China glumly agreed.

One by one they turned to Church.

"What do you recommend we do?" asked the Chinese man.

"In the short term, we can keep the video from going further than the ambassador who received it and the five of us. But we don't know who Punk Press is. They gave the ambassador a chance to respond. I've turned that over to my computer team to post that response. My people will also monitor the page where the response is posted and will use some subtle computer programs—a Trojan horse loaded with trackers and tapeworms. If we can track the source, then we might be able to seize control of their computers, block any further emails, and ID a location so we can send people in to take physical possession of hardware. Ideally they would apprehend the Punk Press people so they can be interviewed in a secure location."

"Excuse me," said South Korea, "but that sounds a bit like Gestapo tactics. Punk Press brought it to our attention in an effort to prevent a global catastrophe."

"Maybe," said America. "Or maybe they're a front for someone with a much different agenda. Not saying I know what that is, but I agree with the Deacon's plan."

"I also agree," said China.

"What happens if they spot the Trojan horse or spot people coming to arrest them?" asked South Korea.

"Then we are in no worse position than we are now," said North Korea. "But containment is critical. Even if we don't like the method used."

"I'm not particularly happy about initiating all of this," admitted Church. "But we have very few cards to play. To that point, we need to get answers, and I have those wheels in motion." He explained about Havoc Team heading to a staging area in South Korea and then using that as a springboard to head to the Island of Frogs.

"You're putting U.S. boots on the ground in North Korea?" asked China, appalled.

"No," said Church. "Havoc—like all RTI teams—is multinational, but they will also be operating as WHO hot zone extraction specialists. They will each have unbreakable credentials ID'ing them as freelance contractors."

"Are there such things as mercenaries working for the World Health Organization?" asked South Korea.

"Yes," said Church. "They are most often active in Africa. It's specialized and very dangerous work, which attracts the most elite operators from around the world. Using those kinds of teams began with outbreaks of Ebola mutations several years ago. They're particularly useful in situations when tribal warlords attempted to abduct infected patients and transport them to cities with dense populations of ethnic groups they opposed. I was consulted by the WHO at the time and since have helped hire, train, and equip some of those teams. Havoc's cover will hold up under scrutiny."

"You said that was a short-term action," said China. "What's your long-term strategy?"

"That's up to you," said Church. "Each of you will have to manage how your governments become aware of this incident, and then exert whatever control we can over how they respond."

"But . . . how . . . ?" asked South Korea. "I'm not in the strongest political position. I don't have a lever to use on my government if any of what's on that video is real."

He ran the Punk Press video of the strike team on the island again. And again.

"It looks real," said China, who—unlike the others, had served in the military. "If the men and women in that video are not American and South Korean soldiers, then they *used* to be."

"Possibly," said Church. "They're not actors, in any case. They move with professional competence, which is difficult to fake."

"It has to be fake," insisted the American.

"I wish we could see their faces," said North Korea. "We could run some kind of facial recognition software."

"We are doing that with the voices," said Church, "but it's a less reliable process. There aren't as many voice clips on file." He went on to explain what Bug had told him about the challenges. "But we may get lucky, so I've instructed my team to keep at it."

They watched it again.

"Who would go to these lengths to stage this?" pleaded South Korea. "I mean, who, outside of one or more of our own countries, would benefit?" Everyone began to answer, but he held up his hand. "No, it was a stupid question. Russia, India, Iran, virtually every country in the Middle East. Several African countries. Others. Everyone who would want to see America shift its focus and its resources away from them and toward Korea and China." He sighed and shook his head.

"I'm afraid your country," said China to America, "has more enemies than true friends. My country understands this. Friendship, in political terms, is fickle and predicated on what our 'friends' can borrow or buy from us, and from how American dollars prop up their own economies."

"And there's another way of looking at this," said China. "If the SEAL team is false, if they weren't actually sent by America, then they create a false flag. Unless they could be irrefutably proven to be fake, then this whole operation could be staged to disrupt any movement toward reconciliation of North and South Korea. And there are a lot of players who would benefit from that."

They spoke for a long time, trading ideas and theories back and forth. Church listened for much of this, eating vanilla wafers, saying little, letting them forge a pathway through crisis together. When they wound down, they turned to him.

"There is a lot riding on your Havoc Team and this man you call 'Outlaw.'"

Church nodded. "There is. Apart from collecting biological samples, his team will attempt to pick up some clues as to the strike team. Until we can find those soldiers and the people who sent them, we have little of substance to serve as a sedative to the rage that will sweep through the upper echelon of your four governments."

"Rage," echoed South Korea, tasting the bitterness of that word. He shuddered as if a cold wind blew past him.

North Korea gave Church a hard stare. "Two of our teams went to the island and both died. What makes you think your Havoc Team will be any safer? Why is this 'Outlaw' of yours the man to handle something as dangerous and delicate as an outbreak of a bioweapon of this virulence?"

Church ate more of his cookie and then dabbed at his mouth with a napkin. "Trust me when I say this, but there is no one more qualified. No one I trust as completely."

"And what if those soldiers, the fake SEALs, are still there?" asked America.

"Then God help them," said Church.

CHAPTER FORTY-FOUR

326-A WHITTLE
AVALON, CALIFORNIA

Petty Officer First Class Norman Cinders sat straight in his swivel chair, his limbs held rigid by the many bands of duct tape. He stared with horror at what was playing out on the video monitor. He saw Frank Swanson's fight with the abductors. Saw him enter his own home. Saw him drop his gun.

Then Cinders watched the clips from a dozen news stories about how a decorated sailor and senior trainer for SEAL Team Six had apparently suffered a mental fracture. How Swanson murdered his wife, sexually abused and murdered his teenage daughter, and then took his own life. Cinders remembered the story from the news, and from things other sailors said within the tight community of SEALs. It had been all anyone spoke about for weeks. A tragedy that no one could understand.

Then the follow-up stories broke. About the child porn on Swanson's laptop. About photos and videos apparently taken with concealed cameras of his daughter in the bathroom. It all turned tragedy into horror and then into shame. After that, no one spoke Swanson's name again. None of them could bear to say it, or even to spit that name out.

But Cinders now saw the truth behind it all.

The murders and the misdirection; the planted evidence and computer manipulation. So sophisticated, so subtle. So monstrous.

And utterly convincing.

Eve, the blond woman, turned the sound off but let the images run. However, she changed one of the monitor screens to show a different bit of footage. Three small windows popped up, showing Norman Cinders' wife, Julie; their son, Levon; and Norman's mother. All of them going about their lives, totally unaware that they were being watched. Unaware that the normalcy—the unpolluted nature of the mundane things they did—was worse than any torture that could ever be inflicted on Cinders.

Eve smiled a brilliant blue-eyed smile. Adam folded his arms and leaned back in his chair. It was clear he had an erection that tented the front of his khakis. From watching *that*.

Rage burned so hot in Cinders' mind that he wanted to tear the man's throat out with his teeth.

Rage, yes. But no power.

"Now," said Eve, "there are three options. A, B, and C . . ."

CHAPTER FORTY-FIVE
OSAN AIR BASE
NEAR SONGTAN STATION
PYEONGTAEK, SOUTH KOREA

We landed at Osan and were taken by nondescript van to a small blockhouse in a remote corner of the airfield, far away from prying eyes. There we were met by Colonel Barry Epps, Commander of the 51st Fighter Wing. Epps was a tall, broad-shouldered black man with a dazzling smile that did not quite reach his eyes. He had a handshake like an industrial vise and held on a second too long as he searched my eyes.

Then he turned and led me to a far corner that was well out of earshot of everyone else.

"I don't know your name, sir," he said, "but I do know your face."

I gave him a bland smile. He was right, of course. I'd first met Epps four years ago while running a very different kind of mission that took Echo Team deep into the heart of North Korea. At the time I'd been introduced as Jim Palmer. Next time we met was two years later when I was chasing down a portable nuke in South Korea. My credentials on that gig said I was Dave McNally.

"What should I call you this time?" he asked. "Zach Britton? Urban Shocker? Steve Barber?" All of those names were among the greatest pitchers in the history of the Baltimore Orioles.

"My call sign is Outlaw," I said.

"Truth in advertising?" He tried to pitch it as a joke but there was too much resentment in his tone to sell it. Epps must have heard it, or he saw my smile go away. "I have pretty damn high security clearance, you know," he said icily. "Being the commander of a base in a critical area of the world."

"Sorry it has to be like this, Colonel," I said, only half meaning it. "You've been briefed, so you understand the stakes."

"I understand that this came through some pretty strange goddamn channels, Outlaw. I understand that I'm breaking every conceivable rule of conduct for an officer in the United States military."

"And thereby helping to prevent a war," I countered.

He breathed in and out through his nostrils like a dragon, but there was no smoke. Just understandable anxiety. Epps was putting not only his career on the line, but was actually committing textbook treason. But Mr. Church had reached out personally to call in an old marker.

Epps looked down at the concrete floor for a few moments, then fixed me with a penetrating glare. "Your boss is unusually persuasive."

"You don't know the half of it."

"Odd feeling to be asked to serve my country by betraying it."

"Tell you what, Colonel," I said, edging closer, "why don't you take another look at the video my boss shared with you. Pay real close attention to the group of sailors on the beach and tell me if you're being asked to do anything unreasonable. No, better yet, tell me what you think would happen if this was allowed to go through regular channels."

Epps met my hard stare and did not look away. Got to give him that. Instead he let out another breath very slowly and said, "Transport to the island is arranged. You can leave as soon as you're ready."

"Thank you, Colonel."

He gave a nod so crisp and tight it must have hurt his neck muscles. "Let me introduce you to your traveling companions."

He gestured to two figures who stood on opposite sides of a stack of equipment cases. Even from a distance it was obvious they were unhappy about being on a U.S. base. Hostility and distrust seemed to shimmer in the air around them. Top fell into step beside me.

"This should be fun," he said, sotto voce.

The two men waiting for me were dressed in uniforms of the Korean People's Special Operations Force. The taller of the two was an

JONATHAN MABERRY

officer and the other a sergeant who was approximately the size and shape of a fireplug. Neither was smiling.

"Allow me to introduce Chungjwai Ho Yong-ju," said Epps. "He is a doctor attached to the Special Threats Group." The STG—or STING—was a new unit that was formed to deal with catastrophic events like reactor meltdowns, biocontainment breaches, and so on. They were ostensibly a non-combative group, but the CIA intelligence analysts pegged them as a kind of special ops team that either delivered or responded to WMDs. If they were merely good guys protecting their country from those kinds of weapons, then they weren't much different from the old Department of Military Sciences, or Britain's Barrier. Ho's rank, *chungjwai*, was a "middle commander," which corresponded to lieutenant colonel.

"*Annyeong hasimnikka*," I said, opting for the formal greeting and even giving it a North Korean inflection. A flicker of surprise registered on his face. Ho's reply, though, was in excellent English.

"It is an honor, sir," he said.

I was wearing loose black pants and a T-shirt and showed no rank of any kind, so Ho did not salute. Instead he used that blend of Eastern and Western greeting, which is a proffered hand and a half bow. I did the same.

Ho introduced his squatty companion, Sergeant Chung, who gave me a sharp bow but did not offer his hand.

"For reasons that are likely obvious to you," I said, "I can't share my name or those of my team. We will operate with combat call signs. I'm Outlaw, and my number two here is Pappy."

I called the rest of Havoc over and went through those intros as well.

"Do you have call signs?" I asked Ho, but he said he did not. "Okay, henceforth for the duration of this mission you're Painkiller and Sergeant Chung is Jeeves."

"Why?" asked Ho.

"Why not?"

Ho almost smiled. "Very well. Shall we get started, Outlaw?"

Epps stayed in the room to hear the mission briefing, but sent his people outside with orders to say nothing about this op.

"Let's get some things on the table here," I said when the door was closed and locked. "First, I'm in charge. This isn't a democracy and I don't care what your rank is. During this operation I call the shots. Understood?"

Ho nodded, and Chung, if possible, stood even straighter to attention.

"I need to hear it out loud," I said.

"Sir," said Ho and Chung crisply.

"Good. You don't have to like it, but that's how this is going to work. We can't have debates on who does what in the middle of a mission. I have experience in these kinds of situations. You don't need to know the details, but you have to accept that as a fact."

"We are not exactly newcomers to this game," said Ho coldly.

"Good, because if you were virgins I'd leave you both behind. The point is, Painkiller, you follow my orders without question. If you're unable to do so, you are welcome to stand down. Is that clear?"

Ho gave me two seconds of a considering stare. Everything about this had to rankle, and none of it squared with military protocol as he knew it. I was, after all, the enemy of his people. A state of war still existed between our countries, even if it was technically on the back burner for more than half a century.

"You are in command, sir," said Ho. After a moment's pause, his sergeant grunted and saluted.

"Good. Oh, side note—no saluting, and you do not have to call me sir."

"Yes, sir," said Ho, but I swear to God I saw a tiny flicker of amusement when he said it. Made me kind of like him. Chung had a strangled look on his face, probably at the thought of *not* saying "sir."

"Okay," I said, "we all know this is off the books. This is not officially sanctioned, which means if we fail, then we will all be disavowed by our respective governments. And rightly so. From here on out this is a ghost op."

They agreed, and my guys gave me a chorus of "Hooah." I saw Chung mouth the word "*hooah*" as if tasting it.

"Chain of command is this," I continued. "Me, Pappy, and then everyone else is equal. No rank. And to that point, I hope you

JONATHAN MABERRY

brought the clothing I recommended. Plain black. No rank, no patches, absolutely nothing that can ID who or what you are."

"What does that matter?" asked Ho. "We will be wearing hazmat suits."

"Because," said Top, "if you get your ass killed and we can't exfil your corpse we don't want you to betray us by being both dead *and* careless."

Ho stared at him for a moment, then nodded.

"Next point," I said. "Right now it *looks* like America and South Korea are the bad guys here. Maybe they are, but the people who sent us don't think so. I have my doubts, too, but I'm going to keep an open mind even if that means I don't like what we find. Either way, we *will* find out."

Ho nodded and we shared a look for a moment. He had a damn good poker face, but there was fear in his eyes and I don't think it was because of whatever killed the islanders. The consequences of America being at fault and being proved to be so could not be anything but catastrophic.

"My boss thinks that the players involved were operating illegally, possibly a rogue cell or something equally shady. Or maybe it's someone else playing dress-up. In any case, when we find out the truth we handle it like professionals. That means all information will be shared with the four governments involved. You know the stakes involved here. Let's act like we actually give a shit about the whole planet. That means we all step outside of our politics and act like human beings. If you can't do that, then you are a liability to the mission." I paused and gave them a very hard look. "If you betray this trust we're creating here, then God help you, because I do not give second chances."

Was I being unduly hard on them? No, I really don't think so. There hadn't been an op like this before. Not with the political ramifications possibly outweighing the outbreak danger, so this wasn't a time to handhold and coddle. Ho nodded to me, and I thought I saw some fires ignite in his dark eyes.

"Sergeant Chung and I—excuse me, *Jeeves* and I—understand the risk and the stakes," he said. "And we acknowledge your complete command for this operation. You can trust us."

"Glad to hear it. Now, I have one last thing before we saddle up," I told them as I stepped back. "Whoever *is* responsible are our enemies. *Our* enemies. We are going to tear their lives apart. But in any instance where we can take a prisoner, we do it. We need answers and we can't ask questions of someone without a pulse. You can defend yourself, but we need to solve this. Is that clear?"

"Yes," said Ho, and there was real steel in his voice. The island was, after all, part of his country. And he was a doctor as well as a soldier.

"Then welcome to the war," I said.

Fifteen minutes later we were on a helicopter to the coast. Locked and loaded and hungry for blood.

INTERLUDE TEN
WILDLIFE ROAD ABOVE THE POINT DUME BLUFFS
MALIBU, CALIFORNIA
TWELVE MONTHS AGO

The basement was modeled after a high-end military tactical operations center. Rows of tables for technicians, big screens showing images cadged from military satellites as well as police and commercial CCTV.

There was minimal staffing at the moment, though. A short hipster kid with too much beard and too much nose was at a console, sending video clips to Kuga and Santoro to review. The clip currently running was the fifth that showed a young couple, both of who were young, blond, and very fit.

"I have been following them for a while now," said Santoro. "They are at the top of my list for my personal team."

"Why them?" asked Kuga between sips of very aromatic Peruvian coffee.

Santoro gave one of his rare smiles. Some snakes smile like that, and it means exactly the same thing.

"Just watch," said Santoro.

Kuga watched. After ten minutes he said, "Yeah, they're exactly what we need."

CHAPTER FORTY-SIX
GAEGULI SEOM
EIGHTEEN NAUTICAL MILES WEST OF NORTH KOREA
SEA OF JAPAN

Havoc Team came in fast, riding across the waves on an RHIB from which all insignia, maker's marks, and identification had been scrupulously stripped. The boat was also rigged with modified thermite and at need any of us could use our tactical computers to turn the craft into a fireball. Our suits, weapons, and other equipment were similarly prepared to prevent anyone from gathering useful forensic evidence. Gruesome? Yes. Scary to walk around with an incendiary device attached to your favorite body? Also yes.

Andrea drove the RHIB and rode a breaker all the way into the sand. Bunny vaulted the side with a rope and lashed us tight to a tree. We all followed and ran for the black shadows under the wall of trees.

We were wearing a special version of Saratoga Hammer Suits, which are chemical and biological warfare agent protective clothing specifically designed for first responders. The versions we had were made special for Mr. Church and are not—I repeat *not*—on the commercial market. Not at any price. The suits rely on special spherical adsorbers, which are engineered for the adhesion of ions, atoms, or molecules from liquid or gas. The suits are air permeable, incredibly flexible, and allow the wearers to move and fight at full speed.

Our versions also have special blends of Kevlar, spider silk, and graphene that will stop any bullet up to an M16. Won't stop a sniper firing high-armor-piercing rounds, but every tool has its limits. They will slow down a knife, which most Kevlar won't; and I have been reasonably assured nothing short of a grizzly bear can bite through it.

Our other gear was generic to the world of independent military contractors in this part of the world. We all carried the same sidearms, the same long guns, the same knives. Our grenades and other nasty toys were RTI make and were laced with the same thermite as the boat. There would be no fragments to analyze.

These toys were all deeply expensive, but worth every penny. I hoped.

Each of us wore ballistic helmets with Google Scout glasses, which are another goody made expressly for Mr. Church. Made by a friend in the industry. We could cycle from normal lenses to zoom to infrared and ultraviolet. And mission intel was fed to one lens. Currently we had ours switched to ultra-low-light night vision, which plunged us into a world of luminous green and white and intense black.

Before the boat hit the beach we'd made sure our wrist-mounted tactical computers were on, with the screens synced to the Scout glasses; and everyone wore the same RTI earbuds. Belle immediately unlimbered her sniper rifle and crouched behind an old fishing boat as she swept the beach and tree line to make sure there was nothing sneaking up on us.

"Clear," she reported.

"Okay," I said, "let's put some birds in the air."

"*Ovviamente*," said Andrea as he opened a waterproof metal case and removed four identical full-sized crows that looked like the real thing, except these were high-end drones. Absolutely convincing at anything more than ten feet. He activated each with a few keystrokes on his forearm computer and tossed them, one by one, into the air. Their wings, which had been folded on the case, deployed and small but very powerful motors sent each bird soaring into the starry skies. The video feeds from their cameras showed up on our screens.

"Okay," I said quietly, "we're going to make for the village and establish our base of operations. From there we'll work the island in sections. Once it's secure then we'll take our samples. Until this, we focus on observation and survival. Everyone is on the buddy system. Bunny and Jeeves, you take point. Mother Mercy and Jackpot, watch our asses. Pappy and Painkiller are with me."

"Rules of engagement?" prompted Top.

"We believe everyone who lived here is dead, as are the two teams sent in to investigate," I said. "Assume nothing until we verify it. If you are attacked by civilians, attempt to restrain, and if things go south, then fall back."

"Go . . . 'south'?" echoed Ho, confused.

"If things turn to shit," said Top.

"Ah," he said, and nodded.

"We're not looking to add to the collateral damage," I said. "But if you are attacked and cannot control the situation, then you are cleared to defend yourself, feel me?"

"Hooah," they said, and even Chung joined in.

"Then let's act like professionals and do this right," I said. "Move out."

We left the beach and the misty stars behind and entered the dense darkness of the jungle. The air was so humid it felt like I had to push through it, even with the barrier of the Hammer Suit. The electronics in the garments fed us constant real-time data and allowed us to adjust what we heard and what we saw.

We saw death and stillness.

What we heard, though, was a forest that was alive. The constant chorus of tree and ground frogs, the drone of insects disturbed from slumber by our presence, and the buzz of flies still busy with their tireless feeding on cold flesh. When we came to our first corpse, we paused in pairs, lingering for a moment before moving on to let the duo behind have their moment to bear witness.

The body was that of a young woman, perhaps twenty, wearing the simple and drab clothing of an islander who lived so far below the poverty line that she'd likely had no perspective on it. She was skinny, with few curves, and a face that, while not pretty, was beautiful in its innocence. When I stopped for a moment to look down at her, what I saw was not someone of a foreign land and not a person who exemplified a political ideology that was alien to my own. I did not even see a Korean, or an Asian, or even a woman. Not really. What I saw was a life stolen. A human being denied the right to life. This person had been murdered by someone, for some reason that mattered more to the killer than did anything that defined the person who'd lived in this flesh. It was a theft of all the days and months and years that could and *should* have come. The level of violation here ran miles deep.

The plan had been to sweep the island before we took samples, but Ho insisted, so I gave the word. Sergeant Chung took out a camera and documented the scene, then spread out a plastic sheet. Bunny helped him lift the corpse onto it, and we all watched as Ho opened a case and removed a number of tools.

Belle unclipped a handheld BAMS unit from her belt and made a slow pass over the corpse. Ho watched, impressed.

"I've never seen one that small," he said.

"Not on the market yet," I said, which told him nothing. The BAMS units we had were several giant steps up from the big clunky ones they use in airports. The device is a bio-aerosol mass spectrometer. It has a vacuum function that draws in ambient air and hits it with continuous wave lasers to fluoresce individual particles. Key molecules like bacillus spores, dangerous viruses, and certain vegetative cells are identified and assigned color codes. Most of the BAMS units on either the commercial or government markets are unreliable because they can only detect dangerous particles in high density. This version had been designed by Dr. William Hu, the former head of the DMS Integrated Sciences Division, and then seriously upgraded by Doc Holliday.

Belle moved it up and down the woman's body and we all watched the little indicator lights. Green means everyone can take a breath; bright red means you're fucked if you aren't wearing high-end hazmat suits.

"That's weird," said Bunny.

We all bent closer. The light was green.

"I . . . don't understand," said Andrea. "This is supposed to be some kind of fast-acting pathogen, isn't it? Or did I miss something during the mission briefing."

"How sensitive is the filter on that?" asked Ho. "Maybe the particles are too small."

"No," said Belle. "It's sensitive enough to detect prions and viroids."

The smallest known infectious agents are prions, which are composed of a single protein, and viroids—simple circles of ribonucleic acid. I saw Ho's eyes bug, and he gave the device a covetous look.

I said, "Bug, Doc, are you getting the live feed from the BAMS unit?"

Doc said, "We are, sugar, but don't get your nuts in a tangle. All that's saying is that there is not airborne in your immediate vicinity. Let's not all get naked and go for a stroll."

Ho and Chung were staring at me in total confusion. I'd briefed them about having our chief scientific advisor on the call, but there isn't really a way to adequately prepare anyone for the phenomenon that is Doc Holliday.

"Call the play," I suggested.

"Get me some blood samples and cheek swabs. Wouldn't mind some other tissue samples, too." She read a list that disgusted me but had Ho nodding. He was sorting out the right tools while Doc spoke. "Keep your BAMS unit on, kids," continued Doc. "You never know what's out there ready to take a big juicy bite out of y'all."

Ho set to work. Belle handed the BAMS unit to Andrea, and then faded back to secure the perimeter. Bunny joined her. Kind of wish I could have as well.

I found myself feeling embarrassed for the dead woman. On one hand, that made no sense since she was way beyond knowing what was being done to her. This woman was dead because someone cared more for their own needs than for hers. Everyone on this island was dead for the same reason. If this was a bioweapon, then it means that a group, large or small, spent time and money and effort to bring death here. This was not heat of passion. This was the icy heartbeat of evil. Indignities don't bother the dead, but they sure as hell tore holes in me. I knelt and pulled the shreds of clothing over the woman's body. Ho glanced over, saw me do it, and our eyes met. He gave me a sad smile and a small nod.

He had work to do, though, and I had to accept it. Ho used special scissors to cut the woman's clothes off, which were then bagged and tagged. Then he proceeded to take swabs and scrapings of her nose, ears, mouth, anus, and vagina. He used a long flexible tube and micro-tools to take additional samples from her throat, from her lungs, and up her rectum into the colon. I had to hand it to him, Ho worked very fast and with obvious professional skill. He wasn't a government flunky pretending to be a doctor, but was the real thing. I watched his eyes, looking for emotion. Saw nothing.

In law enforcement and the military one of the things they will you early on is to not make it personal. They advise staying determinedly *im*personal because that is the perceived safe zone, the solid ground on which to charge or retreat, to plan or pivot. To do otherwise, they say, is to risk letting your emotions cloud your judgment and impair your adherence to your training. Some of that is even true, but when you actually *do* this kind of work you know how naïve that kind of thinking really is. Because if we don't create an emotional attachment then we can easily forget why we're fighting in the first place.

Combat soldiers often say that they don't fight for flag or country, but instead fight for the soldier beside them. That's part of it. Fighting to protect them is fighting to *protect*. That is the definition of emotional involvement in combat. If we fight only for ourselves then we fight for either fear or greed. That turns us into killers rather than warriors. A warrior fights for those who can't fight for themselves, and it doesn't matter if that refers to the living or the dead. Both matter.

I am a warrior. I am also a soldier and a killer. As I stood there, even though it was only really a moment of my life, a moment in this dark night, I knew who I was fighting for. If the bad guys thought they were big and bad and scary and dangerous, then they were going to learn otherwise. There were other kinds of monsters in the dark. I'm one of them. And now I was invested here. Now I was emotionally involved.

Maybe this was what I should try and explain to Junie. It wasn't that I was unemotional during or after combat. It wasn't that at all. If anything, emotion was the fuel I shoveled into the furnace of my resolve. An unemotional soldier—and there are some of those—detaches completely from everyone except his fellow soldier, and sometimes even then. Enemies were dehumanized and given labels—Gooks, Towel-heads, Skinnies, whatever; and civilians were little more than incidental irritants. That wasn't me, and it wasn't Top or Bunny. Pretty sure it wasn't Andrea or Belle, despite his affected joviality and her death-mask poker face. No. I didn't take my emotions off when I dressed for combat. They were there, tingling inside the Killer's skin. Burning in his heart. Boiling the tears out of his eyes so that he could see more clearly and aim all the better. That's what I needed to tell Junie, and wondered why I never had.

JONATHAN MABERRY

Because you're afraid she'll run from the monster you are, said a cold voice in my head. The Modern Man, whispering his truth.

Inside my head, though, the Killer rose up and bared his teeth. He is that part of me who would never hurt an innocent like this, but when he catches the scent of the murderers who caused such harm, he would go to war under a black flag. He would rage war in the ugliest of ways because a murder like this one demanded no lesser response.

Ho finished up and began putting his samples away.

Before I rose, I touched the woman's cheek. I didn't know her name and probably never would. I *knew* her, though, and I loved her. Sounds crazy to say, and maybe most people wouldn't understand, but I don't care. This woman represented everything that's wrong with the world and everything that I fought for. This was why I could pull a trigger over and over and over again and not look for an exit from the field. This is why I wasn't looking to lay down my sword and shield. Not yet. Not when I *knew* that I could still fight this fight. If that was hubris, then so what?

This woman did not deserve to die. She deserved a life and whatever happiness came with it.

So, yes, I was going to find whoever did this and kill them.

For her.

For me.

CHAPTER FORTY-SEVEN
THE TOC
PHOENIX HOUSE
OMFORI ISLAND
GREECE

Rudy Sanchez sat at a disused computer workstation in the TOC, watching the Punk Press video play over and over again. He asked that the same video be sent to the monitor at the workstation, which allowed him to freeze frames, zoom in, study body language and faces. It was sickening work, but it was necessary. His specialty was trauma, and this was trauma.

He blew across the surface of his coffee, sipped, winced, and put it down. Too hot. Instead he sat with his palms cupped around it, seeking warmth for the soul even though the room was not chilly.

The images were horrible, and despite years of this with the DMS and now RTI, Rudy had never truly become inured to it. He did not allow that, preferring instead to walk the narrow tightrope between that mental state of professional detachment. It was a risk, and he knew his involvement, even at a safe remove like this, was corrosive to his optimism, his nerves, and his heart. As it had been since he chose the medical specialty of trauma therapy. He'd been on the ground in the days and weeks after 9/11, had been to various theaters of war, and had helped Joe Ledger and his people clean and dress their emotional lacerations.

Now he was adding this event to his inventory. Just as it would soon be added to the inventory of horrors for Joe Ledger and Havoc Team. He sighed and tried to keep regret from stinging him like a wasp. There had been several opportunities to bring up the subject of Joe's apparent detachment from the emotional cost of this kind of thing. He'd delayed, hoping Joe would broach the subject, and maybe that had been about to happen in the canteen, but then Joe was called away. Again. To venture into a place of horrors.

But none of that was why he sat up very suddenly and then began stabbing the keys to get the video to replay. He watched it through twice, and then switched to the live feed from Frog Island.

"What is it, Doctor?" asked a quiet voice.

"*Ay, caray!*" Rudy gave a violent start, spilling hot coffee on his hands.

Mr. Church stood there, his face tinted a ghostly blue by light from the computer screens.

Rudy plucked a tissue out of his pocket and hastily blotted the coffee. "You scared the living hell out of me."

Church said, "You looked troubled, Doctor. Did you see something of note in the video?"

Rudy crumpled the tissue and set it down next to his cup. "I . . . I don't quite know. Not for sure."

"Then tell me what you suspect," said Church. "I value any insight or opinion."

On the screen the image was showing Top's helmet cam footage of him bending over the bodies of two soldiers who lay with their hands clutched in terminal ferocity around each other's throats.

"Seeing all of that triggered something," said Rudy slowly. "A memory, but unrelated to this matter. At least it seems like it couldn't be connected."

"And yet . . . ?" prompted Church.

"And yet," said Rudy, "do you remember the transcript of my last interview with Rafael Santoro fifteen months ago?"

"Of course. Why do you ask?"

"Well, Santoro made a number of enigmatic comments, but one of them has come back to me rather powerfully. At the end of the last session he said something very strange."

Church stiffened and glanced at the horrors on the screen. In a soft, almost distant voice he recited, *"When the Koreans begin killing each other, then you'll know."*

"Yes," said Rudy excitedly. "That's it exactly."

"My God."

"Surely, though, it can't be connected to this," said Rudy. "Can it?"

Church's face was an uninformative mask.

"I mean," continued Rudy, "Santoro has been in prison for years. In solitary. No TV or internet. No contact at all with the outside world. He could not possibly . . ." Rudy's words trailed off as he studied Church's face. "What is it? What's wrong?"

Church took a small step closer. "When I asked you to discontinue the interrogation sessions with Santoro you asked me why and I evaded the question."

"You said that we had nothing more to learn from him."

"I did, and in a way that was true," admitted Church, "but not because I felt your interviews were of no value or that you were not making progress."

Rudy stood up. "Why then?"

"Because," said Church, "one month after your last visit, the prison was attacked by persons unknown. It was destroyed in a series of explosions, and all of the prisoners and most of the staff were killed."

"Ay dios mío! Rafael Santoro is dead? That's . . . hard to believe. He was always so very much alive. Vital, I mean."

Church nodded. "The facility was a black site under joint jurisdiction by Homeland and the NSA. They each sent forensics teams to conduct exhaustive searches of the rubble and to determine if any prisoners escaped. According to their report, they were able to collect sufficient tissue samples to establish that Rafael Santoro, along with other high-value prisoners, was killed in what the investigators labeled a failed rescue attempt. No prisoners are known to have been liberated. Jerry Spencer is reviewing the forensic data."

Rudy got up and walked a few paces away, running a hand through his dark hair. He turned. "Fifteen months ago? Then it was not the Seven Kings?"

"We don't know who it was," Church admitted. "None of the bodies of the raiding team that were recovered have been useful as leads. They were of mixed nationality, with a slight bias to Central American. Two of them were connected with the Jalisco New Generation cartel out of the Port of Manzanillo. There were key cartel leaders among the incarcerated, but it's uncertain if the hit on the prison was engineered by the cartel or if those two men were on loan. We've hit a number of dead ends running it down."

"Isn't that rather odd?"

"Of course it is. Everything about that event was unusual."

Rudy chewed his lip for a moment. "Does Joe know about this?"

"He does not."

"Why not?"

"Because until now it was not a case that required his attention or his particular skill set."

Rudy said nothing, biting back the words he wanted to say. However, scolding Church was seldom a useful occupation. Instead he turned to the screen.

"*When the Koreans begin killing each other, then you'll know,*'" he quoted. "Am I right to think that there may be a connection to this?"

"That," said Church, "is something we need to find out."

CHAPTER FORTY-EIGHT
HOTEL RYUMEIKAN
TOKYO, JAPAN

It was a party. It was like New Year's Eve and their birthdays and Christmas morning rolled into one big, delicious confection.

Eve made a big bowl of salty, buttery popcorn while Adam opened the champagne. He did it right, too—slowly and firmly turning the knobby head of the cork to ease it out of the bottle's mouth with a satisfying *pop* but without the silly spilling of the bubbly all over the place. She watched him do it and smiled.

"That's hot," she said.

"What is?" asked Adam, reaching for two red Solo cups.

"Don't you see it? The way you opened that?" She grinned. "It's like what we do. Pressure and leverage, with a lot of the right kind of control. Nothing wasted."

Adam paused, considering. Then he smiled, too. "Yeah. Maybe we should use that as a screen saver."

"Or video business card."

"We'd wind up getting hired for weddings and bar mitzvahs."

Eve's grin became something else. A wicked little leer. "And wouldn't that be bunches of fun?"

"Yes, it would," he said, and leaned over to kiss her. The *pop-pop-pop* from the exploding kernels in the microwave sounded like gunfire.

She pushed him back with playful roughness and told him to get the TV ready. He took the cups and bottle to the bedroom of the suite, then busied himself turning on the TV and both of their laptops.

"That's weird," he called.

"What is?" Eve asked as she poured the popcorn into a big plastic bowl.

"Come here for a sec."

She sprinkled salt over the steaming treat and carried the bowl into the other room. The big-screen TV was on, set to CNN, and a panel of experts was talking about a trade bill coming up for vote in the House.

"Did they say anything about Frog Island?" she asked.

"No."

Eve slid onto the bed and sat cross-legged. "Try Fox."

He did, and then MSNBC, BBC News, and a dozen other cable news stations. No one seemed to be talking about what they should have been yelling about.

Eve frowned. Adam stood scowling, stabbing the remote button with his thumb.

"Fuck," he growled.

She set the popcorn aside and pulled her computer onto her lap and began hitting news sites. One after the other after the other.

There was nothing. Not one word.

"Ohhhhh *shit*," said Eve.

They exchanged a worried look. Adam licked his lips. "I know we're supposed to stay dark for now, but . . ."

"Oh, definitely," said Eve, "we need to call Daddy."

Adam took out his cell and started to punch the number, paused, canceled it, started again, canceled.

"Shit," he said. "He's going to be pissed if we break protocol."

Eve pointed to the TV. "He's going to be a fuck lot more pissed if we don't tell him."

"C'mon, Evie, he probably already knows."

"And what if he doesn't and we just *assume*? Want to guess what he'd do to us then?"

They both shivered at the thought. Real shivers, not pretend. They loved their Daddy but he was also the scariest person they knew. Much scarier than they were.

"Shit," said Adam.

"I know," said Eve.

"I'm going to call him."

He steeled himself to punch the numbers into the burner they were currently using. It would have to be destroyed after the call, but that was okay. They had more in the trunk of their car. Eve got up and stood next to him, leaning against him, but she also had her fingers crossed.

The call was accepted on the fifth ring but there was no actual answer.

"We're sorry to call," said Adam quickly.

"But you did anyway, yes?" Daddy's voice was cold. No trace of warmth at all.

"We . . . um . . . had to," said Adam. He rarely stumbled on words and never showed even a flicker of weakness to anyone, even when things were really bad and there was blood on the walls. But Daddy scared him, just as he scared Eve. "We can't find anything on the news. Nothing. Not a word from anyone."

There was a long silence.

"We didn't know if you knew, but . . ."

"Thank you," said Daddy. "You were right to call."

"What do you want us to do?"

"Do . . . ?"

"I mean, do we drop the flag on the families?"

Another pause, then, "Do nothing for now. Go to ground and wait until you hear from me."

"What are you going to do?"

They thought Daddy wouldn't answer, but he did. "Perhaps we may need to shout a little louder."

The line went dead.

Adam tossed the phone onto the bed like it was a scorpion and Eve and he stood there, clinging to one another.

"Shit," she said, half in sustained fear and half in relief. Or, maybe less than half relief. Daddy would be very angry and he would need someone to blame. Maybe the SEALs, maybe someone else.

Adam held her close and all the fun drained from the day like blood from a dying body.

CHAPTER FORTY-NINE
GAEGULI SEOM
EIGHTEEN NAUTICAL MILES WEST OF NORTH KOREA
SEA OF JAPAN

We found the other dead. So many others.

I don't know how Ho or Chung was taking this. It could not have been easy. Even if they, as soldiers, had seen death and violence before, it was damned unlikely they'd seen anything like this. There was almost no chatter. No jokes or banter. The few words that passed were necessary in each moment. Calling attention to this or that.

Andrea sent two of his drones out to circle the island, moving low over the sand to try and find where the SEALs and ROK team landed. It took a while to find it because the tide had smoothed the sand.

"*Trovato*," he said. *Found it.*

We clustered around and watched the screens as Andrea shifted the drones' cameras.

"Tighten in on the boot prints," said Top. "Yeah, see that tread? That's standard SEAL footwear. Same for the ROK."

"You can buy shoes anywhere," said Bunny. "My nephew bought a pair off eBay."

"Yeah, but it helps sell the story, Farm Boy. And see there? The tread is a little worn down, like these are shoes a guy's been wearing on the job. I've seen fakes before where they make the mistake of using everything new. Shit like this doesn't help us prove it wasn't the men with green faces."

That was an old SEALs nickname dating back to the Vietnam War.

Andrea said, "Those footprints are at least a day old. Doesn't look like anyone's been back to the beach since this thing happened."

Ho touched my arm. "If that team delivered a bioweapon here, then we need to determine how they did it. Your BAMS units are still not picking anything up."

"I know. Andrea," I said, "send those drones high and run full-spectrum scans. Run everything. Radiation, chemical signatures, multi-spectrum light analysis. Everything."

"That'll take time, Outlaw."

"Then stop wasting it. Go."

Andrea's fingers danced over the keyboard as he entered the search commands. The video feeds from the two beach drones changed as they accepted the new pattern. He sent two more drones up and quartered the island. The other drones were still looking for the quick and the dead. They were mostly finding the dead.

"Okay," I said, "let's move."

We reached the little town quickly and entered warily, moving well, checking and clearing buildings, covering each other with our weapons while the drones watched everything from above.

"How many?" I asked, knowing that Bunny would be keeping count.

"Hundred forty-nine since we hit the beach," said the big young man. His voice was devoid of emotion, which meant that his heart was hurting. I glanced at him and saw that he was squatting over an old man who lay beside an infant. Both had been beaten to madness with a three-foot length of fence post.

Ho stepped out of the shadows of a line of huts and walked to the middle of the road. Cover did not seem to matter because everything seemed so damned over. The drones confirmed it.

"Okay," I said, "Mother Mercy and Jackpot, secure the street and watch our backs. Everyone else, collect samples. You each have your lists. Let's do this and get the hell out of here."

We all set to work. Doc Holliday and her team worked with us remotely, overseeing every step of evidence collection. Blood stopped flowing as soon as the heart stopped pumping, settling to the lowest points in the body, so we needed to collect it from there in big syringes. We used moisture sprays to help us gather scrapings from inside of cheeks, and swabs for ears and noses. We clipped nails and hair, drilled deep with long needles to take samples from organs. And a lot more.

We also bagged two of the bodies in special plastic envelopes that were thoroughly sealed. A chopper would airlift them out, then settle the bags on a barge that was being towed into these waters. That barge had an emergency lab with staff and equipment ready for whatever we brought back. Everything was to be openly shared, with the process overseen by Dr. John Cmar, one of Church's friends in the industry. One of my friends, too.

The science part of this case was in hand, but I felt like we were behind the clock on finding who did this. Apart from the footprints on the beach there was no sign at all of the SEALs and ROK.

Until there was.

"Yo!" cried Bunny from the far end of the short street. "Outlaw, Pappy, I think I got something."

We came running. Bunny was sitting on his heels by a rickety pigpen near a shack where two people lay in the mud dead. One was a teenage boy who held the cracked end of a rusting oyster knife whose blade was buried in the eye socket of a woman who looked to be his mother. She had her hands locked around the boy's throat. Flies crawled over both corpses, and over a sow and seven piglets who were also dead.

"Look at this," said Bunny as he pointed to the sow. The pig was medium-sized but much bigger than her babies, but it was clear that they had killed her. She was covered in bites from snout to tail. Three of the piglets were bitten and crushed, too, clearly in self-defense. The others seemed to have killed each other. "I mean, seriously, boss, what the actual fuck?"

I called Ho over and he immediately bent close to examine the pigs.

"These are the only animals who were infected," he said.

"The only ones we've seen," I said. "There may be others, but we haven't been looking for them."

"Maybe we should."

I conveyed that to the rest of the team, but told them to finish collecting the samples first. Ho bagged two piglets and several samples from the others. Then Belle called to say she found a couple of dead rats. They lay there, crushed by someone's foot, but showing signs of mutual attack.

"Bag them, too," I said.

Top and I began walking through the town, looking for more animals, but we found something else. Or, he did.

"Hey," he said, stopping to look into the shadows between two huts, "the hell's that?"

He unclipped a flash and used it to chase back the darkness, and there, half hidden by a torn fishing net, lay something that did not belong in this town, or on this island. We crouched on either side of it, making sure we were positioned to let our bodycams get a good look. In my ear I heard Doc Holliday murmur, "Well, butter my buns and call me a biscuit. Is that what I *think* it is?"

"Yeah," I said, "it damn well is."

Top pulled back the net.

There, lying broken and dead, was a drone.

CHAPTER FIFTY
GAEGULI SEOM
EIGHTEEN NAUTICAL MILES WEST OF NORTH KOREA
SEA OF JAPAN

We lifted the drone, carried it out into the street, and set it down on a tarp. There was no maker's mark on it and no serial numbers, but it was clear what this was. Doc and Bug were both ahead of us, though, having run the images through MindReader.

"It's an octocopter," Bug said. "Very similar to the Boeing Farm-Solutions HH13, but not exactly the same configuration. The standard HH13 is a crop-spraying drone. They used a bunch of those for mosquito abatement when Zika started hitting."

"Similar but not the same, sugar," agreed Doc. "The housing is different, and the blade shape is unique. Also, look—most crop drones are built with tanks and sprayers. They're designed for precision variable rate application of liquid pesticides, fertilizers, and herbicides. This one is notably different."

Instead of sprayers, the undercarriage had what looked like shotgun barrels, though they were made from lightweight aluminum. A kind of tank or reservoir was bolted to the undercarriage. The whole thing was pretty lightweight, and Bug said that it normally had a payload weight of about ten kilograms.

"That's twenty-two pounds, give or take," said Bunny. "But of what? Those aren't sprayers."

"Don't mess with it," ordered Doc. "Bag the whole thing and bring it to Mama. If it was carrying a pathogen, and I'd bet my tarnished virtue that it was, then there may be trace residue inside."

"You want us to take the outer housing apart? Look for serial numbers or—"

"I want it pristine, Outlaw. In other words, don't fuck with it or I'll fix your mouth so it won't hold soup."

"Yes, ma'am," I said contritely, and then ordered Andrea and Chung to secure it.

Andrea leaned close, disabled his coms unit for a moment, and asked, "Is it really true that she has a robot velociraptor in her office?"

"No," I said, but before his hopeful expression could collapse, I added, "She has a robot Compsognathus. Looks like a tiny 'raptor. Size of a chicken. Doc told me she built it because someone told her she couldn't. She calls it Pheidough." I spelled it for him. He looked at me exactly the way you'd expect someone to do when you tell them something like that.

"What's it do?" he asked, enthralled.

"It doesn't do anything. Just walks around the lab. Has a speaker inside, so sometimes Pheidough sounds like he's singing the blues."

There was a strange little glaze in Andrea's eyes. "I like men, but I think I am falling in love with her."

I grinned. "Who isn't?"

Bunny knelt down across from him and began removing body bags from his pouch, and Andrea went back to the real world. It took two of the black plastic bags to cover the drone, which were then sealed with duct tape. Ho stood watching them and I clapped his shoulder, making him jump. "Whoa, there. Sorry, Painkiller. This is good news, we have an actual clue."

He turned and gave me a long stare. "We don't manufacture anything like that in my country."

With that he walked away to continue taking specimens.

Ouch.

INTERLUDE ELEVEN
OLD ABSINTHE HOUSE
240 BOURBON STREET
NEW ORLEANS, LOUISIANA
ELEVEN MONTHS AGO

The woman was entranced with her and Eve knew it.

She clung to Eve like a lamprey, bending to listen to every word she said and even managing to laugh in the right places when Eve made a joke. The woman kept touching her. Caressing her back, running her blond hair through slender fingers, copping a feel of her ass when she thought no one was looking. All around them the everlasting party crowds that defined Bourbon Street were doing the full-tilt boogie. Laughing, dancing, drinking, making out, yelling, telling lies, being conned. That was Bourbon Street. It was always that way, day after day, year after year—a permanent frat party with few rules, little common sense, and a full-blooded desire to achieve that unachievable perfect high.

Eve found it all a lot of fun, even when she was working.

The woman's name was Mandy and she was hot, with one of those deceptively petite figures—a handspan waist but with a significant swell of rounded goodies above and below. Caramel-colored skin and eyes the color of fresh spring leaves. And lots of obvious money. The clothes were super high-end made to look like bargain basement. Gold watch, a diamond on her left hand and an emerald on her right, and both so big that muggers would discount them as fakes. Very expensive hair and even more expensive shoes. In the years since she and Adam burned down their past, they'd both learned to spot real from fake. Mandy was rich as hell and from the sly smiles she gave, it was obvious that *awareness* of her money was the bait on the big shiny hook.

Eve had set herself in the right place, a bar frequented by predators of both sexes. She and Adam spotted Mandy a week ago, holding court in a busy corner, fending men off with lethal stares and buying drinks for women of a certain age and type. Mandy clearly preferred blondes. That was obvious at the bar, because when Eve walked past to go to the ladies' room, Mandy caught her wrist and gave a firm but gentle tug, encouraging Eve to bend down to listen.

"I'll have a glass waiting and an empty seat right here when you come back."

"Then," said Eve with a saucy flash of her eyes, "I guess I'd better be quick."

That was several drinks ago and now they were pushing through the crowd, heading for the door, going out into the runaway circus on the street. Mandy paused, pulled her close, and they kissed. A big, deep kiss that made all the boys and some of the girls send up a raucous chorus of approving catcalls. Eve contrived to blush. That was a trick she learned recently. One of many useful things.

They held hands and fought the crowd, sometimes shoving, sometimes smiling their way through the knots of partygoers. When they reached Royal Street they turned toward the Hotel Monteleone.

Royal was much less frenetic, and they slowed to a stroll in the sultry night air. Far above, a fingernail moon was slicing through wispy clouds.

Eve pretended to be surprised that Mandy had a room in so fine a place as the Monteleone. She went positively wide-eyed as if she'd never been there before. The elevator was crowded, so they behaved, but once they were in Mandy's suite things were different. Mandy locked the door, turned, and was all hands and seemed to sprout six more. She shuffled forward slowly but inexorably, making Eve back up to the edge of the bed.

What the woman had not seen was Eve's hand brush against the doorframe as they entered. Had not seen her press a piece of clear plastic over the strike plate. The plastic had been attached to the front of Eve's purse and when pulled free it exposed a strong adhesive. The door closed, but the lock did not engage.

Eve gave in to the moment, having some fun. Mandy could kiss. And she knew how to touch. Eve liked the feeling of the woman's clever hands running all over her. Being with another woman was a rare thing for her, and it had been a very long time since there was one who seemed to understand the art. Her nerve endings were springing alive and warmth flooded her loins. Her nipples were stiff as dagger points and Eve could feel her heart revving up.

It was such a shame it had to end. She wished she'd arranged for Adam to wait a bit longer. Twenty minutes. Maybe half an hour. More.

But . . .

"I'm really enjoying the living hell out of this."

His voice was like a stab through the heart. Too soon. Damn. Too soon.

Mandy shoved Eve away from her and was up on her feet, quick as a cat, eyes flashing, teeth bared.

"Who the fuck are you?" she growled.

Adam leaned against the doorframe, then closed it behind him. Eve heard the click—proof he'd removed the plastic.

"I'd like to talk about our Lord and Savior," said Adam. "Have you talked to Jesus today?"

Mandy moved. Much faster than Eve expected. She was in motion without tensing first, with zero trace of hesitation. She flung herself at Adam with a very sophisticated Thai boxing kick. Adam was very fast himself, but he was not expecting this. The kick caught him in the balls with enough force to fold him in half. Mandy whirled, pulling a black metal cylinder from her pocket. At first Eve thought it was a gun or knife, but Mandy flicked her wrist and several telescoping sections snapped out and locked into place. It was an ASP, a collapsible truncheon. She whipped it across Adam's head, and he managed to duck enough to take it on the skull instead of across the face, but the impact dropped him onto his side. He lay there, his face turning a dreadful purple, while Mandy stalked forward toward Eve.

"I got them," she said aloud. "All units move in."

And then Eve understood. Mandy was a cop and this was a setup and they were well and truly fucked.

Mandy pointed with the ASP. "On your knees, fingers laced and on your head, do it now or I'll knock those pretty little teeth all over the—"

There was a blur of movement behind her that Eve did not quite understand. The door—the locked door—swung open and a dark shape seemed to flow into the room, closing behind Mandy with incredible speed. The cop gave a sudden grunt and her eyes went wide, then her knees buckled. There were several wet whispery sounds as the figure stabbed her over and over again. Then the woman was falling, eyes glazing, mouth coughing blood with a terminal exhalation of surrender and surprise.

The shadowy figure was a man, dressed in black clothes except for a red bow tie. He had a swarthy face and very dark eyes that seemed to glitter like polished onyx.

"They're coming," he said in a heavily accented voice. "You want to live, yes? Then pick up the boy and follow me."

He turned and ran into the hall.

Adam was fighting his way to his feet, but he was a wreck. Blood dripped down his right cheek and he wheezed like a dying drunk. Eve grabbed one arm and pulled him into the hall, following the man in black. They followed him into a stairwell, went down only one floor, exited into a hall and then into another suite. The man locked the door, set the restraining lever in place, and held a finger to his lips.

Adam sank down onto a chair. Eve stood beside him. The man, who was short and looked as wiry strong as a cat, stayed by the door. No one moved for nearly half an hour.

"Why'd you help us?" groaned Adam.

"I've had my eye on you," he said. His accent was Spanish. Cultured and interesting.

Eve tensed. "Why?"

"You've been noticed," he said. "You impress me. Well, maybe not tonight, but everyone has a bad day."

"But—" began Adam, but they heard footsteps in the hall.

"What happens if they knock on the door?" asked Eve when the sound faded. "What if they do a room-to-room search?"

"Then the fire alarm will go off," said the man.

"That's an old trick. They'll think it's just a dodge."

"Not if the building is burning," he said. He smiled, and it was the kind of smile that told Eve and Adam that he wasn't joking.

That was how they met Daddy.

CHAPTER FIFTY-ONE
GAEGULI SEOM
EIGHTEEN NAUTICAL MILES WEST OF NORTH KOREA
SEA OF JAPAN

By the time we'd collected everything—including samples of soil, well water, air, plants, feces from outhouses, items of clothing, and a mile-long list of items—the sun was well up in the sky. Despite the time of year the heat was frying us. Hammer Suits are built for a certain level of comfort and we'd crossed that bridge hours back. Oh yeah, and it's not like we could duck into the bushes, drop trou, and take a comfortable deuce. Everything had to be done in the suit. So, yeah, good times.

"Done here," said Bunny, who was the last of us to check everything off his list.

Ho came over and through the clear visor I could see the sweat running down his face. He looked overheated and weary. Not sure if he was scared or sad, though. Hard guy to read. Wouldn't want to play poker with him.

"The helicopter is on its way," he said.

"Good."

He started to turn away, paused, looked at me, seemed to think better of it, and began again to move off.

"What is it?" I asked.

Ho stopped and this time turned slowly. Then he reached up and tapped the control on the helmet that deactivated the helmet coms from the team network. It was just him speaking to me, and the suit muffled his voice a bit. I hit my own mic.

"Outlaw," he said, "I need to have a conversation with you, but I don't know if I can trust you."

"I thought you got a thumbs-up about me."

"You're American; I'm from the Democratic People's Republic of Korea. My father wasn't even born when the Fatherland Liberation War ended in a cease-fire in 1953."

"Same here," I said.

"Neither of us have lived in a world where our countries did not hate and distrust each other, and there is no end in sight. Our nations might as well live on different planets. There are so few commonalities."

"We both love our countries," I suggested.

Ho nodded. "We do. And I'd like to think we are both adult enough to accept that neither nation is perfect. All political rhetoric aside."

"With you so far."

"The nature of this operation—covert and very much off the official books—suggests that some cooler heads in both of our governments don't want another war."

"Again, no argument."

He nodded to the drone. "Do you know what will happen if we take that drone apart and find proof that it was manufactured in the United States?"

"I have a pretty good idea," I said, "but even if it has a big grinning picture of Uncle Sam stamped inside I'm not sure that proved anything. We export a lot of commercial drones. Second only to Japan in volume. And, hell, China manufactures a lot of the drones we sell."

"It wasn't Chinese soldiers on the beach in that video."

I shook my head. "America has its issues, like every other country, but I can't see the win in us doing this. It's too big, too obvious, and too clumsy."

"Unless it's not," said Ho. "We haven't actually taken the machine apart yet. It may have no identifying numbers or marks at all."

"What exactly are you saying?" I asked.

Ho glanced around nervously, and his eyes lingered on Sergeant Chung, who was working diligently about two hundred yards away.

"There are a lot of ways this points directly and *indirectly* at America," Ho said, leaning close so that he could be heard through the masks we both wore. "And a strong case is being made that this is your military. Even without the video of the SEALs, your own people said that this looks like a Boeing design. Granted, a commercial agricultural model, but that only makes it worse. If we *did not* have the video but did find the drone, the connection to America would be made. The use of a nonmilitary drone for something like this supports the natural supposition that the people responsible did not want it traced to the U.S. military. By itself, that would create doubt, and doubt, reasonable or not, is all that's really needed for saber-rattling to become drawn swords. Do you follow?"

"Yes," I said.

"That fact, plus the gravity of mass murder," continued Ho, "would result—no, *will* result—in an immediate and dangerous escalation of tensions between our nations. Even if we bury the video, that drone will be enough. There will be blood. Now, add the video to it, and *reasonable* doubt is gone. This becomes an irrefutable act of aggression that can only lead to some kind of open conflict."

"That's what we're trying to avoid, Painkiller."

"I know, and I want to assure you that *we* are trying to avoid it. You and me. All of us." He paused. "Look, let me say this. I love my country. The people, our heritage. I chose my profession to serve my country, to protect it." He pointed to where the drone lay, bagged and tagged. "That machine is worse than any nuclear bomb. Its very

JONATHAN MABERRY

existence threatens my country. We are not strong enough to fight America. Everyone knows that. We should not try and fight anyone. Yes, we could inflict great harm on our cousins in the south and on Japan, but in any open shooting war we would be destroyed. Or, we would be consumed by China, who would step in and protect its 'younger brother' state. And, as in the 1950s, North and South Korea would become a wasteland of blood and smoke where China and America fought without openly declaring war on each other. My people would suffer and die. A lot of people would die. The region would become completely unstable. Other countries would suffer. No one would win."

I understood now why he'd disconnected from the team channel. "You're not wrong," I said.

"Tell me, Outlaw," said Ho, "did you see any obvious damage on that drone?"

"No, I did not."

"No. It was in an alley tangled in fishing nets. We are, I think, meant to infer that it flew low, perhaps discharging its payload, then became tangled in those nets and crashed."

"Which seems like a big pile of convenient horseshit," I suggested.

He managed a small smile at that. "A very big pile."

We stood there, feeling the intense heat of what Ho was saying, and implying.

"We're working on preventing that video from leaking," I said.

"That is good," he said, his smile becoming rueful. "Do you think you will be successful?"

"Too soon to tell," I admitted, "but our people are good. The best. If it can be done, then they'll do it."

"That is something. A step in the right direction," said Ho. "But . . . I fear that the existence of the drone is what you would call a smoking gun."

"Yes, it is."

We stood looking at the drone and there was a whole lot more conversation going on that wasn't said out loud. After a while Ho said, "I am not a religious man. Not at all. However, I pray that your country did not do this."

"I'm praying pretty damn hard myself, brother," I told him.

There was a moment of silence between us that could have—hell, *should* have—been awkward. But it wasn't. It was sad, though, because we'd found some solid common ground and as close as we stood, the realities were that there were ten million miles between us.

I suddenly heard Bunny yelling. "*Havoc, Havoc,* we have a live one."

We all turned to see a small figure come walking out of the jungle. It was a little girl, maybe six years old, wearing torn clothing that was stained dark with blood. Her black hair hung in sweaty rattails.

And she was *alive*.

CHAPTER FIFTY-TWO
GAEGULI SEOM
EIGHTEEN NAUTICAL MILES WEST OF NORTH KOREA
SEA OF JAPAN

Sergeant Chung was closest to the girl and he brought his rifle up quick as lightning. Andrea and Bunny were nearby and they rushed in on either side, but Top barked them down.

"Nobody touch nothing," he roared in his leather-throated drill-sergeant's voice.

The child stood there, looking scared and confused. She was filthy and disheveled. Flies and gnats swarmed around her. She was covered in mud and blood, but apart from bruises on her cheek there were no visible wounds. She squinted as she looked around as if trying to understand what she was seeing. As if her eyes were bad and she didn't have her glasses.

"She does not look hurt," said Chung, speaking in Korean.

"Do not, I repeat *do not*, touch her," warned Top.

But Chung slowly knelt a few yards away, shifting the barrel of his rifle away and holding out a hand. Not beckoning to her, but instead showing his palm. Maybe he was trying to get her to stop

where she was, or maybe he wanted her to see that the hand he offered was not the one holding a gun. Not sure.

"Damn it, Jeeves," said Top, moving toward him. "Step away
from her. Do it now."

Jeeves ignored him. Top was ten yards away from the little girl.
Bunny and Andrea were about as far and their weapons were aimed
at the small figure. The little girl looked at each of them, still squint-
ing as if trying to make sense of the blurry shapes. Her mouth was
slack, lips apart, and tear tracks had cut through the blood and grime
on her face.

She said a single word, soft and tentative. *"Abeoji."* Korean for
Papa. Her voice was thin and full of cracks. And it came close to
breaking my heart.

"It's okay," said Chung to her. "Shhh, shhhh, it's okay, little one."

The girl turned toward the sound of his voice and the expression
on her face changed. Became sharper.

"Careful," said Ho.

"I think it is okay, sir," said Chung, smiling, "she seems to be im-
mune."

And she ran at him.

We were all expecting it. All of us. Every gun was on her. We'd
seen this in a hundred horror movies. It always ended this way. It
was fucking cliché, for Christ's sake.

But she was *fast*.

She was so goddamn fast.

The girl leaped like a cat, eyes flaring with madness, fingers
hooked into claws, small teeth snapping. Chung tried to bring his
gun up in time. But there was no time. She slammed into the sergeant's chest, and you would not think a body that small could hit
with such force, but it was backed by a terrifying level of savagery, of
fury.

Of rage.

Top fired. So did Bunny. Chung fell back and her hands clawed at
his visor even as the bullets punched through her and splashed her
blood into the air, onto the leaves of a small tree, all over Bunny. She
collapsed down, dead, the engine of murderous intent switched off

in a heartbeat. We all ran forward, clustered around Chung, pulling the girl's tiny body away.

Ho made a sound that was half laugh, half sob because the girl hadn't torn Chung's suit, she hadn't bitten him. None of that.

No.

But Chung lay there with his visor knocked askew. Not much. An inch. Less. A half inch.

"No . . . ," he breathed, but he did not move. Terror welded him to the spot.

Top leaned in fast and slapped at the visor, smacking it into place. Bunny pulled a roll of duct tape from his pack, ready to repair damage. There was none to repair. It had just been that momentary, tiny gap.

A flicker of time.

Chung lay there, frozen and confused. "I am okay," he said. In Korean and then in English. "I'm okay. I'm fine. She did not get me."

We all knelt or stood around him and slowly, one by one, we turned our guns toward him.

"N—no . . . ," he said. He held up his hands, then plucked at the fabric of his suit to prove to us that he was okay. "Please," he begged.

"Bunny," I said, and the big man moved in, kicking Chung's rifle away. He grabbed the sergeant, half-lifted him, spun him, and then slammed him roughly to the dirt. Chung kept protesting. He tried to fight, to fend Bunny off, but it was no contest. Bunny hit him with a two-knuckle punch between the shoulder blades that knocked words and breath and protests from Chung's mouth.

"Nothing personal, brother," said Bunny.

Top handed him zip ties and before Chung could recover, Bunny had his wrists and ankles bound. Even then the Korean sergeant tried to fight, but Bunny pinched the back of the man's neck and bent close. His words actually went through the team intercom, but Bunny still leaned close to Chung's ear. "You need to stop fighting me, dude," he said. "It's this way or we bag and tag you with a bullet in your brainpan. You make the call."

Chung fought. For a few seconds. Then he sagged down and began to weep.

JONATHAN MABERRY

Bunny knelt then, keeping him down but easing the pressure of his pinch.

Top was looking at the clock on his forearm computer. Timing this. If Chung was going to turn, we needed to know how fast.

Chung lay still.

For ten more seconds.

Then his whole body bucked. It was so abrupt, so incredibly strong a spasm that Bunny was knocked back, losing his grip.

I wouldn't have thought it possible for a man bound like that to get to his feet. It was weird, unnatural, but he rose up like some kind of cobra, every muscle trembling, his eyes wild, and in those eyes no trace of the man he'd been was visible. He had become something else. There was a look of such deep, unfiltered, total hatred in his eyes that we all recoiled. He lunged forward and smashed his helmeted head into Andrea's, knocking the small man back. Andrea fell, losing his weapon and clamping his hands to his visor. Screaming with fear.

Then Chung tried the same thing with Top.

But Top had already shaken off the surprise and he moved into the lunge, twisting as he did so, and smashed Chung across the ear with a crushing forearm. It was an ox-killer of a blow, and if Chung hadn't still been wearing his helmet it would have ended him. As it was it dropped him as quickly and surely as a bullet. The sergeant landed on his side, eyes rolling high, the madness fleeing as he slipped into unconsciousness.

Bunny and I dropped to our knees beside Andrea, pulling at his hands to assess the damage. The heavy plastic visor was cracked, but it wasn't broken. Bunny had the duct tape out and as I held Andrea, he crisscrossed the visor with the waterproof—and air-proof—tape.

Ho stood watching, his gun pointed down. I pivoted on my knees. "Move that barrel right goddamn now."

Ho hesitated and I slapped the barrel high and left, and then Belle was there, coming out of nowhere. She kicked Ho in the back of the knees, and as he dropped she slap-turned him and took his rifle away, handing it to me. Then she straddled him and suddenly her fighting knife was in her hand. Belle took a fistful of cloth in one hand and laid the razor-sharp edge against it.

"Do I cut?" she asked in a voice that was eerily calm.

Ho froze. Not even sure he breathed.

"Stay," ordered Belle. Then to Bunny, she said, "Cuffs."

Bunny produced more zip ties, but instead of cuffing Ho, he cinched them securely around Andrea's wrists and ankles, and for good measure he hogtied him, rolling him onto his stomach and using a third zip tie to connect wrists to ankles. If Andrea turned, he would not be attacking anyone.

"Sorry, brother," he said, and laid a palm flat on Andrea's shoulder.

Top looked at his timer.

"How long?" I asked.

"Jeeves was thirteen seconds," said Top.

We waited. I heard Andrea praying. Not in Italian but in Latin. An old-fashioned prayer to the Virgin Mary. Ho stayed where he was because Belle did not move that knife. The moment seemed to stretch, to pull so tight the world had to break.

"Twelve," said Top, measuring it out in a slow, steady voice. "Thirteen, fourteen, fifteen . . ."

He counted all the way to thirty.

To sixty.

Andrea kept praying.

When Top counted his way through two full minutes, I said, "Belle."

She unclenched her fist and smoothed the material of Ho's suit, gave him a little pat, then stepped back. She did not put the knife away. Nor did she apologize.

We stood there, waiting. Four minutes. Five. No one said a goddamn word until ten full minutes passed. I tapped back into the TOC.

"How are his numbers?"

"Pulse is off the charts," said Doc, "but that's consistent with being scared out of his goddamn mind. Your own pulse is just as high."

"No shit," I said.

Mr. Church spoke quietly, "Jackpot stays bound. Prepare for exfil. This mission is over."

It sounded great. Those were the words we wanted to hear. Even though we all knew—every single one of us—that it was not true.

Whatever this was had just begun.

JONATHAN MABERRY

CHAPTER FIFTY-THREE
PHOENIX HOUSE
OMFORI ISLAND
GREECE

His name was Jerome Leroy Williams, but known to everyone as Bug. Even his mother used to call him that. His smiling face filled the big screen in Mr. Church's office.

"What have you got for me?" asked Church. He was nibbling a vanilla wafer. A silver plate of them sat beside his laptop.

"Been playing with the videos and having some fun."

"Define 'fun.'"

Bug had Coke-bottle glasses and very long hair that he'd recently started wearing in long twists with a sculpted fade. The T-shirt he wore had a Photoshopped picture of him and Lupita Nyong'o getting married, with T'Challa presiding.

"I ran the video of the ROK guys and the SEALs through a bunch of filters and came up with something cool," said Bug. "I isolated a track that I think is the sound of the person taking the video breathing. From the degree of hiss distortion it sounds like the person is breathing right next to a long-distance mic. Trying not to be heard, but it's a good mic if it picked up conversation from the beach. Listen."

He played the track and Church closed his eyes. "Play it again," he said. When it was finished, he opened his eyes and said, "It's a woman."

"Yup. The timbre rings the bells as female, and my sound guys all tell me that she's probably young. Late teens to early thirties. Want me to explain how they came up with that?"

"No. What else do you have?"

"There's a second breathing pattern that's also close, but not as close, to the mic. A guy, maybe the same age or a little older. Stronger breath and more controlled. Less stress in the rhythm." He played it, and Church nodded.

"This is good."

"There's more." Bug was clearly very happy. He loved his job, and it showed. When he was a teenager Bug got into trouble for hacking his school's computer . . . and then he compounded it by hacking Homeland, the CIA, and several branches of military intelligence. Bug had been trying to find Bin Laden. Church offered him a choice between prison or a chance to work with the world's most sophisticated computer system to do some measurable good. Some years later Bug actually helped locate Osama bin Laden in Pakistan. Proof that all he needed was the right computer. That system was one owned exclusively by Church. MindReader.

The MindReader system was designed to intrude into virtually any kind of computer, bypassing security and rewriting the target computer's software to erase all traces of the hack. All other intrusion computers leave a scar, but MindReader does not. Over the years, Bug upgraded the system several times. Most recently merging it with the first truly workable quantum computer, and backed that up with the Calpurnia artificial intelligence software system. The result is a computer, now called MindReader Q1, that works faster than anyone else's by a couple of orders of magnitude.

"I tore the Punk Press thing apart," said Bug. "They were very, very careful to hide the location of where it was sent from. There are some scrambler devices on the market—well, mostly the *black* tech market—that use cyclical 128-bit coding algorithms to bounce everything around so much the source gets buried in its own back trail."

"But . . . ?" prompted Church.

"Well, if this was the only time Punk Press sent out one of these emails then we'd be nowhere. You can't find a pattern from a single instance."

Church chewed his cookie and waited.

"What I did is search for all Punk Press uploads across the Net and the Darknet, and came up with one hundred and fifty-four separate posts." Bug took a sip from a can of Monster. "The first few posts were less well concealed. I mean, they fooled Interpol, and some white hat hackers hired to track it down, but . . . y'know . . . this is me. I tore apart the emails and put Q1 on a pattern search and found the original sixteen-digit computer ID for the sender. The ID tagged the machine as a Dell XPS 13, which is one of the most popular models sold in Malaysia. Now, I know you'll say that model is sold in a lot of countries, but when we backtracked those first messages, there were three with source points at cybercafes in Kuala Lumpur. So, we have four uploads with computer IDs from popular laptops in Malaysia and three actual posts sent from Kuala Lumpur. All seven of those are the seven original posts by Punk Press." Bug shrugged. "After that they got tricky, but I'd bet my mint issue of Fantastic Four number fifty-two, signed by Stan Lee, that one or both of the people doing the heavy breathing on the video are from Malaysia."

"Good work, Bug," said Church, meaning it.

"No, wait, there's more," said Bug happily. "I also had some fun with the email sent to the South Korean ambassador. They used a scrambler on that, too, but it's a different model. Pretty sure it's one of the portable kind that a lot of these WikiLeaks wannabes have been using. Good, but not good enough."

Church tapped crumbs off his cookie. "Stop showing off, Bug, and tell me what you found."

Bug was completely unabashed. "That email did *not* come from Malaysia. I did some noodling, ran a few of my special programs, and I can say with like a ninety-nine percent certainty that it came from South Korea."

"That is not happy news, Bug."

"Not as such, no, but I've been able to eliminate the possibility that it was sent from any of the military bases there. They have uniquely configured firewalls and—"

"Can you find out from *where* in South Korea it was sent?"

"Maybe. I have it narrowed down to the Gyeongsangnam-do region."

"It's my belief that there are several million people living in that region, Bug," said Church.

"I'm working on narrowing it down," said Bug. "It takes time."

"Time is not our friend," said Church.

"I might do better on the ground there. I can take a team and we can—"

"Go," said Church.

Bug grinned and was gone.

CHAPTER FIFTY-FOUR
THE LAB
IN INTERNATIONAL WATERS
TWENTY-FIVE NAUTICAL MILES FROM NORTH KOREA
SEA OF JAPAN

The barge was big and flat and full of people who looked like the Stay Puft Marshmallow Man from that old *Ghostbusters* movie. White or yellow hazmat suits, each with its own air tanks. Lots of bulky equipment. Lots of people with guns, too. And four tower-mounted flamethrowers aimed at a dedicated quarantine space on one end.

The exfiltration chopper had been a bulky Chinook that lowered a metal box like a shipping container. We could not risk using the RHIB to come out here because it couldn't be easily sterilized, so once we were all in the container and lifting off, I triggered its self-destruct mechanism. It's now a lump of unidentifiable slag.

The container they lowered was, in fact, a high-end biohazard unit. We put the zippered corpses into a cold box, and put Sergeant Chung and a very nervous Andrea into isolation cubicles. The drone was isolated in a big plastic box. Havoc Team was strapped into seats with our Hammer Suits on and sealed, while the Chinook flew us to the barge. No one spoke much, though I switched to a secure channel directly to the TOC. Because the hoods of the Hammer Suits are not completely soundproof, I was careful about what I said, and mostly gave them observer's impressions to enhance the telemetry and video feeds from the drones.

On the other hand, Doc and Church were free to be as chatty as they wanted. For Church, that wasn't very much. Doc, on the other hand, is a horse of a different color. She asked about a thousand questions. She asked about skin color and lividity for both the dead and the little girl prior to her death. She had me verify that the girl spoke. This seemed to bother her quite a lot, and she asked me to go over the scene moment by moment.

"It was all on the video," I said. "You can watch the playback."

"You were on the ground, honey-cheeks," she said. Doc is like that. She is about a standard light-year away from being politically correct, and yet her comments never felt all that insulting. Not sure why. I'd need to get Rudy to decode it for me. "Tell it to me the way *you* saw it. Give me all of it, darlin'. Put me in the moment."

And so I did.

I closed my eyes and was back there on the village street, and I told her everything. She did not interrupt. When I was done, she let out a long, sad sigh.

"I'll get back to you," she said, unhelpfully.

I omitted the conversation I'd had with Ho. That would be something to share with Church later on.

The Chinook lowered the biohazard unit onto the barge with only a mild thump, then dropped the cables and flew off. The WHO team, supplemented by hot zone veterans from all four countries, closed around us, blasting the outside of the unit with high-pressure sprays that were designed to kill any living thing, even prions, which are notoriously hard to kill. Then they connected hoses to ports and flooded the inside of the unit with a gas mixture that would do the same. If we weren't sealed into our suits we'd have died along with the viruses, bacteria, fungi, and other unwanted travelers.

They coupled a flexible plastic tunnel to the airlock, sealed it, sprayed the seal, and signaled us to disarm the inside security locks. We walked through the tunnel into a holding chamber that had sanitation cubicles for each of us. They sprayed and sprayed and sprayed, and then we stripped down to our skin and they sprayed us some more. Although I could hear the sprays hitting the other Havoc team members in adjoining cubicles, it somehow made me feel incredibly alone. Maybe this is what it felt like to go through decontamination on the International Space Station. It was not a comforting feeling in any way.

Everything I wore, including all of my equipment, went into a small container that had automatic locks. It sank into the floor for conveyor-belt transport to a holding area. Later it would be studied—as everything was studied—to isolate whatever pathogen caused this. And after that, the stuff would likely be incinerated.

I put on the clothes they left for me—underwear and coveralls made from some kind of plastic that was supposed to feel like soft cotton, but which utterly failed to do so.

Weirdly, they piped music into the cubicle the whole time. Smooth jazz. I'm not sure if it was intended to soothe the nerves, but if I had a hammer I'd have smashed the shit out of the speakers.

It took two and a half hours before they let us out.

A lot can happen in so short a space of time.

CHAPTER FIFTY-FIVE
GOSEONG DINOSAUR MUSEUM
618 JARANMAN-RO, HAI-MYEON
GOSEONG-GUN
GYEONGSANGNAM-DO, SOUTH KOREA

Ainil Tan finished her work for the museum, then spent another hour checking all of the news services for some word of the massacre on Gaeguli Seom. There was nothing on the Net. She engaged her scrambler and accessed the dark web.

That was always a risk.

The dark web was invisible to most of the World Wide Web. Its contents were not indexed by any standard search engines. You had to know how to find specific sites in order to get anywhere, and those HTTP forms were carefully masked. The sites she wanted were also hidden behind paywalls, but Ainil had enough cryptocurrency stored to pay the fees. She'd earned some of the digital funds by selling information on the Silk Road online black market. Her goods were not drugs, which is what comprised most of the commodities sold on Silk Road, but bulk data stolen from corrupt businesses. Data was currency in her world.

She entered the right passwords and went through some verification steps and then she was in. There was one very useful site called RatNest, which was wired in to channels used by the CIA, Interpol, and other groups. She posted some vaguely worded questions, asking if anything juicy was happening in the 2Ks—shorthand for North and South Korea—but there was nothing newer than sixty-one hours ago, and that was a nothing thing about a defector claiming he had photographic proof of human rights violations. Nothing that related to the Island of Frogs.

She chewed her lip. Was no news a good thing? Did that mean the ambassador was actually working on this? Trying to put the pin back into the grenade, so to speak? Or had she been naïve and helped the South Koreans and Americans cover up a crime?

CHAPTER FIFTY-SIX
THE LAB
TWENTY-FIVE NAUTICAL MILES FROM NORTH KOREA
SEA OF JAPAN

I learned that the barge was nicknamed simply The Lab. Bet it took a committee six weeks and a few hundred emails to come up with that.

Dr. John Cmar, the director of the floating team of mad scientists, was a thin, angular guy with steel-rim glasses, a black ponytail and short beard. He looked like the kind of cool professor kids would relate to in college, but there was a cold anger in his eyes if you looked close. He's seen firsthand some of the horrors that governments, terrorist groups, and rogue scientists have cooked up as WMDs, and he's worked on a bunch of DMS cases that had broken his heart and stoked his fury.

When he saw me come out of my sterilization cubicle he smiled and came forward, offering his hand—not to shake, but as a fist bump. Guys who work around diseases tend to go for the more antiseptic bump.

"Tell me you've already figured this out," I said, "and that there's an easy cure that will allow me and my guys to go home, drink beer, get laid, and be happy."

John pursed his lips and gave me a long, assessing look then pretended to dictate examination notes. "So, the patient presented with symptoms consistent with delusional behavior. Possibly a deep-seated psychosis. I'm recommending heavy doses of clozapine and four-point restraints."

"I'm a living weapon, you know," I said. "My hands are knives, my legs are swords. I could chop you into sushi."

"I could have you locked in the quarantine cube for seventy two hours, and pipe in nothing but Nickleback's greatest hits," he countered.

"Touché."

"Come on, I have coffee," said John, gesturing to a structure like a double-wide trailer at the far end of the barge. "And it's real coffee, too, not the . . . wait, what is it you call decaf?"

"Brown sadness water."

"Right. This is definitely not that."

And it wasn't. The coffee he brewed was so manly that halfway through my first cup I wanted to chop wood while wearing a checked flannel shirt. Rudy would have hated it.

The trailer was, in fact, a house trailer, bolted to the deck. Three others were set behind it, each marked as BSL-4—biosafety level 4, which was only used for the direst biological threats. Through the reinforced glass windows of those I could see technicians in hazmat suits. John led me to the only one marked with a much less scary BSL-1, two-thirds of which was a lab, with a cramped kitchen in the back.

"To answer your question, Joe," he said as he slid into the booth across from me, "no, we don't have an answer. I spoke at length with Doc Holliday. We have lots of theories but nothing concrete, which means we don't have a protocol. Not a ghost of one beyond erring on the side of maximum security precautions."

"You saw the video of how fast Sergeant Chung turned?"

"I did," John said, shaking his head. "I've never seen anything work that fast. Not even Seif al Din. It's freakishly fast, which is suggestive."

"Suggestive of what? That we're in the sequel to *28 Days Later*?"

"There already *was* a sequel to that," he said. "It sucked. No, what I mean is that it's suggestive of existing exposure. We're testing Chung now to see if he was previously exposed to something that was triggered on the island."

"Like the super-rabies thing?"

"Possibly."

"What about the drone?"

"I've got a team on that. Too risky to ship it to Doc Holliday until we know more. So far all we've determined is that it's a drone."

"Oh, very useful."

"We're doing metallurgic and materials testing. That may give us point of origin," said John. "As for the tank mounted beneath it . . . it's weird. It has a big fan behind a screen with a very tight mesh. Whatever was inside was clearly blown out through the tube mounted beneath. We don't know what was ejected, though, and unfortunately the tank is contaminated."

"By what?"

"Flies—nasty, persistent little bastards. The whole village was swarming with them. Drawn by the onset of decay, no doubt."

"Why would they climb into the tank?" I asked.

"We're working on that," he said. "Could be that there was some component in whatever was discharged that drew them. Something with a sugar base, perhaps. But that's just speculation, Joe. We don't really know anything."

"So," I said, "any horseback guess as to what we're dealing with?"

"Offhand?" mused John. "It beats the living shit out of me. It's not a drug, and so far we haven't found an active virus or bacterium. No mycotoxins, either. It acts like a chemical imbalance, but that's hard as hell to induce in a group of people. Age and gender differences alone make that tough, and besides, it acted on Sergeant Chung like something airborne. We are processing the samples and sharing that data with labs around the world. There are a lot of people working on this, Joe. And Doc Holliday has her people on it." He gave a wry chuckle. "I'm not actually sure there has *ever* been a larger or more aggressive coordination of medical research focused so quickly on a single biological threat."

"Church . . . ?" I suggested.

"Church."

We had more coffee. He opened a fridge and gave me a wrapped sandwich, which was supposed to be egg salad. It tasted like ass. We ate.

"How come it didn't register on the BAMS units?" I asked.

"Add that to the list of questions that need answering."

"Maybe it's not a virus," I suggested. "Maybe it's some kind of genetic stuff. Couldn't transgenics or CRISPR or that stuff make people go all wonky?"

He grinned. "God, I love it when you demonstrate your incisive grasp of the realities of science."

"Bite me. You're saying it's not that?"

"Genetic manipulation can accomplish significant changes, including radical behavioral changes, but not quickly. Not like this. Gene editing isn't something you can fit into a pill, Joe. So . . . no."

"What if it was some variation on the rabies thing? Genetic manipulation controlled by nanites?"

He was shaking his head before I even finished. "No. Not a chance. The speed of onset and the uniformity of reactions are the keys here, and right now they're not unlocking any useful doors."

"Well, fuck," I said.

"Without a doubt," he agreed.

"The one good thing . . . ," I began, then stopped and tried it a different way. "None of this is good, but the only thing that is the closest to a break we got here is that this happened on a tiny island far away from the mainland."

"How is that lucky? It seems obvious that this bioweapon was delivered *to* the island. Which means that someone has more of it."

"True, and my job will be to find those people," I said, "but it seems pretty obvious that the goal here is to either start a war or destabilize the region. They chose this place pretty carefully, knowing what the political ramifications would be. It could have been much worse."

"Or they were test-driving it," he suggested.

I shook my head. "You don't need a team of phony-baloney Navy SEALs for that. No, man, this was a strike. Deliberate, calculated, and successful."

John leaned back, sipping his coffee, and studied me with his dark eyes. Then he abruptly stood up.

"Then I'd better get back to work."

INTERLUDE TWELVE
HYATT REGENCY
1000 BOULEVARD OF THE ARTS
SARASOTA, FLORIDA
TEN MONTHS AGO

They sat together in the dark.

Adam and Eve snuggled together on a big chaise longue, and Daddy sat on a rattan chair with a huge fan back. The table between them was littered with wine bottles and glasses and spent joints in a ceramic dish. The boats in the marina thumped gently against their fenders. The staff left them alone because everyone who mattered on the night shift belonged to Daddy.

Eve said a name aloud. She said *his* name. Daddy's real name.

"Rafael Santoro." Eve pronounced each syllable, making the Spanish name seem wonderfully exotic. "Rafael Santoro."

"Yes," he said, beaming at her. And at Adam. "This is a great sign of my trust, yes? To know my name means that I indeed trust you. Do you understand?"

Adam licked his lips, then nodded. Eve continued to smile like a happy child on Christmas morning.

"And," continued Santoro, "I know *your* names. The ones you each left behind."

They nodded. It had terrified them when he first revealed that he'd managed to uncover what they each thought they'd erased from the world. At the same time it was somehow exciting that Daddy was that powerful, that smart. He *was* their father now.

"Will you tell us who Kuga is?" asked Eve.

Santoro pursed his lips, then shook his head. "That is not my secret to tell."

"But—"

"Besides, children, how do you know Kuga is a single person? He could be many men. Or women. He could be a thousand people all using that name."

"You called him 'he'," said Adam. "When you told us about him. You always use male pronouns."

Santoro gave a small shrug. "I could be saying that for convenience' sake. Or as a distraction. For all you know *I* could be Kuga."

They frowned. "But . . . you're not . . . ," said Eve slowly. "Are you?"

Santoro laughed. "No, my sweet girl, I am not. Kuga."

"When do we get to meet him?" asked Adam.

Daddy sipped his wine. "When and if he decides to allow it."

"Why's he so cagey, though?" complained Adam. "It's not like we're likely to tell anyone."

Daddy shrugged. "It isn't about what you will or won't do," he said. "It is all about what he wants."

"Well, if we're not going to meet him, then why are we here?" asked Eve.

"Ah," said Daddy, nodding as if it was the question he'd been waiting for. He reached into his jacket pocket and set two thumb drives on the table. It was a peculiar habit of his never to hand things directly to them. "You will find your next assignment on there. Details, identities, account numbers. Physical papers for travel will be delivered to you at the appropriate time."

"Travel?"

Daddy smiled. "Neither of you has ever been out of the country, yes? We will change that. There are some things you will need to do here in the States, and then you will take up residence in Tokyo."

"We're going to Japan . . . ?" said Eve, suddenly excited.

"Yes. Among other places. A language coach will be in touch. You will need to acquire some basic conversational Japanese and Korean. You will be diligent in your studies so that you will not disappoint me."

"I was never all that good with that stuff," said Eve. "They made me study French."

Daddy shrugged. "Whichever of you comes along most quickly will be the point person for certain aspects of the operation. The other will be backup and have other tasks."

"What's the operation?" asked Adam.

Daddy sipped his wine. "We're going to make a lot of people very angry," he said quietly.

CHAPTER FIFTY-SEVEN
YEONPYEONG ISLAND
SOUTH KOREA

Tony Kim loved the place. Yeonpyeong Island had history, it had drama. It was going to make a hell of a location for his movie.

"It's frigging gorgeous," he kept saying. To his location scout, to the cinematographer, and to the scriptwriter. None of them were Korean. None of them thought the place was exceptionally pretty. Or interesting. Or convenient. Tony figured that you had to have Korean blood to have the right kind of insight.

"It's less than three square miles big," said the location scout, named Hector, a mousy little guy who looked like Peter Lorre, except that no one knew who Peter Lorre was anymore. That broke Tony's heart, because Peter Lorre would have loved this place, too.

"It's self-contained," said Tony.

"It's a fucking shoebox," complained Hector. "How do you expect me to find enough location angles to make this look like Seoul?"

"Meh. We'll green-screen some of it if we have to."

The screenwriter rubbed his fingers together in the time-honored way that indicated money. He did it every time Tony made a suggestion like that. Somewhere back in L.A. a line producer was breaking out in hives because shooting here was going to pop the cherry on the budget. Which was the opposite of the actual point. The reason they weren't shooting on the mainland was the skyrocketing cost. Yeonpyeong was supposed to be much cheaper, which would allow them to put more cash into casting and special effects. CGI dinosaurs did not come cheap. Not good ones, anyway. And they wanted someone topping the credits who the general public had at least *heard* of. A solid B-lister, but someone who'd won an award for something somewhere. Like Cuba Gooding, Jr., who had an Oscar. It would allow Tony to shout the phrase "Academy Award winner" in the press releases for the rest of his life.

That was the plan. The screenwriter, Noah Bixby, was trying to hold onto his optimism that there was at *least* a Cuba Gooding, Jr. still in the budget. His optimism kept slipping gears, though.

They were tooling around in a golf cart owned by the board of tourism. Said board shared a storefront with the post office and a little company that wrote copy for mainland tourist brochures. They had only the one golf cart and it looked to be about forty years old. For some reason no one could adequately explain, it had a picture of Donald Duck on the hood. Not a drawing—an actual photograph of someone dressed as Donald Duck. The picture was affixed to the hood with some kind of decoupage.

"The people are nice, though," said Gerhardt, the cinematographer, who was a cheerful German with a shaved head and twinkling blue eyes. He was one of those people who smiled at everyone and everything. Tony loved him for that; but the location scout suspected Gerhardt's optimism came out of a pill bottle. Whatever. Gerhardt was an artist. The documentary he showed at Tribeca won awards. The indie films he did with Julie Delpy had everyone crying at Sundance. Granted, those flicks made pocket change in limited runs in a few art houses, but they were art. Real art.

Now Gerhardt was here to film *Koreanosaurus*. And if Noah Bixby wasn't Derek Connolly or Jordan Peele, then who cared? He could write his ass off.

They rolled along the streets in the golf cart, sometimes doubling back so Hector could take some digital shots of good angles. He liked acting as his own location scout and often micromanaged the cinematography. He was everywhere, clicking pictures. The locals watched, amused. Everyone knew who they were and why they were here. It was no secret. Everyone liked the idea of American dollars flooding into the economy.

Hector slapped at a biting fly on his forearm. "Got these little bastards to deal with, too," he complained.

"Stop bitching," said Noah. "Shoot a film in goddamn Alaska and then you can talk. They got mosquitoes up there who'll pick you up and carry you off."

"Yeah, yeah, whatever."

"Hey," said Gerhardt, "can we stop for some lunch? I'm dying for some kimchi. We just passed a place."

Hector tapped his wristwatch and said, "Light's going to be different by the time we're done."

"So what?" said Gerhardt. "We're not actually filming, man. And I'm hungry. Tony, Noah . . . what about you guys?"

"I could eat," said Noah. "You good, Tony?"

Tony, though, was looking at something across the street. "That's weird," he said.

"What?" asked Gerhardt, scanning the street to find the restaurant.

"Look at that kid."

"What kid?" asked Hector, who was still focused on finding locations and wasn't really looking.

"What's wrong with him?" said Tony.

"Mm?" murmured Hector distractedly. He had a small lens with a frame inside so he could view the street as it might appear on the screen. By adjusting it he could tighten focus. Maybe this wouldn't suck too bad. It was pretty, after all.

"Jesus Christ," cried Gerhardt.

Hector looked up, annoyed, as Noah stopped the golf cart with a jerk.

"The hell, man . . . ?"

His words trailed off into nothing, because nothing he could say would make sense of the moment.

Across the street, a few doors from the noodle shop, was a boy. Ten or eleven. Dressed in jeans and a Ninja Turtles T-shirt. He was eating something that looked like a big, sloppy sandwich. Something covered in too much hot sauce.

Except.

That wasn't what it was.

Hector and Tony, Noah and Gerhardt all knew it wasn't. But none of them could force themselves to accept what it was. Because this was the real world and what they were looking at belonged to the kind of movies they made. Monster movies. Horror flicks.

"No," said Noah.

"God," said Gerhardt.

Hector turned aside and vomited into the street.

Tony Kim just sat and stared.

The boy held an arm. Forearm and what was left of a hand. Tony couldn't process it. He could not even blink. This wasn't special effects.

This wasn't a rubber prop smeared with food coloring, corn syrup, and chocolate sauce. This wasn't that.

This.

Wasn't.

That.

What made it worse, what made it impossible, was that people walked past him and did not even glance his way. As if the child and his grisly feast existed in some parallel dimension; as if it was on a TV screen in a Best Buy and they were shopping for something else.

That rooted them all to their seats.

It was wrong in more ways than Tony Kim could calculate.

"I don't . . . ," began Hector. "I don't—"

He didn't finish his sentence. Because in the very next second he screamed as Gerhardt, still smiling, leaned over and took a big red bite out of Hector's cheek. He did it suddenly. His shriek was so sharp, so loud, so awful that it froze the whole street for one moment.

Then the passersby seemed to be punched out of their mute indifference to what was happening. They stopped and turned. Not toward the boy but toward the men in the golf cart. Noah and Tony were shocked to immobility. Hector shrieked and Gerhardt, no longer smiling, began punching him. Short, hard, vicious punches. To the face, the throat, the eye, the chest. The skin on Gerhardt's fists ruptured and burst. The bones in his hands cracked and shattered. He kept punching though.

Which is when all of the people on the street threw back their heads and screamed. Like a flock of furious birds. Like a pack of hyenas.

High, throat-ripping shrieks of pure, unfiltered, towering fury.

Then they broke into a run. One moment they were still and the next instant they were in full, mad flight, tearing across the street toward the golf cart. Tony and Noah did not try to run. Noah didn't start the cart.

No, because by then they were screaming, too.

In madness.

In rage.

YEONPYEONG ISLAND, SOUTH KOREA

PART FOUR

Hell has three gates: Lust, anger, and greed.

—THE BHAGAVAD GITA

CHAPTER FIFTY-EIGHT
SACHEON AIRPORT
GYEONGSANGNAM-DO, SOUTH KOREA

"Mister . . . ah . . . Bug . . . ?"

The woman wore an official uniform and a tentative smile.

"Just Bug."

They stood on a windy tarmac. The woman met him at the foot of the jet's fold-down stairs. Two hulking soldiers stood by an SUV parked forty feet away.

She introduced herself as Lieutenant Annie Han and stuck out a hand and Bug shook it. He figured she had to be at least in her early twenties to have an officer's rank in the Republic of Korea army, but Han looked like she was fourteen. Tiny body, huge eyes, and obvious nervousness.

"I'm honored to meet you, sir," she said as they walked toward the SUV.

"Really? Why?"

Han looked surprised. "You're *him*."

"Not following."

"You're Coal Tiger."

Bug jerked to a stop and cut her a sharp look. "What did you say?"

Han flushed a sudden and furious red. She leaned close and dropped her voice to a hushed and confidential tone. "On the Dark Web. You're Coal Tiger. I'm right, aren't I?"

"What makes you think that?"

"I . . . I've been studying you for years."

"Wait . . . what? Studying me?"

She shifted so that her back was to the male soldiers, and using one finger drew a small half circle in the air. An arc.

Which is when Bug understood. This young Korean soldier was more than that. She was Arklight.

"My musician friend told me about you," said Han. And that was another code. Musician. Violin.

Bug took a breath, then nodded. Very few people on earth knew about his Dark Web persona. Coal Tiger—a name drawn from Stan Lee and Jack Kirby's original name for the character who became the Black Panther.

"Okay," he said uneasily, "but let's not sling that name around too much, okay? Bug is fine."

"Sure, sorry," she said, but stared at him with a fangirl glow that made him deeply uncomfortable. It was the way *he* probably looked when he met the actors from that movie at a private party in Brentwood.

The soldiers opened the SUV doors. Once Bug and Han were settled in the backseat, she pushed a button that slid a heavy glass panel closed, sealing them in privacy.

"Soundproof," she said.

"You know I have to check you out, right?"

"Oh, sure." Han did not seem offended in any way.

Bug tapped his coms unit and cycled to a private channel. Mr. Church was waiting for him. Before Bug could even say much, Church said, "Lieutenant Han is in the family. Lilith gives her high marks, and she is very close friends with Violin."

"Okay," said Bug. "Good to know."

"Her computer skills are such that if you decide to hire her you have my full approval."

"Thanks."

He disconnected from the call, turned to Han, and smiled. "Have you seen the Punk Press video?"

"I have. And I was told that it was likely sent from here."

"Good," he said, "then let's get to work."

She nodded. "You're my hero, you know. I'm not joking. You're the absolute coolest of the cool."

Bug's face was suddenly hot as flame.

"Um," he mumbled. "Thanks . . ."

Han gave a musical laugh, punched him playfully on the arm, and pulled out her laptop.

JONATHAN MABERRY

CHAPTER FIFTY-NINE
THE LAB
TWENTY-FIVE NAUTICAL MILES FROM NORTH KOREA
SEA OF JAPAN

They let Andrea out of containment.

His blood work was clean. So were his brain scans, CT, MRI, X-rays, and urinalysis. The clincher was when Cmar's people tested his visor and determined that the cracks did not go all the way through. They tested it with gas, dyes, and high-pressure chemicals. The barrier between him and the pathogen was less than three one-hundredths of an inch.

"You better go to church," said Top. "Thank baby Jesus for protecting your ass."

Andrea snorted. "To hell with that," he said. "When we get back home I'm going to cash in my retirement funds and buy as many SuperEnalotto tickets as I can afford."

"Yeah," said Bunny, "that actually sounds like a good plan, because you are officially the luckiest motherfucker I've ever met."

He offered his fist and Andrea bumped it.

We all grinned at one another. Even Belle scowled less, which was her version of a smile.

Then John Cmar came pelting across the deck toward us, waving frantically.

"This is not going to be good," muttered Top.

It wasn't.

He yelled, "There's been another incident."

Andrea closed his eyes. "*Merda*," he groaned. "Say, *miei amici*, I'd be okay with going right back into isolation if it's all the same with you."

CHAPTER SIXTY
IN FLIGHT
OVER SOUTH KOREAN AIRSPACE

Yeonpyeong Island was on the other side of the Korean peninsula, which meant we had to get there asap. The Chinook that brought us was the fastest way of getting there. Those big birds have a top speed of 195 miles per hour, and 195 was about the distance between where The Lab floated and where the outbreak was happening.

However, we couldn't go straight to the island. All of our gear was contaminated, and the hazmat suits on The Lab were not suited for combat. We needed a full refit, but Church assured me that our logistics wizard, Bird Dog, was already at Osan. So we bundled into the Chinook and were wheels up before we'd finished buckling up. Ho wanted to come with us and I agreed.

Once we were in the air, though, I had to call Church to make sure he could finesse the clearance. The Big Man turned it over to Scott Wilson and before you could say "kiss my ass" it was done. Now . . . if everything in government could work with that kind of common sense efficiency we would be a happier species. Just saying.

I went into the back and had a private conference call with Doc, Bug—who was in another part of Korea—and Church. The Chinook didn't have an ORB function, so I put on VR goggles, and there they all were. Doc Holliday was dressed in a cowboy shirt that was about two sizes too small and embroidered with flowers and hummingbirds, bright blue horn-rimmed glasses, and shocking red lipstick. Her blond hair was piled high and there were a couple of novelty Harry Potter magic wands stuck in the bun. Don't ask. There was no humor or playfulness on her face, though. Beneath the makeup and concealer she was drawn and pale.

"Before you ask," she said, "no, we don't know what it is yet."

"I keep getting that answer and it's not very damn useful," I groused.

"When we know, you'll know," she said. "For the moment we need to proceed as if this is every bit as dangerous as it appears to be."

"Roger that." I glanced at Church. "What do we know about the new outbreak?"

"The island has a population of seventeen hundred and ninety people, plus roughly three hundred tourists, crews of fishing and commercial boats, and others. We believe that this disease has spread across the entire island."

"Christ," I growled. "Is everyone already infected?"

"We don't think so," said Doc. "Police and military helicopters are in the air, maintaining a safe distance, but from what we can see through long-range cameras, some people are fighting back or hiding. What matters most is that the infected are aggressive vectors. Any contact with them causes a rapid onset of symptoms."

"Serum transfer?" I asked.

"That's likely, but we can't rule out airborne. The infection rate is so weirdly fast that it's almost like just being in the presence of the infected does the trick. And that shouldn't be the case because cameras have picked up people getting infected while they are clearly outside of the range of exhalation, spitting, or sneezing. But we can't get close enough to understand how this spreads."

"Which is what you want us to do," I said.

"Yes," said Church. "We need to know what we're dealing with. We've never seen anything spread this fast before, and we need to know what the red line is in terms of how we approach containment."

His face was also haggard and there was a deep sadness in the set of his mouth. He wears tinted glasses so it's hard to read his expression, but from the tense set of his shoulders and the tightness of those frowning lips I thought I read fear there. But I could be wrong. People always misunderstand Church. They see how strong and capable he is, they glimpse a towering intellect and a commanding nature, and they take from that a lack of emotion and a freedom from human reactions. That's not accurate and it isn't fair. Church formed the DMS and the RTI *because* of fear. And anger. Those emotions are stoked by his deep understanding of the nature of the threats he asks his people to confront. Church has walked through the burning darkness way too often to be blasé about it. No, his outward calm in most situations is all game face. He needs to be the eye of a hurricane so that the people around him don't panic or lose faith; so that we don't falter in our resolve.

The very first time I met him was when a terrorist group was releasing the Seif al Din pathogen, though by the time he and I had our first conversation, the disease had already been released in a few select places. An infected terrorist had been brought to a hospital in Baltimore, and Church was on-site when the infection began to spread. It spread so fast that one of his crack field teams was overrun, and then it swept like wildfire throughout the hospital. To stop the infected from breaking out of the building—an event that would have created an uncontrollable global pandemic—Church had his people burn down the entire hospital. Everyone who was inside, even those not yet infected, died. It was a horrible act of murder, but I went over all the footage, all the reports, every scrap of information, and concluded that there was no Plan B. He did what he had to do to save the world.

When I called him on it, he gave me the same look I was seeing here, and he said to me, "*To stop this thing . . . I'd burn down heaven itself.*"

I believed him, too. Then, and—by implication—now.

"You said that there were helos in the air," I said. "Where do we stand with containment of information?"

"Oh, hell," said Bug, "this is all over the Net. People were uploading pics and video from their phones almost from the start. There were news choppers up there before the cops even arrived. They've been chased out and there's a no-fly zone now except for authorized birds, but that's closing the barn door . . ."

"The public does not know about the Island of Frogs, though," said Church. "We're still containing that, but expect that grace period to burn off soon. I've been on the phone with some of my associates, and they have been on the phones with all four heads of state. So far we are keeping the Punk Press footage of the SEALs and ROK soldiers under wraps. That's one element of this we can control for now, as long as Punk Press doesn't release it elsewhere, and so far they have not."

"They will, though," said Doc. "You can count on them chickens."

"Add this to the math," I said, and told them about the conversation I had with Ho, where he hinted at making sure word about the drone never got out. That gave them a moment's pause.

"Colonel Ho is a good man," said Church. "This squares with what I've heard about him. It's also a good suggestion."

"*If* the drone is American," I said.

"And if that video doesn't get out," said Bug.

"Regardless of containment," I said, "Frog Island was an act of terrorism. I don't have a shred of doubt about that. Not one."

"But who are our bad boys?" asked Doc. "It's more than rogue SEALs—if that's even who they are—and it's more than drones. Somebody had the brights to cook up some new kind of pathogen. When's the last time you heard of Johnny Cmar's Bug Hunters standing around scratching their heads? When's the last time you ran BAMS units in a hot zone and got jack and shit? No, campers, somewhere in all this is an actual mad scientist and I would dearly love for you and your crew of thugs to bring me his balls. Deep fried, with some grated cheese."

"Count on it," I promised.

"One final thing," said Church. "Because this second outbreak is on a South Korean island, I've agreed to have one of their officers join Havoc for the duration of this mission. She'll be waiting for you at Osan."

INTERLUDE THIRTEEN
EMBASSY SUITES BY HILTON FAYETTEVILLE FORT BRAGG
4760 LAKE VALLEY DRIVE
FAYETTEVILLE, NORTH CAROLINA
SIX MONTHS AGO

Adam and Eve sat on the bed, eyes wide, attentive as schoolchildren.

The curtains were drawn and there was an iPad playing a noisy football game, with small Bluetooth speakers facing the door to the hall and the wall to the only adjoining room. It was the middle of the afternoon, in that gap between the last of the housekeeping rounds and when people in town for conventions returned to their room. The guest next door had been studied and was on day two of a three-day presentation at Fort Bragg. He wouldn't be back until well after six, and later if he went to another dinner on the base.

There was no one to bother them, and the staff at the desk were wonderfully indifferent.

Rafael Santoro stood by the dresser, carefully cleaning his tools and instruments and replacing them in their little fitted slots in the big leather case. It amazed Eve that Santoro had not gotten a single drop of blood on his clothing. Not one.

The blood on the floor was all on the big plastic tarp.

And on the man who sat sweaty, panting, and defeated, on the chair. The man's soft, fractured sobs were muffled by the ball gag he wore. His tears mingled with the blood, turning a pretty pink as it wandered down through the dense forest of his chest hair.

Santoro took a small utility knife from the kit and sliced through the padded ropes that held the man to the chair. He cut them all, and pulled out the ball-gag, and handed the man a towel.

"Thank you," mumbled the man. Adam and Eve exchanged a wide-eyed look. The man had *thanked* someone after everything that had been done—and worse, *said*—to him.

"You may use the bathroom," Santoro said. "Wash thoroughly. Shampoo your hair. Use the toothbrush. There is antiseptic and some Band-Aids. You won't need many. Everything will heal. Nothing will leave a scar. If you are in much pain, there are some aspirin and a bottle of water on the sink. Your clothes are folded on the toilet tank."

Without saying another word, the man rose, naked and trembling, and shambled off to the bathroom. He was a large, muscular man with military tattoos and some scars earned in combat. He met no one's eyes. He looked down at the floor as if afraid it would drop out from under him. The door closed and they heard him vomiting. Then a flush and the shower.

They sat in silence. Adam and Eve held hands while Santoro finished packing up his equipment. He hiked himself onto the bureau and sat. He stared into the middle of nowhere. After fifteen minutes the big man came out of the bathroom, dressed in his camouflage ACU pants and jacket, his cap in his hands. He lingered at the door, looking uncertainly at the three people without actually making eye contact.

"I . . . ," he began, and faltered.

"No," said Santoro. "Just go. Remember our agreement and go. We're done here, yes?"

The man lingered for a moment, and Eve thought she could see the ghosts of his rage and pride and need to kill everyone in the room. Then his gaze crumpled and he looked down at the hand he twisted between his trembling fingers. Without another word he turned and walked out.

The three of them looked at the closed door, then at the bloody and sweat-stained chair, then at each other.

"And that," said Santoro, "is how it is done. He will do exactly what we want, in the precise way we want it, and he will do it with all of his earnest diligence. He will, in fact, let nothing or no one get in his way."

"Won't he tell someone?" gasped Adam.

Santoro did not answer. He studied them both with his dark eyes. His irises were so dark brown they looked black, giving him a demonic cast.

"No," said Eve. "He won't. Because this isn't about what you did to him. It's about what we'll do to the people he thought he could protect, but now knows he can't."

"Clever girl," said Santoro.

After a moment Adam licked his lips. "You weren't joking when you said extortion and coercion were art forms. That they were beautiful."

Santoro pushed off the bureau, walked over, and kissed them both on the head.

"There is so much more I want to teach you," he said with the gentle affection of a father. "There are so many gifts I want to share."

"Thanks," said Adam, nearly tripping on the word. He was awkward, uncertain how to properly react. Until now he and Eve had always been on their own, making things up as they went, taking whatever they wanted from whomever they picked. Now, this strange man was trying to change that, to control them, to recruit them, to make them part of a system. He wanted to tell him thanks but *no thanks*. Adam wanted to grab Eve and get the fuck out of there. To get off the grid and make damn sure they fell off the radar of this man and his organization. He wanted to . . .

Eve stood up and put her arms around Santoro's waist and laid her head on his chest. She was smiling and there were tears in her eyes as she looked up at him.

"Thank you, Daddy," she said.

Adam felt the floor of his stomach drop away, and into the black hole beneath all of his hope and his resistance tumbled down into nothing. Into yesterday. This was what Eve wanted. This was the home she'd been looking for all her life.

He got slowly to his feet and wrapped both Eve and Santoro in his arms.

"Yes," he said, "thank you, Daddy."

CHAPTER SIXTY-ONE
OSAN AIR BASE
NEAR SONGTAN STATION
PYEONGTAEK, SOUTH KOREA

We landed at Osan again but this time Colonel Epps was a little less persnickety. Now it was a major outbreak that was all over the news, so he was able to take overt ownership. Havoc was still running under the cover story of a WHO hot zone team that just happened to be in the area. Epps' boss called us a "lucky break" and a "godsend." Whatever.

Epps met us just beyond the rotor wash of the Chinook. We shook hands as we jogged away from the noise.

"We have the entire island quarantined," he said.

"Are there survivors?"

"We think so. Communications went down on the island about an hour after things started happening."

"How?" I asked.

"Well, that's still up for debate," said Epps. "We know that there are a number of fires burning out of control. No active infrastructure in place. No word at all from police or fire, no contact with the hospital. But I think there's another element in play. Seems pretty clear that something is actively jamming cell and radio communications. If that's the case, it's something high tech, because it's interfering with some drones launched from the *Choe Yeong*, a Chungmugong Yi Sun-sin class destroyer."

"Military-grade jammer?"

"Has to be, but it's weird," said Epps. "My people tell me that it's not stopping civilian radio or cell communication, but it's playing all kinds of games with the drones. Explain that to me."

"Targeted jamming," I said slowly. "Now that's interesting as all hell."

"We can do some of that," said Epps, "but not a lot of other countries can. China, Russia, maybe France. Not too many others. We can beat most jamming attacks, but not this cocksucker."

"Shit. What about satellites? They should be well above any useful jamming range."

Epps rubbed his eyes. "They are considering retasking one, but you know how it is. Hard as hell to convince the CIA to shift eyes from the North Korean missile factories. And so far no one further up the food chain knows about the other thing."

The other thing was the Island of Frogs.

"Understood," I said.

"Okay, there's someone I need you to meet," said Epps, shifting gears. He led me over to where a Korean woman dressed in unmarked black fatigues stood waiting. She was about thirty and unusually tall for a Korean, maybe five-nine.

"Outlaw," said Epps, "allow me to introduce Major Mun Ji-Woo."

Mun held out her hand and when I took it she gave me a very firm, very formal shake.

"Special Forces Brigade?" I ventured. "Which unit?"

There were seven primary units within the ROK's special forces, but Mun shook her head. "I am on special detachment from Kingdom," she said.

"Ah," I replied, and Epps looked a bit lost. Kingdom was a very special and highly secret organization that was similar in structure to Barrier and the old DMS. Small, elite, ruthless, and untethered by the red tape that grinds most military to a stumbling walk.

"I had the honor of working with Talieo a few years ago," I said, and watched her eyes for a reaction. Talieo was the call sign for Captain Kim Daeshim, who was one of the all-time great international special operators. Fierce, smart, and surprisingly funny. We took apart a North Korean factory that was developing DSRVs—deep sea remove vehicles—capable of delivering small nukes into industrial shipping ports or right in the middle of the Seventh Fleet. Talieo and I shook the pillars of heaven on that one, but then he was critically injured, I got him out and brought him home, however he's a paraplegic. Still has that sense of humor, though. Sends me the most hilariously obscene Christmas cards.

Major Mun's eyes were dark brown pieces of polished stone. Not a trace of emotion flickered in them. It was like looking into the eyes of a store mannequin. Odd, and a bit disconcerting.

"Talieo is a great loss to my country," said Mun. "I believe you were in the vicinity when he was injured."

"He saved my life," I said.

"Yes," she said and left it there, allowing me to infer what I wanted.

Epps looked from me to Mun and back again, waiting for an explanation, got none, and sighed. "Your gear's over there," he said, pointing to a hulking Marine Corps MV-22B Osprey, a tilt-rotor vertical takeoff and landing bird that could punch along at over three hundred miles per hour. Fast and big enough to carry us and a lot of gear.

"Thanks," I said and turned to go, but Epps held out his hand. "Outlaw, is there *anything* I can do instead of sit here with my thumb up my ass?"

"Prayers would be useful," I said. "And, no, that's not a joke."

Mun and I headed toward the Osprey.

"Are we going to have some kind of problem, Major?" I asked. She walked three or four steps before she replied.

"I respect your authority in this matter, Outlaw," she said.

"But . . . ?"

"No buts. I will do my duty and serve my country."

That was the end of the conversation. We joined the others.

The RTI logistics man, Brian "Bird Dog" Bird, was sitting on one of a small pile of equipment cases. He was drinking a Dr Pepper and didn't look happy. Guess we weren't happy, either.

I introduced Mun to everyone and noted the brief mutual evaluation and instant dislike evident between her and Ho. They gave each other bows so tight I wondered that they didn't each tear their back muscles. Pretty sure if either was on fire the other wouldn't spit on them to put it out. I stepped close to them and said, "Play nice" in a tone that was not nice at all. Ho looked embarrassed and mumbled something; Mun merely turned away.

Bird Dog got up and offered his hand to Ho.

"I heard about your sergeant, Colonel," said Bird Dog in about the worst chopped-up Korean I've ever heard. Even Ho looked confused and asked him to repeat it in English. "Hope he's okay."

"Thank you," he said.

Bird Dog handed out new coms kits and caught my eye before giving one to Mun.

"Going to need a combat call sign so I can wire her into the network," he said, giving her an almost apologetic smile. "We can pick one for you if—"

"I have one already," said Mun. "Mudang."

I smiled and nodded, and she cocked an eyebrow.

"You know what that is?"

"A female shaman."

"Very good," she said in a way that was supposed to be complimentary but sounded very condescending.

Top cleared his throat and made introductions to everyone else, using only call signs. We all put on the coms units, which consisted of the tiny mole-sized earbuds and mics, and little power packs that were about the size of six stacked quarters. Then Havoc Team boarded the Osprey. We were in the air in under two minutes.

Once we were on our way, Bird Dog opened a big equipment case and began handing out Hammer Suits. We stripped to our skivvies despite the cold December breeze, and pulled on the suits. If Ho or Mun were uncomfortable changing in front of everyone, they kept it off their faces. Points for them.

Once we were suited up, Bird Dog began opening weapons cases.

"Okay, kids," he said, flipping open two identical boxes, "all the weapons are pretty much generic to the mercenary community, and that's still the cover. Pick your handguns and long guns of choice."

I smiled and took a Heckler & Koch G36, which I was very familiar with from my days with the Baltimore PD. It was our assault rifle of choice. And there was a modified Navy Colt 1911 model .45. An old favorite.

Then Bird Dog opened a long case marked with a stenciled image of a horse. Inside were a variety of weapons with bright blue handles.

"What are those?" asked Mun

Bird Dog lifted out a pistol. "This is a Snellig 22A-Max gas dart gun. Proprietary tech. Has very high compression for decent range and solid hits. Will penetrate most clothes except leather or heavy denim. Long internal barrel for accuracy." The guns were about the same dimensions as a Colt M45, but half the weight even with extended thirty-shot box magazines. "Mags are loaded with gelatin darts filled with a nifty new cocktail of goodies built around the veterinary drug ketamine, but with a little bit of BZ to cause intense confusion and DMHP for muscle weakness so bad victims have trouble standing upright. Also some benzodiazepines and chloral hydrate and some other stuff that Doc Holliday calls 'brand X,' meaning you don't need to know what it is. We call it 'sandman.' One dart will put anyone up to and including Bigfoot on his ass right damn now. No one shakes it off, so don't stick yourself. You go down and go out and the psychoactive compounds will give you some peculiar dreams. Goofy over there accidentally shot Pluto . . ." He waved to his two burly assistants. Goofy and Pluto were not their official combat call signs, but Bird Dog refused to call them anything else. "Pluto went down and had very intense sexual dreams about a talking cantaloupe."

"True story," said Pluto dryly. "It was great. Very sexy melon. We bonded."

"It was awesome," agreed Goofy. He and Pluto exchanged a fist bump. They looked like a pair of mouth-breathing Neanderthals, but weren't. They did enjoy playing those roles, though.

"Who is Doc Holliday?" asked Mun.

"She's the head of our Integrated Sciences Division," I said.

"Would that be *Joan* Holliday, formerly of DARPA?"

"It would."

Mun's expression was unreadable, though a bit unpleasant. "Does that mean you are still tied to the United States government?"

"No, it does not," I said.

"Why do I find that hard to believe?"

"Why do I not give a shit what you believe?" I countered.

Colonel Ho cleared his throat, then took the magazine from Bird Dog, removed a dart very carefully, and studied it. "Is there any chance you could share the formula with me?"

"Sure, there's a chance," said Bird Dog with a smile. "There's two chances, actually, and they are Slim and None."

"Ah."

I said, "Doc Holliday suggested these nonlethal rounds and I'm all for it. These are civilians infected with something and the world is watching. We want to contain the situation so that we can study it and offer aid."

"What if there's no cure for whatever this is?" asked Mun.

Ho turned slowly to face her. "We have no proof of that, Major. We only have one living infected right now, and he is my sergeant. Are you suggesting we simply kill everyone who is infected?"

She was unmoved. "I'm asking about the rules of engagement. What if these darts don't stop them?"

"They will," said Bird Dog. "Not joking when I said that you don't shake one off. You get hit, you go down. All you need is a central nervous system and a circulatory system."

"Fine," she snapped, "then what are we expected to do if we're facing too many to be stopped by drugs?"

"If we can't fall back to safety or otherwise control the situation," I said, "then we do what we have to. But the point is to establish and maintain control."

"Hooah," said Top very softly.

Mun's eyes locked on mine for a moment and then flicked away. She bent and took a Glock 17 from the first case. "I'll keep that in mind," she said.

That killed conversation for the moment, so everyone simply began selecting weapons and stuffing as much ammunition into their belt and pouches as they could. Everyone took a lot of it.

Bird Dog scowled at us. "You do know this stuff's expensive, right? I mean, I have to budget all this crap out. Suits, weapons, bird drones. All that. You have any idea at all what my accounting nightmares are?"

Top slapped a magazine into his pistol and the barrel almost—but not quite—pointed at Bird Dog's crotch. He said nothing.

Bird Dog sighed. "You make a compelling argument."

The chopper flew on, taking Havoc Team toward another island filled with death.

CHAPTER SIXTY-TWO

HOTEL RYUMEIKAN
TOKYO, JAPAN

When the phone rang Eve actually screamed. She also peed a little in her pajamas.

Adam flung himself forward to grab the burner phone on the nightstand, clumsied the grab, and overcompensated trying to catch the cell as it slid out of reach. The phone, the lamp, the nightstand, and Adam all crashed to the floor. He cursed as his elbow struck hard despite the carpet, but he snatched up the phone and hit the button.

"Yes!"

"Line . . . ?"

"Clear." The scrambler was already jacked into the charging port, the small light glowing green. "We're good."

"What's wrong?" asked the caller suspiciously. "You sound out of breath."

"Um . . . I was doing push-ups."

There was a beat. "Whatever," said Rafael Santoro. "Are you ready to act?"

"Absolutely," swore Adam. He glanced up at Eve, who was peering over the edge of the bed like a frightened child checking for scary, leering clowns under her bed.

"Are you sure? I'm not hearing confidence in your tone, boy."

Adam drew in a steadying breath and in a more confident-sounding voice said, "Yes, Daddy. I'm positive. We're ready to do anything you need."

"Then I need you to do this." Santoro quickly explained what he wanted done.

"Sure," said Adam, "that's easy. It'll take just a little time. I need to go to the storage locker and get my other laptop. It has the video editing software."

"Do it. Make it convincing, yes?"

"Yes. Certainly. Absolutely. You can count on us, Daddy."

"Then there is a second task for you."

"Anything."

"Clean up the back trail on this. Be thorough."

"No problem, Daddy."

"And one more thing," said Santoro.

"Yes?"

"Don't call me Daddy."

The line went dead and Adam sagged back against the carpet, exhaling slowly. Eve slithered like a nervous reptile off the bed and curled against him. He could feel her heart beating as fast as his own.

"Is he mad at us?" she asked in a tiny voice.

Adam took a moment with that. "No."

"You're sure?"

"Yes," he said. "If he was really mad . . . he wouldn't have called. He'd have knocked."

CHAPTER SIXTY-THREE
ARKLIGHT SAFE HOUSE
GYEONGSANGNAM-DO, SOUTH KOREA

Lieutenant Han was as good as her billing. She had her men take them to a small house that did not belong to the military. Nor, as it developed, did she or her guards. Everything about them was a very clever fraud intended to smooth things at the airport.

"We're all in the system, though," she explained. "If anyone checks, they will find unshakable identification and histories. We officially belong to Department 81, which is an ultra-secret investigative group that really exists."

"I know about D-81," said Bug. "I helped set that up seven or eight years ago. Before Kingdom was created. We needed DMS teams to be able to operate in-country with the appearance of approval from so high no one would ever risk the career backlash to question it."

"That was you?" Han gazed at him with pure love in her eyes. "I should have known. Who else could have made something like that? The structure of misdirection and obfuscation is so . . . so . . ." She fished for the right word and couldn't find one juicy enough.

"Okay, you really need to stop that," said Bug.

"Why?" she asked with such frankness that it gave Bug nowhere to go. And he suddenly wondered if the fangirl thing was a trick to keep him off balance. Probably. If so, it made him like her a whole lot more.

He cleared his throat and began unpacking his gear.

"Arklight uses this place now," she said.

"And those two guys? I didn't know Arklight had any men working for them."

She shrugged. "Allies. Not all guys are assholes."

"Kinda have to agree."

They set up at a big kitchen table. The fridge was filled with Red Bull and the cabinets stuffed with junk food. One of the allies came back in twenty minutes with pizza and soda, left it on the table, nodded, and went out. Neither man had so far said a word.

Han had several monitors set up on a network, and they watched the Punk Press video a couple of times, then went through the information set aside as definitely or possibly pertaining to the case. She had an Oracle substation and Bug had a MindReader Q1 remote field unit. Han stared at it with naked lust.

"That's the actual quantum system, isn't it?" she whispered.

"Kind of."

"Did you marry it to MindReader?"

"You know about MindReader?"

"Mother Lilith told me."

Mother Lilith. Bug shivered. Violin was, as far as he knew, Lilith's only biological daughter, but Lilith was the head of the Mothers of the Fallen, of which Arklight was the militant arm. There was something odd, though, in hearing her called Mother with actual affection. Bug knew that the stories told about Lilith—about the things she and the other senior Arklight women had done to the men they hunted—were all true. All of them. Although Bug knew that Church was probably the single most dangerous person on earth, it was Lilith who actually scared him. At the same time he had an admiration for her that ran miles and miles deep. It was so damn sad that the world needed women like her and the Mothers. It was worse that things like human trafficking and slavery were happening in greater numbers now than ever in history. Ever.

He cut a covert look at Han, who did not look like the kind of

JONATHAN MABERRY

damaged, lethal, righteous warrior he'd come to expect of the Arklight members. It made him wonder what kinds of scars were beneath the glowing eyes, luminous smile, and peppy attitude.

They got to work.

As with the former DMS, the RTI used nicknames for these cases, and this one was given the obvious name of Rage. Bug went through the steps he'd taken to try and crack apart the source of the Punk Press emails. Han had a lot of very good ideas, and she knew the local networks, the tech specs for this part of Korea, and had insight into the fringe culture. She was also very, very good at slicing her way through rerouting programs.

"No one uses that software more than sex traffickers," she said. "Especially the ones who sell kiddie porn to European and American customers. It's mostly Dark Web stuff, but they have to do some stuff on the regular web, and that leaves a footprint. If you know how to track them . . ." She sat back and smiled like a kid who'd cracked the hardest level of the latest *God of War* game. "Gotcha, you bastard."

"What?" asked Bug, bending forward eagerly.

"This is where it was sent from," she said.

Bug frowned at the information on the screen.

"Wait . . . a dinosaur museum?"

CHAPTER SIXTY-FOUR
IN FLIGHT
SOUTH KOREA

I sat in the back of the chopper and watched Havoc Team go through the process of becoming acclimated to their new teammate. I also watched the individual dynamics of Colonel Ho and Major Mun. It was interesting theater.

According to every stereotypical viewpoint, Ho should have been the cold, detached political animal using every opportunity to spout catchphrases from Party doctrine. That was the cliché, but Ho was a kind and rather gentle man, a healer, and seemed comfortable with his own thoughts. My guys liked him, and they're hard sells.

Mun, on the other hand, sat apart and kept her thoughts and her comments to herself. The big rock heads on Easter Island were chattier and more human. There was no time for a quiet chat before suiting up, so I had no idea if her attitude was because she was forced to work with someone from the North, or because he was a higher rank—though I doubted anyone in a crisis would be that petty. That left me with no other avenues of speculation.

So, I moved my coms mic closer to my mouth, cycled over to the TOC channel, and made a discreet call.

"What do we know about the new kid in school?" I asked.

Scott Wilson seemed to be anticipating the call. "She's absolutely top of the line, Outlaw." He ran down her credentials as a first-class officer whose rise through the ranks was meteoric. Enough medals and commendations to fill a wall. "She is fifth-generation military. Seen action all over the world, first with the ROK and then as the first active field operator in Kingdom. If they ever cut her loose she's high on our list."

"Uh-huh," I said, unconvinced. "Psych profile?"

"It's solid. No issues. Devoted to her family. Oldest of three sisters. Parents and grandparents still alive. Father, mother, uncle, and grandfather are all military, all served or are serving with distinction. Uses her leave to go home for holidays. Is godmother to her twin nieces."

I stared across the cabin at her and tried to square what I was hearing with the iron maiden sitting like a vulture in the farthest corner. Her face was a stone and her eyes clicked from one person to another and then out the window. Mr. Spock is ten times more gregarious. It was truly like looking at a robot.

No, that wasn't quite right. I could see the muscles along her jaw clearly defined as she sat there, clenched and tight, clamping it down, keeping it in.

But what was she fighting to control?

"Dig deeper," I said.

"Why?" asked Wilson. "Is something wrong?"

"That's what I need you to tell me."

I signed off and tried not to be seen watching her. Pretty sure she was doing exactly the same thing.

JONATHAN MABERRY

INTERLUDE FOURTEEN
WILDLIFE ROAD ABOVE THE POINT DUME BLUFFS
MALIBU, CALIFORNIA
NINE MONTHS AGO

"We should not linger so long in one place," said Santoro.

He stood in the sunlight, naked to the waist, glistening with sweat, chest heaving from exertion but his eyes calm. The yard was large, with trees and tall fences providing excellent cover from distant neighbors. A tiled patio stretched outward from an indoor gym accessed by a section of wall that opened like a garage door. It provided Santoro with five thousand square feet of training area.

Several men and women, all of them equally sweaty and some of them badly bruised, were working through yet another set of demanding drills. Santoro was a brutal taskmaster. He set very high standards, exceeded those in demonstration, and then encouraged his students to aspire toward excelling him. None did, but many were getting close, which made him very happy.

Kuga, in white shorts and an open tropical shirt, lay on a chaise longue, a bourbon sour balanced on his taut stomach. Watching. Always watching.

"Did you hear what I said?" asked Santoro.

"Sure."

"And . . . ?"

"And you're right," said Kuga. "In fact I have a truck coming tomorrow to take some things down to L.A."

Santoro frowned. "We're moving to the city?"

"L.A.? God no. Place is a cesspit. I should have specified—our stuff's going to be loaded onto a boat. I have a 101-meter motor yacht, a Roberto Curtó that was made in a joint venture with RC Design and Mario Grasso of Navirex. Sixteen-meter beam, draft five meters, and empty is fifty-three hundred gross tons. Round bilged hull displacement. She can cruise at fourteen knots—officially, but I had some guys tinker with it and we can get up to twenty in a pinch. Staterooms for twenty-two people and—"

"I am not shopping to buy it," interrupted Santoro. He snatched up a towel and began drying off. "How conspicuous is this boat?"

"Very," said Kuga. "Big garish thing. But it's registered to someone else. A Canadian billionaire I know. He was born to money and has no politics at all. I, on the other hand, have lots of footage of him with kids, so I own him. Besides, he's Canadian and who the fuck ever looks twice at a silly, rich Canuck?"

Santoro scowled but said nothing, which made Kuga grin.

"You'll love the name, too. *The Soul of Piety.* The owner thinks that's funny as balls. He's a total hedonist scumbag. So, I guess it is. The boat has great range, but we can stop at the usual places to refuel. Make it look casual. There's such an amazing control center aboard that we can run our operations at sea, and I have a gal working for me who knows how to spook her way into telecom satellites without tripping any alarms. Couple of great internet jockeys, too. They look like a couple of stoners. I call them Jay and Silent Bob. One of them worked for Putin. Well, actually, Silent Bob's always worked for me, but Putin *thought* the kid worked for him. You know how that is. Hugo didn't own the patent on building secret networks."

"No."

"The other kid, Jay, was a boy genius who everybody thought was going to be scouted by Apple or Microsoft, but he's such an unlikable asshole that no one wanted to hire him. And when Silicon Valley thinks you're too much of a dick, well . . . So, I snatched him up. Maybe neither is on the same level as that freak, Bug . . . but together? Yeah. They fit like two batteries in a dildo."

Santoro made a small disgusted sound.

The fighters in the yard were setting up cork targets for knife drills. There were two dozen of them, men and women. All of them were former military and each had spent time working for private contractors in places where nobody really looked over their shoulders. They were dangerous as hell before Santoro recruited them, and they'd all come a long way since. No one trained people quite like the little Spaniard.

"Digging the way your new Kingsmen are coming along, by the way. Tough as hell."

"They're not Kingsmen," insisted Santoro. He tossed the towel onto another lounge chair, took a bottle of water from the patio wet bar, and sat. "The Seven Kings are dead."

"Then what do we call them? Henchmen? Minions? No, wait, we'd get sued by Universal. Even I'm scared of entertainment lawyers."

"I am open to suggestions. It was Hugo Vox who picked the name 'Kingsmen.'"

"So it's on me?" mused Kuga. He scooted up and sipped his drink. His fake tan had been replaced with a golden natural one, and the lines of stress had softened around his mouth. In the months since leaving the prison he'd put on ten pounds of useful muscle and shed fifteen years of unearned age.

The two of them batted some possible names back and forth for a while, but discarded most of the choices as either too corny, too obvious, or uninteresting.

"The key," said Santoro, "is to give them what amounts to a flag. A *name* matters. It defines who they are and what they believe in. Kings in so many cultures claimed descent from the gods, or at least divine blessing."

"Okay," said Kuga, "so are you suggesting we call ourselves kings? I mean, Two Kings doesn't have quite the gravitas of *Seven* Kings. What if we go old school? I like the sound of The Immortals."

Santoro considered, lips pursed, and shook his head. "I have never liked that name. It is effective up until one of them is killed by someone who is demonstrably lesser than the standard they hold for themselves. King Leonidas of Sparta proved that at the Hot Gates when he sent his youngest hoplites to gut the first ranks of Persian Immortals. It made a statement that probably cost Xerxes another hundred casualties through loss of heart."

"Point taken." Kuga drained his glass, the ice cubes rattling against his lips. He got up and built another drink. "I like that other group, the cats who worked for Howard Shelton and that Majestic Three program."

"The Closers?"

"Yes. Great name. It was more about what they did than any false claims of immortality or invulnerability."

Santoro chewed on that, nodding slowly.

They heard a yell and turned to see one of the fighters doing a drill in which he ducked, dove, rolled, and leapt while throwing knives at targets on corkboard posts. He hit five of eight targets in kill zones. He tried it again and made six kills. Kuga and Santoro nodded.

"Hey," said Kuga, "what about something *like* the Closers? What about the Fixers? That has a ring to it. And, let's face it, it fits with what's implied with that *Concierge de l'enfer* thing they hung on me."

"The Fixers . . ." Santoro tasted the name.

"The Fixers," said Kuga, giving it some real weight.

And, the Fixers it became.

The two men lay on their chairs and watched the Fixers train. Watched the oil grace with which they moved, the sureness and steadiness, and the coldness.

"They'll never see us coming," murmured Kuga.

"No," said Santoro, "they will not."

CHAPTER SIXTY-FIVE
YEONPYEONG ISLAND
SOUTH KOREA

We flew into hell.

That's what it looked like, even from the air.

Yeonpyeong is actually the name of a group of small islands in the Yellow Sea, roughly fifty miles west of Incheon and only seven and a half miles south of the North Korean province of Hwanghae. The main island is Daeyeonpyeongdo, which means Big Yeonpyeong, but everyone tends to refer to that just as Yeonpyeong. The smaller islands were less important, and right now anyone living on those more remote specks of land were lucky. They were probably still alive.

Yeonpyeong Island was burning.

We circled the island, the Osprey moving like some great prehistoric bird between columns of smoke. Brown and gray from blazing homes; a sour gray-green from the crab processing plant, and oily black from the gas dock in the ferry port. Cars and trucks burned in the streets. People did, too. We could see blackened bodies wreathed in fire sprawled in the streets, their limbs curling as the hellish heat leached moisture from their tendons.

Unlike Gaeguli Seom, though, the slaughter on this island was not past tense. We were not visiting a grave but a charnel house. Figures chased each other through the smoke. Some fought and wrestled in the streets. Some wandered like zombies, their clothes torn and streaked with blood. We saw people hiding from screaming madmen, crouching down behind cars, or hunkered down in the weeds, looking for safety in a place where it might no longer exist. I saw one man standing by a wrecked golf cart using what looked like a shoulder-mounted movie camera to hammer down on a body that was little more than red hamburger. He kept hitting, over and over again, even though the man—if it had been a man—he was assaulting was long dead.

"Everyone get ready," growled Top, and the stridence and power of his voice shook the team out of a hypnotic trance of watching the horror show below. "Let's do it, people."

Everyone broke loose of their shock. They buddy-checked each other's Hammer Suit seals and strapped themselves into their rappelling gear. Even though there were plenty of places to set down, we weren't risking the crew or the plane. As soon as we were down Bird Dog would begin hosing everything down with a powerful disinfectant.

We clipped on, and when Pluto and Goofy opened the hatch we slithered down into the madness. Our landing zone was a field on the edge of town. We disconnected and the Osprey lifted and turned from the LZ, taking its noise and wind and safety with it.

Before the doors closed a flock of drones burst out, large and small. Seagulls and pigeons, and a swarm of insect drones that clustered and swarmed and then followed us down and then spread themselves onto the breeze. Each machine moved like the creature it was designed to imitate, with flight patterns and sounds dictated by ultra-sophisticated software, but they went where Doc Holliday sent them. I needed Andrea's hands on his dart gun and not drone controls, at least for now.

I have spread out and established a perimeter, guns up and out. I saw Top watching Mun, making sure—as I'd also done—that the weapon in her small, strong hands was a Snellig and not a Glock. She must have sensed Top and me watching because she looked over her shoulder at us. There was nothing—no nod, no word; just her letting us know she knew. Fair enough.

I hadn't liked the fact that we were all on a shared channel—though I understood the necessity for it—and now I wished I could have had a few quick private chats. One with Bug to get more background on Mun. Something about her made me twitch and it wasn't merely her lack of social skills. Would also like to have talked to Top. But he must have sensed that—as he often did—and gave me a small nod while cutting his eyes at Mun. He was going to keep an eye on her and was telling me that he had that covered so I could focus on leading this little school trip. Top can compress a lot into a look.

"Call the play, boss," said Bunny.

"We head to the center of town and then see what's what," I said. "Anyone comes toward you, put them down. Don't worry about cuffs. Just dart 'em and move on. We are badly outnumbered and I don't want to risk any other boots on the ground. They won't know how to do this right."

"Hooah," said Top.

"Call signs and common sense. Nobody outside of our official loop should be able to pick up our proprietary channels, but if they do, anything we say is going out prime time. Let's be circumspect."

Our Hammer Suits had WHO and biohazard emblems in bright colors and you had to be real close to see much through the plastic hood visors. The mission channel was being monitored by four friends of Mr. Church, one from each country. They were supposed to be friendlies, but friendship could get seriously strained when actual national security came into play. If we ran into the guys who almost certainly delivered this bioweapon, and if they turned out to be real SEALs and real ROK soldiers, then things could turn south real damn fast. The fact that the Frog Island stuff was still under wraps was kind of amazing, but also scary. None of us believed that the silence would—or could—last.

As if reading my mind, Top asked, "What do we do if we run into some actual bad guys?"

"We take them," I said. "Juice them if at all possible. I need some-one with a pulse so I can have a deep and meaningful conversation, feel me?"

"Hooah," said everyone except Ho and Mun. But they nodded.

We moved out.

INTERLUDE FIFTEEN
ABOARD *THE SOUL OF PIETY*
QUAYSIDE MARINA
VANCOUVER, BRITISH COLUMBIA
EIGHT MONTHS AGO

"I like what you've been doing with the Fixers, Rafael," said Kuga.

They walked slowly together along the finger pier toward the big yacht. Two Fixers walked ahead, two behind. The guards were dressed in boating clothes, but an experienced eye could tell what they were. None of those eyes were looking at the small party.

"I'm glad you are pleased," said Santoro. "Recruitment is up forty percent and attrition is low. We will have more than enough troops for the upcoming operations. We are doing equally well with infil-tration operations and we have an overabundance of minders keep-ing an eye on the families of our unwilling recruits. Everything we set in motion has greatly exceeded expectations."

"Glad to hear it."

"We are so well positioned, in fact," continued Santoro, "that I don't think we need to wait any longer to start several other opera-tions we have been planning."

"That's even better."

"As long as you have the nerve for that kind of expansion."

Kuga shot him a look, but he saw Santoro break into a rare grin. "Ah. Humor. It's a good look on you, Rafael. Maybe I'll book you into some stand-up clubs."

They reached the gangplank, which was guarded by yet another pair of Fixers. Santoro paused, touching Kuga's arm lightly.

"Do you remember our conversation about what to call ourselves? Our organization?"

"Sure. That was the day we picked the name Fixers. Why?"

"I have been giving it some considerable thought. The Seven Kings name was picked partly in support of a propaganda program. The intention was to hijack the mystique and many of the long-standing conspiracy rumors about secret societies and repurpose them to suggest that the Kings was an ancient cult, and one with vast secrets and some supernatural elements. Viewed from a distance that sounds perhaps silly, but when fed incrementally to the internet rumor mill, it was very effective. We had scores of web experts hacking in to databases to change what was there and insert the Kings legend into it. They even modified PDFs of doctoral theses on university websites. And we covertly funded the publication of hundreds of books, paid for speaking tours, bankrolled History Channel specials, and so on. Much of that information is still there, and a lot of people still believe that the Kings were, in fact, an ancient order dating back to Sargon the Akkadian."

"That's impressive as hell," agreed Kuga. "Are you suggesting we do the same?"

Santoro smiled. "I am suggesting we do nothing."

"What?"

"We already have a mystique. Kuga. I have been going through your own records and also conducting deep dives into what is on the Net. Kuga has become far more than your cover name, my friend. You have become the Professor Moriarty of the real world. There are thousands of crimes and actions ascribed to Kuga that I know you had no part in. There are, by my count, forty-three people who claim to be Kuga operating at various levels of the international black market. The name has become a legend." He paused. "At first I was tempted to smash these pretenders, but now I believe that they are useful. They are self-sustaining misdirection, yes? They muddy the water and distract the eye. And because your own organization ran things so efficiently while you were incarcerated, it would be a very difficult thing to attach your real name to the person called Kuga. So, it seems to me that we are looking to name something that is already named, and to build a mystique that already exists."

"Nothing grandiose?"

"Nothing grandiose. You are not a cartoon villain, my friend. You are not political, you are certainly not a religious zealot, and you are not trying to take over the world. What you are . . . is a businessman. Any collateral damage done by my Fixers or our other operatives is not from malice—it is simply the cost of doing business. The name Kuga is the business and the brand, and it's all the mystique we need."

Kuga walked to the end of the finger pier and stared down at the pelicans bobbing in the water. He was smiling. And then he was nodding.

CHAPTER SIXTY-SIX
HOTEL RYUMEIKAN
TOKYO, JAPAN

Eve made the call. They lay in bed together and when Santoro answered she and Adam leaned together to listen.

Santoro answered with, "Line?"

"Clear."

"And . . . ?"

"It's done and it's good," said Eve. "Really good."

"Send it to me."

"I did," said Adam. "It's on your business account." That was code for one of the many coded email accounts on the Dark Web they used for this kind of work. Like the burners, it would be discarded, in this case scrubbed and deleted, with a very nasty virus left like a land mine for anyone who chanced to find the account.

There was a long pause while Santoro watched the video. They could both hear noise and dialogue from the file. Eve tried to massage Adam's crotch while they waited, more of a nervous thing than actual sex, but he pushed her hand away. He was a million miles from hard.

After about a thousand years, Santoro said, "This will work."

Adam closed his eyes and thumped his head against the pillow. Eve bent and kissed his cheek.

Santoro told them when and where to upload it. "After that, destroy whatever computer you used for the upload. Completely. Do not merely wipe it, but physically destroy it, yes?"

"Yes, sure, absolutely."

"You will not under any circumstances disappoint me," said Santoro. He made it a statement and left all of the threats implied. Eve and Adam looked at each other, both of them going pale beneath their tans. They were monsters, but Santoro was a god of monsters. Their god. And in a flash it took Eve back to Haven House, the home for troubled youths in Montana near Flathead Lake. Back to when she and Adam first met.

It was like stepping into a nightmare for her, and that was a journey she hadn't taken in a long time. One she hadn't been broken enough to take since coming to work for Santoro.

That night, though, still burned in her mind like a hot coal. She had died then. Or, at least a girl name Katie McHugh had died then. It had been Katie who'd been arrested all those times for theft and arson. Eve was still waiting to be born.

It was Katie who'd been punched so hard in the stomach by Mike Tillerson that she couldn't breathe, let alone scream for help. It had been Katie who the six older teens dragged into the shed behind the main house. It had been Katie who had her own underwear stuffed into her mouth to stifle the screams as the boys took her over and over and over again. Invading her body in every possible way. Tearing her. Ruining her. Laughing and slapping and punching in places where it wouldn't show. Taking cell phone pictures staged to look like compliance. The boys were wise in their cruelty and thorough in their degradation.

It was Adam who found her. He had already shed the skin of Ryan O'Connor by then. That was why he was at Haven. They thought he was still salvageable, by their standards. They thought he was wayward—the favorite words of the cornball boneheads who ran the place. They had no idea what he'd already become.

Adam was walking back from the lake with a pair of cutthroat trout and a fat rainbow on a hook, whistling a tune that followed no sense or order. He must have heard her, because she was invisible in the dark, under the bushes where she'd crawled. If he hadn't come along Katie might have made it all the way to the lake, and then no one would ever have found her.

She saw the fish fall to the ground, heard the bushes rustle, felt hands reaching in, touching her. Katie screamed. But Adam pulled her out, wrapped her in his arms, held her close. He did not ask what happened. She was naked and there was blood on her thighs and buttocks. He bent his head close and wept with her.

Later, as they sat on rocks by the lake watching the moon roll like a white marble across the black table of the sky, he asked her two questions. Only those two.

First he asked her name. He *knew* it from Haven, but asked it anyway. When she didn't answer—she hadn't rediscovered the mechanics of speaking yet—he told her that although everyone called him Ryan his real name was Adam. He explained that he'd become that after the hundredth night his mother had come into his room. When he still lived at home. When his mother was still alive. He told her, without edit or delicacy, what he had done on that hundredth night. The scissors and hammer and carpet knife and hacksaw. He told her everything. Every. Single. Thing.

One day ago she would have been shocked and horrified. She'd have run from him as fast as she could. She might even have *told* on him. A day ago. Even three hours ago.

That would have been Katie believing. As she listened to the story of Ryan becoming Adam—the first man created in the new world that was inside his head—she felt Katie falter. She felt Katie die. A part of her tried to hold on, to reach back into the gathering darkness to catch Katie's hand, but the tidal pull was far too strong by that point, and Katie McHugh drowned there by Flathead Lake.

She didn't call herself Eve that night. No, that was much later. She first used it when she and Adam got into the car that belonged to Haven's chief of security. In the glow of the burning building, she looked into the rearview mirror and saw only her own eyes and now the burning building.

"I'm Eve," she said.

"I know," he said.

They drove away.

The police looked for the wrong people. They looked for Katie and Ryan, and both of them were long dead. The hunt intensified when it was later discovered that six of the teenage boys at Haven had not died from either smoke inhalation or burns. No. Their bodies were found in a shed set well apart from the house. So far apart, one investigator noted in an interview, that probably no one in the main building could have heard them screaming. The things that had been done to them were so graphic that even the bloodthirsty reporters tended to summarize.

Adam and Eve were never found. Later, once the two of them had begun cultivating a useful set of skills, all computer records of the people they'd been vanished from databases and emails. The living had become ghosts of the useless dead.

Since then, no one had ever really hurt them again. No one had that kind of power.

Until they met Rafael Santoro. Daddy.

He had never hurt them, not even touched them, but what did that matter? He'd taught them the art of pain and coercion and torture. Beautiful arts when used against others rather than directed toward them. So much power. So sexy. No, erotic. Sensual in the truest definition of that word, because it engaged all five senses in ways that made their subjects totally alive and completely aware of every nerve signal.

Santoro had never directly threatened them. Not once. But he'd taught them the cost of disappointing expectations. They'd watched him, the master artist at work, on people who had disappointed him.

Now, hearing him on the phone, Eve felt as if she was the one strapped to one of Santoro's chairs. Naked and vulnerable, with every nerve ending totally awake in dreadful anticipation.

"N-no, Daddy," stammered Adam. "We would *never* disappoint you."

But there was no one on the line anymore.

CHAPTER SIXTY-SEVEN
YEONPYEONG ISLAND
SOUTH KOREA

There was a government building at the edge of town, and we approached it quietly and slowly. There were corpses in the tall grass that edged the parking lot. The grass was stiff and brittle, murdered by the winter cold, and it rustled with a sound like rat claws on old floorboards. Ahead we saw a man standing in the shade of a tree, a big fire ax in his hands. His shoulders rose and fell as if with extreme exhaustion. Top was on point and held up a fist for everyone else to stop.

We covered him with our weapons as he crept forward, the Snellig raised. Top can move like a cat when he wants to. The memory of Sergeant Chung and the little girl was playing on a big movie screen in my head, and I willed Top to be careful. I could feel Bunny fidgeting beside me.

The man with the fire ax was looking off into the blue nothing and was not aware of Top's approach. Maybe he was an uninfected person who'd used the ax to defend himself, or maybe he was something else. The ax was smeared with blood and the man's clothes were spattered. Flies swarmed around him.

The TOC sent the feed from Top's bodycam to a corner of my visor and I saw what he saw. We all did. We saw the red, torn, inhuman lumps of things glistening wetly in the grass. We saw the body of a child—what had *been* a child—sprawled in the dirt, her little arms wrapped around a small dog.

"God . . . ," breathed Bunny. That was the only word anyone spoke.

Top began to circle wide, well out of the reach of that ax. Our weapons all pointed at the man. We watched as Top stepped into the man's periphery, into the line of sight.

The man had been motionless except for the movement of his shoulders. Now his head lifted and turned toward the movement. There was a moment when nothing at all happened. My finger slipped inside the dart gun's trigger guard.

Top knew a little Korean. Just enough. He said, *"Nae mal deuleuseyo."*

Listen to me, sir.

"Dokkileul naelyeo nwa jwo."

I need you to put the ax down.

The pronunciation was fair, the meaning clear, accompanied by a downward patting gesture with Top's left hand.

The man looked confused. He raised the ax a few inches and stared at it as if he'd never seen it before, as if he had no idea how it got into his hand. Then he blinked a few times and shook his head. Trying to clear his thoughts. He looked around, seemingly unsure of where he was.

"Yeon-in?" said the man in a soft and sleepy voice. *"Gaeneun eodi issni?"*

Those words broke my heart.

Sweetheart? Where's the dog?

What a father might say to his daughter.

The ax rose a little higher. Blood ran from the steel head down the shaft and over the man's hand. I saw the hand begin to tremble, to shake. The ax blade wobbled. In another version of reality it would have been because of fear or heartbreak or the absolute terror of understanding.

This wasn't that world.

The shaking became more intense. More violent. I saw the man's confusion burn away, saw the glassiness melt from his eyes to be replaced by something beyond insane. By raw, unfiltered, limitless rage.

He opened his mouth and howled like a demon. The ax rose high.

And Top shot him.

The ax dropped from nerveless fingers and struck blade-first into the dirt. The man collapsed down beside it, making no attempt to break his fall. That fast. No cry of pain, no struggle to bull past the effects of the drug. Sandman whispered and consciousness fled.

Havoc moved forward and stood in a ragged circle around the man. When the poor bastard fell he cut his cheek on the ax blade. Belle knelt and rolled him over, then tore a handful of grass, using it to sponge away the blood. Given what that ax had done and the evidence that lay scattered around, it was a useless gesture and we all knew it. She touched the man's face and then reached over and touched the face of the little girl and the dog.

"Salam ya 'akhi," she murmured.

Peace, my brother.

It came close to breaking my heart. And it also recalled my own moment on Frog Island when I made the promise to the dead woman. Grief, however borrowed, for a total stranger, was the flag Belle would go to war under. I flew my own, and I suspected Top, Bunny, and Andrea had theirs flying. For Ho, maybe it was for Sergeant Chung, or maybe for an entire island of his countrymen.

Only Mun stood apart, looking beyond the horrors there in the grass, studying the parking lot and buildings. She held her dart gun in her right hand, the barrel pointed down. Her head was cocked as she listened to the wind, which was whistling through the trees.

I took the ax and slipped the handle through a loop in my harness, letting that blade hang between my shoulders. Everyone watched me do that, no one asked why.

"Outlaw," said Belle, rising to her feet, "on your six."

I turned to see a woman come out from behind a parked golf cart near the building. Short, fat, and bloody. She looked around like a startled bird, head bobbing this way and that, body hunched unnaturally. Then she spotted us and stared for a long, awful moment. She opened her mouth and let loose a sound like a cheetah. Raspy, raw, and inhuman. She broke into a dead run, barreling straight at us, her breasts flopping under her red-spattered shirt, hands pawing at the air as if trying to pull us toward her.

Andrea walked toward her, raising his weapon, letting her come close. It was a surreal encounter—the frenzied woman running toward a man who stood with apparent calm. I saw the gun tremble, though. I knew.

Andrea let the woman get to within fifty feet and fired. His first round missed. The second did not and she pitched forward, her dead weight propelled by momentum, and slid on the asphalt of the parking lot, sanding off the skin from hands and chin and cheek. Her body came to rest at the very edge of the grass, fingers touching the first withered stalks.

"Outlaw," said Mun. "Listen."

I did. We all did. The wind was louder now. Much louder, swelling moment by moment.

"Oh, fuck," said Bunny.

It wasn't the sound of the wind whistling through the trees. It was a higher, deeper, wetter sound.

It was voices. A lot of them.

They were screaming.

They were coming for us.

CHAPTER SIXTY-EIGHT
YEONPYEONG ISLAND
SOUTH KOREA

It was a tidal surge of madness and murder.

Dozens of people came running, drawn by the screams from the woman Andrea had shot. The sounds they made were inhuman although they came from human throats. It was hard not to think of them as monsters, as *things*. They were people. Sick people.

Civilians.

We ran for a group of parked vehicles to use them as both a shelter and a choke point. The infected would have to squeeze in between the cars and golf carts in order to get us, and we would have the advantage of fewer numbers. We ran like hell and got there first.

As we took up positions, using hoods and trunks to steady our aim, Bunny said, "I'm getting a weird déjà vu about all this shit."

"You thinking about last year in Russia?" asked Top.

"No. Thinking about last week in Syria. Those guys in the lab coats. The way they moved. Like birds. Like these people."

We all looked at him for a moment.

And then the moment was gone.

The infected rushed us, the first to reach us stumbling as the darts hit them and then being slammed into the vehicles by the wave of people behind. Even with the screams of rage we could hear the sharp, wet sounds of bones breaking and flesh bursting. I was behind an old Toyota Camry and the impact rocked it back with such force that two wheels lifted off the ground. Belle, Mun, and I were shoulder to shoulder, firing at them, and there was a change in tone of some of the screams as infected were crushed when the car dropped back down. A boy of about eleven crawled through the golf cart beside me and tried to stab Top with the jagged end of a broken boat oar, but Ho shot him. The boy vanished beneath a mass of seething bodies who crawled over him, smashing the frail body between seat and floor.

At times like this I ask myself—how can a sane and civilized mind adequately process the nature of madness?

We can understand the history of psychosis, we can read the body of work on the pathology of madness, we can discuss the warping effects of tumors and drugs, of diseases and damage. But does any of that really ever prepare you to confront a psychological fracture so severe that behavior appears to be evidence of true evil?

No. And I've been on battlefields and in conflict with the deranged and the diseased, with the ideologically zealous and the hardest of cold hearts. I should have been able to look at what was unfolding on Yeonpyeong with a clinical detachment.

That's not what happened.

Havoc Team was in a world where the victims of a bioweapon were able to think clearly enough to use weapons, to hunt prey, to set traps, and devise cruelties. Most of the victims were completely deranged, pushed to a level of mad vacuity where the harm they were driven to inflict did not need a target other than their own flesh. There was no clear pattern to any of it except that rage.

The attackers weren't even focused entirely on us. As the crowd of them thronged together they turned on one another, committing unspeakable acts.

We saw a man hammering a walking stick down someone's throat with a rubber mallet, the head of the mallet bouncing back, the dying victim kneeling there, fists punching the concrete—weaker each moment.

There was a woman fighting with two crab fishers. She had a boat hook in her hands and it was slick with blood along its length and on her arms to the elbow. There was a look of such profound hatred in her eyes that it seemed to radiate with palpable heat. Her jaw was clenched so tightly that the muscles of her face were etched like stone. The fishermen were unarmed and kept lunging for her with fingers and teeth, being beaten back each time.

A cop walked down the street with a pump shotgun, shooting

anything that moved. People, animals, birds, even a sheet of newspaper pushed by the wind. He emptied the gun and then reloaded with such anger that the slot where the shells went cut and abraded his skin. He screamed continuously, drops of blood flecking his lips.

A group of seven children ran in a pack, with the two fastest flushing apparently uninfected people out of hiding and into the path of the others. Behind them was a wake of destruction as terrible as that left by a tornado.

I heard Belle say something in Arabic that sounded like a prayer. Not for the suffering, but for her own soul. Andrea, a man with no religious beliefs, crossed himself. There was a sob and at first I thought it might have been Bunny, but I was wrong. It was Ho.

We raised our guns and shot them all.

We shot everyone on the town's main street.

We dropped everyone who came at us. Everyone who ran, walked, crawled.

We did not discriminate for age or gender. Men and women, boys and girls. Babies and old folks. Our guns found them.

Maybe we should have felt better knowing that we were firing tranquilizers that would not kill them. Sure. Tell yourself that when you're firing at a group of little kids, or a pregnant woman, or an old lady with rheumy eyes and little cloisonné kitty-cat pins on her sweater.

We fired until our magazines were empty, then dropped the empties and swapped in fresh ones. And fired.

And fired.

INTERLUDE SIXTEEN
ABOARD *THE SOUL OF PIETY*
LIMASSOL MARINA
CYPRUS, GREECE
EIGHT MONTHS AGO

"You've told me a lot about your operation," said Santoro, "but nothing at all about your clients."

"*Our* clients, son," said Kuga. He was stretched out on the deck, naked except for an indecent pair of briefs that were molded to his crotch. Skin glistening with oil, sunglasses pointed upward toward the brim of a hat that was tilted low to cover his entire face. "This is a partnership. Don't know why I can't seem to sell that idea to you."

The marina was packed with dozens of expensive yachts, a few of which were actually bigger than *The Soul of Piety*. That was as it should be. Kuga liked to be seen as wealthy but did not want to stand out in any obvious way.

"You are dodging the question." Santoro sat cross-legged on a cushion under an awning, a glass of iced tea cradled between his palms. "You always dodge the question."

"Well, in point of fact, I have two different clients right now. Two big ones, I mean, and a hell of a lot of little ones. Hell's Concierge is never short on business."

"Who are these big clients?"

Kuga took so long to answer that Santoro thought the man would simply pretend to be asleep.

"One has been a client for a long time now. I've been helping him with a number of interesting requests. Been doing that since before I went to prison. Kept it up inside, thanks to some well-placed friends."

"Like that guard . . . ?"

"Like a few guards," said Kuga. "The prison doctor was one of my people, too. Point is, I've been Uncle Vlad's go-to guy for almost ten years."

"Uncle Vlad?" mused Santoro. "As in Vladimir Putin?"

"Sure. Deep pockets and pays well. Though recently he's taken a pretty big hit. He's bankrolling some kind of big operation in the States. Don't know what it is, but he says it'll help him launch his Novyy Sovetskiy scheme."

"'New Soviet' . . . ?" queried Santoro. "I thought that was only an internet rumor."

"Oh, it's real," laughed Kuga. "Uncle Vlad thinks he has a shot at making it happen, too. Don't ask me how because although I'm happy to take his money we are not drinking buddies. He doesn't drunk-call me and confess his deep, dark secrets. What he is to me, though, is a cash cow. More than a third of what my operation does is tied to him in one way or another."

"Who is the other client?"

"They are a lot more interesting," said Kuga, grinning. "A whole lot. They call themselves Dasuht Myung eh Kangchul Namja."

"I don't speak Chinese."

"It's Korean, and it means The Five Iron Men. Yeah, I know. Sounds like the title of a superhero movie, but it has some ancient cultural significance. Five men representing five very old families who have been deeply involved in some of the most important events in that country's history. Wars, emperors, all that."

"What do they want of you?"

"Of *us*," corrected Kuga automatically. "That's actually a trickier question than you know. These cats won't use two words when only one will work, and they won't use one when they can get away with just a grunt. Hardly the chatty type." He removed the hat and sat up. Despite his usual affectation of indolence and sloth, Kuga moved in a way that spoke of great conditioning. No struggle at all to sit up, no use of hands. All core strength that hid a panther quickness. Kuga stood and padded over to the ice chest, got a bottle of beer, screwed off the top, and drank half of it. "What do they want?" he mused, looking at the seabirds bobbing in the water off the starboard rail.

Santoro sipped his tea and waited.

"There's what they told me," said Kuga, "and what I think they want."

"Meaning?"

"What they said they wanted was for me to engineer a way to so thoroughly discredit the government of the United States that they are forced to withdraw in a big way from South Korea and the entire region."

"Are they North or South Koreans?"

"Yeah, well, that's where it gets interesting. Three of them live in the South and the other two are bigwigs in the North. But all of them have large families that were split when the nation was cut in half."

"So . . . they are for reunification of the two Koreas?"

Kuga swirled the beer in the bottle and stared down the mouth to watch the bubbles pop. "That's what I think they'd like me to be-lieve."

"You doubt them?"

"I doubt everyone," said Kuga. "Except you."

Santoro said nothing to that and instead asked, "What, then, is their real motive?"

"Haven't totally sussed that out yet. I have my computer geeks tearing apart their emails and anything else they can sneak into."

"You have a suspicion, though . . . ?"

Kuga drank. "It's only that," he said, "but yeah. Two of them have pretty strong ties with China. Business ties. And it's not both of the guys in the North. It's one of them and one of the cats in the South. Unconnected businesses. I'll bet you a bottle of Château Pétrus, the 2010 vintage, that all five of them have business interests with China. If the U.S. leaves or their presence is diminished, then China gets to come to the financial rescue of *both* Koreas. China's on the move, becoming a much bigger economy than any Communist ide-ology should allow. I think our Five Iron Men are in this for the money and the stability. Even if there isn't a reunited Korea, if China is Big Daddy, then commerce and travel between the countries will improve. And families will reunite."

Santoro thought about that, and slowly nodded.

"Do you think you can make America retreat?"

"Huh? God, no. Even I'm not that clever."

"But."

"But," said Kuga, "I'm pretty damn sure I can get them *thrown* out."

CHAPTER SIXTY-NINE
THE TOC
PHOENIX HOUSE
OMFORI ISLAND
GREECE

Nikki Bloom, Bug's second-in-command, was on her fifth cup of coffee while hammering away to enter search arguments into the pattern recognition program. Rudy sat a few yards away, rereading the transcripts of his interviews with Rafael Santoro.

Suddenly Nikki leaped to her feet and yelled: "Holy forking shirt-balls!"

Everyone's head whipped around, but before anyone could ask what was wrong, they saw it. Nikki sent a BBC News feed to the main screen. There, larger than life and crystal clear, was a team of men and women dressed as Republic of Korea soldiers and American Navy SEALs deploying a series of small drones into the air above a beach on a remote island. The sound was bad and tinny because the mic was not close to the team, but one voice seemed to cut through the distortion. A male voice. Clearly an American accent.

"When Kim Jong-un hears about this he's going to know not to fuck with Uncle Sam."

Nikki stood aghast, her eyes wide, mouth slack, but her hands were busy as she sent feeds from other global news stations to the other screens. Two, five, eleven, thirty. Bakhtar News Agency, Agence Kampuchea Press, BBC News, China News Service, MSNBC, Ritzau, Suomen Tietotoimisto, Wafa, Agência Lusa, TASS, Tanjug, Channel NewsAsia, Newsis, Yonhap, Associated Press, CNN, Fox, Al Jazeera, Reuters, Khovar, LankaPuvath, Myanmar News Agency, Bernama, Jiji Press, Islamic Republic News Agency, Samachar Bharti . . . Rudy stopped counting. His head swam and he gripped the edge of a desk to keep from falling down.

"Ay dios mío," Rudy breathed. "It's out. Oh my dear God, it's out."

CHAPTER SEVENTY
YEONPYEONG ISLAND
SOUTH KOREA

As the darts hit, the raging people fell. Just like that. There was no struggle, no attempt to shake off the effects. They went down where they stood, weapons falling from slack fingers, eyelids fluttering shut, bodies sagging as the dreadful inner tensions were snapped off as if breakers were tripped inside their heads. We stood in a ragged line, a kind of half circle, with our backs to the wall of a crab shack, loading and firing. Covering for each other during reloads.

The Snellig dart guns' range wasn't great, but the effect was so fast that it didn't matter, and we did not need to make accurate shots. No head shots, as with Seif al Din. The darts had to break the skin, and all of us were good enough shots to do that.

"Are you sure this is safe?" demanded Ho, who had so far shot only three people—two men and a young woman. However there was a rising note to his voice that was not quite hysteria but definitely in that ZIP code.

"It's safe," I said, but Doc Holliday's voice overrode me via the team channel.

"It's been tested on adults of all ages up to seventy and with kids as young as fifteen. We don't know the effect on children or infants. We don't know the effect on pregnant women, but the chemicals should not be able to cross the placental barrier."

Ho looked wildly around as if expecting Doc to be there, but I knew it wasn't her he was seeing. He was looking at the people who lay in silent heaps around us. Some of them were children. Two were toddlers, and there were three women who were visibly pregnant. I could see his mouth through the Plexiglas visor and it was working, forming words that he could not or dared not say aloud. His telemetry was being sent to the TOC and I could only imagine where his pulse rate and blood pressure were. The pistol began rattling in his grip as shudders whipped through his body.

Beside him, Major Mun made a disgusted noise and shoved Ho unkindly aside, firing as a man in mechanics overalls rushed forward. He dropped, and then she took a teenage girl with a shot to the face, and then a mailman. Her eyes were steady, cold, merciless, and I had no doubt that if she'd been allowed to fire live rounds she would have done so with equal efficiency and obvious lack of emotion. That troubled me because it was the kind of military efficiency that crossed a line into a dangerous coldness. Not just hardened to the exigencies of warfare, and not the rancid love of bloodshed, but a complete disconnect from humanity on either end of the gun.

There was a part of me that wanted to take her off the firing line, to stand her down until I could understand who she really was as a person and a soldier. But there was no time for that. The infected of Yeonpyeong kept coming at us, drawn by the sound of conflict and the screams of people who were beyond their minds with uncontrollable fury.

In strange and somewhat perverse contrast, our dart guns made soft sounds. Almost gentle. *Pffft.* Quieter than a sound suppressor. A nothing sound that was lost amid their screams and our own labored breathing.

The scene was surreal. I'd been in firefights more times than I could count, and I've faced down mobs of infected, but in those cases it was a gunfight, or guns against the living dead. This was us fighting people we might actually be able to save, provided we figured out what the disease was and could concoct a cure or treatment. Grief stabbed us with every trigger pull, even though we were not murdering anyone. The emotions were twisted out of shape.

And yet around us, it was a lovely day. The December sky was a hard blue you could scratch a match on. Unseasonably warm sunlight sparkled on the water and there were birds singing in the trees. How was this the world? How did the actions and the environment fit into one dimension? Where in all of this was sanity or God or hope?

"On your left," yelled Top, and I turned as a small pack of them came howling toward us. Nine of them, running together, each of them spattered with blood from the crimes they'd committed; all of them armed with pipes or wrenches or pieces of wood. One had a human arm—a woman's, I think—that he brandished like a club. I wanted to kill him. More him than the others, even though it was obvious every one of this bunch had done awful things to their friends and neighbors. But the man waving the arm was emblematic of the deep horror of this, and the Killer in my head wanted to extinguish that, to erase it and the possibility of it from the tribal consciousness. To deny its potential and prevent such horrors from spreading like an infection.

I fired and tried to hold my ground, but they came fast. Flies were everywhere, drawn by the smell of blood in the air, and they crawled over my visor. They swarmed in the air, too small to be targets of our bullets or of the rage of the infected. Bunny and Belle moved to

JONATHAN MABERRY

flank me and we took them all down. It felt obscene to do it so easily. Nine of them, three of us. Four seconds. I felt bile in my throat as if we'd slaughtered them. How could Junie so misunderstand me as to think I was unmoved by combat?

Or, maybe more truly, how could I be so detached from her as to not explain these things to the one person who cared more for me than anyone else? If there was a failure in perception and empathy, it had to be mine.

The fight—if you could call something as one-sided as this a fight—went on, minute after endless minute. We began making our way through the town, sweating out our fear and horror as we walked beneath the unrelenting sun.

I saw sunlight through the throng and realized that the crowd was thinning. We were gaining the tactical edge here, despite their numbers. Within a couple of minutes the last of the closest ones were down, piled in heaps over their neighbors.

"We need to get to the docks," I said. "That's where the administration buildings are. Everyone reload." They did. We each wore sweatbands around our brows beneath our hoods, but the suits were boiling. Moisture pooled in our eye sockets and ran down to soak our clothes. Dehydration was going to become an issue pretty quickly. I rose up. "Moving," I shouted, and they peeled off and followed, watching left and right and behind.

The streets were like a war zone, with people torn to pieces in very ugly ways. There were no uninfected people along our route. Ho was beside me and pointed to various corpses here and there.

"See that?" he said, indicating where a woman had clearly tried to hide inside a parked car. She was still held fast by her seat belt, but the windshield had been smashed in so that someone could stab her in the throat with a long metal pole. One hand had been punctured and impaled on the pole. "That's a defensive wound. None of the other infected we've encountered tried to defend themselves. They were all postures of pure aggression."

"Which tells you what?" I asked.

"I don't know for sure, but I'd guess that she was uninfected when she died. She tried to hide rather than attack. That's suggestive. I need to take some samples from her."

We paused, standing in a defensive ring around the car while Ho worked.

"Make it quick, Painkiller," prompted Top. "Feel like I'm standing here with my dick out."

"Yes," said Belle, "there's movement ahead, coming fast."

"Done," he said as he used a Sharpie to scrawl notes on a sample container into which he thrust vials of blood and spit.

We moved on. The infected came at us from open doorways, and I noticed that they seemed to react to us once they saw or heard us. There weren't swarms of them actively hunting, or so it seemed. I filed that away for later consideration.

With every person who fell, and every corpse we stepped over, I could feel a gradual shift inside my own head. The Killer was not firing that gun. It was not his kind of gun and not his kind of fight. No, it was the Cop. Cold and professional. Observing everything, seeing what cried out to be seen, pinning it all to the walls inside that aspect of my mind. He was working the case because that's what he did best. That's why his personality was the one I most related to, the one that kept me steady and found a pathway through the landscape of horrors.

"Outlaw," called Mun. "That plant over there. It has a solid wall and good views of the street. We can catch our breath."

"Do it," I said, and she led the way toward the wharf, where a small crab processing plant stood next to a more official-looking municipal building. Swarms of black flies buzzed all around us. They seemed agitated. Many more of them hung in dark roiling clouds around the infected.

Everyone began doing a quick weapons check—reloading, taking a breath, fighting down the shakes. While I fitted in a new magazine of Sandman darts, Bunny's words from earlier came back to me. He was right in that the infected here did move in the same awkward, birdlike way as had the lab-coated techs and test subjects back in Syria. I reached up to tap my coms unit to switch to a private channel with the TOC when I heard Doc Holliday yell in my ear.

"Outlaw, we've lost all video and—" Then the line went dead.

"What the hell?" growled Top.

Suddenly a shot rang out and I heard a big wet cough directly

JONATHAN MABERRY

behind me. Colonel Ho staggered as the entire front of his face mask exploded outward, spraying all of us with red and chunks of gray brain tissue. His body collapsed in an artless tangle of thrashing limbs.

"Sniper!" roared Belle and Top at the same time, and then the whole world seemed to disintegrate into a madness of gunfire.

CHAPTER SEVENTY-ONE
BBC WORLD NEWS
APRIL LLEWELYN REPORTING

"Disturbing news emerged today from the North Korean island of Gaeguli Seom. What at first appeared to be an outbreak of an as-yet-unknown disease form may in fact be the work of terrorists. Video footage has been sent by the radical whistleblower news group Punk Press that appears to show armed soldiers on the beach of that island at around the same time as a presumed bioweapon was released. The Punk Press video shows many casualties among the civilian population . . ."

CHAPTER SEVENTY-TWO
YEONPYEONG ISLAND
SOUTH KOREA

I crouched and spun, but before I could take a step something smashed me sideways. It was Bunny. He had one arm hooked around Belle's waist and had rammed me with his massive shoulder as automatic gunfire filled the air and bullets chewed up the ground where I'd been standing. We fell hard on the concrete beneath the tin roof overhang of a crab shack, then rolled apart. Belle came up on one knee, holstering her dart gun aside and swinging her rifle around from behind her back. She swept the rooftops, looking for targets, firing at anything that moved.

Bunny and I dodged to opposite sides of the crab shack, also swapping weapons. The gunfire was continuous and raining down from elevated positions. There was a lot of it, too. A barrage that chased Havoc Team behind cover. Ho lay on the ground, with his head torn apart but still impossibly—horribly—alive. He twitched and thrashed, caught inside an envelope of personal agony. The bullet had slung his blood seven feet high onto the wall behind which I hid.

Top, Andrea, and Major Mun had scrambled for the cover of parked cars, letting the metal vehicles soak up the rounds. Window glass exploded and the hood and fenders popped as if in a hailstorm. I saw Top looking at me and yelling, but there was no sound in my ear. The coms were dead. That's what Bug had tried to tell me before things went to hell. Andrea was all but punching the keys of his wrist computer, but the machines were not answering to his call.

"So much for gadgets," said Bunny, having to lean toward me and yell. "We need to go old school on these fuckers. But where the hell are they?"

The rounds were coming in so hot he wasn't able to look around the corner. Splinters filled the air like hornets.

"Up there," answered Belle, who had crabbed sideways behind a stack of big spools of electrical cable. "Count twelve. Maybe more."

I took a small mirror on a stick and angled it to give me a quick peek around the corner. Thirty yards away was a one-story dockmaster's office with a cinder block half-wall around the top. A big air conditioner unit and a radio tower dominated the roof, but all along that wall were figures silhouetted against the winter sky. I couldn't make out any details except that there were at least a dozen of them, they were all in black Hammer Suits, and they were all firing down at us.

"Well, to hell with this crap," complained Bunny. He had his big Atchisson AA-12 shotgun in his hands, with a big thirty-two-round drum magazine in place. I saw that the magazine was marked with a little red heart, which was Bunny's way of indicating that it was loaded with explosive rounds instead of buckshot. He didn't dare stick his head out and instead pointed the barrel around the corner, tilted it up, and began firing.

"Merry fucking Christmas, assholes!" Bunny thundered. He was loaded with modified FRAG-12 high-explosive rounds and had his weapon set to full-auto, which gave him a fire rate of three hundred rounds per minute. He burned through the full magazine in seconds, his huge frame braced for the continuous recoil. Each round was a fin-stabilized 19mm warhead that, once fired, arms itself as soon as it travels three meters from the muzzle and detonates on impact. The HE rounds are designed to punch a one-inch-diameter hole through quarter-inch steel plate. The cinder block wall had no chance at all. Neither did three of the shooters behind that wall. I saw bodies leap into the air trailing blood and debris. The other shooters scattered.

Belle reached up and patted Bunny's brawny shoulder. "My brother," she said.

Then there was a shout behind me. "Outlaw, on your six!"

I heard a muffled voice and whirled as Top ran past me, letting his rifle drop to hang from its sling as he drew his dart gun. A swarm of infected were running toward us, climbing over the bodies of their fellow citizens. Some of those bodies were sleeping in the arms of Sandman, but others lay bleeding and gasping out their lives from the bullets that missed us but not them.

Andrea tried to grab Ho and drag him to cover, but the gunfire chased him away.

Mun began firing, but to my horror I saw she had her standard-issue rifle and was hosing the infected civilians with live rounds. Top stepped up and knocked the barrel high. She staggered, then in a moment of apparent anger, kicked Top in the groin. Or, tried to. Top twisted, quick as a snake, and took the blow on his hip then stepped right into Mun, once more slapping the rifle away as she tried to lower the barrel, seemingly to point at him. He hit her in the chest with a hard straight punch that, despite body armor, knocked her back and down hard on her ass. Top tore the gun from her hands and flung it away and pointed at her—not with his weapon but with a stiff finger. I couldn't hear what he said, but she stayed down. Tension and fury emanated from her like waves of nuclear radiation.

Bunny cut me a look and through his visor I saw him raise one eyebrow as if asking if Mun had lost her shit. I shrugged. The situation was too raw and she was an unknown. This was her country, so it was possible the stress was shoving her into some strange psychological shape. Even good soldiers can react wrong if the moment falls apart around them.

I prayed to whatever god was on call that the jammers killed all live feeds from our bodycams. If any diplomat or, worse, head of state, saw her slaughtering civilians, then this whole thing was going to fall down. Maybe that action wouldn't be a cause for war since she was South Korean and so were the civilians, but it could churn already troubled waters. Who knows what political damage it might do?

Andrea began firing at the dockmaster's office, which was now actively burning. I was busy with the infected, using the Snellig to drop them as they came close, but there were a lot of them and they were moving fast. Ho lay between the infected and the rest of Havoc and, despite everything, he was still moving, clawing feebly at the ground with his fingers.

The situation, which at first had been terrible and heartbreaking, had gone through desperate and was about to set its next foot on empty air. The—and I had to assume they were the fake SEALs and Korean soldiers—were on the street level now, sending a new fusillade our way, while the street behind us was filling up with dozens of the infected.

CHAPTER SEVENTY-THREE
THE ECONOMIST
(NO BYLINE GIVEN)

"In response to the Punk Press video purportedly showing South Korean and United States Special Forces deploying a bioweapon on a small fishing island, North Korean President Kim Jong-un issued this boldly worded statement: 'The massacre committed by the United States imperialist aggressions on Gaeguli Seom is proof that they are murderers seeking pleasure in the slaughter of innocent people. They think they can commit such atrocities without impunity but forget that we have new-type intercontinental ballistic rockets with nuclear warheads that can strike to the very heart of their evil cesspool of a nation . . .'"

INTERLUDE SEVENTEEN
DANUBIUS HOTEL GELLÉRT
BUDAPEST, HUNGARY
SIX MONTHS AGO

Santoro looked up sharply as the door opened. Kuga stood there, his blue eyes clicking here and there, taking in the whole scene. It angered the Spaniard. He did not—absolutely did not—like to be interrupted while working. Not even by Kuga.

"Why are you here?" he asked sharply. "I thought you preferred a more administrative distance from the real work?"

Kuga stood in the open doorway, his polished loafers inches from the congealing pool of crimson. Then he closed the door behind him, took a pack of bubble gum from the inner breast pocket of his impeccable Ermenegildo Zegna sports coat, unwrapped two sticks, and chewed thoughtfully. He did not reply to Santoro's comment. Not in words, but he stared at the little Spaniard until even Santoro looked uncomfortable. The little killer cleared his throat and gave a tiny bow of apology.

They stood on opposite sides of a room awash with blood. The sound system was playing a Hollies best-of playlist. The current track was "The Air That I Breathe." A romantic and very sexy song that could not have been more completely at odds with what was going on here. Or, maybe not, mused Kuga. Santoro had a noticeable bulge in his pants. Maybe this was sex to him.

There was one little patch of clean floor and Kuga stood in that. The three figures strapped to chairs barely looked human anymore. Only one of them was actually dead. The others faced the inhuman thing that sagged and dripped. Both of them were gagged and blindfolded.

Beyond them stood Santoro in his plastic blood suit, and in a corner, holding hands, dressed similarly, were two young people. Kuga gave them a long, considering appraisal, the way a hunter examines bloodhound pups in a pen.

"This is them?"

The girl smiled. "I'm Eve and this is—" But Santoro silenced her with a gunshot snap of his fingers. She immediately flushed as red as the blood on her clothes. The boy, Adam, stood staring. He was big and strong and looked dangerous, but he stood shackled by uncertainty.

Santoro said something to Adam, who opened a leather case on one of the room's two queen beds and removed headphones. He placed them on each of the two surviving prisoners, then connected wires to them and adjusted the volume on the music. He nodded.

Kuga leaned back against the door and looked at the three bound people. You couldn't tell much about who they were or where they came from. Their hair was soaked and plastered to their heads and was the color of wet brick. There wasn't a single inch of skin that was not painted with red or purpled with bruises.

He nodded to the dead man. "Who did him?"

Eve started to say something, hesitated, stopped, looked at the floor.

"Eve is particularly enthusiastic," said Santoro.

"Is that a nice word for clumsy?" asked Kuga. He blew a pink bubble. It popped with a satisfying sound and he sucked it into his mouth.

"Not at all," said the Spaniard. "Our guest was very forthcoming. Access codes, patrol schedules, timetables."

"Enough?"

Santoro gave one of his shrugs. "I do not believe he had anything useful left to say."

Kuga glanced at the bed. Clothing stood in three neatly folded piles. Two uniforms and one business suit. He popped his gum.

"These other two going to give us the rest of what we need?" he asked.

"Without a doubt."

Kuga nodded, popped his gum again, and reached for the door-knob. "Then get back to work." He shot cold looks at Adam and Eve but pointed to Santoro. "You two listen to me. This man is my friend and my business partner, but more than that he is an artist. He is the best of the best of the best. You keep your heads out of your asses and maybe—*maybe*—you'll be a tenth as good, which will make you five times better than anyone else you meet. Studying under him is a gift and maybe you're smart enough to recognize how valuable a gift it is. I hope so. He seems to think so. Do not disappoint him. If so, then you won't have him to answer to. Trust me when I tell you that you do not want to make *me* mad." He chuckled, warm as an uncle on Christmas morning. "No, you really don't want that."

He blew another bubble, watching what his words did to their eyes and the shapes of their mouths. Then he gave them a friendly wink and went out.

CHAPTER SEVENTY-FOUR
THE TOC

Church took the call from Jerry Spencer while watching Havoc Team fight their way across Yeonpyeong Island. He stepped into a quiet corner before answering.

"Detective Spencer," said Church. "I've been waiting for your call."

"Yeah? Well, you're not going to like what I have to say," muttered Spencer.

"No," said Church, "I expect not."

CHAPTER SEVENTY-FIVE
YEONPYEONG ISLAND
SOUTH KOREA

There are moments in a person's life that truly define them. It's as if the universe distills everything down in simpler choices, even if those choices are both bad. At least you understand them. You do this or you do that. If you do neither, you die; and maybe that's what you deserve. Inaction is action in its own way—it's the victim's choice: I can't decide, so have your way with me.

In that golden moment, if your will to live is strong enough, you eliminate that weak option and focus on the two bad choices. Which one will kill me first? Or, contrarily, which choice will demand that the universe work that much harder to cut me down? Which choice will *matter* most?

It's not about survival, really. It's about staying alive long enough to make sure that your death serves a purpose. It's you spitting in the devil's eye and telling him to go fuck himself because even if his knights and rooks are about to slaughter your king, you are willing to simply knock over the chessboard.

That was the moment by the crab shack. We had certain death in front of and behind us. But here's the thing about certainty. Just as that old saying "Man plans, God laughs" is true, so is the philosophy of a certain kind of soldier on certain kinds of battlefields. And I'm not just talking about those wearing uniforms and fighting for a flag. It's as true of a bullied kid with his back to a boys' bathroom wall as it is of a woman who will not be punched down to the floor again by her asshole husband. It's true of people who have had almost everything stripped away from them but that last bit of pride, that last spark of fire. And what is that philosophy? It's not some beautifully phrased bit of philosophic insight; it's not a pithy aphorism or a memorable catchphrase. Nah. Nothing like that.

It's just this . . .

If you want me, you have to earn it.

And I'm going to make it very goddamn expensive for you.

CHAPTER SEVENTY-SIX
AL JAZEERA
D. S. MONGOLFI REPORTING

"Many nations have issued statements in support of North Korea and openly condemning the actions of the United States and South Korea in the strongest possible terms. China and Russia are threatening to close American embassies and eject all U.S. government and private citizens. This tragedy comes at a critical time in world politics as North and South Korea, China, and the United States, along with five other nations, have gathered in Oslo for the D9 denuclearization summit scheduled to begin in two days. The nine world leaders are already in Norway, but their embassies and hotels have had their security statuses raised to Severe. It is not yet known whether the world leaders will cancel the summit and return home. There is an air of extreme tension throughout Oslo . . . and the world."

CHAPTER SEVENTY-SEVEN
YEONPYEONG ISLAND
SOUTH KOREA

"Pappy, Jackpot," I barked, "cover our backs. "Dart 'em if you can, but *stop* them."

They rose up without question and began firing.

"Donnie Darko, Mother Mercy, on me."

I took a fistful of Major Mun's Hammer Suit and hauled her roughly to her feet. She tried to slap my hand away but I kept my grip. I had to lean close to be heard. "Listen to me and *hear* me. We're in the shit and you are with us or you're not. Tell me right now and make me believe it. The coms and bodycams are down so if you fuck with me, no one will ever know who put one in your brainpan. Are you reading me on this?"

"Take your hands off me," she snarled.

Instead of that, I gave her a shake that probably loosened her fillings and then jerked her forward until her mask was hard against mine.

"I don't know what your problem is, Major, but right now you are not among friends."

"No," said Belle, shifting close, "you're not."

"Hooah," said Bunny.

"No fucking around," I said coldly, giving Mun another rough shake, "are you with us or not?"

She looked into my eyes. And she did in fact hear me and see me. I could see the understanding in her face.

"Yes," she said hoarsely. "I'm sorry about—"

"I don't give a flying fuck what you're sorry about. Are you *with* us or not? Say it clear and make me believe it."

Something shifted in her. Even her posture changed. She stopped trying to pull away and instead stood firm and straightened. She gave a slow, firm nod.

"I'm with you," she said. I watched her eyes. Mun was tough as nails and she met my glare, but there was a flicker there, as if she wanted, or perhaps *needed*, to look away. It troubled me, but we were in the shit, so I had to accept her word. For now.

I let her go. I didn't shove her back or any of that shit. I let her go. However, I saw Belle point a finger like a pistol and then use her thumb to drop the hammer. Mun stepped away, picked up her rifle, checked the magazine, and turned toward the edge of the wall that was being continually chewed apart by gunfire.

"What's the plan, boss?" asked Bunny.

I was not in a mood for niceties. I plucked two fragmentation grenades from my harness. "Plan? How about a nice big cup of fuck you?"

Bunny grinned and pulled two of his own.

We pulled the pins and lobbed them in a tight arc over the wall of the crab shack. The second they blew I was moving, running low, firing into the smoke, Mun beside me, with Bunny and Belle flanking us. The bad guys had the numbers. We had one moment of utter confusion. That's my kind of math.

I saw shapes reeling in the cloud of red-tinged dust and fired into it as I ran. Bullets punched through the air, but I didn't care. This wasn't a fight. This was murder. We took it to them, closing to zero distance as we hosed them with rounds. I heard Bunny cough out a cry of pain as bullets hit him, but he powered through the foot-pounds of impact, letting the body armor do its work and making the bad guys pay for the searing pain in his chest. One of the ROK soldiers, his weapon empty and no time to fish for a new magazine, swung his rifle stock at Belle but she shot him in the face and kicked him at the same time. He reeled back, his dead weight screening her as she closed on a second man and killed him, too.

Belle, small and wiry and fast, emptied an entire magazine into a pair of soldiers who were trying to shift away out of the smoke in order to get a better look at their targets. They wasted a second doing that, and she killed them for their stupidity.

On the other side of me, Mun was firing with a handgun, holding it in both hands as she walked forward, aiming, firing, killing, aiming. I thought I'd seen her hesitate for a moment at first, but now she was doing her job.

There were a total of eleven of the bad guys left after Bunny's earlier barrage and my grenade. We could have hidden behind obstacles and spent all afternoon sniping at each other. This wasn't that kind of fight. We had that moment of advantage and we took it.

And we killed them all.

When I lowered my gun and turned around, Top and Andrea stood side by side, chests heaving, dart guns hanging at their sides, in front of a mountain of infected.

I looked around for more enemies to fight. Saw none. Beyond the tiny town was the bright blue water, the wave tops traced with gold, and a line of clouds peering with frightened interest over the horizon line.

CHAPTER SEVENTY-EIGHT
CNN
THE SITUATION ROOM WITH WOLF BLITZER

"We begin this hour with breaking news from North Korea. A shocking and deeply disturbing story is unfolding. The video you are about to see contains strong images and viewers are cautioned . . ."

The graphic for Punk Press fills the screen.

CHAPTER SEVENTY-NINE
YEONPYEONG ISLAND
SOUTH KOREA

They were all down.

They were not all dead. We formed a tight circle, guns up and out as we turned like a dial, scanning for targets—maybe hungry for them. Birds, shocked to silence, stood like witnesses to what we'd done. Nothing moved except the smoke.

One of the soldiers—a slender man with a Korean face—was on his knees, his body running with blood. He had a pistol in his hand but it was pointed down. Mun was moving toward him, her gun pointing at his heart. Bunny pointed his shotgun at the man, too.

"Drop the weapon," he bellowed. "Do it right now or I will kill you."

The man did not drop the gun, but Bunny never had a chance to follow up on his threat, because the soldier swept the pistol up, jammed the barrel under his own chin, and pulled the trigger. The bullet punched a big red hole in the top of the Hammer Suit hood and then the man was down, reduced to cooling meat in a microsecond.

Mun, who was closest, was splashed with blood and bits of bone. She stood stock still, eyes wide, mouth open, her gun pointing nowhere.

"What the actual fuck . . . ?" gasped Bunny.

"Check the others," I ordered, and Havoc began moving among the dead.

One of the attackers was still alive, body torn by grenade shrapnel. He crawled slowly away from the scene of slaughter, leaving a glistening red slug trail behind him. I removed my nearly empty magazine and replaced it with one heavy with unspent potential. The man on the ground was looking over his shoulder, and through a cracked and torn visor, I saw an American face. A SEAL. Or someone masquerading as one. He made a sound that was unnaturally loud in the sudden silence—a whimper of fear and pain—and tried to crawl faster. I began walking toward him. The darkness in my heart was beginning to scream.

Then, all at once there was a sudden sharp electronic squawk that stabbed through my head and Scott Wilson's voice was in my ear. ". . . *Outlaw, do you copy?*"

"I'm here," I said.

"The jammer just went down," Wilson said. "Don't know why, but it's good. All channels are open and we have the feeds now from your bodycams."

I glanced at Belle, who hurried over with something she just pulled from a dead soldier's backpack. I took it and turned the thing over in my hands. It was a ruggedized laptop in a thick plastic case. Three bullet holes puckered the cover.

"Yeah, we found and disabled the jamming device," I said. "It's trashed but I'll bring you what's left. I don't recognize the design, though."

"Maybe Bug's team can salvage it and find out who made it," Doc said. "Right now, though, all lines but one are clear. Check Pain-killer's telemetry feed—something seems to be wrong with it."

Top and Andrea, their rearguard work done for now, were kneeling on either side of Colonel Ho. I could see Top's shoulders rise and fall with resignation. He raised his head, found me, gave a small shake. I felt a pang, deep and acute. I'd come to like and respect Ho. "Painkiller's down," I said.

"Oh, dear God," said Wilson. "I'm so dreadfully sorry."

It occurred to me then how this was going to look. The only representative of North Korea was dead, and on South Korean soil. During an illegal operation, because it would come out that he hadn't cleared his involvement in this with anyone higher up the political food chain. I wondered if the North Korean official who was a friend of Church's was still on the call and deliberately broke protocol by using the fallen doctor's real name.

"Colonel Ho was a hero and he died like one," I said. "He took an incredible risk to participate in a mission to save his country and maybe the whole region. Dr. Ho did not want his country torn apart by war, especially one that does not need to happen. He believed, as this whole team believes, that whoever did this—on Gaeguli Seom and here on Yeonpyeong—is trying to manipulate the governments of both Koreas, and probably China and the United States, into declaring war. They used a bioweapon in both places and tried to sell the false narrative of this being a secret plot by the U.S. and South Korea. Ho didn't believe that any more than the rest of us. Of *course* he didn't believe it. He was too good an officer, too insightful a man, too wise a doctor, and too loyal and honorable a soldier of the Korean People's Army to be fooled. His death was tragic, but he died fighting for his country and his people. He died a hero and I am proud to have served along with him. I will gladly work with the governments of all four nations to hunt down the people responsible and scorch the ground on which they stand."

It was a speech, and I spoke slowly, crafting my sentences, making sure that the message was clear. While I spoke I looked at Major Mun, who stood a dozen yards away. Her body was ramrod stiff and her eyes burned into mine. I waited for some acknowledgement, some sign that she was truly on the same page as me. All I got was that stony silence.

I gave her another nod, though, with a different meaning that I figured she was sharp enough to read. Letting her know that this was far from over. Telling her that we were going to have a conversation off-coms. Soon. Maybe one she wouldn't like. Beyond her, I saw Belle and Top studying her. Belle's rifle was still slung from her shoulder, but the barrel was pointed ever so slightly in Mun's direction. Belle was making her own eloquent statement. Top didn't have to. I always know where he stands. The major looked hard at Belle and over the com channel I heard a soft grunt of dismissal, as if Belle was nothing to her. Who knows, maybe she even believed that, but if it came down to gunplay I knew where my bet was going to fall.

I glanced down at Colonel Ho and felt a fresh wave of sadness sweep through me. Poor bastard. Because of the bottomless bullshit of international politics, guys like us might never have met. I admit to sometimes falling into the trap of demonizing the citizens of adversary countries because it's easy to conflate everyone there with the far more visible policies of their leaders. Kim Jong-un is a hard guy to like and I'm not sure I'd piss on him if he were on fire. But he's only the *head* of North Korea, he's its mouth and fist and noise. He isn't the *people*. Lieutenant Colonel Ho Yong-ju was a doctor and a humanist, and he died trying to prevent a war. I didn't know him very well, but I knew I would mourn him and count him among the chosen few with whom I've served, and who have been swept from the chessboard while lesser men like me somehow survive.

The speech I'd just given, however, hadn't just been a testament to Ho. No, it had been for Church's four "friends in the industry." I assumed they were all listening in and maybe watching bodycam feeds as well. That was fine. Maybe they could use what I said in whole or as sound bites as part of the spin control needed to keep the missiles in their silos. I only hoped I'd given them enough.

I bent and placed my hand on Ho's chest for a moment. Being with him.

"Sorry, brother," I said, but not loud enough for anyone but me to hear.

CHAPTER EIGHTY
FOX NEWS
CHRIS WALLACE REPORTING

"The White House has issued a firm rebuttal to the accusations of hostile acts committed on the North Korean island of Gaeguli Seom—the Island of Frogs. White House Press Secretary Alexandra Marini says that the president sends thoughts and prayers for the people of Gaeguli Seom and will make a formal televised statement later today . . ."

CHAPTER EIGHTY-ONE
YEONPYEONG ISLAND
SOUTH KOREA

I rose from Colonel Ho's body and walked over to the dying SEAL, came around and stood in his path. Nobody had stopped him from trying to crawl away, because he wasn't making any real headway.

Bunny had turned him over and pressed compresses into the red ruin of his chest and stomach. Through the blood I could see purple coils of intestines and the sharp white edges of bone. The Hammer Suit the man wore was a ruin and there was a big chunk missing from his visor, though his face was unmarked. There was blood around his nostrils and on his lips, and more leaking from one ear. From the look Bunny gave me, and the evidence of my own eyes, it was clear this guy was not going to make it.

Bunny took a syrette and gave the guy a shot of painkiller. Not enough to drop him into darkness, but enough to help with the agony. The stuff worked fast and the man's frantic shallow breathing slowed noticeably.

The dying man looked up at me and I could see so many emotions in his glazed eyes. There was, strangely, no hate there. None of the *fuck you* gallows bravado of the dying soldier. None of the disingenuousness of the discovered traitor. None of that. In his blue eyes I saw fear and shame and horror. And, I think, a kind of regret that drills all the way down to the marrow. The emotions in his eyes changed the words I said to him; they changed the conversation we would have.

"Who are you?" I asked, and the gentleness in my voice surprised even me.

It took a lot of effort for him to answer. Breathing was a challenge. "B-Burke . . ."

"Give me more," I told him.

But before he could speak the left lens of my goggles filled with raw data. Not only was the jammer down, but Bug had clearly taken images from my body camera and run facial recognition. I scanned the information and felt my heart sink.

"Petty Officer First Class Cletus Burke," I said. "You're actively U.S. military. You're a SEAL, currently serving as a trainer."

His eyes widened for a moment, then he mouthed the word *yes*.

Behind him I saw my guys moving among the other dead, turning them over, letting Bug take a look. Names began appearing on my visor screen, and some of them broke my heart. Not because I knew them, which I didn't, but because one in four were actual soldiers and sailors. Real Navy SEALs. Real Republic of Korea soldiers. I heard Top sighing a lot. Heavily, the way you do when, against all efforts to the contrary, the goddamn truth turns out to be bigger and uglier than you thought.

The other dead men and women were more of a puzzle. Some were pinged as ex-military, but from a variety of countries. England, Russia, Egypt, both Koreas. Both honorable and dishonorable discharges. Some with known ties to the shadier private contractor groups. Blackwater. Blue Diamond.

And one of them was a suspected member of the group of highly trained mercenaries who used to work for the Seven Kings, known as "Kingsmen." We'd put that organization down and locked up or killed a lot of their foot soldiers. Like bad pennies some of the survivors turned up here and there. Never in good places. Like now.

"This is getting pretty weird," said Bunny. "Even for us."

I leaned close to Burke, all compassion for him burning away as fast and hot as a magician's flash paper.

"*Why?*" I snarled. "Why did you do this?"

"We . . . *had* to . . ."

JONATHAN MABERRY

"Don't give me that bullshit, Burke. You're active military and so are some of the others, but you're running a kill op against civilians and most of your team are contractors. Tell me how that makes sense. Who cut your orders?"

Burke gave a feeble shake of his head. "Please, you have to help me . . . my wife . . . my kids . . ."

I wanted to hit him. I wanted to rant about all the wives and kids dead on Frog Island. Dead here. Infected and ruined. But the Cop and the Modern Man inside my head told me to listen. To *hear* what Burke was saying.

"What *about* your family?" I asked.

Tears boiled up in his eyes and fell onto the bloody dirt. "*They'll* hurt them."

"They? Who?"

"The . . . blond kids . . ." His voice was fading.

"What are you talking about? Burke, listen to me. Tell me what happened here."

He shook his head. His fists were clenched as he tried to hold onto life long enough to talk. "They . . . blindsided me. The blond kids. They . . . looked like nothing. Like maybe . . . college kids. Jesus . . . you have to swear to me that you'll save my family . . . my wife . . . my kids . . . oh, God, what have I done?"

He coughed and red blood ran over his chin.

"Listen to me, Burke," I said. "You're dying. Nothing can change that now, but you can change what your death means by telling me what is going on. Who sent you here? Is this a sanctioned military operation? Are you working for the government of the United States?"

If his answer was a yes, even if it turned out to be a rogue cell, we were all fucked. And by "we," I mean most of the population of planet Earth.

Burke shook his head. "Not . . . not official."

"Is this a black op?"

"No," he said, and sounded surprised that I even asked such a thing. Maybe he didn't know about the Punk Press video. I dearly hoped the TOC was getting this all in high-def video and good-fidelity sound.

"Then who sent you?"

"I . . . told you . . . the blond kids . . ."

"Who are they? Is that a code name for a group? Give me details, Burke, give me names."

Blood ran from the corners of his mouth.

"Boss," said Bunny quietly, "this cat's circling the drain."

"Talk to me, Burke," I pleaded. "Don't die with this on your conscience. Who are the blond kids?"

"Don't know who they are. The boy . . . he called her Eve . . . I think . . . Don't know who they work for. They're . . . Americans, I think. Young. Twenties. They . . . they took me to see this other guy. Their boss, I think. Not American. Spanish, I think. Spain . . . not Mexico or Puerto Rico or like that. They called him . . . Daddy. They took me to see him and he said . . . oh, Christ, he said they would . . . would . . . hurt my wife, my kids . . . oh Christ . . . they said . . ." Words failed him. A man like this, a professional sailor and special operator, was unable to repeat the things these three strangers said they would do to his family. Jesus Christ.

"Give me more," I demanded. "Give me some details. Names, locations. What is this bioweapon? Why these targets? Why North and South Korea both?"

"Please . . . ," he begged in a ghost of a voice, "please send someone to save my family . . ."

"Give me *something* and I promise to do everything I can. But you have to tell me something I can use."

Burke looked at me with eyes defined by pain and the knowledge that he was dying. So much fear, but not of me, and not—I think—of his own death. His breathing was getting bad, stopping and starting.

"They . . . they said it wouldn't . . . kill them," he wheezed. "They said it would just make them . . . a little crazy. They swore." He coughed and fresh blood ran from his nose and mouth. "My . . . my . . . locker . . . I . . ."

"Burke, you're not making sense."

It was all the sense he was ever going to make. He closed his eyes and there was a settling of his body, not just as the last air left him and muscular tension relaxed completely. No, it was more than that.

JONATHAN MABERRY

It was almost as if I saw his troubled spirit leave the broken shell of his house of life.

CHAPTER EIGHTY-TWO
YEONPYEONG ISLAND
SOUTH KOREA

I stood slowly, feeling as if my body was burdened with ten times as much mass. A burden of pain and doubt and confusion. Not only because of what Burke said, but because his visor was shattered, with pieces missing, exposing him to the outside air. He had not gone insane. Or, at least, not violently so. What did that mean?

"Did you get all that?" I asked.

"Every word," said Church. "We have people already working on everything he said."

"He said something about his locker."

"On that," said Scott Wilson. "He's stationed in Tokyo. We have his hotel and gym targeted and investigators are en route with all clearances pending."

"Make sure they have bodycams," I told him. "We share every damn thing."

That was for the benefit of anyone watching, of course. Wilson said that he would insist upon it.

To everyone at the TOC, I said, "We need to dig deep. We need to know the connection between the active-duty military and the contractors."

"On it," promised Bug.

"Two blond kids and a Spanish guy," I mused. "Maybe that's a start."

There was a slight pause, then Church said, "I look forward to your field report with great interest."

I stiffened. Church and I had agreed on a handful of code phrases before Havoc rolled out. Using a shared channel was useful for the diplomats, but it was a severe pain in the ass for the kind of unfiltered communication I was used to having with him and the field support teams. "Field report" was a signal that he wanted to have a private chat, and ideally soon; however, "great interest" meant that there was something very important he needed to tell me.

"Copy that," I said as calmly as I could manage. But something else needed to be on the record for whoever was listening. "Burke and the others were renegades, that much is clear. Someone wants us to think that this is some kind of government-sanctioned plot, which we all know it damn well is not. This is criminal, not political, and we have to work together to stop it."

It was another speech, a little more of the "we're all in this together" rhetoric that I hoped would throw water instead of gasoline on the fire. I'm not great at keeping things calm, though. I think we can all agree that's not my most well-polished skill set. Even so, it was worth a try.

That done, I needed a clear space for that chat, and I needed it right now. "Mother Mercy," I shouted, "find an elevated shooting position and watch our backs. Jackpot and Donnie Darko, start a sweep along the docks. These bastards came here in some kind of boat. Find it. Preserve all physical evidence."

"Hooah," they said.

"But before you do, Jackpot, I want every UAV we have in the air. Complete aerial survey, all wavelengths. If there are uninfected survivors, I want them located so we can bring them here. The crab plant is our shelter point."

"On it," he said. Andrea and Bunny ran for the equipment bags.

"Pappy," I said, "you take Mudang and work the buildings around the harbor. Flush out anyone in a hazmat suit. Dart guns only unless you have no choice. That includes any more of these phony-baloney soldiers and SEALs. I want to drag some of these bastards in chains before a world court and I need them alive."

"Hooah," he said; however Mun said nothing. Instead she gave me a lingering look that was impossible to read. What the hell was her game? I have an intense dislike of going into critical situations with people I don't know and haven't trained alongside. I've done a lot of operations alongside various divisions of the ROK and my personal estimation of them is very high. Mun, however, was an X factor. I had an uneasy feeling there was more to her attitude than just the sometimes off-kilter social interaction of someone working for a black ops team like Kingdom. Hell, I'm black ops and I know I'm weird. No, there had to be more story to be told, and the situation hadn't allowed for me to get to know someone who was walking into battle alongside me and my team.

Mun seemed to be studying me, too, then without a sound she turned and followed Top. I watched to make sure she was drawing the dart gun only. She was. That was something, but only cold comfort. However, I trusted that Top was going to keep a close eye on her. He's a tough man to fool, and his tolerance for bullshit or shifty behavior is notoriously thin. She would cross him at her peril, and neither gender nor nationality would be a buffer against his wrath.

"TOC to Havoc Actual," said Scott Wilson quickly, trying to catch me before I disconnected from the main channel, "we have a support team inbound. Medical personnel and a coalition team to help secure the island. ETA thirty minutes. They will drop supplies but not land or deploy personnel until you give the all-clear." He gave me the coordinates for the drop zone.

"Much appreciated, Grendel," I said, using his call sign. "In the meantime, we've got a lot of work to do."

"Yes, we do," he said.

I moved off into the shadows of the crab shack and tapped my coms unit to cycle out of the main channel. As soon as I engaged the TOC-only channel, Church was waiting for me.

"How much of what's going on here is making it onto the news?"

"Virtually everything that happened before you arrived," he said. "Very little since. Our enemy seemed quite interested in allowing civilians to upload images of a military team attacking them and getting it onto social media. The jammer started when you were about to come in conflict with them, suggesting they did not want the public to send video of good guys riding to the rescue. It's clever, but we now have some useful material to counter that."

"Will that keep the missiles in their silos?" I asked.

"There is considerable saber-rattling and some grandstanding with fighter jet flybys, but so far no one has fired a shot," said Church.

"Well . . . that's something. Stopping World War Three is way high on my day planner."

"You don't say," drawled Church dryly. "By the way, your feeds are being shared with officials in the four governments, and that goes all the way to the top. Your speeches and pointed commentary have been particularly useful. Grendel says that if you ever retire from field work you have a promising career in public relations or politics."

"Politics? I'd rather be eaten by rats."

"I told him as much."

"Tell me something, though, our feeds are shared, but what about our names?"

"No," said Church firmly. "We insisted on that. Combat call signs only, and your cover as a WHO team is still intact. Bug has buttressed the backstory and it is unshakable. John Cmar is fielding questions about hiring you, and is doing a creditable job. I don't think anyone will feel the need to try and deconstruct your cover."

"Well," I said sourly, "hooray for that."

"We take our wins where we can find them," said Church philosophically, but then his voice turned much more serious. "Now, listen to me, Outlaw, there is another critical matter I need to tell you about. The Punk Press video file has been released to all major news services. The story is exploding. It is eclipsing the outbreak on Yeonpyeong Island, and the usual talking heads are already howling for blood."

"Ahhhhh . . . fuckballs." I closed my eyes. "How bad is it?"

"No one has declared war," Church said, "but that word is on the lips of several heads of state, and it's all over the media. Warships are already closing on one another and there are jets doing dangerous flybys of our fleet. North Korea and China are trying to provoke a response and unfortunately that may happen. They are clearly willing to sacrifice one or more of their aircraft to further justify a strong military response."

My heart was racing, which I know they could see from the suit's telemetry. Bet theirs were, too.

"What are we doing to encourage cooler heads to prevail?" I asked.

"Everything that can be done."

"Sounds like a platitude, boss."

"It's a statement of fact," said Church crisply. "We have people well placed in each government and they are pioneering new levels of spin control. It's important to remember that heads of state yelling into press cameras may be alarming, but the generals and admirals who would actually carry out the physical actions of pressing buttons or pulling triggers tend to be cooler and far more professional. It is in no one's best interest for this to escalate to an armed conflict, and right now everyone—hawk or dove—is having to step away from what got them elected or appointed and think very carefully about what will keep their constituents alive."

"Are we talking mutiny if they're ordered to launch nukes?"

"That's flexible but not outside the bounds of probability," said Church.

"Good, so I can unclench my sphincter."

"The situation is fluid and volatile," warned Church, "and the fact that the strike team were, in fact, active U.S. and South Korean military is critically bad for us. I don't think we're getting out of this without at least a proportional response."

"Shit. I don't suppose we can sell Yeonpyeong as that response?"

"Right now the fact of a similar attack on a South Korean island is the *only* thing keeping North Korea and China from firing on our fleet. We are selling the story that an unknown terrorist organization is behind this, possibly to either prevent Korean reunification, or to disrupt the D9 conference. The intel from Burke and the identities of the military contractors you put down will help with that, but it's brand-new intel and has to be massaged."

I waved away some blowflies and leaned my back against the shack wall, and stared across the stretch of bloody ground. Past Colonel Ho's body to where Burke lay. "About that," I said, "the things he said are eating my lunch right now, you dig? Two blond kids and a Spanish guy? And Burke's terror that something was going to happen to his family. On the face of it, I thought he was talking about retaliation for what he and his team did, but . . ."

"Say it, Outlaw."

"There is something really familiar about this. I feel like I've had this same conversation before."

"Perhaps on Fair Isle?" suggested Church.

Fair Isle was a small island in the North Sea, off the coast of

Scotland. By some very weird twist of international politics, a bio-weapons research facility known as the Fair Isle Research Endeavor was located there. It was officially anything *but* what it really was. During one of my early DMS gigs, I had to go into the facility to get information from a scientist. The entire facility had been compromised and the scientist tried very hard to kill everyone there, even to the point of disabling the facility's safety protocols and releasing a deadly pathogen that killed everyone. Among the dead was his own son, whom he'd brought to work that day in order to kill him. Which is so messed up, because the scientist loved his son very much. But he was willing to let his son bleed out from exposure to a weaponized hemorrhagic bioweapon rather than allow some very bad people to get their hands on the boy. And he destroyed the entire facility via contamination to make it a tomb for his child and himself.

Why commit murder rather than go to the authorities? Ah, that took some figuring out. What we learned is that a truly evil little man named Rafael Santoro, who worked for the Seven Kings organization, was a master of the art of coercion. He could get virtually anyone to do anything. Sure, he mainly targeted very specific people, those with a predisposition to weakness or with exploitable vulnerabilities. But not always. Santoro had a genius for breaking social values and even military conditioning, because he made the alternatives so unbearable. It wasn't merely threats, but video documentation of what had been done to those people unwise enough to call his bluff. Santoro never bluffed. That was the key. He had a large network of people so well positioned—and so utterly ruthless—that the slightest slip in cooperation had unbearable results. The Spanish Inquisition had nothing on Santoro. Or, maybe it was that he learned their secrets and then took it further, away from religious insanity into big-ticket criminal endeavors.

During that case the DMS heard, more than once, pleas to protect children, wives, husbands, whole families. Sometimes we were able to do that. Sometimes we were too late because Santoro had planned for that. When an operation was as big as the Seven Kings, there were ten times the risks as with ordinary criminal conspiracies—which meant there were ten times the safeguards. And it was always planned years in advance. By the time the DMS collided with the

Kings it was almost impossible to stop them. And, sure, we did, but a lot of innocent people were destroyed along the way. I don't say just "killed" . . . they were destroyed. Consider that word for a moment, let the implications run wild, and maybe, just maybe, you'll get a hint of the enormity of it.

All of this ran through my head like fevered lightning.

"Yes," I said, "a lot like Fair Isle. Are we thinking that someone's taking a page out of Santoro's playbook?"

It took Mr. Church way too long to answer the question. The day, bright and sunny, suddenly went cold around me.

"That's *not* what you're thinking, are you?" I asked, dreading to both ask the question and have it answered.

"Outlaw," said Church, "there have been some developments."

INTERLUDE EIGHTEEN
ABOARD *THE SOUL OF PIETY*
KIEL CANAL
RIVER ELBE, GERMANY
FOUR MONTHS AGO

"Let me ask you a straight question, Rafael, and I'd like a straight answer. It's just the two of us."

Santoro looked up from his work. He had a whetstone and was sharpening a row of knives. "What is it?"

"Well, first, take a snapshot of this," said Kuga. He was smiling but there was no amusement in it. "You are—by anyone's standards—a mass murderer. You've killed more people than the average person ever meets. And here you are, sharpening your knives aboard my boat, which amounts to our secret lair."

"That is a silly way to view it."

"I know, but I want you to tell me why. I mean, for fuck's sake, look at us. We are actual supervillains. Or as close as, and sometimes even I can't stand myself. We're clichés from a James Bond movie. Both of us were part of shadowy criminal organizations that, had we been successful, would have done immeasurable harm to the world."

Santoro set down his tools, took a deep breath and exhaled through his nostrils, controlling his irritation. "Anything can be mocked when viewed from a certain perspective, with a certain skewed frame of mind. So what?"

Kuga came and sat on a padded bench seat.

"So what?" he asked. "Here's the thing. I know I'm corrupt. By any legal standard I'm nothing but a bad guy. I'm a criminal and—quite frankly—I enjoy being one. I rather enjoy the power and the risk."

"What is your actual question?"

"It's this . . . when you look in the shaving mirror each morning, what do you see? I mean, do you actually see the face of someone evil?"

Santoro leaned back and considered him. He searched Kuga's eyes, looking for mockery or humor, but instead saw other emotions. Confusion, doubt, and even pain.

"This matters to you?"

"I think it does."

"Are you having doubts about what we're doing? About Korea and the other matter?"

"That's the thing," said Kuga. "I'm not."

"Not at all?"

"No."

Santoro picked up a knife, studied the edge in the light from a desk lamp, sighed and set the weapon down.

"Do I see evil when I look into my own eyes each morning?"

Kuga nodded.

"No," said the Spaniard. "That is not what I see. I see desire. I see purpose, but I do not put that kind of judgment on myself."

"Ever?"

"No."

"What about the first time you did the . . . well, when you did the kind of stuff you're famous for?"

"No."

Kuga grunted. He leaned back and looked up at the ceiling.

"I used to believe in what I was," he said quietly. "I was a soldier and then I went into the CIA. I was a case manager. I worked jobs in the field that put me in direct opposition to people like us. People like me. I arrested some, popped caps in others. Never blinked. And, frankly, never bothered with trying to crawl inside their heads. Oh, sure, I used whatever psych profile our teams generated, but at no time did I try to *be* them, like some agents do. I was never into the Method-acting version of law enforcement. I was all tradecraft."

"So . . . ?"

"So, then I began stepping over the line. Skimming some cash from arms dealers, pocketing hard drives of information on key players and then using that data for some lucrative blackmail. Like that. It never felt like crime to me, because I was stealing from people who were very corrupt. People who were worse than me." He laced his fingers behind his head and closed his eyes. "Even when I had to cut a throat or two, it was no big thing. I was never the bad guy. In fact, I felt a little like P. T. Barnum. You know who he was? The circus guy? Well, he said something about there being a sucker born every minute, suggesting that if people are dumb enough to get taken, then it was on them rather than any fault of whoever took them."

Santoro shrugged.

"That's where I was," said Kuga. "I had absolutely no pity for whoever got in my way. Over time, my plays got bigger, involved more risk, and I guess I lost sight of where that line in the sand was. I became a criminal—and a really bad one, or good one, depending on how you see it—without ever having a shaving mirror moment where I saw my face and said 'yeah, that fellow there is evil as shit.'" He shook his head. "Even when I got involved with the Majestic program and developed my own scheme with a bioweapon and some Cold War mind-control stuff, I still didn't see anyone in the mirror I would have called evil."

Santoro said nothing.

"For a long time, especially in prison, I actually did some soul searching. Looking inward to find my flaws. It was like having some of your lights off and searching in the dark for the breakers. But I guess here's the important part, here's what I found."

"Oh," said Santoro, amused, "do tell."

"I found I like the darkness. No, wait, don't give me that look. I'm not saying I really am evil. I still don't see myself that way. It's just that I recognize and accept that my personal code of ethics is truly my own. It isn't defined by the Ten Commandments or the Constitution of the United States or any oath I swore. I am who I am. Not evil, not good, but beyond that. Or, maybe . . . apart from that."

"You are dangerously close to describing sociopathy."

"Maybe. But that's better than evil, isn't it?"

Santoro sat down and crossed his legs, brushing a few flecks of metal dust from his thigh. "Evil is something I have spent much time contemplating," he said. "Except in very rare cases it is nothing more than a concept constructed by civilized man, and therefore it is subject to civil laws and either judicial or sociological interpretations. If all humans had an innate sense of good and evil then everyone would have to own guilt for what they do. However we know that is not true. Before there was a society structure, even before formalized tribes, people did whatever they had to do in order to survive. There was no good and evil at all. There was survival or death."

Kuga glanced at him. "And . . . ?"

"Evil as a concept is a reflection of the laws people created once they chose to live together. Evil is representative. It is the thing we fear when the cement that holds society together is disregarded by someone who does not accept its absolute nature. Conquerors should, by standard and especially contemporary civilized assessments, all be evil. And yet look at how you Americans revere Christopher Columbus. The Greeks worshipped Alexander, but do you think the people he conquered hold him up as an icon of *good*? They were forced to laud him openly, yes? But in their hearts? Genghis Khan was a hero to his people and the devil to many. Kings and great generals are both god and devil. This was Napoleon, Pol Pot, Hitler, Tamerlane, Hannibal Barca, Francisco Pizarro, Cyrus the Great, Attila, Julius Caesar, Hari Singh Nalwa, and so many others. People like you and me, my friend, do not take the path of the sheep, accepting values merely because society says we should. We stand on a higher ground so that we look over the rabble to see what is, for us, the promised land. The reward for our efforts."

"You make it sound grand," said Kuga, "but it has an overtone of religion about it. I'm not the Goddess and I'm not one of the Seven Kings. Neither are you."

"No," conceded Santoro with a shrug, "but we are conquerors. Even if we have not conquered all of the worlds we yearn for, we are on the path of those great generals. Had we won our previous campaigns, history would have written about us and used the same adjectives as were used for Hannibal and Alexander. Had Hitler won his war, he would have been an emperor greater than the Caesars."

"We didn't win, though," said Kuga.

"We did not die in defeat," said Santoro. "We are free. You have your network. You are the go-to person for so many things. My guess is that even the Deacon knows less than a fifth of the activities in which you are a player, and of those most are minor, or are misunderstood by the intelligence communities. Those same spies will misunderstand what we are doing in Korea. They will think it is one thing if we succeed, they will think it is something else if things go wrong, but they will never understand what it really is. Quite frankly, I doubt your—excuse me, *our*—employers will ever understand. Those Five Iron Men—who I have not met and do not care to meet—will probably even applaud us when their plan fails. As it must fail."

"Yes, it really must."

"Those five men will think that we did everything we could to help them, and some good—as they interpret that word—may even come out of it. After all, given the stagnation of the political situation in the region, any change is profitable. They will profit."

"Sure," said Kuga dubiously, "but what we're doing isn't nation building. Hell, we're only dicking around with politics to shake up the market. It's all about the buck for me."

Santoro smiled. "How is that different from what *any* conqueror has ever wanted? Name one conqueror, one great king whose driving passion was not to acquire something he did not have. Hitler probably did not hate the Jews—he wanted their money, their businesses, and he needed a devil for his people to revile. Even the Crusades were only marginally about religion. Money, land, expansion of trade . . . those things were what mattered to the power players. The rest was for the tourists, the faithful."

"The rubes."

"Yes."

"So, you're saying evil does not exist?"

Santoro smiled. "Did I say that? No, I said that it was rare. In fact, I have only encountered true evil once in my life. In one person."

"Oh?" prompted Kuga, raising his eyebrows.

"Yes. A man. Or, at least, he took that form. He had many faces and I believe he was very old. Unnaturally old. I do not know where he came from, and I am not at all sure that he was even human."

Kuga frowned. "You trying to scare me with a ghost story?"

"No. He was not a ghost. *Is* not. I am not certain if he is alive or dead, but he was flesh and bone when I knew him. And he was the soul of evil. He called himself Nicodemus. He, my friend, was evil."

"Nicodemus . . . I've heard that name. Seen it in a few reports, but I thought he was a myth. Hell, I built some of my Kuga personality around him. The man with a thousand faces and no face. All of that voodoo shit. You're telling me Nicodemus was an actual person?"

"Oh yes. He was real and he will always represent evil to me, in concept and in practice." Santoro made a sign in the air. An ancient warding against the evil eye.

The yacht shifted as another boat motored past. A gull cried out in protest and then fell silent again.

"So, to answer your question," said Santoro, "when I look into the mirror I do not see an evil man looking back at me. I see a conqueror. As I believe you do. And neither evil nor good applies to such as us."

CHAPTER EIGHTY-THREE
RAPPORT HOTEL
SACHEON-EUP, JINSAM-RO, 1485-7
SACHEON-S
GYEONGSANGNAM-DO, SOUTH KOREA

Ainil sat perched on the edge of the couch, knees pressed together, fingers knotted together, eyes burning from not blinking as she stared at the TV.

The live feed on KNN showed the president of North Korea screaming—actually screaming, his face flushed an awful red. He thumped his fist down on his desk as threats of nuclear retaliation spewed from him. This was an act of war, he screeched. An act of war.

Of war.

"God . . . no . . ."

Ainil snatched up the remote and changed the channel. Her cable service provided her with several stations from South Korea, Japan, the United States, and a scattering throughout Southeast Asia. The faces of the reporters were different, the languages were different, but the story was the same. There was only one story.

But it was wrong.

Wrong.

This was her story.

And yet it was not.

It was wrong. It was different.

How, though?

She flung the remote down, grabbed her laptop, entered the complex password to log into her Punk Press account, and loaded her video. Ainil played hers all the way through. Then she watched the screen for them to replay the footage—which seemed to be on a continuous loop as reporters and talking heads shouted about it—and synced it to her file.

It was close. So close.

But it was not the same file. That voice, ringing out from the TV screen, made no sense. *"When Kim Jong-un hears about this he's going to know not to fuck with Uncle Sam."*

Ainil had been there. Right there. None of the SEALs or Korean soldiers said a word. Not one word.

It was at that moment when Ainil heard the knock on her door. She shot to her feet, heart pounding. The apartment was tiny and it took her only three strides to reach the door. She peered out through the peephole. The person in the hall stood with his back to her. Tall, muscular, and blond.

Familiar.

Suddenly several things made sense, but in very, very bad ways.

She put her hand to her mouth and began backing away slowly. There was nowhere to go, though.

It was then Ainil knew she was about to die.

CHAPTER EIGHTY-FOUR
ASSOCIATED PRESS
WIRE STORY

North Korean Leader Kim Jong-un has made a formal and incendiary response to the alleged attack on the island of Gaeguli Seom: "I call for the president of the United States to resign. I demand that he take full responsibility for this egregious act of unprovoked slaughter. I demand that the United States remove all military presence from this region of the world, to openly admit their guilt, to explain their actions, and to turn over the criminals who invaded our country. This must be done or the United States will cease to exist on this planet."

CHAPTER EIGHTY-FIVE
YEONPYEONG ISLAND
SOUTH KOREA

Mr. Church told me about the attack on Area Ninety-Four, the black site to which some truly vile sons of bitches had been exiled. I'd only heard about that facility once, and then only in passing during a conversation with Aunt Sallie. When I asked what and where it was, she told me to mind my own damn business. I tried to follow up with Church, but he stonewalled me, saying that the topic was not of value to any of my current operations.

I have rarely wanted to kick his ass or tell him that he was wrong, but man, that was burning in me right then. With dead bodies to my left and a couple of hundred tranquilized infected to my right, I felt intense anger with him. Fuck him and his fetish for compartmentalization and secrecy.

He came clean, though, and I listened.

The short version was that the people we sent to Area Ninety-Four had no value at all except in what information could be pried or coaxed out of them. The fact that Rudy Sanchez was one of a team of interrogators sent in to interview them made sense, but that also pissed me off.

The facility was attacked by a strike team fifteen months ago, and was utterly destroyed in what had been written off as a failed but catastrophic attempt to free key prisoners. Because the facility was shared with one of the more covert groups within the Department of Homeland Security, as well as four different National Security agencies whose names you never saw in a news story, the story was squashed. A forensics team was sent in, and their conclusion was that all of the prisoners and all but two guards had died in the attack. The whole thing was a clusterfuck and the kind of embarrassment that would have sent heads rolling, and so it was quietly filed away and that was that.

Except, Rudy remembered Rafael Santoro making a weird and otherwise anachronistic comment about Koreans killing each other. And so Church somehow got Jerry Spencer to review the forensic data and samples.

His report was every bit as terrifying as what I saw lying sprawled around me.

"Say that part again," I asked, my throat dry, and the day suddenly way too bright.

"Detective Spencer says that the forensic report is wrong," said Church. "The remains found in the ruins add up to three hundred and eleven inmates. There were three hundred and *thirteen* people being held there."

"Meaning two got away?"

"So it would seem."

"I don't even want to know who made it out, do I?"

There was a beat, and then Church said, "One of the missing inmates is Rafael Santoro."

"No . . . ," I breathed. Then I took a breath. "Christ . . . *Daddy!* Burke said that the two blond kids took him to see a Spanish guy. It has to be Santoro. Who else has the skills, the vision, and the balls to try and extort a bunch of Navy goddamn SEALs!"

"I fear you may be right," said Church glumly.

"Who's he working for, though? Santoro was Hugo Vox's man, and then he was the Goddess's creature. Do we think Santoro has gone from pet scorpion to evil mastermind? I don't buy it. He's lethal as hell, but he's a follower. A zealot and believer. This doesn't fit his profile."

Then the full weight of what Church said about the attack on Area Ninety-Four sunk in. "Whoa, wait a minute. You said there are *two* inmates missing. Who's the other one? Who else is missing?"

My legs wanted to buckle because I thought I knew the name he was going to say. A person who was the most dangerous person we'd ever faced, alive or dead. I didn't want him to say it. I wanted the name to be someone else. Anyone else. A stranger, maybe, who'd been jailed by Homeland.

Church said the name anyway.

"The other prisoner was Harcourt Bolton, Senior."

CHAPTER EIGHTY-SIX
RAPPORT HOTEL
SACHEON-EUP, JINSAM-RO, 1485-7
SACHEON-S
GYEONGSANGNAM-DO, SOUTH KOREA

There were only two ways out, Ainil reasoned. Well, two ways to die at a time like this. She could simply be murdered or she could die fighting.

She did not know how to fight and had no real weapons, but she had to try something.

There was another knock on the door. A little harder.

"Hold on," she yelled. "Let me put something on."

Instead she grabbed a wooden kitchen chair and placed it quickly and quietly under the knob. She had no illusions that it would stop him, but it would slow him down.

Ainil went from stillness to motion all at once. She snatched up her laptop and charger and shoved them into a battered old leather courier bag, looped it across her body. She unlocked her cell and dialed the police emergency number and when the call was answered she told the dispatcher that some strange man was in her apartment and that she was barricaded in the bathroom. She tossed the phone onto the bed, the call still engaged. If she got out of this she could always buy a burner.

The doorknob rattled.

Ainil ran to the tiny kitchenette and grabbed one of those boxes of cheap party wine from a shelf, opened the microwave, and stuffed it inside. She turned the setting to high and started the power.

Then she opened the little window over the sink. It didn't want to move, but she used a big bread knife as a lever, snapped that right off, found a screwdriver in a drawer, and forced the sash to move. The microwave was already starting to rattle as gasses built up inside. There was a heavy thump as something big and hard hit the outside of the door. The man was trying to force it. Another heavy thump. Too sharp a sound to be his shoulder. He was trying to kick it in.

Ainil crawled onto the sink and began squeezing herself through the miniscule window. Small as she was it was a brutally tight fit, and the frame bruised her and fought her.

Behind her she heard the front door burst inward, accentuated by the splintering crash of the kitchen chair. Footsteps, a snarl of anger, and then a hand closed like a vise around her ankle. Ainil kicked backward with all her strength, but the man was hauling on her, using his greater weight and strength. The courier bag snagged on the outside of the window and for a moment the laptop inside was enough of a brace to keep her from being pulled all the way in.

And then the box of wine in the microwave exploded in a huge fireball of superheated plasma and burning alcohol. A hot fist of heat punched her the rest of the way out of the window and she fell onto the stairs fifteen feet below. Something detonated with red-hot fury in her elbow and she struck her head, then tumbled down three steps, hitting cheek and shoulder and the edge of one hand until she wedged to a stop between the bottom step and the rail. The world spun drunkenly around her and pain seemed to define everything.

Even with all of that, even hurt in ways she could not yet catalog, Ainil did not stop. She forced herself up, dragging agony with her.

When she glanced up she saw smoke curling out of the window and tiny fingers of flame. In the distance there was the alley-cat wail of police sirens.

Ainil ran.

Not well. Not fast. But she ran.

Past neighbors who came to see what was happening. Through gathering crowds. Down side streets and backyards and along alleys.

She ran and ran for her life.

CHAPTER EIGHTY-SEVEN
YEONPYEONG ISLAND
SOUTH KOREA

"Bolton is alive?"

I felt as if the ground was tilting under me and I was going to slide down into a big pot of boiling oil.

"Yes," said Church. "We don't know if he and Santoro are working together, but we have to be open to that possibility. Listen to me, Outlaw, there is a lot more, but you can't be off the team channel too long."

"To hell with that. Tell me right goddamn now."

Church gave me the rest of what Jerry Spencer found. The forensic collection specialist tasked with overseeing the chain of evidence relative to the dead prisoners was an FBI agent named Michael Mallory. However, Mallory was killed in a single-car accident five weeks after the Area Ninety-Four investigation was closed. Jerry Spencer believed that Mallory was working for whoever orchestrated the release of Santoro and Bolton. Spencer was currently coordinating with some of Bug's people to do deep background searches on the rest of the staff there. Financials, health, the works. If this really was the kind of manipulation that we'd seen before, even if it was overseen by new management in the absence of the Seven Kings, then there were patterns we could follow.

"I've been in touch with some friends in DHS and various military intelligence services," continued Church. "They're putting people on the families of each of the SEALs and Korean soldiers.

We know from experience that Santoro kept close tabs on each family member, and if that is still his pattern, then we may be able to detect the surveillance. We have equipment now we didn't have then. Q1 and our drones."

"Sure, but we don't have our old DMS field teams ready to act to protect those civilians."

"That is in hand," said Church. "We still have quite a few friends in the States."

He didn't explain and did not need to. A lot of DMS field agents retired but were still reliable if they got this kind of call. Plus we had friends in other agencies, and freelancers we've worked with who might like to come and play. Sam Hunter, a private investigator in Philly; former Echo Team sniper Sam Imura in California; police detective Tracy Cole in Atlanta; freelance investigator Jean McGee in Fort Lauderdale. And others, including key players in Sigma Force, MHI, SEAL Team 666, Chess Team, and some players so far below the public radar their teams had no actual names. The war was big and it never ended and thank God there are other knights out there in dented armor, riding off to fight dragons here and there.

"Any idea who the blond couple are?" I asked. "Eve and whoever the boy is?"

"None, but we are looking. And that includes accessing CCTV cameras in the areas around the homes and bases where the strike team's families live. We may get lucky."

"Some luck would be real frigging useful right about now," I said. Flies were everywhere now, drawn by the scent of blood, and I was having a duel with one who kept landing on my visor. "Rafael Santoro and Harcourt Bolton are alive and maybe they're working together."

"We don't know that for certain," said Scott Wilson.

"Only two guys busted out of a supermax black site?" I said. "Fudged forensics. Come on. That took some major planning. Hugo Vox–level planning, and since Vox is bones in a box, who's the next scariest long-range planner of really bad shit? Begins with a *B* and rhymes with Harcourt fucking Bolton."

"It's a working theory," admitted Wilson. "Bug and his team are looking into it."

"Glad to hear it," I said sourly. "So, where were we? Oh yeah, Bolton and Santoro are *maybe* working together and they have a rage virus. Well, that's just swell. That's just peachy. That's better than petting a puppy while you get a blowjob. Jesus jumped-up-Christ on a—"

"It's not a virus," interrupted Church.

"Wait . . . what?" I snapped.

"It is not a virus or a bacterium or any disease form."

"How can you be so sure, boss? Are you saying we've actually *gotten* somewhere?"

There was, despite everything, a musical laugh, and I realized that Doc Holliday was on the call, too.

"Oh, hell, sweetness," she said, "we've been busy as a hive of bees on Adderall. And our own Johnnycakes just won the blue ribbon at the science fair. Here, let me put him on the line."

John Cmar, who I imagine was not a fan of that nickname, said, "Outlaw, I think we've figured out what the bioweapon is, and this is a doozy. It's so simple that we would never have thought of it. I didn't, actually, until that discussion you and I had about speed of onset. I kept knocking down your theories because nothing in nature could cause that specific a personality change in so short a time period. Well . . . I was wrong. Granted, no virus, spores, fungi, or bacterium could do that, but we were looking in the wrong place."

"Skip to the part where this makes sense," I barked.

"Sure, sure," said John, and his excitement crackled like electricity. "I started looking into causative agents of behavioral change in *all* known species with notably unusual onsets. I found several, but one really stood out. *Loligo beta-microseminoprotein.*"

"What in the wide blue fuck is that?"

"It's a protein. Loligo beta-MSP for short," he explained. "Oh, and get this—it's found in the longfin inshore squid."

"Squid? As in a *squid* squid?"

"*Doryteuthis pealeii*," he said with a weird kind of pride. "A species of squid of the family *Loliginidae,* common in the North Atlantic."

I found an old chum bucket outside of the crab shack, turned it over, and sat down. "And this is a bioweapon?"

"In a way," John said. "Look, here's the skinny. Males of a variety of egg-laying species are attracted to the sight of eggs, which is what drives them to produce sperm to fertilize them. That's shorthand, but you get the idea. But the female longfin squid covers her eggs with the Loligo beta-MSP protein and it causes the males to fly into a violent rage and attack any other male in the vicinity. The upshot is that only the toughest and most aggressive male gets to fertilize the eggs. Darwin would *love* this."

"Whoa, slow down a sec," I said. "This thing didn't just affect the men. Everyone on Frog Island and here on Yeonpyeong went batshit."

"That's the difference between what exists in nature and what someone did to it in a lab," said John. "The protein was the basis for the weapon, but it was significantly modified. And, no, we haven't cracked the modification yet. What we can infer is that the bioweapon is sight reactive. It triggers when an infected person sees another human. Or, in some cases pigs and monkeys, both of which have some biological similarities to humans, which is why they're used as lab animals."

"Sight reactive, eh," I mused. "That might explain the little girl. She was okay until we approached her."

John grunted. "And I bet if we could identify her home we'd find glasses with a strong prescription."

"Okay, that's sad and creepy. What about Burke, though? He was exposed because of the broken visor. Why didn't he turn?"

"Actually, I'm going to hand you over to Doc," said John, "because she thinks she already has that part figured out."

"Oh, I don't *think* I know, honeylumps," said Doc. "I know I know."

"Okay, impress me," I suggested.

"You see any flies around?" asked Doc sweetly.

"It's a fisherman's wharf and there are corpses everywhere," I said. "I'm ass-deep in flies."

"Then keep your Hammer Suit zipped up, honeybunny," she said, "because you are surrounded by the delivery system for this thing."

"Flies? How? They're not all that bitey. I mean, if it was mosquitoes or wasps or something then I could see it . . . but how are flies spreading this thing?"

"You tell me," she said slyly.

"How the hell am I supposed to do that?"

Doc said, "How closely have you looked at them?"

I looked down at a pair of flies crawling on my left knee. They were fat blowflies, one a little larger and darker than the other. I was about to swat them when I stopped and gaped.

"No . . . ," I breathed.

"Ahhhhh," said Doc. "I think our favorite stud-muffin just figured it out."

The flies were similar, but they were not identical. I bent closer to look and saw that only one of them was really a fly.

The other one, the slightly larger one, was a goddamn drone.

And jutting out from under its head was a very thin, very sharp needle.

CHAPTER EIGHTY-EIGHT
KOREA NEWSWIRE
KIM YUNG REPORTING

"Military tensions have escalated to a critical point in response to accusations by North Korean leader Kim Jong-un that joint special forces from the United States and South Korea have launched an unprovoked attack on the island of Gaeguli Seom. China has spoken out in support of North Korea and there are reports of Chinese and North Korean jets buzzing U.S. warships in the troubled waters off the Korean peninsula. Fighters from the USS *Ronald Reagan*, the *Theodore Roosevelt*, and the *Nimitz* were scrambled. . . ."

CHAPTER EIGHTY-NINE
YEONPYEONG ISLAND
SOUTH KOREA

I talked with Church and the crew at the TOC a little longer, letting them give me details that seemed to steady the ground under my feet. Sort of.

Havoc Team was out there, on the move, trying to get one set of answers. I was processing other answers and finding that it opened up a whole lot of questions.

Here's the thing. RTI, much like the DMS, is a rapid response organization. Emphasis on *response*. We can't be directly active because we don't know where to aim until someone else fires a gun. We're not patrol officers out looking for people who might be about to commit crimes. The CIA and other intelligence networks are better at that than we are. They have fifty or a hundred times the manpower, and it is their job to spot trouble before something blows up. We wait for that big, ugly bang and then while first responders are tending to the dead and dying, we go hunting for whoever made the bomb. Not as direct punishment, but because experience has made us wise enough to know that terrorists seldom commit a single terrible act. They usually have an agenda, and they learn from what they've done, and from how people are affected by it.

At times like these I remember a conversation I once had with Church. It was during the King of Plagues matter. It was while we were still on Fair Isle, in fact. I'd been in a similar place. Events had pushed my team and me around. There was blood on the ground and on our hands. But we did not yet know the real shape of what was going on. I was feeling that when Church took me aside. He told me that sometimes we don't get easy answers and clear targets, and that was how the world was wired. It wasn't any kind of fair fight.

I said, "Are you saying you don't think we'll catch them?"

"We don't even know who they are," Church said. "We're miles and miles from certain knowledge of any kind. Even the things we've learned today could be carefully seeded misdirection. This is the nature of the war on terror. Sometimes there is no face, no name, no target for us to point a gun at. It can be disheartening and daunting, and the frustration of it has forced a lot of players out of the game."

"But not you," I said. I wasn't sure if I meant it as a statement or a question.

"Not me."

"Why not?"

Church didn't answer that. Instead he said, "The darkness is all around us. Very few people have the courage to light a candle against it."

"I'm not that kind of an idealist."

"Nor am I. We are of a kind, and neither of us is holding a candle against the darkness. Like the unknown and unseen enemy we fight, people like you and me—we are the darkness. In some ways we are more like the things we're fighting than the people we're protecting. We are part of the darkness. Granted our motives are better—from our perspective—but we wait in the darkness for our unseen enemy to make a move against those innocents with the candles. And by that light, we take aim."

I could hear him say those words as clearly now as if he stood beside me on the bloodstained street on that small Korean island.

Now, as then, Rafael Santoro was conjuring a special kind of evil magic. I hoped Church's friends in the industry were going to be able to protect Burke's family and those of the other coerced soldiers and sailors my team had been forced to kill.

Even if they did, though, it would be a win, sure, but how big? Santoro's schemes, when working with the Seven Kings, were on a scale so grand it was truly terrifying. Tens of thousands, and possibly hundreds of thousands would have died. Many people did die.

It was worse with Bolton. His Kill Switch plan would have used drones to deliver weaponized smallpox against which there is no known cure. Bolton was willing to slaughter *millions* of people, most of them children.

Now they were together.

So far they had murdered everyone on Gaeguli Seom and hundreds here on Yeonpyeong. I did not for a minute believe this was their endgame. Both of them were long-range planners and big-picture thinkers. What then was their endgame? How many more people would have to die before they were stopped?

If they *could* be stopped.

I turned and looked at the dead men. One of them had been a Kingsman. Was that significant? Or just some of the gutter leavings scooped up by those two madmen?

I was standing in the darkness of my unknowing, waiting for someone to light a candle so I could see the gleam reflected on someone's gun barrel. The Cop inside me wanted more pieces of the puzzle. The Killer wanted to rise up in the shadows and take aim. And yet somehow I felt shackled, crippled. I stood there not knowing which way to turn.

In that moment, it was not really Cop or Killer who whispered to me. Nor even the Modern Man. I heard Junie's voice. Soft and loving.

"I love you with my whole heart. You are also the bravest man I know. But you are human, too. You are not indestructible. If you think there is even the slightest chance that you are becoming disconnected from the truth of what you're doing, from the humanity that made you who you are, then I need you to stop. Take a breath. Step away. Allow yourself to feel."

"Not now," I whispered.

"Say again, Outlaw," said Top.

I cleared my throat. "Nothing. It was nothing."

CHAPTER NINETY
PHOENIX HOUSE
INSIDE THE ORB
OMFORI ISLAND
GREECE

"Calpurnia," said Church as he settled into a chair in his apartment, "activate the ORB."

"ORB activated," said the AI. "Your guests are already signed in."

His office once more became a dark chamber with five chairs. As the audio kicked in he was assaulted by the four members of the group yelling at each other at the tops of their voices.

"Enough," he roared. They fell immediately into a silence so pregnant with tension that he knew the shouting could resume at the slightest provocation. *"Factaque pace maestus vigilantiam."*

They stared at him as if he was a madman. They glanced at each other in obvious surprise.

The Chinese man said, "Do you really think now is the time for silly rituals?"

"Silly? No," said Church. "I encourage all of you to remember what brought us together in the first place. *Peace through vigilance* and *action.* Our vigilance was not enough given the tradecraft used to launch these attacks without our being aware there was even a threat. And to do so in a way that endangers us all. I believe it is now time for action, and that cannot be recriminations or accusations. I am not a fan of bickering at the best of times, and this situation demands the best of us."

There was a brief and very heavy silence.

Then, China said, "*Factaque pace maestus vigilantiam.*"

After another moment, North Korea, South Korea, and America said it, too, their oaths overlapping. Church nodded.

"Thank you," he said. "Let me start by filling you in on what we've discovered."

He told them about the weaponized protein from the longfin squid.

South Korea said, "Is there a cure?"

"Not as such, no," said Church. "With the squid, the effect only lasts for a short time, and as long as male squids don't come into contact with it again, the protein eventually dissolves into seawater. The half-life within animals in nature is relatively short. Although Dr. Cmar's team has not fully reconstructed the bioweapon, tests indicate that the effect will wear off naturally. In fact, Sergeant Chung is showing signs of recovery. He is the only test subject we currently have under observation, so there's no way to make too many guesses. Dr. Cmar is hopeful, though."

"That's good," said America quickly. "If he becomes lucid he can testify to the cooperation between Havoc Team and Colonel Ho."

"Havoc Team was never on that island," said Church. "A WHO field team was there and they operate under no flag. The sergeant's testimony would not only break Havoc's cover story, but would likely result in his imprisonment."

"Not 'likely,'" said North Korea. "It would be certain. Chung would be executed offstage. Ho would have been, too, if it became known the field team was actually attached to the United States."

"That's not actually true," said Church.

"It could be made to appear so," said North Korea. "Colonel Ledger has a certain reputation as an American special ops cowboy. He is not exactly unknown in my country."

"Nor mine," agreed China. "He would be a very useful target of propaganda."

"Let's set Sergeant Chung to one side for now," said Church. "We've also cracked the delivery system for the bioweapon."

He told Calpurnia to display the recovered crop-spraying drone and several samples of the blowfly drones.

"The larger UAV was fitted with tanks with a high-powered air-jet delivery system. The drone was also fitted with a thermal scanner with tracking software. My people tell me that the tracking software is sophisticated enough to uniquely identify each human target and then tag them a target number. As the blowfly drones are deployed, their own GPS system targeted those tags and then zeroed in to deliver the bioweapon. It takes very little of the weapon and it is engineered to act with the speed of a neurotoxin. The assault team either used a large number of UAVs to tag and infect all of the population of the two islands, or they worked for a long time to accomplish this. My guess is somewhere between the two."

"Who manufactured the drones?" asked China.

"That gets complicated," said Church. "The design patents are held by companies in the United States, however virtually all of the parts and some of the assembly is done in Japan. A few parts are manufactured in South Korea, and the operating system—including design and patent—on the UAV we recovered is Chinese."

"*What . . . ?*"

China and America cried out at the same time.

CHAPTER NINETY-ONE
YEONPYEONG ISLAND
SOUTH KOREA

Bunny and Andrea moved quickly, quietly, and very carefully along the marina. There were dozens of boats, but most were covered in tarps, or were open skiffs, drifters, center-console boats, jon boats, bay boats, and cut-down trawlers. The rest ranged from gillnetters with squatty cabins, seiners, and one big longliner that was essentially a fish factory boat.

Andrea used all of his stock of bumble bee drones to invade the shadows of the moored watercraft while the two of them crouched in safety and watched the feeds. They found very little to either draw their fire or break their hearts. The infection did not seem to have had much of a presence on the boats.

Or so they thought.

As they stepped aboard the longliner, creeping up the gangplank to the steel deck, a figure rose up from behind the coaming and Bunny very nearly shot him. But the figure threw up his hands.

"Don't shoot!" cried a skinny boy of about twelve. "Please, God—don't shoot!"

He was Korean and spoke in heavily accented English. He was filthy and spattered with blood, but there was no fury or madness in his eyes. He dropped to his knees and begged for his life, tears burning furrows down his grimy cheeks.

"Please," he sobbed. "Please."

"Don't move," ordered Bunny as he moved forward. Behind, Andrea pivoted to clear the deck, the barrel of his rifle seeking movement behind stacked deck cargo or in patches of shadow.

"Topsides clear," he said.

Bunny grabbed the kid by the shoulder, jerked him to his feet, pushed him against a big crate, told him to put his palms against the wood, kicked his feet wide, and kept his barrel pressed between the boy's shoulder blades as he did a fast but thorough pat-down. He removed a cell phone with a cracked screen, some coins, and a wallet with ten thousand South Korean won and two American one-dollar bills. A combined total of about ten bucks. An identification card gave his name as Kim Bong. Bunny fished zip cuffs from his pocket and secured the kid's wrists. Then he spun the boy around and pressed his back to the crate.

Bong wore jeans stained with fish guts and engine oil, and an Aquaman T-shirt under a soiled anorak. No gloves, no hat. Cheap rubber-soled deck shoes. Bunny studied his face, looking for signs of the homicidal madness and finding no trace of it. He did not lower his gun, though. Not after what happened to Sergeant Chung.

"What happened here?" he asked.

Kim Bong began talking so fast it was like everything in his head wanted to spill out at once. It was often incoherent and went off on desperate tangents, but Bunny was able to pick some details out of it.

A boat had pulled into the dock. Not an RHIB, like the one at Frog Island, but a battered old cabin cruiser that Bong recognized as belonging to Old Mr. Kim—no relation to the boy. As soon as it pulled up to the pier, two men jumped off and secured the lines. They were wearing strange clothes, a kind of uniform, the boy thought. They were Korean, but they were not from the island. Bong, who knew everyone, did not recognize them. He even went over to ask what happened to Old Mr. Kim. The two strangers ignored him. They began hauling up a series of large black plastic cases and placing them on the cruiser's deck. Not stacking them, but placing them side by side. There was a moment when only one man was on deck, the other having gone below to fetch another case. Bong took that moment to again ask the guy on deck what was going on, and that was when the story took a very weird turn. The man on deck looked up at Bong, who was leaning over the side of the bigger boat. There were tears running down the stranger's face.

"Do yourself a favor, kid," said the weeping man, "go find someplace to hide."

"Why? What's going on?" asked Bong.

There was a sound below and the weeping man glanced at the hatch, then back up at the boy. "Do you go to church?"

"Sure," said Bong, "when we're not out fishing."

"Next time you're in church . . . say a prayer for me, won't you?" the man sobbed. "Tell God I'm sorry. Tell him I had to do this."

Then the other man came up with the last of the plastic cases. The weeping man wiped his tears away. He turned away and as Bong watched, the men took hoods from pouches on their uniforms and pulled them on. When Bunny asked what kind of hood, the boy described the type worn by the soldiers and sailors Havoc had just killed.

"What happened next?" asked Bunny.

"They opened those big plastic boxes and took out some of those flying things. You know, the ones they sometimes use on TV. Eight of them. And they went flying away into town."

Bunny understood what that meant. Drones.

"Where are those men?" asked Bunny.

The boy jerked his head toward the port bow. Bunny guided the kid to the rail and they peered over and down. The cabin cruiser lay there, rolling in the chop. The eight cases were still there. Andrea came over and peered down as well, having heard the story via his coms unit.

"I'll go look and . . . ," he began, but his voice trailed off. As the waters lifted and shifted the boat against its moorings, they caught a brief glimpse of the interior of the cabin. A figure lay slumped just inside the housing. He wore the same clothes, same hood, but the shape of the hood was wrong, and the top of it was torn open and splashed with gore. A speck of sunlight gleamed off the barrel of a handgun.

They went to investigate, and took the boy with them.

Aboard the smaller craft they found not two but four bodies. The skipper—Old Man Kim—and his mate, Park. And two dead soldiers. One had been shot in the back of the head, and the other clearly from a self-inflicted gunshot wound. All dead.

Bong pressed himself against Bunny and began crying.

CHAPTER NINETY-TWO
PHOENIX HOUSE
INSIDE THE ORB
OMFORI ISLAND
GREECE

The five of them in the virtual conference sat in thoughtful silence for a long time. Church watched the others, reading them. They were each, in their way, good poker players, well used to guile and misdirection, to bluff and boldness. They could not have climbed to their positions of power and influence, nor clung on through regime changes, without exceptional skills.

The revelation of the Chinese component of the UAVs was significant, and it changed the kind of poker they were playing. That device was not for sale on the open market. It was proprietary, reserved for drones used on state-controlled farms attached to military bases. Technically not military in design or use, but not used anywhere else.

Church had a good idea why it was used, and a better one for what the response to its inclusion in the two island strikes would be, but did not share his thoughts. Events like this were better handled by letting others pick the best next card to play. It took them a while to process everything, but Church was a very patient man.

It was the South Korean man who came up with the idea.

"None of our countries can look weak," he said without preamble. "None of us can look like villains, either. So . . . I think I know how we can actually *use* this."

The others came to point like a pack of bird dogs. Not because of his opening comments, but because South Korea was smiling as he spoke. A tentative smile, but a hopeful one.

Church smiled, too.

"Tell us," he said.

CHAPTER NINETY-THREE
YEONPYEONG ISLAND
SOUTH KOREA

We joined Bunny and Andrea on the docks and studied the equipment cases. They confirmed everything Doc Holliday and Bug said about the drones. We even found some dead blowflies, and by dead I mean ones with broken wings that had been tossed aside as useless. I called it in.

"We're seeing all those goodies," said Doc brightly. "Any chance you can find l'il ol' Buggy-bear a serial number?"

On the shared line I heard Bug say, "Jeeez."

Andrea checked. "Nothing."

"Well, I'm as confused as a fart in a fan factory," said Doc. "They keep giving us some clues and then being plum stingy with the rest."

"She's right," said Bunny. "Video points us at the U.S. and South Korea, now we find out that the parts are made in Japan and South Korea, but the tracking module's from China. I mean, like . . . what the actual fuck? This keeps up we won't know which direction to shoot."

He said it casual, as a joke. But we all looked at him.

"What?" he asked, then he grunted as if hearing his own words like an echo. "Well . . . shit."

"Huckleberry," I said, using Doc's call sign, "what are the chances that these cases carried all of the UAVs necessary to infect this entire island?"

She and Bug had a rapid-fire and highly technical back-and-forth, and then Doc said, "Not a chance, sugar."

"Shit," I growled. "Jackpot, talk to me."

Andrea was already bent over his computer, looking at feeds from his own drones, which he retasked to fly low and close over the boats. We found two other craft. Not RHIBs, but pirated midsize fishing boats. There was no one on deck, but that didn't mean anything. They would almost certainly have left someone aboard, and it was unlikely in each case that the anchor watches would have committed suicide.

We split into two teams. Mun, Top, and Bunny went east; I took Belle and Andrea with me. We ran fast. Everyone knew what we needed to find. Someone alive. Someone who could tell us more than Burke told us. Though, boy howdy, it was going to suck to be them if they were still alive.

Top's squad found their boat first, about two klicks along that side of the coast.

"Pappy to Outlaw," he said, and I held up my fist for my team to stop and hunker down behind a big cargo container.

"Go for Outlaw."

"Looks like there was a party here," he said. "Two men left on board, but they must have miscalculated with their squid-bug or whatever it is. Count about eleven dead civilians and both of the bad guys. They made a fight of it, but they're deader'n shit."

"Copy that, Pappy. Secure the scene and wait on my call."

We got up and moved on. The third boat was almost four kilometers from where we'd started out, and we were broiling in the oven bags we were wearing for protection. At some point I will find the designer of this particular generation of Hammer Suit, make him put one on, and then leave him in the middle of the goddamn Sahara. I was pretty sure I'd sweated off every slice of pizza and every cold beer I'd ever consumed.

Andrea was puffing beside me. On my left, Mun ran as lightly as a gazelle, and if I hadn't already taken a strong dislike to her, then her apparent comfort would have soured me. I kept fighting the childish wish that she would trip.

She did not.

The GPS on the drone sent clear directions to the screens inside our hoods and we slowed from a run to a careful walk when we were a few hundred yards away. The target was a big fifty-two-foot Trintella 52 C, a lifted-keel sailing vessel that had clearly seen better days. Where it was once sleek and elegant, it had obviously encountered a series of calamities because it had all the sad and faded grandeur of a thousand-dollar-a-night call girl who now did ten-dollar hand jobs at truck stops. Dirty, unkempt, patched, and nondescript.

We crept close and Andrea sent a hummingbird drone to scout for signs of life, but before it was even close there was a subtle shift of weight out of sight and an audible change in the sound of water slapping against the hull. The hummingbird landed on the rail and Andrea turned the speaker gain all the way up. We could hear someone talking, but faintly, clearly belowdecks. I had to strain to hear him.

"Alpha Four to Alpha One, do you copy?" This was repeated three times, and then there was a single frustrated expletive. I smiled and wondered which of the dead men back by the crab plant was Alpha One. Burke? Or someone else.

In my ear I heard Scott Wilson begin to say, "There is another jammer—" Then the coms went dead.

Mun started to rise and I saw that—once again—she had her standard handgun instead of the dart gun.

"Mudang," I snapped, my voice low but harsh, "check your weapon."

It was tough to make her hear me with the muffling effect of the Hammer Suit while being quiet enough not to alert whoever was on the boat. I used pretty emphatic gestures to make my point.

Mun turned to me and smiled.

And then shot me in the chest.

CHAPTER NINETY-FOUR
YEONPYEONG ISLAND
SOUTH KOREA

I saw her finger slip into the trigger guard and was moving before she pulled the trigger. It didn't matter. The bullet punched into my sternum with the force of a mule and I would have gone down hard if it wasn't for the body armor. The catalog says that it diffuses up to 70 percent of the foot-pounds of any round fired from within twenty feet. Yeah, and maybe that's literary license.

With standard Kevlar I'd be down with a broken sternum and maybe whiplash from the impact. I was in motion, though, and the pain slowed me by a quarter second. It hurt. A whole fucking lot. It did not stop me, though.

I swatted the gun from her hand with a hard, fast palm, and her second shot blew past my knee. There is no protective gear in the world that can adequately protect a flexible joint from a hollow-point round. I don't know how much it missed by, but I found Jesus in the space of that gap. I brought my own gun up, but Mun used her free hand to chop at my wrist. It was an expert blow, precise and very fast and my gun went flying from numb fingers.

Then she tried to kick me in the balls the same way she'd tried to kick Top earlier. A short, savage front kick that would have crushed my protective cup into my groin hard enough to stall me and give her a chance for something more lethal.

I turned and took the blow on the side of my thigh and it hurt like a bastard. But I was mad now. Mun whipped a knife from a thigh sheath, but I was closing on her now, smashing chest to chest, using my greater weight, trapping the blade between us. I clamped my numb right hand around her waist to keep the knife right there, then headbutted her just about as hard as I could. She must have seen it coming and ducked her head, so instead of smashing the front of my skull against her nose, we hit head-to-head. Our visors crashed together and cracked. I had the better angle, though, so the huge crash drove her to her knees. Stars exploded in my eyes, but I fought through it, caught her knife wrist, and gave her arm a savage wrench. And this time she did kick me in the balls. It was not a great kick, but it folded me in half.

Mun used that moment to try and cut my throat, but I caught her arm and jerked her half around and then swept her standing leg out from under her. She landed on her back and I stamped her wrist to the ground, trapping the knife. Mun tried another kick, this time catching my thigh. She was cat-quick, but I was ready and slipped it.

Then Andrea pushed between us. "*Scusami, Colonello*," he said and shot her four times with his dart gun. Not sure how many darts penetrated the Hammer Suit, but suddenly Sandman dragged the squirming Major Mun down into darkness and stillness.

I staggered back, but immediately turned as a figure rushed up from the cabin of the boat, opening up with an automatic rifle. Andrea and I dove for cover, but he—less damaged and more nimble—rolled to a kneeling position and fired the rest of his magazine at the shooter. The darts dropped him as surely as a bullet to the brain.

We stood there, not looking at the unconscious soldier but at Major Mun.

There was a burst of squelch in my ear and then Wilson was telling me the jammer was off. Telling me everything was okay.

Which it damn well was not.

CHAPTER NINETY-FIVE
ABOARD *THE SOUL OF PIETY*
KIEL CANAL
RIVER ELBE, GERMANY

They sat in leather swivel chairs and watched the screen. Kuga and Santoro. Forgotten drinks stood sweating on a galley table. Two senior Fixers were behind them, bending forward to watch the feed from the bodycam of Petty Officer First Class Cletus Burke.

The bodycam was hidden, covered in a nonreflective one-way film that made it invisible against the material of the Hammer Suit. The clarity of image, however, was unimpaired. The four of them could see the team of soldiers in similar protective gear. They saw everything and heard everything.

"Can you zoom in on that big guy's face?" demanded Kuga.

Santoro did. The visor was at a bad angle to the sun, catching flares of reflection. It took a while, including running the footage back, before they found a few seconds where the soldier's face was visible. Santoro froze the image and they sat staring at the screen.

"Jesus Christ," breathed Kuga. "It's him. Shit, Rafael, it's fucking him *again*."

Santoro shook his head. "I do not understand. How is he there? That team is supposed to be with the World Health Organization. How in hell is *he* leading them?"

One of the Fixers—a burly Russian—leaned close. "Do you know him, sir?"

Kuga wheeled around so fast that the Fixers recoiled.

"*Know* him?" he snarled savagely. "Yes, I fucking well know him."

Santoro laid his hand on Kuga's arm, but Kuga whipped toward him and slapped it away. Or tried to. Santoro held on, though, and despite the difference in their size and forty pounds of weight, Kuga could not knock that grip away. The rock steadiness of it, though, also steadied him. He let himself be pulled down to his chair.

"How?" said Kuga hoarsely. "I don't understand this. How is it even possible he's there? First Turkey and now this?"

"Sir," said the other Fixer, a former member of the Filipino secret police, "who is that guy? Is he U.S. Special Forces? He sounds American . . ."

"He's the goddamn devil is who he is," growled Kuga.

Rafael Santoro turned to his men. "That is Joe Ledger," he said.

"Whoa, *that's* Ledger?" gasped the Russian. "*Bozhe moi.*"

"I thought he'd look tougher," said the Filipino.

"If you think that, then you're an idiot. Both of you. He'd cut both your dicks off and make you eat them," snarled Kuga. "Now shut up and let me think."

Kuga launched himself from his chair and began pacing like a nervous tiger. The Filipino started to speak, but the Spaniard quickly gestured for him to be silent. The boat lifted on a swell as another watercraft moved past.

"What I do get is the timing of this," said Kuga. "I can understand Turkey. He was with Violin, and Arklight has been hunting me for a while. Or, at least, they've been hunting the *myth* of Kuga.

That's okay. We anticipated that, provided for it." He paused and considered Santoro. "And, even if Ledger somehow recognized you at the café in Izmir, how did he make the connection to our operation in South Korea?"

"Excuse me, sir," said the Filipino, "but I thought the Department of Military Sciences was closed down."

"It is," said Santoro.

"So . . . maybe this Ledger guy got cut loose. From what I heard he didn't have a lot of friends in Washington. Maybe he *is* with that World Health team. They were hiring experienced operators. This could just be a coincidence."

Kuga considered that, standing there with his hands shoved down into his back pockets, face caught halfway between a scowl and a thoughtful frown.

"I can check on that," suggested Santoro. "I know some people I can ask."

"Do it," said Kuga. "Though, I'm getting a bad feeling about this. I don't much believe in coincidences."

He stood in silence, looking at the face of Joe Ledger.

"With or without the DMS, with or without the Deacon holding his leash, Ledger is just too damned dangerous."

"You want him taken off the board, boss," said the Russian, "just say the word. There won't be enough of him left to bury."

Kuga kept watching the screen.

"Make it hurt," he said. "Make him scream."

CHAPTER NINETY-SIX
ABC NEWS CHANNEL 6 IN PHILADELPHIA
JIM GARDNER REPORTING

> **JIM GARDNER:** We have disturbing breaking news about the growing tensions in the troubled waters near the border of North and South Korea. An hour ago a Chinese Shenyang J-11 fighter jet buzzed the USS *Ronald Reagan* in the Yellow Sea, coming within one hundred feet of the flight control bridge. The *Reagan* immediately launched two F-18s to challenge the Chinese fighter, and were able to encourage it to withdraw without shots fired. However the

situation escalated when a Chinese Luyang-class destroyer sailed within two hundred feet of the USS *Curtis Wilbur*. It is believed this was not an action but was instead a deliberate act of provocation.

CUT TO CLIP OF WHITE HOUSE PRESS SECRETARY ALEXANDRA MARINI: Such a move by the People's Liberation Army naval warship was nothing short of a calculated, deliberate act.

JIM GARDNER: This is the most aggressive and dangerous action China has taken since a similar Chinese warship nearly collided with the USS *Decatur* several years ago and is another dangerous step in the direction of open conflict. This is a developing story and we'll update you as things unfold.

CHAPTER NINETY-SEVEN
YEONPYEONG ISLAND
SOUTH KOREA

There was no more to do on the island.

Now that we knew that the bioweapon was being delivered by drones, I asked Church if anyone in the neighborhood had an e-bomb they weren't using. Since the drones were mechanical, the brief but intense energy pulse from an electromagnetic bomb would kill all of them in a microsecond.

Doc Holliday said, "Oh, honey, that's sweet that you had an actual idea, but think of the optics. We fire a cruise missile from a surface ship or sub and suddenly everyone thinks that's a good idea. By the time you explain what we fired and why, the Korean peninsula would be glowing in the dark."

"Yeah, yeah, damn it," I complained.

"But don't get your Speedo in a knot," she continued. "Those little darlings are way too small to carry much of a battery, and from what I can tell they aren't rigged for solar recharge. I bet half of them are down already. Go find a quiet place to read a book. By the time the choppers get there with the medical teams and backup, I bet you can all strip naked and skip tra-la through the town square."

"You worry me sometimes," I told her, but she laughed at me.

We used the time to finish combing the island, and used golf carts to do it. Not sure I have ever seen a group of Special Ops shooters in full combat hazmat suits and armed to the teeth tooling around at a stately fifteen miles per hour. I left Andrea with Mun and our prisoner. He spent his time feeding us real-time intel from the UAVs.

"*È silenzioso come un cortile della chiesa, Colonnello,*" he said.

Quiet as a churchyard.

That was almost true. We found more than eighty infected people, many of them horribly injured. We darted them all. We found more than three hundred uninfected people huddled in a big warehouse. Before we entered we checked for drone flies. Saw too many of them crawling on the windows and doors. I called to the people inside and told them to stay there, to keep all of the doors and windows closed. Help was coming. It was not a massive victory, but we'd take all the wins we could get.

As for the kid, Kim Bong, he seemed to be fine. No signs of aberrant behavior. Even so, he would have to go into quarantine at The Lab.

Doc Holliday was right in her prediction. Right around the time the last of the drone flies stopped buzzing and fell to the ground we heard the sound of helicopter rotors beating a comforting *thump-thump-thump* off to the east. There were a lot of them. Maybe fifty. As they landed, it lifted my heart to see that there were U.S. military birds, South Korean helos, and four others. Two each from North Korea and China. Flying together in formation. Coming to help.

It made me want to cry.

TSUSHIMA ISLAND, JAPAN

PART FIVE

A soft answer breaks the rage,
a tough answer encourages the fury.

—SOLOMON

CHAPTER NINETY-EIGHT
AOI OTERA (THE BLUE TEMPLE)
TSUSHIMA ISLAND, JAPAN
THE KOREA STRAIT

We flew to Tsushima Island, off the coast of Japan, which was the closest neutral ground. A place where we had a lot of friends, and enough of a military presence to allow us to vanish into the woodwork. There was a shared facility there, known as the Blue Temple for some reason I have never been able to discover. It's neither blue nor a temple. It looks like a warehouse for some security-minded corporation, and isn't. There are a lot of surveillance gadgets like motion sensors, cameras, and an electric inner fence-line beyond a normal chain link. There are also guards where you wouldn't think to look.

The place was officially designated as a secure testing facility for the diseases of aquatic animals. Great if you're an oceanography nerd but otherwise a big ho-hum, which is precisely the point. About 15 percent of the facility actually was legitimately studying fish gill fungus or something. Never did get the actual story because I overwhelmingly didn't give a shit. The rest of it was actually privately owned by a mysterious financier named Mr. Kyōkai. That's Japanese for Church, so . . . well, you figure it out.

The reason we were in Japan was because Burke had been living there. Wilson had some kind of cooperation deal in place with the Tokushusakusengun, the Japanese counterterrorism special forces, and they were doing the legwork to run down Burke's activities. There was some very cautious involvement by NCIS, but trust was a big issue lately. I told Wilson to keep me posted.

The guy from the boat—Pavol Benka—and Major Mun were taken to separate interrogations rooms. Both were examined by doctors and left to recover. Sandman does not wear off quickly.

Havoc Team shucked our hazmat suits—no quarantine now that

we knew about the blowfly drones. We were checked out by the medical staff and given clean bills of health. All except for my bruised forehead and a throbbing nutsack from where Mun kicked me. It made me walk like an old man recovering from hip replacement.

I tried to get Bug on the line, but although he'd dialed into the TOC earlier, I couldn't get him. He was running his own field op somewhere in Korea, running down the Punk Press thing. I instead talked with Nikki Bloom, one of Bug's senior researchers.

"I want everything on Major Mun," I told her. "Everything. Dig all the way down to her potty-training. She worked for Kingdom, which means she got vetted nine ways from Sunday, but they missed something. Or someone turned her. Maybe it's Santoro and Bolton. I don't know but I want to know."

"On it," she promised.

I tried to arrange an ORB conference with Church and Doc Holliday, but they were both busy. Doc had the drone now from Gaeguli Seom and was tearing that apart, while also coordinating with John Cmar and his Bug Hunters on the squid protein weapon.

I checked with Scott Wilson, and he told me that the political situation around the Korean Peninsula was on a lower boil. Church and his friends inside the four governments had somehow negotiated a temporary truce. Pending a full debrief by Havoc and a lot of discreet political levers being pulled.

"It's not over, though," I said.

"Well, no," Wilson conceded, "but right now everyone has retreated to their respective corners and are content to merely glare."

He made it sound like no big thing, but it was actually huge. One minute we were on the brink of war, and now everyone was taking a breather. This is a very, very weird world. Not a news flash, I know, but at least this minute's weirdness was erring on the side of sanity.

I wandered into the mess hall, found a quiet corner, and made three calls.

The first was to Violin, who was in Oslo as part of the Arklight team. Lilith had her and a select few others scouting for very bad guys on their "list." Events like the D9 conference drew certain kinds of people like flies. Political opportunists, lobbyists, and also terrorists. Arklight wasn't there to protect the world leaders; they were there to take some shitbags off the board. Violin was, after all, first and foremost an assassin. One of the very best in the world.

I told her about Area Ninety-Four and the possible escape of Harcourt Bolton, Senior.

"Harry doesn't know about that," she said. "Do you want me to tell him?"

"Can you do it in a way that won't ruin the poor kid?"

"I didn't think you cared about him, Joseph."

I sighed. "He's a doofus, but he's *our* doofus. And he deserves a better father than the one he has. Break it to him gently."

She laughed. A musical sound. "You pretend to be such a gruff old bear, Joseph, but you are really a sweet man."

"If you tell anyone that I'll deny it."

My next call was to my brother, Sean. He'd been on my mind a lot. Even though he was a cop working homicide cases, his life was normal. A smart and beautiful wife, two amazing kids, and actual stability. He was the kind of sane and normal person that I ached to be, but knew I never could be. That had been taken from me years ago, and now all that the three people living in my head could hope for were brief moments of calm, of a pretended normalcy.

"Hey, Joe," he said when Ali handed him the phone, "you better not be calling to tell me you're going to miss Christmas. I will hunt your ugly ass down and—"

"I'll be there," I said. "Would not miss it for the world."

"Junie, too?"

"Junie, too."

"Bring that silly dog of yours, too. Hey, did I tell you I'm getting the kids a dog for Christmas?"

We talked for a long time. He'd spotted a four-month-old monster of a shepherd-mastiff-Doberman mix at a local shelter and put in for adoption. The approval came through the day before and the shelter agreed to hold the dog until Christmas Eve as a favor. The dog's name was Buck, but he figured the kids would want to rename him. We talked dogs, we talked about the kids, we talked baseball, and we talked about our dad, who was going to be stepping down as the mayor of Baltimore in January.

"Dad's going to rebuild Uncle Jack's old place in Robinwood," said Sean. "And between you and me, I think he's going to ask Cassie Edwards to marry him."

Cassie was a social sciences professor at Loyola. Mixed race, elegant, exceptionally graceful, and very much in love with our widowed father.

"That's really wonderful," I said, and meant it.

Sean must have heard something in my voice. "Everything okay, big brother?"

It was a tentative question because Sean knew better than to ask specific questions about where I was or what I was involved with. He'd been tangled up in one of my cases and it nearly got Ali and the kids killed.

"Been a busy couple of days," I said, and let that hang.

"Big hug, man," he said.

My third call was to Junie. I rarely get her on the phone, but this time lucked out.

"Joe!" she said with such light in her voice that it made me want to cry. After that argument in Greece we hadn't had any time at all to make amends. And I very much wanted to do that.

"Junie, listen, I—"

She cut me off. "Don't, Joe. Please. I was out of line. I shouldn't have said what I said. I know you're a good man with a good heart. I know that you aren't arrogant or cold or detached."

"You weren't entirely wrong," I said. "Maybe I've become disconnected as some kind of defense mechanism. I don't know. I'll talk to Rudy about it, though. Promise you that."

"I never wanted to hurt you . . ."

"Doing a pretty good job of that myself, babe." I tried to make a joke of it, but the delivery was flat.

We switched the subject, shelving important stuff until we were face-to-face. That was our way, and it was the best way. If the Korea thing was not going to explode, then Church might not need his shooters for the next part. Politicians and spin doctors were no doubt warming up in the batter's circle. That was fine. Christmas was coming and I did not want to spill a single additional drop of blood.

Well, that's a big a fat lie. I would love to have been in a room with Rafael Santoro, Harcourt Bolton, and those two blond kids. Yeah, I bet that would even put me on Santa's Nice list.

CHAPTER NINETY-NINE
AOI OTERA (THE BLUE TEMPLE)
TSUSHIMA ISLAND, JAPAN
THE KOREA STRAIT

I had some food, sitting alone in my corner.

John Cmar sent me a quick message to say he had a whole team of people working to reverse-engineer the weapon in order to understand its full functionality. He had that vague and dreamy quality to his voice scientists of my acquaintance get when they have something they'd love to publish but may never be able to do so. It's a danger when working with a covert ops group. His fascination with the bioweapon was obvious. He nicknamed it Rage, which made sense.

Major Mun and the mercenary were still sleeping. Sandman packs one hell of a punch, and Andrea had shot them each multiple times. Doc Holliday sent a formula for the right stimulant to bring them out of it moderately quickly and with few side effects. We did not need them dopey and hallucinating. We needed answers so goddamn much I could scream.

All of those people on the two islands. So many dead. So many brutally hurt. And those who survived? What would happen when the effect wore off? Would they remember the awful things they did to friends and family? To neighbors? To their own children? How could they ever bear it?

I wanted to know the *why* of this.

A tech rang me to say that Church, Doc, and Wilson were all available if I still wanted an ORB conference. I did, and headed to a room set aside for that. Top, Bunny, Andrea, and Belle came with me.

"Calpurnia," I said once the door was closed and the security seals in place, "activate the ORB."

"It would be my pleasure to do that, Joseph," purred the AI system. "It's wonderful to see you again. You look fit. Have you been working out?"

Someone—either Doc or Bug, I haven't found out which—programmed my personal Calpurnia interface so that it speaks to me in this smooth, sexy late-night jazz radio voice. Top and Bunny turned aside to hide smiles. Belle cocked an eyebrow and Andrea laughed out loud.

The lights dimmed and for a moment we stood in total darkness, then a whole different world seemed to appear as if by magic around us. Figures materialized. Mr. Church, somber in a dark suit, seated behind a large desk. Scott Wilson in shirtsleeves, quick and slightly nervous, his face haggard; Doc Holliday, her lab coat open to reveal her embroidered cowboy shirt; her masses of blond hair piled into a sloppy bun, magic wands sticking out of it like hairpins.

"Colonel," said Wilson briskly, "very fine work today. That goes for all of you. It was an exceptionally ugly mission and for a newly formed team you did exceptionally well."

"Yeah, hooray for us," I said. "Before we go any further at all I need to say for the record that operating with active bodycams and coms that are shared outside of the RTI family is bullshit."

"It was necessary," countered Wilson.

"It was intrusive. It cut down on our operational efficiency. It made us careful in ways that shifted some awareness from combat and teamwork to an audience."

"Noted," said Church. He said it in a way that let me know he would ask the same of us again if it suited his needs. I was under no illusions that my life—and the lives of everyone on my team—was expendable under the right circumstances. Needs of the many and all of that. His eyes were unblinking behind the lenses of his tinted glasses.

Wilson, diplomatic as ever, said, "Despite the awkwardness of all that, Colonel, Havoc Team performed brilliantly."

"Glad you think this was a good day for the good guys, but from where I was standing this was a shit show from the jump. Colonel Ho is dead and Major Mun is either a traitor or a psycho. The guys who did this are two-thirds mercs and one-third actual active military. So, can anyone tell me what in the wide blue fuck is going on?"

Andrea pointed to me. "Ditto."

CHAPTER ONE HUNDRED
LUCKY KIM INTERNET CAFE
SACHEON-S
GYEONGSANGNAM-DO, SOUTH KOREA

She ran as if the hounds of hell were chasing her.

It felt as if that was true.

After leaving her apartment, Ainil tried every trick she'd ever read about in novels, everything she'd seen in cop shows. Entering a store through one entrance and sneaking out the back. Making random turns. Doubling back and going different ways. Checking for people following her by looking into reflective store windows and the windshields of parked cars.

She saw no one. She thought everyone was looking at her, though.

The man who'd broken in was the same man who'd tipped her about the massacre. The same one who'd taken her there.

So, why try to hurt her?

What was the real story? Who was he really working for?

The whole world felt like it was ready to blow itself up, and Ainil twice went into fast-food restaurants and hid in toilet stalls, her fist jammed into her mouth to keep from screaming.

On one side street she saw a sign for an internet café. It was an old place, looking like it had not changed—or been cleaned—since the late nineties. Grimy tables, old-school computers with bulky monitors. However, against one wall was a row of wall sockets and a sign for pricing of high-speed Wi-Fi. Ainil paid cash for tokens that would buy her access in fifteen-minute intervals. Two teenagers sat huddled together at one end of the bar, and she climbed onto the stool farthest from them, plugged in her laptop, read the Wi-Fi password off the card she'd gotten from the clerk, and logged onto the Net. She fitted her rerouting device into place and turned on the encryption. It was not a real wall, but she felt safe behind it. The screen resolved.

Then she nearly screamed out loud.

There were three emails from *him*.

The guy she thought she'd blown up.

Two from before he showed up. One from ten minutes ago. Telling her he wasn't mad. Saying it was a weird accident. Asking to get together so he could explain.

Ainil nearly slapped her laptop shut and fled.

Then a message pinged onto her screen.

> *I am a friend.*
> *I know you sent the Punk Press video.*
> *We need to talk.*

She stared at it. Her messaging was turned off, she was sure of it, and when she checked it was definitely off.

> *I am a white hat.*
> *We are trying to stop a war.*
> *How can I prove myself to you?*
> *Set the rules for this conversation.*

Ainil was totally unable to move. There was not enough air left in the world. Everyone and everything faded out into a white nothing, taking all the sound with it.

> *Tell me what you want me to do to prove myself.*

It was him. It had to be him.

And yet . . .

She frowned at the screen. This wasn't how he approached her before. It wasn't the way he phrased anything. Before it was all about stroking her ego, offering her a huge jump in her reach.

This was different.

She looked around. Grabbing her laptop and running would be easy. Six steps to the door and then gone. Could she risk a response?

It took her so long to decide that the token box started pinging. Ainil fed in a token. Waited. Bit her lip. Checked that the rerouter and encryption tools were fully functional. Waited some more.

And then she typed a reply.

Who are you?

A moment later . . .

I'm a computer geek for the people trying
to stop everyone from doing stupid shit.
If you use the Dark Net, my name is Coal Tiger.

Ainil felt her heart jump.

Coal Tiger.

She knew that name.

Everyone knew Coal Tiger. He was a legend. People told wild stories about him. The kid who could walk through walls. What they used to call a hacker's hacker.

How did you find me?

Coal Tiger replied very quickly.

I'm the only one who could.

There was a pause.

I want to help you.

And I need your help.

Pause.

Help me, Ainil.

And behind her a voice said it aloud.

"Help me, Ainil."

She shrieked and whirled, falling sideways off the stool. A hand caught her before she crashed to the floor.

CHAPTER ONE HUNDRED ONE
AOI OTERA (THE BLUE TEMPLE)
TSUSHIMA ISLAND, JAPAN

"We have a lot to cover," said Church, "and we have some answers. Everyone has been busy. This meeting should allow us to compare notes in a useful way. A picture is emerging, though it is still incomplete. So, let's start with an update on the political ramifications of the two attacks."

"If there are missiles in the air, boss," said Bunny, "please tell me when to duck."

"No missiles," said Church, and even managed a little smile. I wonder if it hurt. "In fact, the various military forces are in the process of standing down."

"What?" grunted Belle.

"Although wearing bodycams and being on a communication channel that was shared with certain officials in the four concerned governments was an inconvenience—"

"More like a pain in my ass," muttered Bunny. Andrea offered a fist and they bumped.

"—the intended effect has exceeded expectations," continued Church without a pause. "Havoc Team, though still believed to be on contract to the World Health Organization, was the voice of reason in an otherwise unreasonable situation. The fact that it was multinational was very useful." He nodded to Belle and Andrea. "The humanity demonstrated by Sergeant Chung with the little girl, the sad but heroic loss of Colonel Ho, and Havoc's obvious efforts to use nonlethal force against the infected civilians all played key roles."

"And you're saying that's why we're not in the middle of a shooting war right now?" I asked. "Are you telling me all four governments just simply accept that this wasn't the U.S. and South Korea going off the reservation?"

"In essence," said Church, "yes."

"Can they afford that, though? There is so much currency in it being some kind of American plot."

"Because I've made it clear," said Church, "that I can prove otherwise, and that I am willing to do so at the United Nations, via the world press, via social media, and through other means."

"'Other means'?" asked Belle.

I didn't think Church would reply, but he said, "Rogue Team International is not the Department of Military Sciences. We do not have a state-sponsored charter and we are not beholden to any government. There are people who know me and know that it is a mistake to assume that I—or my people—are under the thumb of any special interest group. I have made that very clear to people positioned within a number of world governments. Not all of those people are my friends, but they are not interested in becoming my enemy. Please do not think I am boasting."

We were all silent. I more or less spoke for the group by simply shaking my head.

Church continued. "When this matter began I used this same ORB technology to have a series of meetings with key players in the four governments. They were able to help me set up a meeting that ended twenty minutes ago. Bedlam Team, currently in Oslo for the D9 summit, established a secure ORB link with the president of the People's Republic of China, the supreme leader of North Korea, the president of the Republic of South Korea, and the president of the United States. We spoke at length and I laid out what we knew about the attacks on Gaeguli Seom and Yeonpyeong Island. I explained the nature of the bioweapon and the drones used to deliver it. I made it clear that this drone was intended to be taken as an American device, but is not. The identities of every man and woman belonging to the strike teams were shared. I also made the connection between several of the dead mercenaries and the criminal known as Kuga."

"Since when are you Mr. Candid?" I asked.

"Since someone tried very hard to start a third world war," said Church.

"Ah," I said, "Point taken."

"Understand me, Colonel, this was not an easy sell. North Korea in particular wants the political leverage this situation so easily offered."

"And Kim Jong-un just went with the flow?"

Church gave a thin smile. "North Korea very much needs to remain in the good graces of China, and China does not want a war. Cooler heads prevailed."

"Yay?" said Bunny, posing it as a question.

"Don't get me wrong," said Church, "this situation is far from resolved and it is every bit as fragile as it sounds. We need more than this. We need resolution, answers, and the names of who funded this."

"I am confused, *Signor Chiesa*," said Andrea. "Don't we already know this? Isn't Kuga our *furfante* . . . our villain? Him and this Rafael Santoro *bastardo*?"

"I find it highly doubtful," said Wilson. "Remember, they are a concierge service. They are hired to manage an operation like this, but we don't think they are the actual villains." He paused. "Beg pardon . . . perhaps I phrased that wrong. They are not the ones who *ordered* this done. They certainly *are* villains."

"Then do we have even a damn clue who hired them?" asked Top.

"We're working on that," said Church. "Nikki Bloom said she'll have something for us very soon."

"How soon is soon?" I grumped.

I felt restless and began to pace. It meant, of course, that I walked through the holographic people. Rudy once told me that this was considered bad form, but I offered the counterargument of fuck you. Wilson seemed disconcerted; Doc was delighted and gave me a bawdy comic wink. Church was completely indifferent.

"If you have questions, Colonel," Church said, "ask them. You were a detective before you were a case manager for matters of this kind. I can almost hear your gears turning. So, it might be the easier way for us to move this forward."

I nodded, but paced another few turns. Then I stopped and turned.

"Okay, let's take it point by point," I said slowly. "Tell me about the strike team. Some of them were Kingsmen. And . . . ?"

"It's more complicated than we told the heads of state," said Wilson. "We have Kingsmen, we have Closers, we have people who worked for the Jakoby organization, we have former contractors for Blue Diamond Security, including two who were with Majestic Three. And we have one who we know for sure worked security for Harcourt Bolton."

"Why am I not surprised?"

"So, can we remove the question mark about whether Bolton and Santoro are partners?" asked Top.

"At this point," said Wilson, "it would be quite extraordinary if they were not."

"What about these blond kids Burke mentioned? Eve and the guy?" asked Bunny. "They're what? Jedi apprentices?"

"Sith apprentices," corrected Andrea, sotto voce. "Get your pop culture references right, *mezza sega*."

"We can assume," said Wilson, "they are pretty much that. Learning the trade from Santoro, which is a deeply frightening thought. They may be young and impressionable people he recruited and corrupted."

"No," I said, "I'm not really buying that. Or not exactly that. They were referred to as 'kids,' so we can assume early twenties, maybe late teens, but I doubt that. Let's figure twenties. With Santoro being away for years and then only out for fifteen months, I can't buy that he could corrupt two people that completely in so short a period of time. To do what he does takes a kind of pathology with years and years behind it. This is guesswork, but like Church said, I was a cop. People don't just wake up one day and decide they're evil psychopaths."

"So?" asked Andrea.

"So," said Belle, "they were probably doing something similar before Santoro recruited them. There may be a record, a pattern of behavior."

"Right," I said.

Another person suddenly materialized in the ORB with us. Nikki Bloom.

"I'll start running a check on that," she said, clearly having heard the conversation so far. "But we need more to go on."

I looked at my watch. "Our prisoner should be waking up in about half an hour."

"Well, then it downright sucks to be him," said Top.

I turned to him. "You and Belle are on him. The second he's awake I want him begging to unburden his soul. Do what you have to do, but he *talks*, feel me?"

Top and Belle both gave me the kind of grins you never want to see on the faces of someone looking down at you when you're at their mercy. Then exited the ORB.

"I'll get moving on a behavioral pattern search for the blond kids," said Nikki. "All we have is the one name, though, right? Eve? Nothing for the guy?"

"It's what we have until we talk to the prisoner," I said.

"Okay. On it." She vanished. The ORB thing was useful, but also a bit disconcerting.

"What about Major Mun?" I asked. "What if she's not a bad guy but more like Burke? Under coercion?"

"We already thought of that," said Church. "A team has been sent to take her family into protective custody."

I turned to Wilson. "How about Burke? He said he was afraid for his family. If they were intimidated, they might have seen Eve or the guy."

Wilson nodded. "Actually, an FBI hostage rescue team is heading there right now."

CHAPTER ONE HUNDRED TWO
LEACROFT COURT
FAYETTEVILLE, NORTH CAROLINA

The house was a white two-story with an attached garage. The siding looked old, but it was clean, and the live oak on the front lawn was tall and sturdy. There was a tire swing swaying in the breeze and a couple of bicycles on their sides in the driveway. Grackles chattered in the trees and the sky above was clear.

A white Ford Edge rolled along the street, reached the end of the cul-de-sac, turned and drove out again. Beyond that everything was still.

Until it wasn't.

The quiet of Leacroft Court was suddenly shattered by the roar of engines and then the sharp squeal of tires on asphalt as six vehicles rushed toward the white house. They screeched to a stop, doors opened, men and women in body armor, ballistic helmets, and assault weapons swarmed the house. The letters FBI were stenciled on chests and backs.

"Go, go, go," yelled a stern-faced woman in her mid-forties. Special Agent in Charge Connie Malgar ran toward the front door, her Glock in her hands, as other agents surrounded the house. They did not wait to announce their presence. The orders were to go in hard and fast and secure the entire Burke family.

Burly agents with breaching tools smashed in the front and back doors; another pair of agents with long crowbars forced the garage door open. More than two dozen agents rushed inside, all of them now yelling. So much yelling.

And then none at all.

Malgar had gotten as far as the end of the entrance hall and then stopped. Still as a statue. Dead still.

Because dead was the defining word.

She stood there, her gun pointing down at the floor. Eyes wide. Mouth slack.

Everywhere she looked she saw red. She saw horror.

She was so dazed and horrified that she almost did not notice the tiny sting on the back of her hand.

Someone made a gagging sound and she turned to see one of the younger agents turn away, a hand to his mouth. He lumbered toward the door.

"No," said Malgar.

She thought she said it quietly, but like a muffled echo her word came back to her so much louder. Bigger. Raw and filled with emotion.

"Oh," she said, "I'm sorry."

The younger agent turned in shock and surprise, because those words had been shouted, too.

Special Agent in Charge Connie Malgar shot him in the face.

CHAPTER ONE HUNDRED THREE
AOI OTERA (THE BLUE TEMPLE)
TSUSHIMA ISLAND, JAPAN

We stood there in the ORB, watching a horror movie.

Except it was in real time and in the real world.

The feeds from the FBI bodycams were projected in high definition and vivid color onto a screen. Standing in a home filled with some of the most appalling horrors I'd ever seen—a family cut to pieces and hung like decorations for some insane holiday—a dozen agents were slaughtering each other. With guns and fists. With teeth.

The SAC, Connie Malgar—a woman I'd worked with in the past—stood in the middle of the room shooting anything that moved. Her mouth was moving but her words were drowned out by the gunfire and screams. I could read her lips. "Oh, I'm sorry." That's what she kept saying. As she murdered her colleagues and friends.

It was what she was saying just as a bullet took her in the forehead.

Malgar went down like a broken toy and lay amid the carnage she had helped to create.

No one said anything. No one asked a stupid question like "Why?" We all knew.

It was Rage.

That was how Santoro kept control. It was the surest punishment for any of his victims of coercion who broke faith. It was how he cleaned up. No risk to any of his people.

I bowed my head, heartsick.

Feeling a great deal of my own rage.

CHAPTER ONE HUNDRED FOUR
AOI OTERA (THE BLUE TEMPLE)
INTERROGATION ROOM TWO
TSUSHIMA ISLAND, JAPAN

Top Sims placed a wooden chair backward, sat down on it facing the prisoner, who was in wrist, ankle, and waist chains, and secured to both a steel chair and the floor. The man wore a plain orange jumpsuit and paper slippers. Belle went and leaned against the wall—slim, quiet, patient, and unexpressive.

"Okay now," said Top in an almost fatherly tone, "let's see what we got."

He removed a folded piece of paper from his shirt pocket, opened it, and read.

"Let's see now . . . you are Pavol Benka. Born in the city of Bratislava, in the Slovak Republic. You're thirty-four and used to be a sergeant in the . . . hold one, let me see if I can pronounce this right . . . 5. *Pluk špeciálneho určenia, 5. PŠU*. Did I get any of that right? The Fifth Special Purpose Regiment. Uh-oh . . . says you were dishonorably discharged after a charge of aggravated sexual assault. Then you skipped the country as soon as a civil suit was filed by the family of the fourteen-year-old girl you sodomized. You were recruited by the Seven Kings organization and completed training as a Kingsman. Since then you fell off the damn world and now you turn up on a boat in South Korea where a whole bunch of innocent people are killing each other." He sighed and folded the paper again. He kept folding it until it was a paper airplane, which he soared over the prisoner's head.

Benka glared at him, jaw set, eyes hard.

"What have you got to say for yourself?"

Benka leaned forward. "Fuck you, nigger."

Top smiled as if it was a pleasant old world. He had a very warm smile. "You know how long it's been since anyone called me that? I mean, heck, it was back before the PC crowd started calling it 'the N-word.' Been a long time."

Belle chuckled.

"And that goes for the nigger dyke, too," sneered Benka.

Top looked at Belle. "He's got a way about him, doesn't he? Knows how to make friends."

She snorted. "He's not exactly reading the room, Pappy."

"Okay, okay, that's fair."

Top stood and fished a key from his pocket. Benka watched with the narrowed eyes of a wary rat as Top bent to unlock the shackles. The metal clattered to the floor.

At all once Benka was in motion, rising from his chair, hooking an arm around Top's neck, pulling the big Sig Sauer from the holster round Top's waist, pressing the barrel against the thin hair on Top's temple. It took a second.

"Hold it right there, bitch," he said, even though Belle had not moved at all. "You assholes are going to help me get out of—"

Suddenly everything went wrong for Pavol Benka.

The big, older black man with the sleepy eyes and laid-back voice was gone and instead he held—or tried to hold onto—a whirlwind. Top turned inside the grip, twisting head and body toward Benka's shoulder, which unlocked the hold. A dark forehead snapped forward, crunching into Benka's nose, knocking him back. Two iron-hard fists and a lightning-fast kick chased him, caught him, smashed him against the wall. Benka somehow clung to the pistol, pointed it, fired. Nothing. He staggered backward and racked the slide to put a round into the chamber. Fired. Nothing.

Top took the pistol away from him like a disappointed teacher snatching the chalk from a dull student's hand.

"Oh, for fuck's sake," said Top. "You can't even tell from the weight that there's no bullets in the magazine? We won't even talk about how rude it is for you to assume I'm that slow and stupid as to bring a loaded gun into an interrogation room."

Benka spat blood from his mouth and threw a vicious hook punch at Top's head.

Top walked into the swing, checking the punching arm on the point of his left elbow and driving his own fist into the center of Benka's chest. It was a heavy punch, using only the prominent big knuckle of his forefinger. A spear punch to the center of the sternum that felled the mercenary as surely as a bullet to the heart.

Benka hit the wall and slid down, coughing, gasping, fighting for breath.

"A smarter man would have known this was a setup, son," said Top. "But, clearly you were never the brightest one in your class."

"F-fuck you," he wheezed, and he tried to fit a triumphant smile onto his face. "You don't even know it yet, but everyone you love is already dead. And if you think I'm going to tell you a goddamn thing then you're out of your fucking minds."

Top squatted down slowly, hooked a finger under Benka's chin, and raised his face until they met eye to eye. "I guess that means you probably haven't figured out how this works. The whole good cop, bad cop thing? No? Well, here's the scary part." He leaned close and whispered, "I'm the good cop."

Smiling like everyone's favorite dad, he stood up, swapped the empty magazine for a loaded one, winked at Belle, and left. The door locked solidly behind him.

Benka looked through the pain-induced tears in his eyes at the slim woman who still leaned against the wall. He saw her eyes. Saw her smile.

And knew he was lost.

CHAPTER ONE HUNDRED FIVE
LUCKY KIM INTERNET CAFE
SACHEON-S
GYEONGSANGNAM-DO, SOUTH KOREA

Lieutenant Han sat on one chair and Bug on the other. Between them was Ainil Tan. The café was empty except for one of Han's bodyguards. The other was outside somewhere. The shades were pulled down.

"He said his name was Adam," said Ainil.

"Last name?" asked Bug.

"Just Adam."

"And he was in his twenties?"

"Sure. Yes. Maybe my age. Twenty-five or so. He looks a little younger when he smiles—like a big kid—but his eyes are older."

"And this is what he looks like?" Han held up her laptop to show the face Ainil had painstakingly described. The identity replication software was very sophisticated and Bug was impressed by how skillfully Han led the younger hacker through the process. The face that emerged was that of a very handsome young man who looked a lot like a younger version of the actor who played Captain America. A square jaw, blue eyes, full lips, good cheekbones.

"Oh," said Ainil, "he had a scar, too. I forgot. It's small. Two scars, really. On his left cheek. A dot and a crescent. It's funny because it looks like a semicolon."

"How badly was his face burned when you blew up your apartment?" asked Han. "Would he have had to go to the emergency room?"

Ainil chewed her lower lip for a moment, then shook her head. "I don't know. I hope his whole head burned off."

Bug tapped some keys on the laptop he balanced on his knees, then shook his head. "The police and firefighters reported no one home. No casualties. No one presenting at a local hospital with burns."

"All the pharmacies in town have CCTV," said Ainil. Bug grinned at her and hit more keys. Frowned. Tapped some more. Finally he turned his screen toward Han. A camera feed from a pharmacy sixteen blocks away showed a non-Asian woman picking up her bag at the checkout. Bug rolled it back and zoomed in, showing the gauze, ointment, and other supplies.

"Wait," said Ainil sharply, "you found it that fast? How? Who *are* you people? And don't tell me you're cops because I know what kind of computers cops have. I've never seen *anything* like that." She stabbed a finger toward Bug's MindReader Q1 substation and then at Han's Oracle. "Or that. I know computers. I know everything about computers, but I don't know either of those. So, tell me who you are."

Bug cleared his throat. "We can't. Or, at least not yet. First we'd like you to tell us everything from the beginning."

"Again? I already told you six times."

"And each time you remember some detail you forgot the first time," said Han.

"A lot depends on it," said Bug.

"Will you guys promise to keep me safe?"

Bug and Han both smiled. "You can count on that."

Ainil wiped away a tear, sniffed, then nodded.

CHAPTER ONE HUNDRED SIX
AOI OTERA (THE BLUE TEMPLE)
TSUSHIMA ISLAND, JAPAN

The ORB conference fell apart.

Church stepped out in order to help local authorities in North Carolina understand the nature of the Rage threat. Nothing came officially from him, since he has no actual legal authority in the States, but he knew who to call. It seemed to me that since we left the U.S. over disputes with the current administration, key members on both sides of the political aisle have stepped up to form an unofficial network truly dedicated to the security of America. It was surprising but heartening to see big-picture thinkers take actions that earned them no party advantage but actually spoke to a level of patriotism that ran deep. Made even a cynical old son of a bitch like me want to shake some hands.

The first action was to quarantine the area. Agents in hazmat suits were dispatched into adjoining homes to find neighbors and isolate them in place. What that meant in practical terms was to put each of them in separate rooms in their own homes, bind them with zip ties, and tranq them with Sandman. How the FBI got so many doses of Sandman that fast is something neither Church nor Wilson seemed to want to explain. Infants and very small children were transported to the local hospital.

Teams armed with electronic scanners went hunting for the blowflies, with orders to try and catch them in nets or bags so they could be studied.

I sent Bunny and Andrea to check on Major Mun, with orders to let me know as soon as she woke up. Because she was substantially smaller than the bad guy we bagged, her lower blood volume meant she'd sleep a bit longer.

While I waited, I talked with Doc Holliday.

"I'm trying to make sense of this," I said. "Forensics people on the scene estimate that the time of death of Burke's family roughly coincides with when we bagged him. How's that possible? I mean, why kill them at all? They couldn't know Burke told us anything."

"Well, dang," said Doc, "I finally get a chance to fit a word in edgewise. I can answer that." Her tone was sprightly, but that was forced. Her hologram was so sharply defined that I could see the horror in her eyes, and I felt certain she'd seen images from the Burke house.

"What've you got?" I asked.

"I had the boys there at Aoi Otera strip your prisoner down to his skivvies, and search his gear. Turns out he has a very sneaky and very nifty bodycam. Don't know the make and model yet, but it's high end and covered in film so it can't be seen unless you're looking for it. It has some software built into it, and I'll bet you a dollar to a donut that the code is aligned to their jammer so their signal gets out while everyone else's is scrambled."

"Which means Santoro and Bolton saw us," I said.

"Sure would. Your visors would spoil long-range views, like from a news helicopter or someone forty feet away with a cell camera, but up close . . . yeah, they'd be able to see your faces."

"Well, that's a sobering thought," I said. "Bolton and Santoro both know my face."

"Well, honeylumps," said Doc, "they know it even better now."

Wilson rejoined us, and he looked gray and worn out. I knew it was going to be bad news. "I . . . I don't even want to . . ."

"Go on," I said. "Hit me."

"On the odd chance that Major Mun is compromised, we sent people to take her family into custody. But . . ."

He shook his head.

"All of them?" I asked.

"Yes," said Wilson. "Her entire family is dead. Even the bloody dog. All dead. All by their own hands. It's bloody awful."

His choice of expletive seemed to catch up with him and he turned away, his hologram blinking out.

I stood there with Doc, each of us on different continents, thousands of miles apart, yet caught in the same bubble of sadness, anger, and dread.

"This is worse than a damn pathogen," she said bitterly, her cowgirl burlesque bawdiness falling away. "At least with a disease there's a logical pattern to the spread. This is more like a sniper. You can't hunker down and hide because you don't know which way is safe."

"Is there some kind of antivirus? And, no, don't say it, I know it's not a virus, not a bug. But you know what I mean? A counteragent?"

"For a weaponized protein?"

"I take that as a no?"

"Honey, whoever designed this Rage thing is damn smart. Possibly a genius."

"Yeah?" I said. "I thought you were a super genius. Didn't Church hire you because you're supposed to be smarter than everyone else? Now might be a good time to prove that."

She gave me a long, withering look. "Joe," she said mildly, "use that tone with me again and I'll beat you like a tented mule."

Her image vanished, and I was left alone. Standing there in darkness, wrapped in the barbed wire of my frustration and anger.

"Calpurnia! Lights, goddamn it."

"Please use respectful language, Joseph," scolded the AI.

I resisted punching the computer interface mounted on the wall. Instead I stalked out of the room, but with no clear direction where to go.

CHAPTER ONE HUNDRED SEVEN
AOI OTERA (THE BLUE TEMPLE)
INTERROGATION ROOM TWO
TSUSHIMA ISLAND, JAPAN

I saw Top standing outside of one of the interrogation rooms. He was eating sushi from a plate. He had a piece of *gunkan maki* caught in the pincers of his chopsticks but when he saw my face he stopped from putting it in his mouth.

"You going to tell me there's more shit coming down the pipe, aren't you?" he asked.

I pursed my lips for a moment and looked past him at the closed interrogation room door.

"He talking yet?"

"Belle's with him," said Top. "She's been in there for ten minutes now."

"That's enough time. Come on."

He tossed the sushi into a trash can and unlocked the door.

I could smell the blood as soon as we stepped in. There was not a lot of it, but it was fresh. That coppery smell is distinctive and fades to something else as the cells die and thicken.

Pavol Benka sat weeping in the chair. The prison jumpsuit we'd put him in was rags. His body trembled as if with a fever. He sat rigid as if afraid to move a muscle. As if doing anything at all was so terrifying that his muscles struggled to keep him there on that chair. I saw a pile of shackles in a corner. Benka was not tied or restrained by anything except terror.

Belle leaned against the wall. She was breathing heavily but affected a resting state. Like a cheetah who'd just outrun an unfortunate impala. Sweat jeweled her dark brown skin and there were really unpleasant lights in her eyes. Her hands were red to the wrist.

Without looking at the man, she said, "Tell them about the Fixers."

"I'm . . . I'm sorry . . . ," he said, his voice disintegrating into blubbery tears. But Belle snapped her fingers, loud as a pistol shot, and his tears stopped.

"Tell them."

Tears and snot ran down his face, into his mouth, dripping onto his chest.

He told us.

CHAPTER ONE HUNDRED EIGHT
AOI OTERA (THE BLUE TEMPLE)
TSUSHIMA ISLAND, JAPAN

"They're called Fixers," I said.

The ORB seemed to be a crowded house. My guys, Church, and everyone at the TOC. Even Rudy was with us now. I made it a point not to walk through anyone this time.

"Our prisoner, Pavol Benka, knew Santoro from before, and confirmed that he is training a new team. A large one. Multinational. They are heavily funded and well equipped."

"Is Santoro working with Harcourt Bolton?" asked Wilson.

"He didn't even know that name," I said. "But he has seen Santoro with a tall American who fits Bolton's description. So, we can probably make that leap. And, I think we can also connect Bolton to Kuga. What's not clear is whether Bolton *is* Kuga, or is employed by him. The reason that's unclear is because Benka talked about Kuga as if it wasn't so much a person as an organization."

"I can understand that," said Rudy, "though I actually think that supports a supposition that Bolton is the man running that organization. Consider his past. He was in the CIA most of his life. He was a field operative used to submerging into whatever country or culture was necessary for his mission. Then, when he became a criminal, he never self-aggrandized in the same way as, say, the Seven Kings. His focus was on his goals. Sharing a name with the organization is useful obfuscation."

"So you think Bolton is both Kuga and the head of an organization called Kuga?" asked Church.

"I do."

Nikki spoke up. "Rudy's right, I'm sure of it." She went on to explain how the name Kuga has been picked up and used by a lot of criminals active in the black market and mercenary communities. "He's like Macavity the Mystery Cat." She looked around, saw a lot of blank faces. "From *Cats* . . . ? The one who everyone blames for everything but no one actually sees."

"Moriarty," said Wilson.

"Sure," she said. "Whatever. I think that's also why he calls his guys the Fixers. After all, *he's* the ultimate fixer."

Church gave her a nod of approval. "Your job now is to peel back the layers of deceit and misdirection and find the man. We need a better idea of the shape of his organization."

"What did Benka tell you about the attacks on the islands?"

"Not a lot that we don't know," I said. "He wasn't in on planning. Burke set it up and trained everyone for the missions. Benka was muscle. They used the blowfly drones. On Frog Island they collected as many as possible, but my guess is that a good forensic sweep will find them. I suggest that be a team effort, with experts from all four countries. Make a show of it. Share the effort and share the win when they find stuff."

"Agreed," said Church, and Wilson said he would arrange it.

"Benka said that the hit in South Korea was the only other one he knew about. Those two hits."

"Do you believe him?" asked Wilson. "He could be lying to you."

"He was not," said Belle. Everyone looked at her for a moment and she met the stares. Her eyes were about as human as those of a statue to some goddess of vengeance and slaughter. That's not a joke.

"Fair enough," said Wilson, looking uncomfortable. Rudy looked down at the floor and sighed. This kind of thing was so hard for him. Hell, it was hard for all of us, but what else could we do? Innocent people were dying and we had no real idea how to stop it.

"After Frog Island," I continued, "the strike team was to head here to Japan, split up, and make their way to a pickup point in Tokyo."

"That's where we may have caught our first useful break," said Wilson. "The site is a warehouse—Kamikaze Jitensha—a bicycle manufacturer owned by Haruki Hong. He is half Korean, and when Nikki tore apart Hong's emails, she found some communication with businessmen in South Korea. By itself that's nothing, because the firm buys parts from the South and also sells bikes there through a large number of retail outlets. Nikki, want to tell them the rest?"

Nikki flushed a little and in her rapid-fire chipmunk voice said, "Kamikaze Jitsensha makes mostly rental bikes for tourists. South Korea is their biggest market, and Mr. Hong visits several times a year. When I dug deeper I found that Hong's grandfather was stuck

JONATHAN MABERRY

in Pyongyang when the borders were closed and Korea split up. More than half the family was there, actually. Still is. And despite all of the filters and restrictions the North Koreans put on any kind of internet or email, Mr. Hong has been swapping emails and even Skyping with his family there."

I said, "Ah." And meant it.

"I have six people digging deeper," said Nikki, "but so far we've already found some dirt. Mr. Hong's uncle, also in the North, is a big industrialist up there. Publicly he's a good Party member and supports North Korean isolationism, but he takes a whole different view in emails. And, for the record, the Hong family uses a type of pattern encryption that I've only ever seen before used by people in the North. They send family photos, but when you blow up the images so that you can see the individual pixels, there are characters there in Korean. These are placed randomly by a 128-bit encryption program in order to hide the pattern and not trigger code search software."

"But you found it anyway?" asked Rudy, smiling.

Her flush went five shades darker. "Well . . . um . . . sure. I mean . . ." She coughed and met nobody's eyes and finally found her way back to her point. "I, um, ran some filters and other stuff on the emails and we're starting to be able to read some of them. The Hongs are complaining a lot—and I mean a whole lot—about how living in the North is killing their business and stifling growth. They have to pay too much to the State, and the trade sanctions imposed by America and other countries are crippling them. Lots of stuff like that. There's also a lot of bitching about China for fueling the North's hostility and keeping it locked in place as a buffer against the South, and by association America. Hong's dad has made some cryptic comments about how the current situation is more fragile than it looks and only needs a push to fall down."

"Ah," I said again.

"Boom," said Bunny.

"We're still decoding. So far, except for the use of the bicycle warehouse, there's nothing directly tying the Hong family to Kuga. We've still got a lot of emails to go through. I also have some of my guys writing a tapeworm program to get deeper into all the Hong family computers. We plan to attach it to Mr. Hong's next email. In the meantime, though, there was a reference that I found kind of odd. Something that seems to be out of place. Four different members of the Hong family—Mr. Hong in Japan, his brother in Seoul, and the two elder Hongs in Pyongyang—have all made kind of cryptic references to something called Dasuht Myung eh Kangchul Namja, which means—"

"The Five Iron Men," I translated.

Church leaned forward, sharp as a hawk. "What was the context?"

"That's just it," said Nikki, "there was no context in terms of the emails. That was all they said. Just that name. What struck me, though, was the timing. Each of the family members sent the same email just before the attacks on Gaeguli Seom and Yeonpyeong."

Church turned slowly toward me. "Now isn't that interesting," he said slowly.

CHAPTER ONE HUNDRED NINE
AOI OTERA (THE BLUE TEMPLE)
TSUSHIMA ISLAND, JAPAN

Now that we had an actual solid lead, Church put the full machinery of RTI into motion, coordinating with Kingdom, with Arklight, and with a select few groups in the region where we had friends we could trust. It was a small list, though.

After the ORB conference wrapped, I indicated to Church to linger a bit for a private chat. When we were alone in that strange virtual setting, I asked if he knew who these Five Iron Men were, because I got the impression he knew something.

"Not personally," he said, "but that name has come up before. There have been groups using that name for a thousand years in Korea. Always very political but always tied to mercantile interests. The DMS hasn't had to go after them, but other organizations with which I've been associated have been aware of them. They were active during the Second World War, even during the Japanese occupation, working behind the scenes to make sure that trade flowed. It may be that they have been more aggressively active than was previously supposed."

"Why didn't you say so to the group just now?"

"Because, Colonel, I may be culpable for some of the damage which has been done."

I gaped at him. "*How?*"

He studied me for a moment, then sighed. He looked sad. "There was a time—some years ago—when I was involved in a matter in Korea and brushed up against the Dasuht Myung eh Kangchul Namja. It was a crossroads moment, and I could have gone one way or the other, but not both. Had I chosen differently, then it is entirely possible that organization might have ended then. I chose what seemed like a better target and helped take that down." He paused. "It was one of the first missions I undertook with Aunt Sallie. Quite a long time ago. She wanted to go after The Five Iron Men, but as senior agent I made a different call."

"Who was the other target?"

"You would not have heard of them," he said. When it was clear I was going to wait for an actual answer, he said, "They called themselves the Builders. They pretended to be part of the Freemasons, but that was a lie. And they were not interested in building anything. Outwardly they were a group of well-funded militant anarchists sowing hatred and violence throughout Southeast Asia."

"What made you pick them instead of The Five Iron Men?"

His eyes were black jewels behind the lenses of his glasses. "Because they were associated with Nicodemus."

"Oh," I said. "Shit."

"Yes."

Nicodemus was a strange little man who has been involved in some of the worst and more frightening moments in my career with the DMS. I first encountered him during the King of Plagues matter. He was in a supermax prison at the time, but somehow managed to be actively involved in what the Kings and the Goddess were doing. Then he showed up again and again after that. In Iran, during the Assassin's Code case, in the Predator One case in San Diego, and then with the Dogs of War fiasco. Top and Bunny were fighting Nicodemus—and losing badly—when Church showed up. He chased my guys out and, as far as we can tell, killed the evil son of a bitch. Church absolutely refuses to talk about what happened, and evades every conversation about Nicodemus that strays from what's in our main case files. They have a connection, though, that much is sure, and it is an old one. How old? Good guess, because I can't even accurately figure out how old Church is. He looks like he's in his mid-sixties, but there are rumors about him going way back. Some of it is probably bullshit, like the rumors around the name Kuga. Even so, it gives me a serious case of the wiggins when I think about it.

Church scares me.

Nicodemus scares us all. Is he dead? Even Church won't say for sure.

"You didn't take Nicodemus down that time with the Builders," I said, aware of how unkind it sounded.

"No."

"Did you stop the Builders?"

"Yes."

"Well . . . you have that, at least."

Church is not a man much given to outward displays of emotion, but he looked like he'd been punched a few times in the gut. Hard. He shook his head.

"I try not to carry regrets around, Colonel," he said quietly. "Regrets are a cancer that can eat you alive. I'm not clairvoyant enough to look forward and see the full consequences of my actions. None of us have that luxury. We do what we think is best in the moment and then try to keep making the best choices based on the information we have. It's staying in the fight that matters."

"The war is the war," I said. It was an important catchphrase for him. For me, too; and for many of us in this field. The ones who understand that individual battles may be won or lost, but the war—that big, essential, endless struggle that puts guys like us between the devil and the world—goes on.

After a moment, I said, "This case . . . maybe it's because it's the first for our new outfit, or maybe because it's so *international* instead of being contained within the overall politics of the U.S. of A., but there is something deeply off about all this."

"In what way?"

"I don't know . . . that's the problem. It doesn't feel right. It feels like we're—"

"Only catching a glimpse?" he said.

We looked at each other.

"Yeah," I said. "A frustrating goddamn glimpse."

As I turned away, Church said, "I'd like you and Havoc Team to stay in Japan for a few days. The political situation there is calming down, but still tense. Since the leaders of the four countries are all in Oslo for the D9 summit, I'm going there. I've arranged a private meeting with them. Call it a calming-down session with some creative spin control."

"About that . . . if you're able to do that, then Bolton and Santoro have failed. Their larger purpose, I mean. If these Five Iron Men hired them to stage those bioweapon attacks, they got the small and ugly win, but they didn't really shake up the political situation. In a big-picture way, our bad guys lost."

"Perhaps," said Church. "Stay here and find out for sure. Talk to Major Mun. Bug is in the South now and is interviewing the woman from Punk Press. Check with him to see if he has anything that could be a lead. I'll go play diplomat, Colonel; you stay here and be a cop."

"And if we wrap it up here?"

He smiled. "Oslo is lovely this time of year. Come and join the party."

As he turned his hologram vanished, leaving me standing, once more, in the dark.

I ended the ORB and tapped my coms unit to see if Bug had anything at all.

CHAPTER ONE HUNDRED TEN
AOI OTERA (THE BLUE TEMPLE)
INTERROGATION ROOM THREE
TSUSHIMA ISLAND, JAPAN

Top caught up to me on the way to the interrogation rooms.

"Are you going to talk with Major Mun?" he asked.

"Yeah. They said she's coming out of it."

"Scott Wilson sent over a file." He held out a blue file folder. "He wants you to read this before you do the interview."

"What is it?"

There was a strange look in Top's eyes. "Seems Nikki's people did a full background check on her. A very deep dive. And we also did a physical workup. Blood, prints, everything."

"Has she been compromised?"

"Best you read the report," he said, gave me a strange smile and a nod, and left me there. I flipped open the folder and read.

"Well, damn," I said aloud. I leaned against the wall and read it all through again.

"Yo, boss," said a voice, and I looked up to see Bunny and Andrea coming through the doorway at the opposite end of the hall. I handed them the folder and they leaned together to read it. At first they looked blank. Then they looked confused. Then they looked mad.

"Yeah," I said. "Life just keeps on getting more interesting, doesn't it?"

I looked in through a small grilled window at the woman seated at the interview table. Cuffed. Bowed and broken. I quietly slid the panel shut.

"I'll talk to her alone."

Andrea punched in the lock code and held the door for me. Mun's head jerked up as I came in and she watched me with hostile cat eyes as I walked around and sat down across from her. I said nothing for a long time. Maybe two full minutes. She did her best to meet my eyes, but eventually her glare faltered and she turned to look at the wall.

"So," I said, "you want to tell me who the hell you are?"

CHAPTER ONE HUNDRED ELEVEN
AOI OTERA (THE BLUE TEMPLE)
INTERROGATION ROOM THREE
TSUSHIMA ISLAND, JAPAN

She said nothing.

I sighed. Very theatrical. The kind of sigh that says: *We can do this the easy way or the hard way, and you just made the wrong choice.* That kind of sigh.

"Where is Major Mun?" I asked.

Nothing.

"How did you infiltrate Kingdom? Are there other agents in that organization?"

Nothing.

"Okay," I said, "then let me tell *you*."

That got a flinch, but she still stared at the wall.

"Your name is Staff Sergeant Soon Hue Kang. You are not a member of Kingdom. You're not even a Korean national. You're a citizen of the United States. You are separated from Mr. James Kang. You have a seven-month-old daughter but do not have custody. Everyone thinks you are on leave from Fort Story in Virginia Beach. Won't they be surprised when you don't turn up for duty on December 27? Did you think you'd be back by then?"

She tried to glare through the fear, but I wasn't fooled.

"To anyone who doesn't know Major Mun personally, you're a good fit. Same height, about the same weight and age. Someone gave you a hell of a lot of training so you could pass muster as special forces. I'm impressed. Mind you, I'm pretty unhappy, but I am impressed."

I let silence beat her up for a bit.

"Here's the thing," I said. "I don't yet know if your actions were because you are under duress, or because you are a spooky psycho lady. Right now I'm leaning more toward the latter, because after evaluating your actions last night you clearly tried to thwart our mission. Notice that I said 'thwart.' I don't often use that word with a straight face, but I am not laughing right now. This is my serious face. This, in point of fact, is my really unhappy face."

She stared at me as if I was insane. Fair enough.

"If Major Mun is alive, and if you can help us find her, I will legitimately argue for leniency on your behalf. You don't walk, but you don't go to a black site where no one who works there ever heard of the Constitution or the Bill of Rights. Look into my eyes and tell me if I'm joking."

Sweat beaded her upper lip.

"If you go a step forward and tell me everything—and I do mean every goddamn thing—about Rafael Santoro, Kuga, Harcourt Bolton, the Fixers, and The Five Iron Men, then you might actually get out of prison while you're still young enough to enjoy your AARP benefits. Are you following me?"

There was the tiniest of movements of her head. Not sure if it was a twitch or a nod. I cupped my hand around my ear. "Sorry, didn't hear you."

"I . . . I want a—"

I slapped my palm down on the table so fast and hard that she jumped and screamed. In the coldest voice I own, I said, "Be very careful what you say next. If the word 'lawyer' plays any part of that sentence you are going to fall into a world of shit."

She started to cry. They were not weak tears. None of that girlish tears chauvinistic bullshit. This was a strong, dangerous, capable woman. No, these tears were pure terror. Then she said the four most horrible words a person could say. They broke her. They twisted her mouth into such an ugly shape that it turned everything in my stomach to icy slush and robbed all the heat from the world.

She said, "*They have my daughter.*"

CHAPTER ONE HUNDRED TWELVE
AOI OTERA (THE BLUE TEMPLE)
INTERROGATION ROOM THREE
TSUSHIMA ISLAND, JAPAN

I stood up and hurried to the door, knocked to be let out, and pulled the door shut behind me.

"You heard?" I asked. Bunny looked and looked through the grill.

JONATHAN MABERRY

"Fuck me," he said softly. "These pricks are lower than whale shit. We need to be cutting some throats here."

Andrea was already speaking on a wall-mounted telephone. "He's right here," he said and handed me the phone. "Wilson."

"Scott," I said, "what can we do? Who do we have in that area? I'm almost afraid of sending in more Feds because I think they've been infiltrated, too. The way they took out Burke's family . . ."

"Well, Colonel, there is someone in the area, but he's not military. He's one of Junie's FreeTech colleagues, down there working on some disaster relief from the last hurricane."

I closed my eyes. "You're going to tell me it's Toys, aren't you?"

"Mr. Chismer is the closest capable asset available."

"Shit. Okay, do it."

CHAPTER ONE HUNDRED THIRTEEN
CROMWELL PARK DRIVE
VIRGINIA BEACH, VIRGINIA

Alexander Chismer—Toys to everyone who knew him from before his days as CEO of FreeTech—leaned back against the stucco wall of the FEMA building in Virginia Beach. He closed his eyes and exhaled a long, slow, sad chestful of breath.

"Bloody fucking hell," he whispered.

He heard a crunch on the gravel. "You okay, Mr. C?"

Toys opened his eyes. His chief of security, Maxine Rudd, loomed over him. Toys was slender and average height, but Maxine— affectionately known as Mad Max—was six feet three inches of scowling muscle. She wore camo pants, a green FreeTech T-shirt, and a Sig Sauer 9mm in a nylon shoulder holster. Her partner, Croc Peters, stood a couple of feet behind her. They both looked worried.

Toys looked at them. Mad Max and Croc were ex-DMS field agents who now worked for him. Mostly they drove cars, checked security at venues, liaised with local law, and ran interference because Toys generally did not like to talk to people. Among the staff, the assignment to protect him was called minding the dragon. They never bothered him with chitchat, and did not question why Toys' first stop in any town was a visit to a church. Mostly Catholic, but for the boss any church will do. They each carried cash in case he ran out and needed some for the poor box. Toys did not know how much they knew about his past other than that he'd once been employed by the Seven Kings and had left that organization and come to work for Mr. Church as the head of FreeTech. Junie Flynn was the public face and, inarguably, its heart; but Toys was the money and the useful deviousness that sheared through red tape and political resistance.

"Do you know where Cromwell Park Drive is?" asked Toys. "And how fast we can get there?"

"Sure," said Mad Max. "Finding it is nothing. How fast do we need to be there?"

Toys pushed off the wall and began walking briskly toward the helicopter parked on the landing pad out back.

That was answer enough.

The pilot had the rotors turning and the bird was in the air in no time.

The chopper cut through the air.

As they flew, Toys explained the situation. Mad Max and Croc did not waste time with foolish questions. They unfolded a laptop and brought up Google Maps, switched to satellite view, and made decisions on where to land.

"It'll be a seven-hundred-yard run," said Croc. "Or I can steal someone's car."

"How fast can you do that?" asked Toys.

Croc merely laughed and began sorting through a metal case of electronic equipment. He shoved a few items into his pockets, and then accepted a combat shotgun from Mad Max.

The flight was seventeen minutes. They put down in a parking lot of an abandoned Kmart. Before leaving the machine, Toys grabbed a clipboard and the pilot's unmarked gray ball cap. It was mundane and functional, though in any other circumstance Toys would rather be eaten by rabid voles than wear that kind of hat.

The residential area was a short block away. Mad Max and Croc split off from him, while Toys slowed to a walk and then a saunter, pretending to look from his clipboard to addresses painted on curbs, mailboxes, or homes. He knocked on the door of the house next to the target, asked directions of a sleepy old lady, smiled a big fake smile, and went to the target house.

He could see no one but felt eyes on him. That was fine. He was no virgin when it came to deception and playacting. He walked right up and knocked on the door. While he waited he made a subtle show of studying the clipboard, idly flipping a page or two. Beyond the door he heard a baby cry and felt only marginal relief.

As he always did in moments when he was out in public, he felt the presence of his ghosts. So many of them. All of the people he either murdered, ordered killed, or whose deaths he enabled by his association with monsters like Sebastian Gault, Hugo Vox, and the Seven Kings. Although Toys believed in the biblical promise of redemption, he did not believe that he deserved it. No matter how much good he did now through FreeTech. No matter how many people he saved with his investments, charities, and covert philanthropy. It was his unshakable belief that damnation waited for him after death. No limbo, no purgatory, no resurrection of the soul. He did not want to be redeemed, and accepted Hell as the natural and fitting punishment for his many sins.

Jobs like this—favors for Joe Ledger or Mr. Church—might put blood on his hands, but it would not darken his soul. That was already painted a toneless black.

Footsteps clicked along a tiled floor and then the door opened a few inches. Enough for a four-inch slice of a man's face to scowl out at him.

"What do you want?" demanded the man. He was some mix of Asian, mused Toys. Japanese and something else, possibly Thai. A good-looking man in his mid-thirties.

Toys waved the clipboard. "Mr. Kang? I'm from the Independence Middle School. We're fundraising for Bobby Miller, perhaps you've heard about him on the news? His parents' car was hit on the way home from practice and they're okay—thank the Lord Jesus—but Bobby's in a coma and the medical bills are just piling up. We're collecting donations to help defray those costs and show love and support for the Millers."

The man stared at him with dead eyes for a three count and then actually dug into his pocket, peeled a ten-dollar bill off a roll, and opened the door wide enough to hand it over.

"Sure, whatever," said the man.

Toys reached for the bill but missed it. The ten fluttered down and the man automatically bent to catch it.

Toys brought his knee up so sharply the man had no chance at all of blocking it and his nose exploded with a wet crunch. Then Toys shoved him back, pushing his way into the living room. A woman sat on a couch, holding the crying baby to her in a rough embrace. She gaped at Toys, dropped the child onto the floor as she scrambled for the Glock on the coffee table. She was very fast.

She was not nearly fast enough.

Toys cleared the nine feet between door and couch, hooked the table with a foot, and kicked it halfway across the room. The gun flew straight up in the air; he caught it, pivoted, and whipped the barrel across the woman's face as she shot to her feet. The blow slung blood and teeth on the curtains. Toys spun back to the man who'd answered the door and who was on his knees trying to pull his gun out of his waistband, but it was slipping on bloody fingers.

"Sodding amateurs," growled Toys as he took the gun away and repeated the action, this time crashing the barrel against the side of the mouth. The man went down.

He glanced at the baby, who was crying even louder now, screaming, but otherwise seemed to be okay.

Croc appeared in the doorway to the kitchen, grinning the way he did when things got ugly. He had a Marine Corps Ka-Bar in his left hand and it was red to the crossbar.

"Two of them," he said. "Mad Max is cleaning the rest up. No noise."

"Clear the house," ordered Toys. Croc unslung his shotgun and went up the stairs, returning in seconds, nodding that all was okay. He repeated the action with the cellar and garage.

Mad Max came in, her face aglow as if they were all on holiday. "Two watchers. One in a car, the other in an empty house across the yard. No muss, no fuss," she said, as she always did.

"Well, a little bit of muss," said Croc, right on cue.

"Can we interrogate either of the watchers?"

"With a séance, maybe."

Toys nodded to the baby. "Do something with that."

He preferred not to touch children. Ever.

Croc squatted down and picked the child up and bounced her gently. The baby began to settle at once, which pulled a surprised grunt from Toys. But then Croc brought the baby over and held her up to show her legs. There were cigarette burns on both legs and the bottoms of the tiny pink feet. Not new—weeks old, but badly healed. Two of them were infected.

Toys turned away. "Kitchen," he snapped.

Mad Max dragged the two dazed and bleeding survivors into the kitchen and tied them securely with flex cuffs. The woman was mostly conscious and glared death at the three of them. Toys wasn't fooled. He saw the fear there, too.

He pulled over a plastic chair and sat on it.

"We're going to have a lovely chat," he said amiably. "You can save yourself a great deal of discomfort by not forcing us to go through the process of you pretending you're tough enough to endure what I'm willing to do. You work for Rafael Santoro, so you must know it never works. I *knew* Santoro. I've seen him in action. I know you are Fixers. So, be a useful little cow and just tell me everything."

"Fuck you," said the woman, and tried to spit on him. Her attempt fell short.

Toys sighed and drew a slender knife from his inside pocket.

"Very well," he said wearily, "let's begin, shall we?"

CHAPTER ONE HUNDRED FOURTEEN
AOI OTERA (THE BLUE TEMPLE)
INTERROGATION ROOM FOUR
TSUSHIMA ISLAND, JAPAN

This is how it is for us. The DMS and now RTI. There is nothing, then there is way too much random information—like pieces from twenty different jigsaw puzzles jumbled together. Then some kind of dam bursts and the information floods in. So much that it's like getting caught in a barge when a levee breaks.

I went into an empty interrogation room and sat down on a chair with my heels up. It's a trick—putting the body into a posture of calm nonchalance sometimes tricks the mind into relaxing. Andrea was next door minding Kang, and was apparently attempting to amuse her by demonstrating card tricks. Not that the woman was at all interested, but Andrea has some issues. Bunny came and leaned his big shoulder against the doorframe. He was sipping some kind of blueberry Korean soda.

Bug called and I put it on speaker. He and an Arklight agent named Annie Han had found and interviewed Ainil Tan, the woman behind the Punk Press video. After sifting through the bits she knew and the stuff we were learning, it was clear that a man named Adam—who was almost certainly the partner of Eve—had approached her with a hot tip. Adam had excellent bona fides from all sorts of underground whistleblower groups.

"Those credentials were probably retrofitted onto the right websites," said Bug. "Some pretty sophisticated work, but Annie and I will be able to take it apart."

He said "Annie and I" with an unusual amount of emotion.

"I've uploaded an identikit picture of Adam," said Bug, "and we're getting a lot of hits. Maybe fourteen different aliases in two dozen places. Surveillance camera footage has him with a cute blonde. We figure that's Eve. Those images have been enhanced and shared with our whole network, and with Arklight. Both were last seen in South Korea. So, they're here."

He explained that Adam sold Ainil on a story that he was in U.S. military intelligence and caught wind of something illegal his government was doing. He could not risk blowing the whistle himself, because he would go to jail, or have to run like Edward Snowden. So, instead, he used his connections to find Punk Press, and flattered Ainil by saying no one else had the right blend of integrity and guts. Bug said that Ainil Tan was very smart, but young and probably too optimistic. She bought the story, and went to the island with Adam, both of them in hazmat suits.

"Here's the thing that unplugged her from believing in this guy," said Bug. "When they ran the video on the news, there was that bit of dialogue where an American sailor was talking trash about Kim

Jong-un. Ainil said they didn't record anything like that. I guess Santoro's crew figured she would be freaked by that and sent Adam around to shut her up."

He told me how she blew up her kitchen and burned Adam. A second identikit was made with probable burn marks.

"Is she willing to go on record with all of this?" I asked.

"We finished recording a full statement half an hour ago," he said. "Mr. Church has it already and it's being shared with the four governments. We can prove Adam has never been in military intelligence, or in any government job. He's a ghost, though, which is frustrating on one hand because I know you'd like to have a long talk with him, but on the other hand it sticks a pin in the American conspiracy theory. I think, as far as war in this area goes, we can all go take a shower and get a foot rub."

"Spectacular work, Bug."

"Should I preen?"

"You should."

Bug said he and Annie were going to get Ainil out of the country. I suggested Phoenix House and he said they were heading to the airport at that moment.

"Hey," said Bunny dryly, "we won one. What's that make it? One for two? Yay us."

Bug ended the call and Toys called a few moments later.

"Ledger," he said, in about the same way someone would say "testicular cyst." There wasn't a lot of love between us.

"Toys," I said, giving it the same inflection. "The baby?"

"Alive."

"But?"

He told me about borderline malnutrition, an unchanged diaper, and cigarette burns. He said that the father's body was wrapped in black plastic trash bags in a basement closet. I sat there very still and stared a burning hole through the wall. I saw a look in Bunny's eyes that was ugly and deadly. And probably a match for my own.

"We took two of the four-person team," he said.

Very calmly I said, "Were you able to get anything from them?"

There was a sound. Could have been a laugh, or a sob. Hard to tell. Toys said, "I got everything from them."

"Hold on," I said, and conferenced Scott Wilson, Doc, and Church in on the call. "Okay, the gang's all here, Toys. Give us all of it."

He did. The people Toys interrogated were part of a group of a hundred freelancers being trained to be Fixers. It was possible that hundred was only a single training group. Santoro called it a "century," and had made some reference to a cohort and a legion. That was significant and scary. A cohort was an old Roman designation for a group of six centuries, which in turn formed one tenth of a legion. We did not believe Santoro had managed to build an army of six thousand mercenaries. Not saying it was impossible, but it was very unlikely, given the time needed to do it and what would be required to hide, train, equip, and arm an army of that size. No, but if he had one or more cohorts, that was bad enough. Worse than bad.

The Fixers said they worked for Kuga, but from what they told Toys, it seemed like "Kuga" was the name of the organization. If there was a person of that name, the Fixers didn't know that for sure. They believed Santoro answered to someone, or to a group, but that was above their pay grade.

The Korea gig was some kind of "client job," which seemed to verify what Nikki found out about The Five Iron Men. It seemed obvious those five pricks were our collective Big Bad.

The Fixers thought that there were other operations ongoing, but they were only told about their part of the Korea op.

They knew about Adam and Eve and Toys said he detected animosity and jealousy, because the blond kids were teacher's pets to Santoro. They called him Daddy, and he called them his firstborn.

They also gave us some locations. Recruiting centers near four different U.S. military bases; others in South Africa, Turkey, Iraq, Pakistan, Somalia, South Sudan, and Thailand. One of Toys' captives was involved in recruiting before graduating to field operations. They also gave up two training facilities. One in Yemen and one near Dryden in Washington State.

And that was all. It was a lot, but the Fixers did not know where Santoro was. They didn't know where the Kuga headquarters were. They had no idea if there was more to the Korea thing.

"How sure are you about the Korea situation?" I asked. "Because it feels to me like there's another shoe to drop."

"If there was more to give," said Toys, "they would have given it."

He dropped out of the call, but I stayed on with the others.

Wilson said, "We can act on all of this. If we move quickly enough, we might have a chance to cripple the Kuga network."

"Do it," said Church, and Wilson was gone.

After a pause, Doc said, "Well, boys, I don't know whether to shit or wind my watch here. And I'm with my honeybunny in that I can't believe this whole thing is just going to peter out into a simple mop-the-floors and dust-the-shelves thing. One minute we're about to bend over and kiss our asses goodbye, and next minute the president of these United States and the little psychopath from North Korea are acting like they just blew each other."

"How well you sum it all up," said Church.

"You know what I'm saying, Deacon. If everything's coming your way then maybe you're driving in the wrong lane."

"I think we're all on the same page," admitted Church, "but if there is more to this then we are absent the proof. What we know is that Kuga attempted a big play and failed. Perhaps it is a matter of overreach. Trying to incite a war with two of the world's great super-powers is bold. The fact that it very nearly worked says a great deal about the sophistication of our enemies."

"And their weaknesses," I said.

"So it would seem. However, I believe Doctor Holliday has a quaint saying for that."

"Something about counting chickens?" suggested Doc. "Now, Outlaw, as much as I like agreeing with you, take a step back and see what they accomplished. They killed hundreds of people with a brand-new bioweapon. Maybe it was developed in that lab in Aleppo that you and your lovely band of cutthroats blew into orbit, but I don't believe so. I can see a lab that small being used for some kind of testing, but nothing you described speaks to something sophisti-cated enough for large-scale biological weapons research."

"Which means the lab is still out there," I said glumly. "Fuck me."

"Oh, I think Junie would spank me hard if I did that."

"Cute. So, if the Korean Peninsula isn't about to become a battle-ground, then we're talking some serious mission creep. Looking for that lab, and hunting for Kuga and Santoro."

"Yes," said Church. "That has to be high priority, though whether it is an RTI case or not remains to be seen. We have been very frank with the four governments, and they will be throwing their considerable assets into that hunt. The intel provided by Mr. Chismer is extremely useful. I will decide which agencies to share it with. Arklight will want a piece of it as well. As will Kingdom, since Major Mun was one of theirs. I can also imagine the SEALs would like an opportunity to avenge their own."

"So what do we do? Eat popcorn and watch from the sidelines?"

Church thought about that for a moment and we listened to the silence.

"Given the possible size and reach of the Kuga organization," he said slowly, "I think you should bring Havoc Team here to Oslo. You, Top, and Bunny are the only active operators who have experience with Santoro and his former Kingsmen, and you can provide useful advice to other players on our in-house teams and to our friends."

"What about Harcourt Bolton? *Is* he Kuga or not?"

"Frankly, Colonel, I do not know. My gut says yes, but we do not have any corroboration of real substance. It's possible he is simply in hiding. It's possible he, also, works for Kuga without being its head. We don't know and we will have to find out."

I sighed. "I'm going to interview the Kang woman," I said. "I'll tell her that her kid's alive and what happened to her. Maybe she'll have something to say. I know how I'd be if someone tortured my nephew and niece. She's an actual mother, and her kid is safe. She's out from under Santoro's control and might want some payback."

"Go talk to her," said Church. "I'll see you in Oslo as soon as you clean up things there."

The line went dead.

"For the record, boss," said Bunny, "I think this one's ending weird, too."

CHAPTER ONE HUNDRED FIFTEEN
AOI OTERA (THE BLUE TEMPLE)
INTERROGATION ROOM THREE
TSUSHIMA ISLAND, JAPAN

The three of us talked with Soon Hue Kang. When I told her that her baby was safe, she began to cry.

When I told her what they'd done to her baby, she screamed.

It took a while to calm her down. She jerked at the chains. She thrashed about, cutting herself, spit flying, eyes filled with madness. Andrea got up and wrapped his arms around her and held her, despite the violence, despite the attempts to bite him and headbutt him. He held her through the immediacy of that storm. Bunny and I exchanged a look. We both felt enormously embarrassed, and sad.

The screams, like any storm, passed. She sagged back against the chair, dripping with sweat, tears running down into her nose and mouth, shudders like earthquake aftershocks rippling through her.

I got up, fished a key out of my pocket, and unlocked her chains. Andrea stepped aside and I squatted down and took her hands in mine. She stared at me in total surprise.

"Soon Hue," I said gently, "Santoro and Kuga and the others are still out there. Adam and Eve are still out there. If there is anything you can tell us that will help me and my team find them, then you—"

"I'll tell you everything I know," she cut in. Her teeth were clenched, her lips peeled back. "As long as you promise me you'll fucking kill them all."

"That," I said calmly, "is the only plan I have."

She told us everything. An hour's worth of unfiltered truth. She gave us better physical descriptions of Adam and Eve. She gave us the names of nine other people at Fort Story who'd been compromised, and six here in Japan. She gave me locations for blind drops of money and equipment. She gave us the locations of two safe houses.

She gave us everything she had.

I put it into our network.

Scott Wilson assured me that people would go out to investigate all of this. People.

But not us.

CHAPTER ONE HUNDRED SIXTEEN
TSUSHIMA ISLAND, JAPAN

We spent a couple of days in Japan watching things happen and feeling moderately put out about the fact that we were no longer running the show.

I called Church, and Wilson, and Doc about a dozen times each. Church was busy in Oslo, hosting meetings with the heads of state who needed their egos massaged. Wilson was there, too, keeping those same world leaders from using the incident as proof that (a) the situation in the region of the Korean Peninsula needs to radically change or (b) the situation in the region needs to remain the same. Wilson is rarely flustered, but the last time I spoke with him he seemed ready to strangle kittens.

I called Rudy about it, and got a lecture about being a control freak. He did not use those words, because he's too urbane and compassionate and civilized. No, he phrased it so that I didn't feel like a hurt teenager who can't get a date for the prom. His closing remark was, "The world has changed and your role in it has evolved, Cowboy. Try and take comfort from the fact that there are now many organizations ready to do their share of heavy lifting." It took great effort not to tell him to go piss up a rope.

After a suitable period of sulking—with plenty of good local beer to grease my cognitive wheels—I called Junie and told her what I was feeling, what Rudy said, and that I, in actual point of fact, *was* guilty of hubris. I was annoyed that useful, reliable, dependable ol' Joe Ledger wasn't the one being seen to save the world. Because Junie is immensely more mature than me, she did not give me any species of "I told you so." Instead she told me she loved me and said that spending Christmas with Sean and the family in Maryland would do us both a lot of good.

It was oddly sobering. I spent the rest of that day in a dry suit doing nothing more useful than scuba diving off the island. Tsushima has the coldest and most northern coral reef in the world, with all kinds of newly discovered coral species. There is a warm current that brings tropical fish into the area, and they were such an unexpected delight that I felt my heart lift. There is something both

　　　　　　　　　　　　　　　　　　JONATHAN MABERRY

otherworldly and deeply grounding about diving reefs, especially those as untouched as these. Gorgeous, tranquil, and about a million miles away from pain and bioweapons, from tortured babies and slaughtered families.

Somewhere down in the blue-green waters, I felt something change inside my heart and head. Yeah, maybe I was guilty of thinking I was the one permanently on deck to save the world. And, yeah, I could see now that this was far from the truth. I knew that now—even after all of my victories with the DMS and RTI—I was still trying to redeem my soul for being unable to save Helen. Among the coral and fishes I found a measure of perspective on that, and a grudging acceptance that those terrible events long ago were not my failure but simply beyond my control. I could not have saved her. Wanting to did not change that. Trying to be the champion of the world wouldn't change it, either.

I thought about the unknown woman on the Island of Frogs. The one I'd made a mental promise to. I could not save her, either. Even if I caught and killed every single person who was part of the Kuga machine, she was still going to be dead. I was not a demigod capable of restoring life to the unjustly slain.

I swam beneath the waves and tried to release the strictures of my pride that held onto the things I could never control.

A few brightly colored fish, of a kind I did not know and couldn't name, swam with me for a time and, one by one, peeled away, as if taking fragments of my darkness with them.

I would tell Rudy about this. I would tell Junie.

But not yet.

Instead I swam and swam and was, in some small way, healed.

CHAPTER ONE HUNDRED SEVENTEEN
DIVERS' BATHHOUSE
TSUSHIMA ISLAND, JAPAN

They tried to take me quick and quiet.

I was naked as an egg, covered in soap and shampoo, alone in the shower stall. My dry suit was on a bench and my tanks hug on a peg. The spray masked the sound of them entering, but I felt a cool breeze and turned to see shapes rushing me. Three of them. Not big, but big enough; dressed in black, moving fast. There was a flash of steel. Knives. Black-bladed commando-style field knives. You don't use them to go hunting unless you're hunting men.

Fixers. Had to be.

The lead guy slashed low and hard, trying to gut me. I twisted out of the way and felt the cloth of his sleeve brush my hip instead of the cold point of the knife. I turned the twist into a spin and chopped him in the back of the neck with my elbow. Real damn hard. He staggered forward and I heard him hit the wall; but I was going straight after the other two. They were fast and they had the advantage, but they did not know how to fight together. Most people don't, not even most killers. They both tried to slash at me at the same time, both trying to disembowel. If they'd thought it through and went high and low, they'd have had me.

Maybe.

I slid to my left and chopped the closest arm and then shoulder-checked him so that he stumbled into his buddy. They were wearing sneakers but not the right kind for a soapy tiled floor. They both slid and I helped them along by hitting the guy I'd just checked with four very fast, very hard palm shots to the ear. He screamed as his eardrum burst. I slapped my hand down against the wrist of his extended arm, pinning it against my wet thigh, and then used both hands to take the knife away from him.

Now it was two armed thugs, one unarmed and injured thug, and me with a knife. Bare-ass naked, sure, but with a knife. That is much better math.

For me.

For them the math sucked ass.

They gave it a good try, though, pushing off the wall, coming at me again, trying to spread out and circle me. If I was an idiot I'd have backed away, and been killed. Or charged them, and been killed.

Instead I faked left and went right, sliding across the floor to engage the first man. He tried a throat cut this time, but I ducked under it and sliced the outside of his lead knee. The knife was excellent and honed to razor sharpness, and it cut through the hamstring tendon with shocking ease. He screamed and went down onto that same knee while I checked my cut, reversed, and took him in the right eye with the point. Not deep. I didn't want to lose the knife to suction.

I shoved him toward the others, but the soap on the floor made me slide backward and for a moment I pinwheeled for balance. Then I dropped into a squat like a surfer on a wild board, reclaimed my balance, and dodged left to get to the outside of the two men coming at me. The one whose eardrum I burst dove down to try and take the knife from his crippled friend, but I chopped down with the butt of my knife and the extra force slammed him belly-and-chin-first onto the unforgiving tiles. I stepped on him and over and slashed at the thrusting arm of the third man, catching it with a shallow slice across the forearm and then crashing into his side with my shoulder and chest. We crashed back and fell. Since I knew that was the likely result of our impact, I rode the fall and used the confusion to half roll onto his knife arm, pinning it between us.

He dropped the knife and damn if he didn't reach down and grab me by the balls. He grabbed real damn hard and the pain sent ten million volts of white-hot agony up through my stomach and into my heart. I screamed.

I did not stop fighting to scream, though. Idiots do that. I used the pain to kick me into aggressive overdrive. I headbutted him, elbowed him across the temple, bit his nose, and when I could get my hand into position, I cut his damn throat.

He gurgled and collapsed back, vomiting blood and thrashing wildly. His fucking hand was still locked on my scrotum and I had to cut his wrist tendons to free myself.

I rolled off him, sick and dizzy, in time to see the guy with the burst eardrum come up off the ground. His chin was split and blood ran over his lower lip, but his face was twisted into a mask of hatred. He dove at me before I could get away, and we fell back hard, rolling all the way to the edge of the shower. He was about twenty pounds lighter than me, but he knew how to wrestle. He knew a lot of dirty tricks, and he tried them all. Twisting joints, sticking his thumb in the hollow of my throat, headlocks, an armlock that would have shattered my elbow if I hadn't locked my frame, twisted my hips, and bit his calf.

Yeah, I know a lot of guys dig that MMA bullshit. Those supposedly unbreakable holds, the floor pins, the mounts.

Oh, please.

If you're in a ring, with rules, with a ref, and you can tap out, then sure, it can be pretty intense. But even cage fights have rules. I, on the other hand, am not a sportsman. Never was. I tore a chunk out of his calf, then pivoted more and bit his balls. Weird, sure. Nasty, sure. Worked, though. His scream hit the ultrasonic and he lost the integrity of his lock. I took my arm back and then spent the next ten seconds breaking everything of his that I could break while still leaving him alive.

One of his buddies was dead, the other was in shock with a pierced eye and blood loss and was maybe half in a coffin. This asshole still had a pulse and I really—*really*—wanted to have a meaningful chat.

When I finished, he wasn't going anywhere. He lay there, quivering, too hurt to do anything but whimper. I crawled to the wall and used it to climb up, wheezing, gasping, my nuts on fire, my nerves shot to shit.

My gear bag was on a bench outside and I grabbed my gun, crept to the exit door, and looked out. No one in sight.

I went back and looked down at the three men. They were total strangers. The guy with the pierced eye looked Korean. The dead one was maybe Italian or some kind of swarthy Mediterranean. My wrestling partner was Caucasian. None of them were Santoro or Adam.

The injured man looked up at me with terrified, pain-filled eyes. He looked into my eyes and saw something there. Maybe it was like looking into a magic mirror that showed him what the next few minutes of his life were going to be like.

"Please . . . ," he begged.

I smiled.

"No," I said.

CHAPTER ONE HUNDRED EIGHTEEN
ABOARD *THE SOUL OF PIETY*
KIEL CANAL
RIVER ELBE, GERMANY

Santoro set down his phone and looked up at the ceiling.

"Did they get him?" asked Kuga, who was alert and impatient. "Is the son of a bitch dead?"

"No," said the Spaniard.

"How many guys did you send?"

"Three. Good men. Excellent fighters."

"You told me it would be a simple cleanup operation."

"It should have been."

They sat staring at nothing for a long time, each chewing on the bitter reality of it.

"Next time why don't you just throw some grenades at him. Ledger's a maniac but he's one of the most dangerous people I ever heard of. Blow the fucker up next time."

Santoro gave him a thin smile and said nothing.

CHAPTER ONE HUNDRED NINETEEN
AOI OTERA (THE BLUE TEMPLE)
THE ORB
TSUSHIMA ISLAND, JAPAN

"They were a cleanup crew," I said. "At least that's what my shower buddy told me. I am convinced it's what he believes."

Church's hologram sat there taking small bites out of a vanilla wafer. Doc stood on one side of him and Wilson on the other as if they were all in the same room. But Church was in Oslo and they were still in Greece.

"Did he give a list of other potential targets?" asked Church.

"A few. Colonel Epps, the rest of Havoc Team—which, by the way, he called Echo Team, so we know that Kuga's network doesn't have ears inside RTI."

"Thank God for small mercies," said Wilson.

Church nodded. "Anything else?"

"He corroborated some of what the Fixer Toys, um, *questioned* told us. A few new targets, and I've uploaded them to the TOC mainframe."

Doc Holliday was grinning fit to bust. "And all of this while you were buck naked?"

"Yes. Sorry I didn't take pictures."

"Boy howdy, me too!"

"We have some news to share, Colonel," said Wilson. "Doc, if you would start us off?"

"Sure, sweetie. So, we sourced all of the parts in that drone, and, yes, the computer systems were manufactured in China, but one of the key designers at the tech firm in question is Li Hong."

"Hong . . . ?" I mused. "As in the Hong family who are tied to The Five Iron Men?"

"Nephew once removed," she said. "That's one thing. The next is some digging I had Nikki do about Syria. Even though the lab is all blown up, the equipment had to come from somewhere. Mind-Reader Q1 just busybodied its way into Mr. Assad's government computers and in two shakes of a sheep's tail we have all kinds of purchase orders and shipping manifests. Now, I just bet you can guess where they bought their parts."

"The Hongs?"

"Yeppers. From companies and very shady private firms in Hong Kong, Shanghai, and all over North Korea. And some off-market stuff from sources unnamed, so we can assume that's black market, and black market means—"

"Kuga," I said.

"You go straight to the top of the class."

Church said, "I briefed the four heads of state about this an hour ago. Arrest warrants have been issued for nineteen members of the immediate Hong family and fifty-four others tied to their businesses. As to The Five Iron Men . . . three are in custody, and two committed suicide."

I sat down on a chair.

"Well . . . kiss my ass," I said. And smiled while I said it.

"Come to Oslo," said Church as he brushed cookie crumbs from his tie. "The *tørrfisk* is delicious."

OSLO, NORWAY

PART SIX

An eye for an eye will only make the whole world blind.

—Mahatma Gandhi

CHAPTER ONE HUNDRED TWENTY
IN DARKNESS

The woman woke in darkness.

Bound. Bleeding. Bruised over every inch of her body that she could feel.

She lay there, feeling the damage. Listening for any sounds, fighting for a sense of where she was. The pain in her head was so ferocious it crowded everything else out.

Almost.

She felt movement before she heard sound.

It made no sense to her.

The floor on which she lay was moving. Tilting. Back and forth. Very slowly, but very steadily. She strained to make sense of it but the darkness around her seemed to flood into her mind and she was gone.

For a while.

There was no way to know how long she was out. Minutes? Hours? She did not think it was much longer than that because the level of pain was about the same. Cuts hurt less over time, deep bruises got worse. She ran a tongue around the inside of her mouth and discovered that several important teeth were missing. The gums hurt worse than any other part of her.

That was when a small door of memory opened for her. The teeth. She remembered losing them.

No, that wasn't right, and she forced her mind to be precise. She remembered them being taken from her. Torn out. Rocked back and forth in their sockets with pliers and then pulled from the roots. She remembered the taste of her own blood. She remembered the screams that had tried to claw their way up from her lungs and out through her mouth. She remembered fighting them down. Refusing them. Refusing to gift her torturers with those screams.

Not with the lost teeth. Not with the small cuts on her nipples and between her toes. Not even when they ground the lit cigarettes into her cheeks.

She had not screamed once.

Now, here in the fetid darkness, she wanted to let the screams out.

She did not.

The floor moved and a sound, muffled and odd, snuck through walls to whisper in her ear. A slapping sound. Soft, unemphatic.

Water.

I'm on a boat, she thought, and knew it to be true.

But . . . whose boat?

Did that Spanish bastard—the *monster*—have a boat? Why had he brought her to it? Why was she even still alive?

She lay there, testing her bonds, assessing the damage, inventorying her strengths.

Planning her escape.

Planning her revenge.

CHAPTER ONE HUNDRED TWENTY-ONE
D9 CONFERENCE
RADISSON BLU PLAZA HOTEL
SONJA HENIES PLASS 3
OSLO, NORWAY

The place looked like a miniature version of the United Nations. Flags everywhere, and not just those of the nine nuclear nations. Other countries were in attendance as well. Some as allies of the denuclearization process, some because they had nuclear energy programs and their centrifuges and waste would be topics of discussion. Thirty-one countries in all.

Every hotel in Oslo was crammed with dignitaries, the press, anti-nuke protestors, more press, government officials, and—yeah—more press.

Havoc Team was there as event security, meaning we were supposed to be in the employ of the Norwegian government. That was some of the combined sorcery of Scott Wilson and Mr. Church. They made quite a formidable team.

We were dressed in standard upper-level security clothes: black suits, white shirts, dark ties, wires behind our ears. We were armed, but with Snellig dart pistols loaded with Sandman.

The conference was scheduled for the big convention room at the Blu Plaza, which is also where all of the heads of state and their entourages were booked. They filled the entire 678 rooms, with some of those suites set aside for ops centers, security team staging, very select ticketed press, and a few high-profile guests. You had to know God personally and be able to show vacation selfies with Him to get into that place. Even Top—who was notorious for his disdain of most security setups—kept grunting his approval.

"You sound like a boss hog, Old Man," complained Bunny. "Grunt, grunt, grunt."

Top gave him two seconds of a withering look. "You know, Farm Boy, it is actually possible to kick a two-by-four up someone's ass if you try real hard."

Andrea snorted and offered a fist to Belle for a bump. She stared at it, shrugged, and bumped.

We walked the crowded halls on the conference level. It seemed like every third person we saw wore the same kind of clothes we did. They gave us the same uninformative stares we gave them. They teach that at tough guy school.

"*Scusami, Colonello,*" said Andrea quietly as we rounded a corner and walked past an ornate stairwell that looked like a piece of art, "but do we actually have an assignment?"

"Not as such, no," I said. "We are vagabond thugs."

Bunny said, "Not sure I've ever seen this much security."

"You complaining?" asked Top.

"Not even a little. Even my virtue feels protected."

Top grunted.

"You think this is security," said Andrea, "you should see how they guard the Pope's porn collection."

"If something happens," said Belle, pointedly ignoring Andrea's comment, "what actions do we take? Who owns the trigger pull?"

I snorted. "Scott Wilson has been pulling his hair out all night trying to figure that out. Short answer is, we are—at best—support. The badges we have are legit, but each world leader has his or her own people, and we do not want to get between them and any bad guys. I don't want us to be the collateral damage on somebody's after-action report."

"Hooah," said Top.

"Hoo-fucking-ah," said Bunny.

"Colonel Ledger?"

I turned to see a thin man hurrying toward me. One of the many Norwegian officials who was there to massage overblown political egos and keep things chugging along. I fished for his name and pulled it out of my ass.

"Mr. Møller," I said. "What can I do for you?"

He leaned close and lowered his voice. "Colonel, I've been asked to escort you to a small private reception."

"Now? Isn't the conference starting soon?"

"This, um, will not take long, and I believe you will find it rather interesting." Møller had a soft, high-pitched voice that, for some reason, reminded me of how a ferret might talk. "Your associates are free to wait here or continue patrolling. Now, sir, if you please . . . ?"

I gave Top a nod and followed Møller through a guarded doorway and through a series of service hallways to another door that was even more heavily guarded. My ID was checked and my retina scanned, then Møller ushered me into a small conference room crammed with a dozen people. Security, translators, Scott Wilson, Mr. Church . . . and the four heads of state for China, North and South Korea, and the United States. They all looked up as I entered.

It was one of the strangest moments of my life. The president of the People's Republic of China was closest to me and came over to offer his hand. His translator came with him, but the president spoke in very good English.

"Colonel Ledger," he said, "I will be frank. Your name is well known in certain circles within my government."

I said, "Okay."

His dark eyes searched mine, and he wore an enigmatic half smile. "There have been quite a few times when my countrymen had cause to curse your name. There are many of my generals who wanted to make a special project out of you." He gave the words an emphasis that left no doubts as to their meaning.

"I'm okay with that, Mr. President. Send them along."

He shook his head. "No," he said, "not today. In fact I hope that you can understand and appreciate what I am about to say. As of this moment, all past transgressions are forgiven. If your name is on any list, it will be taken off. In this moment, and unless your future actions require it, you are no longer an enemy of the People's Republic of China."

"That's nice to know. But, here's the thing . . . I don't have a beef with China. Actually, I don't have a beef with anyone. I do, however, have a beef with anyone who tries some big play to do a lot of harm to innocent people. As long as your people don't do something that forces me and mine to come hunting, then we'll get along fine. I'm not going to turn a blind eye, though. Not for you, and not for anyone in this room. Or any country anywhere. I'm not political. I'm a shooter. Guys like me react when someone else starts a fight. As of right now, sir, I have no one in China on my list, however if future actions require it, they'll hear from me in ways they won't like."

His smile flickered, then firmed up. "Then we understand each other, Colonel."

"I hope we do, Mr. President."

He offered his hand again and we shook.

After that the president of South Korea thanked me and clutched my hand like someone who'd been saved from drowning. He shook my hand, held on, and leaned close. "If you ever need a friend in my country, Colonel, you reach out to me personally."

When he released my hand I could feel the stiffness of a folded piece of paper against my palm. I quietly slipped it into my pocket.

The next two meetings were surreal. Kim Jong-un was a short, round young man who spoke with great diction and clarity via a translator—though I could understand him quite well.

He made a mini-speech that, to my surprise, steered clear of political rhetoric. Instead he vilified The Five Iron Men, the Kuga organization, and lamented the unfortunate death of the Frog Island villagers. He did not mention Colonel Ho, however, which kind of pissed me off.

Kim was, by all accounts, a psychotic dictator; and yet when I looked in his eyes I saw a great deal of fear. As if he was trapped in the role he played. For about a second I felt a tendency to buy it, and to carve off a slice of sympathy—but I couldn't manage it. I'd read too many reports about the inhuman conditions in North Korea, the murders and disappearances, the starvation of people, and more. No, he did not get a pass. I shook his hand because Mr. Church was watching and gave me a tiny nod, but I didn't like it. When I turned away I wiped my hand on my trouser leg.

And that left me with the president of the United States. As I'd told the Chinese president, I was not political. I'm neither left nor right. I'm an idealist and a humanist, but if all politicians suddenly vanished into thin air I would shed damn few tears. I did not like this president and wasn't a huge fan of any of his predecessors. However there was bad blood between us, because his policies and stubbornness helped the Russians do a great deal of harm to us during the Deep Silence case. It doesn't matter one bit that he later claimed that his intelligence people did not properly warn him of the dangers. The captain of a ship is the one who takes the blame. Any ship, anywhere.

All that said, he offered me a very gracious and effusive thank-you, and when he was done talking I shook his hand, too.

Have I mentioned lately that it's a weird goddamn world?

Church walked me out. In the hallway, we stood out of earshot of any of the guards.

"That looked like it hurt," he said.

"Not sure I'd piss on any of them if they were on fire."

"You have no future at all in politics, Colonel."

I grinned. "Well . . . thank God for that."

CHAPTER ONE HUNDRED TWENTY-TWO
IN DARKNESS

They had tied her well, but not well enough.

She vaguely remembered someone else in the room with the Spaniard. A beefy man who looked like a thug straight from central casting. A smiling mouth and soulless eyes. She was sure he'd been the one who tied her up. She could remember his hands on her bloody breasts, groping between her thighs. Had the Spaniard snapped at him for that? Rebuked him? There was a fragment of that in her recollection, though it seemed strange. As if torture was okay as long as there was a point to it, but random sexual abuse was not.

The thug had said, "Why are we bothering with her at all, boss? She's chum for the sharks, right?"

"Not yet," replied the Spaniard.

"You think she's going to stop acting like a bitch and talk to us?"

"Everyone talks eventually." There was a small, terrible pause before he repeated one word. "Everyone."

They cut her loose from the chair and she tried to fight, but did not know if she did any damage. She had no memory of what happened. Instead there was a huge furnace of pain on the back of her head. Memory, like consciousness, had been bludgeoned out of her.

The thug had tied her well.

He had not done it expertly, though. He'd tied her the way people do when they think the other person is helpless. As if the victim has no nerve, no imagination.

In the darkness, the woman smiled. She worked her wrists against the bonds, letting the rope cut her. Making fists and flexing her muscles to make herself bleed. Blood was useful. Blood, after all, was liquid. Thick, and viscous, and in its way an excellent lubricant.

In her darkness, she smiled as she worked.

CHAPTER ONE HUNDRED TWENTY-THREE
D9 CONFERENCE
RADISSON BLU PLAZA HOTEL
OSLO, NORWAY

Havoc Team had split up and was wandering the halls. Top and Belle were one level up and Bunny and Andrea were on the ground floor. When I checked in I found, to my great relief, that everyone was bored because no damn thing was happening.

Which is exactly what you want to happen.

Of course, it wasn't surprising. The security here was on par with the other big summits like G8. Lots of thugs like me in suits, lots of undercover operators, lots of uniformed types.

Over the loudspeaker they began calling people to the big exhibit room where the opening remarks and introductions for the summit would take place. Masses of people began moving toward stairs, escalators, and elevators.

I told Bunny I was coming down to the lobby to begin an upward floor-by-floor sweep, when I saw someone on the far side of the big central stairwell. A woman dressed in the coveralls of hotel maintenance staff and carrying a small toolbox. Slim, pretty, young . . .

And blond.

I stopped and stared at her. She seemed to turn away as soon as I looked in her direction.

"No fucking way," I breathed.

Then I was moving, going the opposite way of the crowd, fighting to swim upstream through hundreds of people. Was it her? I couldn't be sure at all. It was only a glimpse. How could Eve even be here? Why would she be here? With all this security how was it even possible? My uncertainty tore what I thought I'd seen to shreds. Doubt kept me from yelling, from calling it in to the house authorities.

Instead, I tapped my coms unit. "Outlaw to Havoc, I'm on the mezzanine level. Possible sighting of target Eve."

I gave them a quick description of the woman I'd seen. Because of the density of the intervening crowd, the tiny camera on my lapel got nothing.

Belle asked, "What is the confidence in the target?"

That was a good question. "Fifty percent," I admitted. "Maybe less. Look anyway."

I got a chorus of *Hoouhs*, but as the seconds ticked by and gathered into minutes, none of them saw a damn thing.

Great. Now we can add paranoia to being arrogant. And crazy. I was batting a thousand.

CHAPTER ONE HUNDRED TWENTY-FOUR

IN DARKNESS

She tried for hours.

How many hours was impossible to know. Two? Three? The thin ropes sawed at her, tore at her, filling the black room with blood smell. With fear smell and anger.

There was every chance someone would come before she worked loose.

There was a very good chance her attempt to slip out would fail.

There was no chance she would give up.

She lay there. In pain and darkness. Curled in a pool of blood and her own urine. Her breath rubbing like hot sandpaper in her throat. She did not curse or complain, even to herself. That was not who she was, because none of that would contribute one iota to getting free. All it would do would be to admit defeat.

She never admitted, or even accepted, defeat. Even now.

She worked and worked.

Suddenly the rope slipped halfway down her hand, over the bloody bulge of her thumb.

And Major Mun Ji-Woo was free.

CHAPTER ONE HUNDRED TWENTY-FIVE

D9 CONFERENCE
RADISSON BLU PLAZA HOTEL
OSLO, NORWAY

Nobody saw a thing. I didn't, even though I went down all of the halls and peered into suites and conference rooms and closets. There was no trace of the slim blonde.

Until there was.

Suddenly she was there, thirty feet from me. She had her toolbox and came out of a hall, walking in my direction. As she approached she reached into a loose pocket and began pulling something out.

I could have shot her. I could have made a scene, flashed a badge, started a panic.

Thirty feet was a forever distance if it was a gun.

I ran at her. No shouting, no waving my own pistol. I reached her in nine very long strides and was suddenly up in her face, my hand clamping onto the wrist.

"Don't," I said.

The woman yelped from the pain of my grab, flinching back, but I held her and shifted to use my bulk to block what was happening from the crowds who now stood watching the opening ceremonies on big-screen TVs mounted on all the walls.

"What are you doing?" she cried in Norwegian.

The door behind her opened and five other maintenance people came out, each carrying an identical toolbox. Four men and a brunette woman. All young. They saw the woman and my grip and they stopped and frowned. I looked like security and they suddenly looked confused and scared.

"What's going on?" asked the oldest of the men. He was maybe thirty and had pockmarked cheeks. "What is this?"

I ignored him. To the blonde, I said, "Take it out using two fingers."

She blinked and then gingerly removed a cell phone clutched between thumb and forefinger. It was vibrating. I took it from her and glanced at the screen display. It said MOM.

I released her and stepped back, holding onto the phone. My lapel cam was now feeding her face to MindReader and almost at once I heard Bug's voice in my ear.

"Outlaw, be advised, that is not Eve. Detainee is Hilda Winnersein. I have her whole history right here. School ID, driver's license, hotel security clearance. It's close, but it's not her."

"I need to see IDs," I said, also in Norwegian. Pitching it with an edge of command to make them think I was more important than I am. It worked. They all produced picture IDs. Bug verified all of them.

The man, who turned out to be the supervisor, said that they were told to report to the press room to fix a speaker issue. I called that in, got verification, and then let them go. I felt more annoyed than foolish, though it is always better to check than not.

JONATHAN MABERRY

I saw more maintenance people, another two men—one with a brown buzz cut and the other with a lumberjack beard and wire-frame glass—a chunky black-haired woman, and a redhead hurry in the same direction. All four of them glanced at me, or at least in my direction, but they seemed to be casual glances. I saw them glance at other people, too. They were too far away for me to stop, and I did not see the point. My spider sense was still tingling, but now everything wanted to trigger it.

"Outlaw to Havoc," I said when I stepped into a quiet corner, "situation negative. Continue foot patrols. Stay sharp."

On the TV monitors the prime minister of Norway was making a speech and smiling as if the world was a big happy place.

I hoped like hell she was right.

CHAPTER ONE HUNDRED TWENTY-SIX
IN DARKNESS

Major Mun lost no time. Once free of her bonds she felt around the room in which she'd been held and discovered stacks of folded material. It was sticky and smelled of salt, and that told her she was in a sail locker aboard a large boat. The patty-cake slaps against the hull, and the relative stability of the floor suggested the boat was moored, possibly at a dock. She pressed her ear to the wall and heard sounds. The natural creaks of a watercraft. A faintness of conversation that was strangely muted. TV? Or perhaps a radio.

There was no door handle inside the locker, but she traced the outline of the door itself, found the hinges. That was good. Hatches of this kind had doors that opened out.

Mun had decisions to make. On one hand she was stiff, sore, weak, and injured. On the other hand if the boat was moored there was a better chance of escape than if she waited and the thing set sail. No, the smart risk was to make a break for it now.

Before that, though, she felt her way through the room again, looking for some kind of weapon. The sails were too big, and the nylon rope threaded through the grommets too sturdy and long to be of practical use. So, she scooped up the bonds they'd used on her. By untying the knots Mun found that she had two six-foot lengths of medium-strength nylon rope that was soft and flexible. She smiled, because she could do a lot of damage with that.

She wore only her underwear—functional panties. Mun coiled the rope around her waist and tucked the ends into the waistband of the pants. Then she groped her way back to the door. Her head hurt horribly and in a way that suggested she probably had a concussion. That would mean once she was through the door there would be disorientation and light sensitivity. Maybe dizziness and more of the nausea that was a constant. Those things were factors to be weighed but she did not accept them as limitations. What was required was to adjust her expectations of her physical skills, and then use what she had. Mun was a practical woman, and she'd been injured before while on missions with Kingdom.

The door, when she pressed against it, felt pretty tight, which meant it was a good locker that had been well installed. The actual panel of the door was a piece of particleboard built into a pine frame. The panels were thin because interior lockers don't need to be strong. Mun gave it a few experimental pushes with the flats of her hands. There was give in the center. Good.

She dragged the stacks of sails over and made a thick and very heavy backrest, then leaned against it, braced her hands on the wall and deck of the locker, raised her right foot, took a breath, and then exhaled as she kicked.

The door held.

She kicked again. A third time.

On the fourth kick the center panel of the door did not break. It simply popped out of the frame and fell flat. Weak light splashed into the locker, but Mun had a hand up to shield her eyes. She took just a moment to allow her eyes to adjust, and then she crawled out. The door was small, but so was she.

Mun found herself in a long, narrow corridor of what had to be a very large craft. Probably a motor sailor. Private. There was no whiff of military about it. She could smell a faintness of bilgewater, and also coffee. She tensed, straining to hear for anyone coming to investigate the sounds she'd made.

There was nothing. No yells, no footsteps.

Mun got slowly to her feet, fingertips touching the walls to steady herself as she assessed balance and dizziness. The deck wobbled and the corridor took a few lazy half turns, but then her head settled down. She removed one length of the rope, tied a thick knot on one end, and wrapped the other end around her hand and wrist. One experimental flick produced a nasty whipcrack. Not loud, but with vicious force.

Thus armed, and smiling the coldest smile she owned, Major Mun went hunting.

CHAPTER ONE HUNDRED TWENTY-SEVEN
D9 CONFERENCE
RADISSON BLU PLAZA HOTEL
OSLO, NORWAY

I found Top and Belle on the floor where the big show was unfolding. Top has the ability to look like just another guy when he wants. It's a shift of body language and a pulling in of his considerable personal power. He manages to look shorter, less muscular, and far less alert than he actually is. Belle, on the other hand, looked like a very hungry panther. People tended to walk around her rather than expecting her to get out of their way. And, to my amusement, I saw that Top was using that as a distraction. He walked a dozen paces to her left, and as people passed to one side of her, he got to see them while they were distracted.

I indicated a quiet spot near some potted ferns and we drifted over. Just some folks taking a moment on a busy day.

"Anything?" I asked.

"Negative, Outlaw. Not a goddamn thing."

Belle shook her head. I'd gotten the same report from Andrea and Bunny.

"Hate to say it," said Top, "but I think we are pretty much fifth wheels here."

I nodded. We stood. The speeches droned. Time burned itself away.

"Off the record," said Top. "You invited me to Christmas and I said I couldn't. Well, I can. My thing fell through."

He had a daughter in Georgia, but they were estranged. She'd lost her legs in combat and his being an active operator seemed to trigger episodes of PTSD for her. She was the only blood kin Top had, and it had to hurt him. Especially this time of year.

"I can't promise there won't be deeply ugly holiday sweaters and corny Christmas movies. The kids are addicted."

He smiled, even though I saw some pain in his eyes. "Long as I'm not an inconvenience."

"Believe me, I'm going to need some grown-ups to talk to. And Junie would cry if you weren't there."

Top nodded, pleased. I knew better than to ask Belle. She'd volunteered to be duty officer at the TOC. Christmas was not her thing.

The prime minister was about to begin introductions of the world leaders, each of whom would make a short prepared speech. Then there would be a reading of the denuclearization proposal, followed by a break, and then break-out sessions to wrangle over finer points of negotiation.

I kept looking for blond heads. Yeah, in Norway. Like looking for sand in the Sahara.

"Bug," I said, "go through the security cameras again. Run everyone's face through the software."

"There are a lot of people there, Outlaw."

"Cry me a river," I told him.

CHAPTER ONE HUNDRED TWENTY-EIGHT
IN DARKNESS

Major Mun ghosted along through the hold and up the companion ladders. She checked staterooms and closets, finding no one. She did, however, find a cupboard with a stack of extra life jackets, each of which was stenciled with a name, *The Soul of Piety*, and a port of registry of Vancouver.

Was she in Canada? Or still in Korea? Her memory was faulty from the blow she'd received. Traumatic amnesia. Mun was sure she'd lost time, but how much? When she'd awakened her body had been very sore, but as if she'd slept for a long time. Something occurred to her and she checked her arms and thigh—and there it was. A pinprick inside her left elbow. A needle mark. They'd not only beaten her, they'd drugged her. For how long? And *where* was she?

A voice called out, startling her, and Mun whipped around, ready to strike, but no one was there.

"Going to get my smokes," said the voice, and she realized that the acoustics bounced the sound to her, but the speaker was still in the corridor. She heard him coming closer, the footsteps quick but heavy.

Mun faded to one side of the open doorway, slipping behind a yellow rain slicker hung on a peg. A man entered the room. Big. Six feet tall, broad-shouldered, very fit looking. He wore khakis, a T-shirt, and a weapon belt with a holstered pistol and sheathed fighting knife. He passed by her and went straight to a duffel bag on the floor below the porthole. He bent over to unzip it and Mun made her move. She brought the heavy knot overhand and down as fast and hard as she could and hit on the base of the skull. The rope was not a killing weapon, but Mun knew how and where to hit. The sudden shock of the blow drove the man to his knees and then Mun was moving. She looped the slack of the rope over his head, stamped one foot between his shoulder blades, and pulled with every ounce of desperate strength and speed. The 110 pounds of body weight would not have mattered much in a stand-up test of strength, but it was a lot of dead weight to suddenly jerk the slack of a nylon rope against a windpipe. She heard the hyoid bone crack like a wet eggshell. The man flopped down, clawing at his throat, turning a hideous purple as he tried to drag air past an impenetrable obstruction. Mun darted forward and whipped the knife from its sheath, jerked the dying man's head back, and cut his throat.

She let him drop so that his body blocked the spray of blood.

Mun wasted no time. The gun belt was too big to bother with, so she tied the rope around her waist, snugged the knife between it and her hip, took the pistol and a spare magazine, and left. The hall was empty. She ran. Barefoot in the direction the dead man had come. There was a TV on somewhere and Mun heard the measured tones of someone giving a speech. At the end of the hall were three steps up to a lounge. Two men sat on a big couch watching someone in a suit talking from a podium. There was no one else in sight, and the men were relaxed.

She shot them both in the head from six feet.

Then she found cover and waited for someone to come and investigate the noise.

No one came.

Mun searched the entire ship and found no one. The craft was anchored about three hundred yards from the shore of a broad river. It was bright daylight.

Back in the lounge she began scrambling through papers, looking for some answer to where she was. She found a wrench and smashed open a locked side room, and in there she found something that took her breath away.

The room had a worktable on which were laptops, a high-end graphics printer, other devices used for affixing holograms to plastic, to attach security chips, and a laminator. And a whole pile of security badges. Duplicates, discarded failures, and some that looked ready to use.

On the upper left of each card, faded to be a background graphic, was a letter and a number.

D9.

Mun stared at the badges as she felt her ice turn to snowmelt.

Then she raced off to find the radio or a phone to call this in to Kingdom. To warn everyone of what was about to happen.

CHAPTER ONE HUNDRED TWENTY-NINE
D9 CONFERENCE
RADISSON BLU PLAZA HOTEL
OSLO, NORWAY

Bug got back to me while the third of the nine world leaders was nattering on about international brotherhood, a shared desire for peace, and the spirit of cooperation. On one hand I was all for those concepts; on the other hand I was too cynical to believe any of it, at least in this circumstance. This same president had two days ago accused the leader seated next to him of some truly vile human rights violations. So, they were selling the usual pack of platitudes and lies.

Mind you, if the nine nations actually *did* reach a true binding denuclearization agreement, I'd give them all foot massages and sloppy kisses. But . . . I've never known politics to move at the speed of common sense or simple truths.

"What've you got, Bug?" I asked, once more stepping away from the crowds.

"We hijacked the feeds from the hotel's security cameras, and . . . um . . . the private bodycam feeds from most of the teams on-site."

"I won't tell Santa Claus you've been naughty."

"We've found a couple of anomalies, which we'll sort out," said Bug, "but one bothers me. When you were talking to the blond gal, there were other maintenance around. The ones who stopped with her and more."

"I saw them. What did you find?"

"There's one we can't match to any staff records. She had black hair, a little heavy?"

"What about her?"

"The facial recognition software kicked out a possible match with the gal we're calling Eve. Not a high percentage, though. Forty-seven percent. I mean, she could be wearing a wig and padded clothes. Padding could be just that, or body armor, or something else."

I tapped the coms earpiece to bring the rest of Havoc onto the call. "Scout," I ordered, and we all put on aviator glasses with a subtle tint. The left temple piece was a Bluetooth receiver that sent data and images to one lens. The surveillance photo of Eve was there next to the blurry image of the black-haired woman. The computer began pinging corresponding facial orientation points and measurements.

"Close," said Andrea, "but I would not bet my retirement on it."

"Let's find and detain her," I said. "Sweep the building. Bug, see if you can pick her up on the camera feeds."

"Been looking, but so far nothing."

"Starting to get that itch between my shoulder blades," said Top.

"Right there with you," I said. "Let's find her. In the meantime, Bug, pull up the maintenance logs. The woman I spoke with, and her friends, were heading to the press room to fix some speakers. The black-haired woman was heading toward the service corridor. Where were they heading?"

I walked while I waited, using my height to look above most of the crowd.

"Outlaw," said Bug, "they were checking on one of the HEPA filters in the main hall. There was a rattle that was being picked up on the mics. I'm scanning that area now to see if she's around."

Suddenly Scott Wilson's voice broke into the call. "Outlaw, Outlaw, we have urgent intel."

"Go for Outlaw."

"We just received word from the assistant director of Kingdom. He said that Major Mun is alive and contacted him via satellite phone. She was held as a prisoner aboard a motor sailor, *The Soul of Piety*, which is currently moored in the Kiel Canal on the River Elbe. She described one of her abductors and it is a perfect match to Rafael Santoro. The others were Fixers. She got free, eliminated three Fixers, and called it in."

"That's great but the River Elbe? Why is she even in this part of the damn world?"

"Outlaw, that's the critical thing. Mun found equipment and samples of identification badges and a contact lens maker which can imprint new retina patterns. This is high-end stuff. And, Outlaw, the passes are for the—"

"D9," I finished. "Jesus Christ."

And then everything hit me. All of it. In a microsecond all of those jumbled puzzle pieces *fwapped* down on the table and fell into place. The lab in Syria. The poor bastards in the glass cages being sprayed by some chemical mist. How crazy they went. What I'd first thought was fear and anger and a desperation to escape that hellish lab, now meant something entirely different.

The flies at the café in Turkey were the same as those on the islands. An aerial drone delivery system. That's why the customers went nuts. They weren't Santoro's men, they were civilians turned into weapons.

I looked around, seeing everything as if with new eyes.

There were no bugs in a place like this. A single fly would be noticed. Everything was clean and sanitized and prepared for the presence of nine world leaders. They wouldn't tolerate flies in here.

I looked in the direction of the service hall. The maintenance crew had gone to fix the air filters. The big hall was right around the corner, sixty feet from where I stood. Pieces, pieces, falling into place. Created a much bigger picture.

Air. Mist.

A delivery system appropriate to the venue. Flies for an island or a small café. But for a place with high security and filtered air . . . ?

Suddenly I was running.

"It's airborne," I yelled. "Wilson, clear the conference room. It's the air filtration system. Shut it down. Christ, shut it down . . . *they have an airborne version of Rage!*"

I barely had those words out when all of the lights, everywhere in the hotel, went out.

CHAPTER ONE HUNDRED THIRTY
D9 CONFERENCE
RADISSON BLU PLAZA HOTEL
OSLO, NORWAY

My run turned into a blundering collision as people did what people do—they panicked. There was reflected light from the big glass windows, but it was around the curve of the hall behind me, leaving everything in front of me in roiling shadows. This room had been chosen partly because there was no direct window access—no vantage point for a sniper to shoot through the glass.

As I pushed and yelled and fought my way in the direction of the big room.

"Where the hell are the security lights?" I bellowed, but all I got was static on the coms unit. Another damn jammer. I heard other security people yelling into their sleeves or lapel mics in a dozen languages. Reporters and others who'd gathered in the hall to watch on the monitors were yelling and demanding explanations. There were grunts and curses and a sharp yelp of pain as someone fell or was stepped on. It was the Tower of Babel in near total darkness.

Then some pale battery-operated security lights came on. None very close to the conference room doors, though. Were the closer ones sabotaged? Of course they were. We were in a no-coincidence zone.

Small lights flicked on—people with cell phones and some presence of mind. I could just make out the closest door, where four agents were clustered together to block the entrance with their bodies. They had not yet drawn weapons.

"PST," I snapped, using the shorthand for Politiets Sikkerhetstjeneste, the Norwegian Police Security Service. I held the badge up and one of them peered at it and me.

"What is happening?" he demanded.

"Power is out and all radio communication is down," I said. "Cell phones will be down, too. It's a jammer."

His hand flashed to the butt of his pistol. "Is this an attack?"

"I think so. Get the prime minister to safety. We need to pass the word to the other security teams. Get me inside. *Now.*"

The man turned and pushed past his comrades; he pulled the door open and I followed him into the big hall.

Inside it was a little calmer, and there were flashlights and cell lights. The world leaders were down, pulled to safety and surrounded by their teams. Supervisors were yelling to the crowd to settle down, to remain in their seats. It was a shelter-in-place solution for what everyone in there probably thought was a bad, and very unfortunately timed, technical glitch. The news people had the brightest

JONATHAN MABERRY

lights, driven by power packs on tripod-mounted cameras. These played on the nine clusters of world leaders.

"Outlaw, Outlaw," yelled a voice and I half turned to see Top and Belle come hustling through the same door I'd used.

I hurried along the side aisle, following the guard. I held my badge up and yelled the security crisis evacuation word for the day, "*Longship, longship, longship.*"

The security team leaders immediately went into action, rising, yelling orders, shaping each exit huddle and pushing them toward their assigned evac routes.

A scream—huge, towering, shrill, and filled with madness—tore its way across the big room, and even in the midst of evacuation everyone turned. By the side wall, a Pulitzer Prize–winning, internationally famous reporter for BBC News grabbed a shoulder-mounted news camera from her assistant, swung it into the face of the senior political analyst for Al Jazeera. It was a murderous attack—savage and fast—and the analyst's face broke apart in a spray of blood.

That's when I saw the vent above where the BBC reporter stood. In the glow from all those small lights turned in that direction I could see the millions of tiny droplets of mist shooting into the room at high speed.

God, I hated to be right.

All around the reporter, people began twitching, growling, snarling, howling. They turned on one another, baring their teeth, grabbing anything they could—cameras, microphones, pens, clipboards—or used their bare hands and snapping teeth. The room became a madhouse of murder and death.

CHAPTER ONE HUNDRED THIRTY-ONE
D9 CONFERENCE
RADISSON BLU PLAZA HOTEL
OSLO, NORWAY

I saw the security huddle around the Chinese president moving toward the left stage exit. Two of the guards rose up, guns in hand,

and led the way, while another pair faced the rioting crowd. They were making good time, and covered their leader so well I couldn't see him at all. The other groups were shifting toward the sides, all of them looking like bizarre turtles.

Until one of the PST officers ran onto the stage, drew his pistol, and opened fire at the Chinese guards. Six fast shots and both of the guards in the lead crumpled backward, blood splashing their team members and their huddled principal. The knot of Chinese guards—as a unit—flinched back, confusion colliding with training. Then the Norwegian fired directly into them, trying to get the president.

One of the Chinese shot him, but missed because of jostling, and a second later took a round in the throat.

By then I was at the rostrum, put a hand on it, and vaulted up onto the stage, pulling my own gun. The Snellig wasn't lethal but it was fast and I yelled at the Chinese, telling them that I was a friendly as I fired two shots at the Norwegian. He went down.

Top and Belle spun and put their backs to the stage, facing the crowd. They were far enough away from the wall vents that most of the people around them were not infected by the Rage protein. But a Pakistani reporter suddenly pulled a pistol and began firing indiscriminately at the huddled groups on the stage. I cut a look at him and saw no trace of madness in his eyes, no face of rage.

"Fixer!" I yelled, and Belle swung toward him and shot him with a Sandman dart.

As if that was a call to arms, gunfire erupted all through the room and it seemed like everyone was shooting at everyone else. Security guards of different nations opening up to kill other guards in an attempt to get clear shots of the world leaders. There was no way at all to tell who were good guys and who was a bad guy. A third of the room was tearing itself apart as the vents continued to spew Rage onto the crowd. Top and Belle were turning and firing, turning and firing, and there was no way to know if the targets they dropped were Fixers, people driven mad by fear, or victims of Rage.

I thought about how much ammunition we each had. One magazine in our guns, two extra mags. That was it.

Not enough.

Not nearly enough.

I spun in place, looking at the nine huddles. More gunfire was coming from offstage. Both sides. Guards went down, the huddles shrunk. The Fixers clearly wanted the world leaders to stay in the hall.

Above me I heard a metal *clunk* and a sharp hiss and looked up in horror to see dense vapor begin shooting from a vent directly above the stage.

"Cover your mouths," I roared, first in Chinese, because they were closer, and then in English, Korean, and every other language I could manage. "Get out from under the vent. They're spraying a bioweapon. Move, *move.*"

I fired at Fixers and shoved security people. I could see the American president hunkered down, Secret Service body-blocking him. He looked terrified. Couldn't blame him. I was scared out of my mind because everything was falling apart and I did not see a single path to safety.

The Fixers backstage were kneeling behind some equipment cases they'd pushed into place to act as a shooting blind. If the huddles stayed where they were they would be torn apart. If they moved, they'd be sprayed by the Rage.

Abruptly one of the guards from the Indian huddle stood up, pressed the barrel of his gun against the temple of the man next to him, and fired. The bullet took off the top right corner of the victim's head and then punched into the cheek of the guard next to him. Things went to shit from there. The gunman wasn't a Fixer. His insane and inarticulate howl told the awful truth. He was driven out of his mind, beyond sanity, and had become a creature of pure rage.

I shot him with Sandman and he went down but then I was staggering back from a mule kick as two rounds hit me center mass. The vest saved my life but the impact knocked the air from my lungs and drove me to the edge of the stage. I pinwheeled my arms for balance and only by dropping into a low crouch did I keep from flopping down into the screaming crowd. Even then I tottered and then something caught me. I twisted to see Bunny there, propping me up. Andrea was behind him, and soon the four Havoc team members had formed a defensive half circle hard against the edge of the stage. I crouched above them.

"We don't *have* this, Outlaw," yelled Top.

"There has to be a shut-off switch somewhere," said Andrea. "We need to turn the whole air-conditioning system off or this will get through the entire building."

"The power's out," growled Bunny.

"There has to be a battery backup. Maybe I can—"

"Havoc!" roared a voice and I turned to see three Fixers stagger out from stage right. They were stumbling, bleeding, dying, and they fell as Mr. Church came striding out. He had no gun but was instead armed with a short piece of pipe—God only knows where it came from. Church waded into the other Fixers and for a moment I just stared. I've rarely seen the Big Man in action, and it was always an awesome sight. He is much faster than you'd expect a man of his size and age to be, and he moved with an almost clinical precision. Nothing wasted, nothing flashy; his movements were quick, brutal, and constant. Wilson was right behind him, a Snellig dart gun in his hand. Wilson was bleeding from a bad gash through his right eyebrow and cheek.

"This way," yelled Wilson, but then he took one step too far onto the stage and the mist got him. A drift of particles dancing in the air, sucked in after he cried out to try and show the way to safety. There was one frozen moment when I could see his face change. The eyes went empty for one blink and then they filled with something hot and red and wild. He turned and fired his gun at Church, and although it seemed as if the dart struck the big man in the chest and side of the neck, Church did not drop. Instead he stepped into Wilson, quickly twisted the dart gun from his hand, and shot Wilson in the cheek.

Belle had climbed onto the apron of the stage and was firing over the heads of the huddles toward the Fixers on stage left. Bullets burned around her as she drew their fire, but her accuracy was chilling. One after another of them dropped.

"Donnie Darko, Pappy, Jackpot," I shouted, "focus on the infected. Stop them before they can hurt people. I'll see if I can find the shut-off."

"We're running out of time," warned Andrea.

I looked for the best route out of the madness. It was a tough call because we needed shooters in the gunfight, but at the same time we were there to protect the innocent, which meant stopping the flow of Rage throughout the crammed hotel. At the moment it looked like we were going to fail in both fights.

Church began grabbing guards in the Chinese huddle and propelling them toward stage right. "It's clear behind me all the way to the safe room," he bellowed. "Get your president to safety. Go, go, go."

One of the guards began twitching and abruptly swung on Church, but then the man fell and I had the wrong angle to see what Church did to him. Whatever it was, it was damn fast.

"It's Rage," I hollered in Church's direction. "Cover your mouth and nose."

Church nodded and plucked his pocket square out and pressed it to his face. I heard him telling the survivors of the Chinese huddle to do the same. They used ties and sleeves. The president buried his face in a handful of a guard's jacket. Would that be enough? I hoped so. The Rage protein was a vapor, so unless it got into a mucus membrane it shouldn't be a danger. Eyes, though. They were a vulnerable spot, but there was nothing we could do except try not to be sprayed there.

The situation was this—the nine huddles were on the big stage. The stage-left exit was blocked by a Fixer fire team, but their angle was bad for wholesale slaughter because of how far offstage they were. Only when someone tried to escape did they come into a merciless line of fire. The right-hand exit was clear, but to get there the huddles would pass under the spray from one vent. Offstage, the riot was expanding as the bioweapon poured from vents on all the walls. There was a relative safe zone in the orchestra pit, but it was already overcrowded. Infected people were hurling themselves into the crowd, with three of Havoc fighting them back, using a very limited supply of Sandman rounds.

To confuse the math even more, this was the ultimate diplomatic nightmare. The security teams were critically aware that everyone around them represented a foreign government, and—given this was a summit on nuclear weapons—a well-armed government. Shoot the wrong person, no matter what the circumstances, and the fallout would be devastating. So, how does a guard keep his principal safe in that kind of circumstance? You tell me, because no one has ever trained for something like this. There is no response protocol for this on file.

More gunfire crackled behind me, tearing the edge of the stage into a storm of flying splinters. I dove toward the American huddle and drove them down and back. I scrambled up, whirled, and saw more Fixers coming in. I recognized them as the second maintenance crew from earlier. The tall man with the beard, the black-haired woman, and two others. They fired at the stage, bullets tearing into the guards, who tried to return fire but did not know where to shoot.

I realized who they were, of course. Even with the disguises. Adam and Eve. Hatred and hope surged up together in my chest. I wanted to end both of those psychos, but at the same time, they might know how to shut the sprayers off.

Before I knew I was going to do it I was in the air, leaping from the stage, landing running. Adam and Eve laughed—actually laughed—and whirled around, fleeing before me. Adam tore off his fake beard and flipped it arrogantly in my direction.

Like a fool, I chased them.

CHAPTER ONE HUNDRED THIRTY-TWO
D9 CONFERENCE
RADISSON BLU PLAZA HOTEL
OSLO, NORWAY

As I charged toward them, one of the others—a redheaded woman—went down as Eve shoved her into the path. Eve and Adam turned and ran. The fourth Fixer tried to hold the door, to block me, to gun me down. I shot him in the face and one of the Sandman darts hit his eye. He started to shriek in agony but then the drug slapped the scream from his mouth and dropped him. I vaulted his body but stopped at the doorway, crouching for a fast look. And immediately jerked my head back as a bullet chunked into the frame an inch from my eyebrow.

I flung myself forward into the hall, rolling like a log low to the floor, turning, bringing the gun up, but my quarry was already running away. They ran fast, shoving people aside. Eve shot two people and jerked them backward to block pursuit. I ran zigzag, shamelessly using people as cover. I could not let the blonds take me down.

We ran through a crazy darkness filled with indistinct moving shadows, some of them painted with stark blue light from phones, throwing goblin shadows on the wall. It was a fun house in some deeply twisted nightmare version of an amusement park. Nothing was real. And it was so strange—so deeply frightening—that something as orderly, well managed, and planned out as this summit could be torn to pieces so quickly. Control the lights, jam communications, rig the sprayers in the vents, and start a wave of violence. The summit had only been announced four months ago, so for this to have come off so smoothly, it spoke to an organization that was huge, subtle, well funded, and tightly run.

Kuga. The plague.

Yes. Very much that.

So, if Korea was a job for The Five Iron Men . . . who was the client for this? Was it Putin, looking for payback after he got spanked during the Deep Silence case? Or was this Kuga making a statement? Look at us. Look what we can do. Look at how powerful Hell's Concierge truly is?

My gut said it was the latter. A statement piece that would never be forgotten. Even if the world leaders all survived, this would be talked about for a hundred years.

This attack, the Rage disease launched against nine world leaders, was the most audacious plan I've ever heard of. It would hit the global economy like an asteroid strike. Governments might fall. Blame would be hurled around before sense and sanity prevailed. The Korea thing had been bad enough, and could have started a war, but this was the big play. This was an incalculable disaster and we hadn't seen it coming in time.

I felt like a fool. An imbecile. The pieces had been right there. Why hadn't I taken a better look? Christ, was all of this because of my arrogance? Because of my lack of vision? If so, every drop of blood was on me. Every ruined life, every crack in the globe was mine to own.

Adam kicked open a door to a side corridor with me only steps behind. I bashed through, firing as I went. It was nearly pitch dark in there. My last dart missed Adam and hit a confused security guard who was blocking the exit door on the far side of the room. He dropped onto his face. Adam lost a half second glancing at him, and that was enough time for me. I threw the Snellig and hit the back of his forearm. His gun went spinning and struck Eve in the mouth, splitting her lip. She was closer to me and tried to bring her gun around, but I look the long reach for a brutal overhand right and caught her in the side of the biceps with enough force to send her gun spinning through the air like a flying saucer.

Eve wasted no time being surprised. The fat suit disguise she wore did not slow her down one little bit. She came at me, quick as a cat, snapping out a kick intended to knock my kneecap loose. Very hard, very fast. I jerked my leg up and counter-kicked her with a ball-of-the-foot to her hip that sent her stumbling back. As if they'd choreographed it, Adam jumped past her, slapping a hand against her shoulder to stabilize her as he came at me from a quarter-angle. He threw huge hook punches—big ones that he swung from the floor, pivoting to put maximum power into right and left fists. I'd seen this kind of thing before. If you're smart, you build a cage of muscle and bone and try to ride it out. Try to be clever and counter-punch and you're likely to catch a good one. He was fast as a snake and strong as a bull, but I tucked my head down behind my shoulder, kept my fists against my skull, and gave him nothing but elbows and the edges of bones to punch.

As soon as the flurry began to slacken, I drove at him, using my forearms to shove Adam back. Then I gave it to him with a bit more precision. A lot of quick injuries in different places can make a person feel like they've been tumbled into an industrial dryer filled with rocks. I stamped on his foot, thumbed him in the socket of his throat, popped a cupped palm against one ear, drove a single-knuckle punch into his left sinus, whipped him across the throat with a backhand blow of my fingers, and hooked him a heavy one in the floating ribs. He stumbled and dropped to his knees.

As I'd hit him, I'd shifted around to try and put him between me and Eve. That saved me because she had one of the two fallen pistols.

She brought it up fast and shot from the hip, but I shoved Adam toward her.

Her bullet took him in the mouth.

The big hollow-point exploded his white teeth and shredded his lips and blew a hole the size of an apple out of the back of his skull. Blond hair, pieces of bone, gray brains, and bright red blood splashed my thigh and hips as the slug exited and burned past me.

Eve stared in absolute, uncomprehending horror.

And then she screamed louder than I've ever heard anyone scream. A rising wail of total horror that was filled with unbearable loss.

Still screaming, she swung the gun toward me, her finger jerking on the trigger, firing wildly, bullets filling the air. I dove in and down and forward and tackled her. The last round hit me on the side, slamming the Kevlar and then ricocheting off to hit Adam's corpse where it sat slumped against the wall. Eve was freaking out— torn apart by grief and shock and hate. She hammered at me with the butt of the pistol and caught me over the ear, dimming the lights for a moment. But I didn't let that stop me. I bashed the gun hand aside and hit her in the stomach about as hard as I've hit anyone in my life. I brought the punch up from the floor, pivoting for maximum velocity and depth of penetration, and the blow lifted her completely off the ground. She collapsed down on kneecaps and elbows, gagging, trying to breathe, and then vomited violently.

I staggered to my feet, picked up the fallen gun, and checked it. The slide was locked back. I tossed it away. Through the open door to the hall I could still hear screams and gunfire.

Eve was writhing on the ground, weeping and trying to crawl to where Adam lay in a wretched sprawl. I bent and grabbed her by the collar and hauled her roughly to her feet and slammed her against the wall, clamping a hand around her slender throat. I bent close and heard the Killer's icy voice speak to her. It was as if darkness itself spoke.

"You got one chance, kid, and that's to tell me how to stop this thing."

"Fuck . . . you . . ." she wheezed. Then she tried to kick me, but I punched her thigh with my other hand. Hard, driving two knuckles deep into thigh meat and giving them a corkscrew twist. She screamed. I pulled her off the wall and slammed her back again, making her eyes go momentarily blank.

"How." *Thump*. "Do." *Thump*. "I." *Thump*. "Stop." *Thump*. "This?" *Thump*.

I was not gentle. I don't give a fuck. Her head hit the wall. She cried out in pain and protest. I lifted her to her toes and then completely off the ground, pinning her to the wall by sheer force and my grip on her throat. She tried to hold out. Maybe she thought she could because she was a monster. It didn't work. It might have. Perhaps if she hadn't spent so much time proving to her victims that everyone breaks, she might have held out longer. But even in the dim light, Eve looked into my eyes and saw ugly things. She saw her own future and the horrors that were promised by the monster in me, which in that moment was bigger and less human than the one in her. Her hand fluttered and at first I thought she was reaching for a gun in the oversized clothes she wore. I slapped her hand away and reached into the pocket, and there, nestled against the fake blubber, was a metal box. I removed it and recognized it as the same kind of jammer the SEALs had used on Yeonpyeong Island.

I snatched it from her, letting Eve slide coughing and spitting down the wall. There were several small switches below a row of red lights. I flipped them all and saw the lights go green. Then winced as voices began yelling in my ear.

"Havoc, Havoc, Havoc," I growled, "Havoc Actual. Jammer is down, repeat jammer is down."

"Hooah," called Bunny, but behind him I could hear more yells and shots.

"Bug," I barked, "we need the lights on and—"

"We're in," he said quickly and the room was flooded with fluorescent light.

"I need those fucking vents shut down," I barked. "The entire air-conditioning system. Shut it all down."

There was a pause as tight as a fist and then Bug gasped, "Shutting it down now, but . . . shit, Outlaw, the blowers are still functioning. They . . . they must be connected to some other power source. Something I can't get to remotely."

"Can't use that answer, Bug. Find me something."

"If you can keep that jammer off I can keep the lights on. But you're on your own with the blowers. Sorry!"

I dropped the jammer and stamped down hard enough to burst the device into fragments. It gave a single puff of smoke and then died. With the lights on I was able to find Adam's gun and his two extra magazines. I took the sleeping guard's weapon, too.

I looked at Eve, laying in a weeping pile, then went over and crouched in front of her. I placed the barrel of one of the guns under her chin and, despite resistance, made her raise her head and look at me.

"How do I stop this?" I demanded.

Eve shook her head. I placed the barrel of the pistol hard against her kneecap. "I can make this last," I said. "You know that. So, tell me right now. How do I stop this?"

"Each . . . each blower is self-contained. Battery operated. You . . . you'd need to turn them off individually."

I gaped at her, my mind racing on to process that and at the same time figure out how to stop the machines while taking fire from Santoro's crew.

"How many Fixers are in this building?"

"Th-thirty," she said, tripping over it.

Shit. That was a lot. It was going to take so much to figure it out, to find the infiltrators.

"Are they all Fixers or are some of them under your thumb?"

"All . . . they're all Fixers. A strike team."

I leaned closer and spat the next question. "Where is Rafael Santoro?"

She stared at me but said nothing. Her mouth firmed in a way that told me she'd endure a lot before giving him up. I didn't think it was fear of the Spaniard. No, this was deeper, more ferocious. It was more like love. Like a family thing. He was what they called him— *Daddy*. Shit.

"Who is Kuga?" I asked. "Is he Harcourt Bolton?"

There was a flicker on her face, a brief appearance of a line between her brows. Confusion, I think. No trace of recognition of that name.

"*Where is Kuga?*"

She licked her lips. "Everywhere."

I gave her another thump. "Not the best time to be mysterious, kid. Where?"

"I . . . I don't know . . . we only really ever see Daddy."

"Is he here? Is Santoro in this hotel?"

Eve did not want to answer. She tried not to. But the Killer was asking the questions and she could see him in my eyes. She nodded.

"Where?" I asked.

"I *don't know*. He doesn't tell us where to find him. He finds us."

I pressed harder with the barrel. With my other hand I tore off her black wig and saw that a slender wire mic was hidden by the hair. "Is there a team channel?" She nodded. "What is the stand-down order?"

Her eyes shifted away. Some reserves of courage seemed to rise up in her, but she shook her head.

"Fuck you," she said, spitting the words at me.

"I warned you," I said, and shot her through the knee.

Her scream tore the air in half, rising to the supersonic. I placed the barrel against the other kneecap. That was as effective as a slap across the mouth. She stopped screaming and sat there, shaking, sweating, bleeding, terrified, staring at me.

"What is the fucking stand-down order?"

Eve did not want to give me the code. For whatever such stubbornness or loyalty or stupidity is worth, she did not want to give it up.

And yet . . .

CHAPTER ONE HUNDRED THIRTY-THREE
D9 CONFERENCE
RADISSON BLU PLAZA HOTEL
OSLO, NORWAY

I didn't waste a Sandman dart or another bullet on her. I left her there to bleed. If she bled out, then what a damn shame that would be.

"Bug," I said as I moved into the hall. People were running and yelling, some crouched down, but the Rage pathogen did not seem to be out here. Small mercies. "I have one of the Fixer's coms units attached to a booster unit. I need you to access their system and send the following message: '*Icarus Falls.*' Repeat that back. Good. I'm plugging the coms unit into my Q-box."

The Q-box was a device the size of a deck of playing cards, with various kinds of ports on three of the four sides. The unit I found in the wig had a standard double-end cable and I plugged that in. An encouraging little green light flicked on.

"Got it, Outlaw," said Bug, "but whoa! There's some serious protection here. Firewall and encryption."

"I don't care if it's guarded by dragons. Kick your way in and send that code."

Eve said it was not a surrender order, but instead directed the strike team to exfil by any possible means. That was fine. Better than what was going on. It would give me a chance to pull people away from the sprayers and maybe enlist some of the security personnel into protecting the uninfected and corralling those driven mad with Rage.

"Bug, get Bedlam and Chaos Teams in here. We're going to need a lot more Sandman."

"Be advised, Outlaw, that the hotel went into hard lockdown when the power went out. It's all on a private generator and we have heavy seals on all the exterior doors. Bedlam is trying to breach the door and Chaos is being airlifted to the roof."

"What about the vents?" I asked. "Can you shut down the blowers?"

"The AC is down, but Pappy confirmed the stuff is still blowing out at high speed. Unless you can access each vent and manually shut the units down we may have to wait until their cannisters are empty."

"Then send the shutdown code and get those Fixers out of here."

"Working on it. Whoever wrote their security software is good. Really, really good."

I said some very ugly ten-letter words and ran for the main hall.

A bleeding reporter staggered into my path and thrust a microphone toward me. "Sir, are you state security? Can you give us an update on—?"

I pushed him aside and kept running.

The area around the entrance to the main hall was empty except for three silent bodies and four men who stood in the doorway firing into the room. Two were dressed in maintenance coveralls, two were in black suits like the one I wore. I took my gun in two hands and slowed to a fast walk, mindful that they all wore body armor, firing at the backs of their heads. Eight rounds. Four dead Fixers. Only the last one was able to turn, but my last round went through his temple.

Then I stepped into hell.

There were many more of the infected now, and they were like a storm tide crashing against small islands of uninfected. Bodies lay everywhere. Many people were bleeding. Everyone was fighting. On the stage, three of the huddles were still there, inching their way toward the stage-right exit. I saw more than a dozen dead guards. Church was up there, standing beside a kneeling Belle. Church had a regular handgun, while Belle still had her Snellig.

Below them, in the orchestra pit, Top, Bunny, and Andrea were using bare hands to fight the infected. Heaps of unconscious people explained why they no longer had darts to fire. Those same darted people created a crude barrier that forced the attackers to come at them through a choke point at one end. And come they did. As the infected came in, the three fighters took turns tripping them, spinning them, clubbing them down, occasionally breaking a leg or an arm. Writhing infected were all around them. Bunny kept grabbing them and tossing their bodies onto the barricade. It was brutal work and I could see that they were tiring. No one could maintain that kind of fight for long.

I raced down the central corridor, bashing people out of my way.

"Havoc, Havoc, Havoc!" I yelled as I vaulted the barricade. I pressed my Snellig and two magazines into Top's hand, then climbed up onto the stage close to the left side, out of line of the shooters. I saw, to my amazement, that one of the huddles was the American president. He should have been second off. Then I saw that every man in his Secret Service detachment was injured, some badly. I could read what happened—they'd tried to get out and took a full fusillade, then retreated to the dubious safety closer to the rostrum.

Out of the corner of my eye I saw someone enter the room from the door I'd just used. He was dressed in maintenance coveralls—a short, slender man who moved with the oiled grace of a panther. He stopped, looked across the mêlée at me. We made eye contact. He smiled.

Santoro. Right there.

If anyone knew how to stop this, it would be him. If anyone knew what *else* was coming, what new horrors the Kuga organization was about to unleash, he would. And I needed to make him tell me.

I began to shout his name, but then his hands came up holding a Colt Canada C7 assault rifle. It was not pointed at me, though. He aimed it at the stage. Not at the huddled world leaders. No.

He opened fire on full auto at Mr. Church.

I bellowed a warning, but not in time. I saw Church stagger, his clothes popping as the bullets hit him. Blood slapped the curtains behind him and splashed Belle.

Mr. Church fell.

CHAPTER ONE HUNDRED THIRTY-FOUR
D9 CONFERENCE
RADISSON BLU PLAZA HOTEL
OSLO, NORWAY

I ran, screaming in fear and fury and despair, straight at Santoro. I fired at him until the slide locked back, but he was moving, dodging and turning the way good soldiers are taught to move. He was trying to swap in a new magazine but someone blundered into him and the mag went flying, so instead he threw the weapon at me with great force and accuracy. I clubbed it aside with my empty pistol.

Santoro ran for the exit, bashing people aside, hitting them with crippling blows and flinging them behind him to hamper pursuit. A Fox reporter staggered toward me clutching a shattered nose. A Pakistani reporter dropped to her knees in front of me, eyes bulging as her desperate fingers clawed at a smashed throat. I had to shove her aside and stop the murderous madman. This was not a time for mercy, it was a time for murder.

Santoro burst into the hallway and kicked the door shut in my face. I was moving so fast there was no time to stop. It was like hitting a brick wall. I rebounded, staggered, nearly fell, caught myself by grabbing the shoulder of a screaming dignitary.

"Sorry," I said, but then the man lunged for my throat with his teeth. Fuck. I backpedaled and swung a heavy right to smash the heel of my palm against his ear. The blow sent him sprawling into the arms of another infected. They fell thrashing and snarling to the ground.

I jumped over them and kicked the door, expecting it to be locked or braced. It flew inward so quickly I almost fell on my face—and that fall saved my life as a blade sliced through the space where my eyes had just been. As I hit the ground I rolled sideways and kicked up with both feet, catching Santoro in the knee and stomach, and sent him reeling backward. He hit the edge of the doorway and used the jolt to reclaim his balance. I rolled away again to avoid a stamp that would have crushed my throat. I kept rolling and then on the fourth turn I crunched my body and was on fingers and toes. Santoro was too smart a fighter to charge and shifted hard left, dropping into the springy crouch of the master knife fighter.

I pushed back off my hands and grabbed for my Wilson Rapid Response folding knife, which was clipped to the inside of my right pants pocket. A sharp snap of my wrist locked the three-and-a-half-inch blade into place. My knife's total weight is less than five ounces, which reduces drag—I could use it at my normal hand speed. And I am a very fast fighter.

We faced each other, eyes meeting. *Knowing* each other. We'd fought once before. Years ago, aboard the *Sea of Hope*. I'd never fought a tougher opponent, and even with Ghost's help the little bastard nearly killed us both.

There was that one moment of stillness and awareness. Then he came at me with a flurry of vicious cuts, fake stabs followed by shallow slashes, and devious feints that drove me back six full steps. I cut left and then jumped right, and tried to take him with a deep cut on the back of his knife arm, but all I got was sleeve.

"The Deacon is dead," he said as he circled with me. "That alone makes today a beautiful holiday. A sacred day."

He was trying to bait me, to make me angry enough to do something stupid.

"And when you go back to Harcourt Bolton to brag, will he pat you like a good puppy and give you treats?"

I looked for surprise or recognition, but he was too good a player and gave me nothing.

"You should have stayed in America," he said.

He faked a lunge to try and make me go for a counter-cut. I fake-flinched and snapped a shallow kick, hoping he'd try and cut my leg. It didn't work any better than his fake. We were too evenly matched for those kinds of tricks. Mind you, part of me was in shock, maybe starting to grieve for Church. I could not imagine the world without him. Certainly the RTI needed his vision, his strength, his guidance to do the kind of work we were there to do. The world needed him. And he was family to me, though we would never say such things aloud. There was "the family," which was made up of trusted allies in our war, but he was family on a deeper level.

If he was dead, I don't know how we could survive it.

Maybe we wouldn't.

But those thoughts were in the back of my mind. The Cop and the Modern Man could handle the potential loss. The Killer had work to do, and he wanted this man's blood. He wanted to tear the heart from Santoro's chest and chase the light from the Spaniard's eyes.

Santoro feinted, double-feinted, and came in with unbelievable speed, ducking low and slashing at my leg from an unexpected angle. His blade was razor sharp and suddenly there was a line of fire across the outside of my right leg. If I'd tried to backpedal he'd have gutted me. So I closed with him, slamming chest to chest with him, using my greater weight, and the angle of my upper body mass against his slimmer, shorter body, to jolt him backward off balance. It earned me a second slash, because even off balance he was that fast. However the angle was wrong for a lethal cut, and his blade merely gouged my hip and sliced through the Velcro holding my vest on beneath my shirt and suit coat.

I headbutted him and slashed him across the throat, but he brought a forearm up and took the cut there. I felt my blade hit bone, but he was moving the arm and his balled fist caught me on a nerve cluster at the end of my wrist. My hand went numb and I lost the knife. He tried to stab me, to end it right there, drilling his knife upward under my chin, but the proximity of our bodies foiled the thrust and instead his blade caught in my lapel. I headbutted him again and he staggered back without his knife. I heard it tinkle to the floor. Then he kicked me and I twisted to take it on the hip, saving my groin but getting knocked back against a row of chairs. The mad screeching of the infected was rising in volume, drowning out everything except the gunfire.

I straightened, feeling an alarming weakness in my injured leg. He'd gotten the muscle. Shit.

We were both bleeding now and unarmed. He flicked a glance at the stage and the exit. Belle was kneeling over Church, firing and firing. Was there less return fire? I couldn't tell.

"What's the point of all this?" I demanded. "What's the goddamn win here for you motherfuckers? Since when are you political, Rafael?"

He laughed. "Political? I spit on politics," he said, and did.

"Then *why*? At least tell me that."

His dark eyes were filled with a strange light and he frowned, as if surprised at the naïveté of my question. "Does there need to be a cause? Does there need to be an ideology?"

"You went to war for the Goddess."

"I waged war for the Seven Kings," he corrected. "My love for the Goddess was separate. As for this . . ." He waved his good arm at the crowd and the stage. "This? This is business. A happy, peaceful world does not need people like me. This world . . . *does*."

"Business?" I said, inching to my left, favoring my good leg. "That's all Kuga is? A fucking businessman?"

"Of course . . . what else? How are you naïve enough not to grasp that?"

"All this damage . . . all this pain. Jesus Christ," I said, "what the fuck is *wrong* with you?"

He did not answer. Instead he rushed at me, lunging, pivoting, attempting a Muay Thai kick to my bad leg that would have dropped me. I knew it was what he'd do. It was the best possible move, and he counted on his appalling speed to sell it.

I sucked in my gut and skipped both feet back like a matador avoiding a low slash with a bull's horn; and as the foot missed by a millimeter I drilled a punch into the side of his calf, into the meat, packing all of my 215 pounds of muscle, all my fury and heartbreak and fear, into that blow.

He cried out in agony and dropped down at my feet, but even hurt like that he was a scorpion at heart—he'd fight as long as there was breath in his body. He used his slashed forearm to chop my bad leg, buckling it. I tottered sideways, fighting for balance. Then he piled on me, smashing me across the face with his bloody forearm, obscuring my vision. Unlike Adam, who'd tried to smash me to pieces, Santoro was much smarter and more skilled. He tried to do to me what I'd done to his apprentice and rained down awful blows to fragile targets. He straddled me and hit, hit, hit. He smashed my nose and split my lip and hammered my left eye socket apart. I could feel my face burst apart, feel bone cracking and cartilage crunching. I felt two teeth break.

I was blind and I was losing this fight.

In my head the Killer roared in mingled fear and fury. The thing about beating someone like me to death is that you have to take their heart to make it work. One slip, one missed blow, one inadvertent mercy because of choosing the wrong target was a doorway for coun-terattack. He had a moment's advantage where he could have—and should have—killed me. He could have used the punch that knocked out my teeth to crush my throat. He really should have. But he wanted to make it last. He was trying to hurt me before he killed me, to *defeat* me because I had defeated him.

That was his mistake.

I tucked my chin and turned to one side and took his next punch on my cheekbone. I could feel his knuckles shatter. I spit my broken teeth into his face, bucked my hips, and rolled sideways, slamming my left hip against the inside of his right leg. The leverage toppled him sideways and I gave his body a vicious twist, driving that same hip into his crotch. I did not need to see him—we were touching, entwined in a sick embrace, and I could extrapolate where every part of him was. I grabbed his crotch with my left hand and used my right to punch my palm just about as hard as I could. It was a hideous, smashing, crushing overhand right that caught his scrotum between knuckles and palm. He howled as loud as Eve had screamed

I caught him by the hair and rammed his face into the floor. Once, twice, again, and again. Breaking him. For Church and Colonel Ho. For everyone on those islands. For every dead child and family. For the blood of my friends and for strangers whose names I would never know. I blinked my eyes clear and saw the ruin of him.

I pulled what was left of him close to me, so that my bleeding mouth was against his bloody ear.

"Die, you evil little motherfucker," I wheezed, and slammed his face onto the floor again.

Suddenly the air above and around me was filled with gunfire. Bullets tore stone chips from the floor and walls. One ricocheted off the marble and struck me hard in the floating ribs. I fell sideways, losing my grip on Santoro. At the far end of the corridor I could see a group of Fixers running toward a service exit. Others joined them. A mass exodus. Bug must have cracked the system and issued the shutdown code. The rats were fleeing the sinking ship.

But there was more gunfire behind me and I wheeled drunkenly around to see a squad of men and women in dark suits running in a cluster, firing past me at them. I pawed blood from my eyes and saw that the person in the lead was Steve Duffy, my old Echo Team sniper. Which meant this was Bedlam Team and the goddamn cavalry had arrived.

Something splashed me in the face, and I recoiled, spitting and cursing, and looked right up at the liquid vapor spewing from the vent on the wall three feet above my head. As I stared, the spray twitched, dwindled, and then died as the tanks concealed behind the vent went dry. Empty. Done.

I turned to see that most of the other vents had already stopped.

I saw Santoro crawling away from me. He was laughing.

I laughed, too.

Except it wasn't a laugh.

What came from my mouth was a full-throated roar of pure, savage, intense rage.

CHAPTER ONE HUNDRED THIRTY-FIVE

D9 CONFERENCE
RADISSON BLU PLAZA HOTEL
OSLO, NORWAY

My vision changed from clarity to crimson distortion. I saw monster shapes all around me. Leering, slavering beasts who wanted to kill me. They came at me with fangs and black talons. There was a black knot of fear deep inside my chest, but it was buried beneath a thousand layers of fury.

There was no Santoro, no Eve, no Kuga, and no Fixers. No Bedlam Team, either.

There was no Church or Belle, no Top, Bunny, or Andrea. No presidents or guards or press or civilians.

I staggered into a big room, to where people were fighting. It made me happy. It made me mad. I should be doing this. All of it. The stabbing and biting. That was mine to do. Mine.

All there were, everywhere I looked, were people I hated. No, more than hated. Despised with every fiber of who I was. It was a loathing that tunneled down into my DNA, into my soul.

I saw a big man on the stage. Familiar. I knew him and hated him more than all the others. He was bleeding from gunshot wounds, but still sitting up. Still firing a gun. The bastard. I despised everything about him. He needed to be stopped. He needed to die. I ran toward him. Something was wrong with my leg. I could not run as fast as my hate.

God, I wanted to kill them all. Now. In bad ways. In ugly, ugly ways that would ruin them and everyone who loved them. My muscles were tight with the need to hurt them. The pain in my side and my leg—that was fuel for the fire that burned inside of me. I found my knife on the floor and snatched it up with a howl of triumph. Sweet, beautiful knife. Red and silver and perfect. Now I could do it. Now I could cut into them, cut them apart, cut the evil from them and rub it all over me. I wanted—needed—to bathe in their blood. To drink it and spit it back in their faces. I wanted to crack their bones open and suck out the marrow.

I ran toward the injured man. Howling at him. Telling him the things I was going to do to him. I wanted to paint the walls with the red lies of their lives and—

"Sorry, boss," said a voice and Belle—that hateful bitch who deserved to die like the backstabbing traitor she was—pointed a gun at me and fired.

I swung my knife forward, stabbing, wanting to bury my blade into her traitorous heart and . . .

CHAPTER ONE HUNDRED THIRTY-SIX
D9 CONFERENCE
RADISSON BLU PLAZA HOTEL
OSLO, NORWAY

I woke in semidarkness.

Every goddamn thing hurt.

My leg, my side, my mouth, my face, my body. My heart.

Images lingered in my head. Top Sims, Duffy. Adam and Eve. Santoro. Church. Others. Their faces seemed weirdly overlaid with distorted Halloween mask versions of them. Even the familiar faces of friends had loathsome monster masks superimposed. As I stared, though, the freak masks faded and faded.

I lay on a couch in an empty office.

Zip-cuffed. Heavily bandaged. An IV drip hanging from a pole. Too much pain to catalog. Shadows in my mind. A clock on the wall insisted it was the wrong time of day. It said that it was evening. But . . . how was that even possible.

"Hey," I called. No answer, so I yelled it. Yelling hurt my mouth. It hurt everything. My soul. There were footsteps outside and then the door opened. Violin stood there. Tall, lovely, intense, her long hair falling loosely to frame her patrician face. Eyes filled with concern.

"Hello, Joseph," she said.

"Um . . . hello, Violin . . . ?"

She came in, pulled a chair over, and sat next to me, searching my face. "Is it you in there?"

"As opposed to . . . oh," I said, and that quickly I understood. "Rage?"

"Oh yes. They tell me you got it full in the face."

"Christ. Please tell me I didn't kill anyone."

She smiled and shook her head. "You tried to stab Belle. She had a dart gun."

"Is she okay?"

"She is. Though, I think you should buy her something nice for Christmas."

My words were slurred from pain, swollen tissue, and two missing teeth. "And . . . Church? I remember seeing him there . . . I had a knife . . ."

Her smile dimmed. "St. Germaine is alive. You never reached him. He has been medevacked out, though. He was shot in the thigh, lower back, the chest and left arm. A lot of blood loss, but he was still fighting the whole time, still protecting the presidents when Chaos Team found him." She laughed and shook her head, making her hair sway. "I don't know what it would take to actually kill him."

"Guess his body armor saved him," I said. "We have pretty good stuff. I got hit a couple of times."

Violin laughed. "He wasn't wearing body armor, Joseph. He is simply lucky. Strangely, consistently lucky. He has been taken to a local hospital where, no doubt, he has friends among the doctors and specialists there."

"He'll live?"

"Oh yes, Josephy, he'll live," she said, her smile enigmatic. "I know for a fact he has been hurt much worse than this in the past."

I looked at her. "How much do you know about him? About his past? Maybe who he really is. Or *what* he is."

Her smile faded except for a tiny Mona Lisa curve. "He is a good man, Joseph, but make no mistake, he is a man. He's no angel or demon or anything else. People tend to mythologize about him, but he is flesh and blood."

I said nothing, mostly because I knew she was lying, but not which parts of what she said were a lie. So, instead I raised my cuffed wrists. "Mind?"

Violin drew a slender blade from inside a sleeve and cut me loose, then helped me sit up. My exploring fingers found a turban of gauze wrapped around my head. I could see brown antiseptic goop around the cuts on my hands, and a red-soaked dressing on my thigh. When I tapped my pocket I found a Ziploc baggie with my two broken teeth in it.

"I could use an aspirin."

"I'll see what I can arrange," she said. "You're on the list for the hospital, but they've triaged you as lower priority. There are a lot of badly injured people here. My team was outside when this all happened. The hotel went into full lockdown and it took considerable time to get in. We were able to assess the situation thanks to intel from Top, relayed through Bug. My people took down a number of Fixers attempting to leave and helped Havoc with controlling the infected."

I rubbed my eyes. They were grainy and blurry, and the room was a bit too bright. "I think I have a concussion."

"I'd be surprised if you did not."

There was a lot of noise beyond the closed door. People dealing with what happened.

"Did we win?"

She smiled. "They won't give anyone a parade, but yes, Joseph, we won."

"What's the butcher's bill?"

Her sigh was long and slow and weary. "It's bad, Joseph. It's very bad."

At the beginning of the conference, there had been a total of 3,019 people in the hotel. Diplomatic and presidential teams, hotel staff, press, security, and others. Of those, 91 had been sprayed with Rage. Between the Fixers' gunfire and the attacks by the infected, there were 137 dead, and almost twice as many injured. Eleven critical.

Of the nine world leaders, seven were unharmed, one had been injured in the hand by a ricochet, and one had been bitten on the face by one of his own guards. Almost every member of the nine security teams sustained injuries, and a third had died protecting their principals.

There was a knock on the door and Scott Wilson came in, looking tentatively at me and my uncuffed hands.

"He's fine now," said Violin. She bent and gave me a light kiss on the top of the head, patted Wilson's shoulder, and left.

Scott sat in her chair. He gave me the rest of it. Once the jammers went back on, some of the people inside the main hall had started using cell phones or press cameras to record the incident. They didn't help people or try to find safety; they grabbed the story instead. For their networks or, in many cases, for their own social media feeds. Stuff like that can make you hate people.

But, as Wilson explained, it did some good. Wilson controlled the message and was able to use the network of contacts he and Church maintained to make sure the right story got out. There had been a terrorist attack on the D9 summit. The terrorist organization called itself Kuga, and was believed to be a criminal rather than ideological group. Kuga used a bioweapon that caused violent outbursts on the crowd. They also had active shooters there to attempt assassinations of all nine world leaders. Only the combined efforts of the well-trained and thoroughly professional security teams of the nine nations and the host country of Norway prevented a disaster from being even worse than it was.

"There will be speeches and medals," Wilson told me. "None of the nine presidents was seen to be acting in any cowardly way. All of the security personnel looked like heroes."

"And the fallout?"

"Don't expect another nuclear summit anytime soon," he said glumly.

"So, after all this shit, from Syria to Korea to here, Kuga *wins*?"

Wilson gave an eloquent sniff. Very Eton. "If his goal was assassination, then no," he said slowly. "However, if it was to stop the D9 summit, then yes."

"We don't know which, though," I said.

"No. Quite frankly, Colonel, this feels a bit like Pearl Harbor. A sneak attack that lets us know we're at war with an empire."

"Shit."

"If you were hoping for a big dramatic finale, this is not that. We *won,* but only on a sliding scale. It was pretty clear they wanted to assassinate as many of the nine world leaders as possible. Ten, if you count the prime minister of Norway. They failed in that, and may actually have strengthened the unity of those nations. So, if we view it through that lens, this is a great victory. But it is a battle won, not a war."

"Santoro told me that this was all just business," I said. The bitterness was clear in my voice, slurred speech or not.

Wilson nodded. "Very big business, to be certain. As soon as the story broke, the global stock markets plummeted, of course, until trading was suspended. I have no doubt Kuga was positioned to profit from the first wave of flight to safety. Depending on how many people he had positioned to buy as the stocks dropped, and depending on how well they're concealed, he could have scored billions today."

"Jesus Christ. That could have been their whole damn plan in the first place."

"Yes," he said bleakly, "it could have. A gigantic con game to create a massive stock market price drop. If so, then we really have lost. The stock market swing would have been the same whether we saved presidential lives or not. It was the failure of D9 that ignited the sell-off. There is already an uptick in black market and open market arms sales. I expect there will be an even greater uptick in hiring of private security."

I leaned my forearms on my thighs, feeling old and used and empty.

"You didn't arrest Santoro, did you?" I asked.

"No. Sergeant Duffy said he saw two Fixers helping him out of the hall but couldn't get to him. Santoro is gone. So, by the way, is Eve. We did manage to arrest three Fixers, and they are being interrogated, but it doesn't appear that they know enough."

He went to the door and paused. "Kuga is still out there. So now we begin preparing for what comes next."

"The war is the war," I said.

He studied me for a moment, nodded, and left.

CHAPTER ONE HUNDRED THIRTY-SEVEN
THE LEDGER COUNTRY HOUSE
ROBINWOOD, MARYLAND
DECEMBER 24, 11:41 A.M.

The war was the war, but it was over for me. For now.

Because of my exposure to Rage, and because neither Doc nor John Cmar knew if there were any lasting effects, I was put on administrative duty, but then a message came from Mr. Church to tell me that I had the holidays off.

I called the private hospital where he was recovering from surgery and was surprised to be put through.

"Hey, boss," I said, "how the hell are you?"

"Alive," he said. "And you?"

"Alive." I cleared my throat. "Look, with you on the sidelines, maybe it's better that I stick around the TOC for a while. Just to . . . you know . . . keep the search going."

"Colonel," said Church in a tone that held no hint of weariness, injury, or weakness, "the world is quite capable of turning without you constantly needing to push."

"Ouch," I said.

"Go spend Christmas with your family," said Church. "Give them my love."

Before I could say anything else, the line went dead. I'd made that call from my own hospital room. I was covered in stitches and staples and tape and looked like a reject from a Frankenstein movie. They were going to fit me with a bridge to replace the missing teeth. The concussion was still ringing my chimes, my face was the color of a ripe eggplant. But it was Christmas and nobody wanted me to go shoot anyone. Not at the moment.

Which is why I was in a car with Junie, driving down country lanes in Maryland. The leafy trees were all bare but the pines were a rich, dark green under a sky littered with cotton-candy clouds. Ghost sat on the edge of the backseat, his big white head leaning forward onto the armrest between Junie—who drove—and me. Ghost's eyes drifted to me over and over again in the hope that something yummy would magically appear in my hand. As it often did.

"He's going to get fat," scolded Junie.

"He's not fat, he's big boned."

We drove.

Since my return from Oslo, she and I had spent a couple of nights doing little more than holding each other. Frankly because I was incapable of anything else. There were days filled with deep conversations and long, comfortable silences. She knew that I was working things out. Junie is one of those rare people who knows when talk is good and when silence is better.

In the big rental SUV behind us were Rudy and Circe, their son, and Top. And Banshee, their Irish wolfhound. Two of Banshee's puppies—who looked suspiciously like Ghost—were in the back. Both cars were filled with wrapped presents. Bunny was back in California with his fiancée, Lydia, who was six months pregnant. Belle was in Egypt with Arklight, and I have no idea what they were doing. Andrea and his husband had taken their daughter to a little villa in Tuscany. Bug and Annie Han were, I was surprised and delighted to hear, holed up in a swanky bed-and-breakfast in Santorini.

Poor Scott Wilson was working, running the ever-expanding global search for anyone connected with the Kuga organization. And making inroads. Hitting a lot of dead ends, too. He had not yet established that Harcourt Bolton *was* Kuga. We all believed that, but there were too many mysteries. Some pieces that were left out of the puzzle.

One interesting turn of events was that Major Mun had applied to RTI. I hadn't yet met her and wanted to. She seemed like a good fit for us. Mun wanted to be part of any hunt for Rafael Santoro, no matter where it led.

That, though, was for another day. It was Christmas Eve and there was even a chance for a white Christmas, corny as that sounds. Corny seemed really appealing at the moment. On the car radio Josh Groban was singing "O Holy Night." Corny, too, but kind of nice.

"Here we are," said Junie, turning off the road onto a winding drive. The house looked cheery and right out of a Christmas card, down to the green wreath on the red-painted door. A FedEx truck was parked on the far side of the crushed-shell turnaround, and I saw the driver trudging toward it. He wore a huge white costume beard and a Santa hat with a bouncing pom-pom. In the doorway, I caught a glimpse of Sean holding a big box. He saw us coming, grinned, and hurried to take the box inside so he could come out for handshakes and hugs.

The FedEx driver, a smiling little guy with mirrored sunglasses, gave us a cheery wave and a huge pleasant smile. He had one of those port-wine skin discolorations—a firemark, my grandmother called them—that was every bit as dark as my bruised mug. Junie tooted at him as he drove away. We parked and I got out, careful of my leg, which was healing but sore as hell. Ghost bounded ahead, but stopped on the bottom porch step, sniffing at something. As Junie and I approached I saw that it was a folded piece of paper.

"Dropped the delivery receipt," I said, and picked it up. When I opened it, I saw that it wasn't a receipt at all. Just a note written in flowing and elegant scripts.

> *You have taken something of mine.*
> *Now I will take something of yours.*
> *Merry Christmas*

My blood went instantly cold.

I turned to see the FedEx truck hit the blacktop and accelerate away with a scream of tires. I turned back, seeing in my mind the big box Sean had carried inside. It looked heavy. The Santa wore a beard and glasses. Not a firemark discoloring him but facial bruising.

I opened my mouth to scream my brother's name.

And the house blew up.

EPILOGUE

The world was a white too bright to look at.

Then it turned orange and I felt it burn me.

After that it was all painted in featureless black.

Then red.

A dark red that smelled of copper. I blinked and the red was everywhere. In my eyes. On my hands when I lifted them.

When I turned my head I saw Ghost lying there. His white coat was red, too. He was panting weakly, eyes staring at nothing, tongue lolling.

I turned my head the other way. It hurt to do it. There was something wrong with my neck.

Junie lay there, only a few feet away. Might as well have been the far side of the moon. She was also painted red. Her mouth worked like a dying fish. Gasping. Trying to speak. There were pieces of wood—splinters thick as my little finger—standing up from her chest and stomach and thighs. I saw her turn to me. It took a million years. Her hand twitched. It crawled toward me like a broken spider. I made my hand move toward hers. Our fingers met, entwined, locked. We held onto each other.

Beyond her was the house.

No.

That was wrong. There was no house anymore.

There was nothing but a place of broken stone and burning wood. The arms of the fire reached all the way into the sky.

I tried to say the names. Sean. Ali. Em. Lefty. Dad. Tried to speak them, but I had no voice, and those names weighed too much. The fires swirled upward, taking their souls away from me.

-2-

Somewhere, millions of miles away, I heard a muffled sound. Car doors slamming. Voices calling. Yelling.

Top.

Rudy.

Circe.

Screaming. I heard my own voice screaming the loudest.

-3-

I don't remember all of it.

They say that—even burned and bloody, with eight broken ribs, a broken nose, lacerations everywhere—I kept Top and Rudy and four firemen busy trying to keep me from entering the conflagration of my uncle's house.

They say that helicopters came to take Junie to a hospital for emergency surgery. And an ambulance took Ghost away for the same.

They say that I broke away, snatched Top's gun, and ran down the road, screaming Santoro's name. Top had to drop me with a Sandman dart.

They say that there is justice in the world, and that the good guys always win in the end.

They say.

-4-

Doctors repaired the parts of me that could be fixed.

Rudy did not try to tell me everything was going to be okay. He's not that unkind. He told me he would be with me, and that he would help me. He wrapped his arms around me and we wept together. Even Circe joined us. So many tears, but no way to douse the flames that would burn forever.

Mr. Church flew in and sat with me by Junie's bedside, his hand resting on my forearm. For hours. Days. Watching machines beep and ping, watching digital readouts insist that she was alive.

She hovered there on the edge for so long.

But then that remarkable strength of hers won out, and she came back to me. By slow degrees, she came back. When she was able to open her eyes and speak my name, just that one word was filled with more sadness and awareness than the world could hold. Church, swathed in bandages, was wheeled out and left us alone, and in our privacy Junie and I let the world break around us.

-5-

People had to sift through the charred debris to find my father, my brother Sean, his wife Ali, the two kids, and the unborn baby. Doc Holliday took care of the identification with DNA sequencing. No one was cruel enough to ask me to look at what was left.

Jerry Spencer arrived and took over the forensic collection. Whatever he found was shared with Wilson and Church. Not with me.

There are no Ledgers left. My family line ended right there. Junie can't have kids, which means *we* won't have any. The Ledgers are done.

Because Sean was a cop and Dad had been the mayor of Baltimore, the funeral was immense. Thousands of people. A motorcade of flashing lights more than a mile long. Folded flags and guns fired in volleys. Pipers in kilts playing "Amazing Grace." Top and Bunny made sure that the press did not get within a quarter mile of the church. I sat in the front row, with Junie—who was still in a wheelchair—beside me. All of Havoc Team was there. Rudy and Circe were there. Major Mun and Colonel Epps were there. Violin and Lilith sat behind me and both of them put hands on my shoulder when I began to lose it. Other old friends. Colleagues from my own days as a cop, former DMS agents. Bug and Annie Han. So many others.

I have no idea what the minister said, or what any of the people who came up to speak said. Bunny helped me up to the podium and I stood for several long minutes as silence owned the church. Then I shook my head and he let me lean on him as he took me back to Junie.

We buried them in a row. Five neat headstones. Five futures stolen. Five holes in the world in the shape of my family.

-6-

What do you do when they turn off all the lights?

All of your lights?

I asked myself that every day. As I healed. As I threw myself into rehab and reclaimed my strength. I took that question with me to the dojo and the firing range.

What do you do when they turn off all your lights?

On a cold day in mid-February, I sat with Church in his office at Phoenix House. I knew he was looking for Santoro and Kuga. He was looking harder than anyone has ever looked for anyone. All of the resources of Rogue Team International. The field agents, the MindReader team, our network of allies around the globe.

They were not looking hard enough, because Santoro's head was not on a spike. Neither was Kuga's—whether he was Harcourt Bolton or not.

Church and I sat there, saying next to nothing for a long, long time.

Then, he said, "Whatever resources you need, whatever clearances, whatever freedom of action, Joe, you will have them."

Joe. Not Colonel Ledger.

I nodded and got slowly to my feet. So much of me hurt and so little of that pain was from the injuries. Burns heal, bones knit. I took my pain and stood looking out the window. I didn't say a goddamn word. My hands hung at my sides and every now and then my fingers twitched as if aching to close around guilty throats.

Church said, "Good hunting."

-7-

What do you do when they turn off all your lights?

You learn to use the darkness.

No.

No, that's not it. That's not enough. Not for me. Not for my family. Not for all the families who lost people to these bastards.

What do you do when they turn off all your lights?

I'll tell you.

You *become* the darkness.

The End